NYC ANGELS: REDEEMING THE PLAYBOY

BY
CAROL MARINELLI

NYC ANGELS: HEIRESS'S BABY SCANDAL

BY
JANICE LYNN

Step into the world of NYC Angels

Looking out over Central Park,
the Angel Mendez Children's Hospital,
affectionately known as Angel's, is famed
throughout America for being at the forefront
of paediatric medicine, with talented staff
who always go that extra mile for their little patients.
Their lives are full of highs, lows, drama and emotion.

In the city that never sleeps,
the life-saving docs at Angel's Hospital work hard,
play hard and love even harder. There's always time
for some sizzling after-hours romance…

And striding the halls of the hospital, leaving
a sea of fluttering hearts behind him, is the
dangerously charismatic new head of neurosurgery
Alejandro Rodriguez. But there's one woman,
paediatrician Layla Woods, who's left an
indelible mark on his no-go-area heart.
Expect their reunion to be explosive!

NYC Angels

*Children's doctors who work hard and love
even harder…in the city that never sleeps!*

NYC ANGELS: REDEEMING THE PLAYBOY

BY
CAROL MARINELLI

MILLS & BOON

With love and thanks to Wendy S. Marcus x

First published in Great Britain 2013
by Mills & Boon, an imprint of Harlequin (UK) Limited.
Harlequin (UK) Limited, Eton House, 18-24 Paradise Road,
Richmond, Surrey TW9 1SR

© Harlequin Books S.A. 2013

Special thanks and acknowledgement are given to Carol Marinelli
for her contribution to the *NYC Angels* series

ISBN: 978 0 263 89881 1

Dear Reader

New York City is my favourite place on earth. I love it, and one day want to spend a decent amount of time there. For that reason I was especially thrilled to be involved in a Medical Romance™ continuity set there.

I have loved working with wonderful authors and helping to create a series I really hope you enjoy.

Angel's Hospital is as busy as the city it is located in, and Jack and Nina kick the series off. I felt as if I knew Jack the second he came into my mind's eye, but Nina simply refused to conform to any preconceived image I had of her—which is rather how she is. Nina gave me a few surprises in the process of getting to know her.

She gave Jack a few too.

Happy reading!

Carol

Carol Marinelli recently filled in a form where she was asked for her job title and was thrilled, after all these years, to be able to put down her answer as 'writer'. Then it asked what Carol did for relaxation. After chewing her pen for a moment Carol put down the truth—'writing'. The third question asked—'What are your hobbies?' Well, not wanting to look obsessed or, worse still, boring, she crossed the fingers on her free hand and answered 'swimming and tennis'. But, given that the chlorine in the pool does terrible things to her highlights, and the closest she's got to a tennis racket in the last couple of years is watching the Australian Open, I'm sure you can guess the real answer!

Also by Carol Marinelli:

Mills & Boon® Medical Romance™

HERS FOR ONE NIGHT ONLY?
SYDNEY HARBOUR HOSPITAL: AVA'S RE-AWAKENING*
CORT MASON—DR DELECTABLE
HER LITTLE SECRET
ST PIRAN'S: RESCUING PREGNANT CINDERELLA†

†*St Piran's Hospital*
*Sydney Harbour Hospital

Modern™ Romance

BANISHED TO THE HAREM**
PLAYING THE ROYAL GAME††
AN INDECENT PROPOSITION
A SHAMEFUL CONSEQUENCE
HEART OF THE DESERT
THE DEVIL WEARS KOLOVSKY

***Empire of the Sands*
††*Santina Crown*

These books are also available in eBook format from www.millsandboon.co.uk

CHAPTER ONE

'NINA WILSON.'

Jack kept his face impassive, but his cynical grey eyes rolled a little when he heard that Nina was the social worker who was dealing with baby Sienna's case.

Nina was hard work, and well Jack knew it, because they'd clashed on more than one occasion over the past couple of years.

Paediatrician Eleanor Aston had asked Jack, who was Head of Paediatrics, to join her in the case meeting that was to be held at nine this morning.

'The social work department seems intent on discharging Sienna home to the care of her parents,' Eleanor told him. 'I've been up nearly every night for a fortnight witnessing Sienna's withdrawal from methadone. The mother has already had two children taken off her. I personally looked after her newborn son last year.'

Eleanor's lips tightened at the memory of that time, but Jack chose not to notice. Instead, he flicked through the case notes as Eleanor's voice heightened with emotion, which Jack didn't respond to—he preferred facts.

'I just don't see why we're giving her a chance with her third baby when we know how she's been in the past.'

'You won't win with that argument against Nina Wilson,' Jack said, and as he read through the notes he saw that some of them had, in fact, been written by him.

One entry that he had written was just over a week old: *Five-day-old, unsettled, distressed...* He'd been called by the night team for a consult, he noted, but as Jack tried to picture the baby he had written about just a few nights ago he felt a slight knot of unease that he couldn't place baby Sienna.

He told himself that it was to be expected—Angel Mendez Children's Hospital was a phenomenally busy free hospital in New York City. Not only did Jack head up the general paediatric team, he also dealt regularly with the board, Admin and the endless round of socialising and networking that was required to raise vital funds for the hospital.

The Carters were a prominent New York family and, as the son of a Park Avenue medical dynasty, Jack, with his endless connections and effortless grace, was called on often, not just for his impressive medical skills but also because of his connections and therefore the donations his family name alone could bring.

Still, this morning it was all about baby Sienna and making the best possible decisions for her future.

Jack finished with the medical history and read Nina's meticulous notes. They were very detailed and thorough and, Jack noted, very dispassionate—unlike Nina herself, who was incredibly fiery and fought hard for her patients. She was young, a little angry with bureaucracy and out to set the world to rights, whereas Jack, at thirty-four years of age, was just a touch more realistic as to what could and could not be achieved.

'Nina always comes down on the side of the parents,' Eleanor said.

'Not always.' Jack shook his head. 'Though I do know what you mean.'

He did.

Nina believed in families. Of course there were tough calls to be made at times and then she made them, but as Jack read through the notes he realised this was going to be a very long meeting.

Arguing with Nina was like an extremely prolonged game of tennis—everything that you served to her was returned with well-researched and thought-out force. He wasn't in the least surprised that Eleanor had asked him to sit in on the case meeting—Nina would know every inch of the family history and would have arguments and counter-arguments as to why her findings should be upheld.

'Come on, then.' Jack put on his jacket. He didn't need to check his appearance in the mirror—a combination of genes and wealth assured that he always looked good. His dark brown hair was trimmed fortnightly, his designer attire was taken care of by his housekeeper. All Jack had to do in the morning was kiss whatever lover was in his bed, head to the shower, shave and then step into his designer wardrobe to emerge immaculate a few moments later—more often than not just to break another heart.

As he headed to the meeting Jack thought briefly about Monica's tears that morning.

Why did women always demand a reason for why things had come to an end?

Why did they always want to know where they had gone wrong or how they could change, or what had happened to suddenly change his mind?

Nothing had changed Jack's mind.

He simply didn't get involved and there was no such thing to Jack as long term.

And so, as he entered the meeting room, Jack readied himself for his second round of feminine emotion that morning. Nina had already arrived and was taking off her scarf and unbuttoning her coat. There were still a couple of flakes of snow in her hair and as she glanced over and saw him enter the room Jack watched her lips close tightly as she realised perhaps that Eleanor had brought in the big gun.

'Morning, Nina,' he greeted her, and flashed a smile just to annoy her.

'Jack.' Nina threw a saccharine smile in his direction and then turned her back and took off her coat.

Damn.

Nina didn't say it, of course, she just undid the belt and buttons and shrugged off her coat, but despite her together appearance she was incredibly unsettled and not just because Jack was Head of Paediatrics.

They clashed often.

Jack, always cool and detached, often brought her to the verge of tears, not that she ever let him see that. Just a couple of months ago she had been part of the team that had worked hard with a family struggling with a small baby who had been brought in to the emergency department. Jack had been reserved in his judgement that Baby Tanner should be discharged home to the care of the mother, but her team had fought hard to ensure that it happened. But just two weeks ago she had been called to the emergency department to find out that Baby Tanner had been brought in again, unconscious, a victim of shaken-baby syndrome.

Jack had said not one word to her as she had stepped into the cubicle.

His look had said everything, though—*I told you so.* Nina could still see his cool grey eyes harden as they had met hers, and she still carried the guilt.

But it wasn't just that that had Nina unsettled this morning.

Jack Carter was more than good looking and, of course, that didn't go unnoticed. He was known for his playboy ways and his charmed, privileged life, and the acquired arrogance that came with it irked Nina.

But, no, it wasn't just that either.

What really got to Nina was that *he* got to her.

He was arrogant, chauvinistic, dismissive—in fact, Jack Carter was everything Nina didn't like in a man, and, no, logically she didn't fancy him in the least—it was just that her body said otherwise.

It noticed him.

It reacted to him.

And Nina didn't like *it* one bit.

She could feel his eyes lazily watching her as she took off her coat, was incredibly aware of him as she hung up the garment and headed to the table to commence the meeting. She almost anticipated the slight inappropriateness that would undoubtedly come from his smirking lips.

He didn't disappoint her. 'Nice to see someone at the meeting with their clothes on,' Jack said as she made her way over, because everyone apart from Nina and Jack was wearing scrubs. Everyone present laughed a little at his off-the-cuff remark.

Everyone, Jack noted, but Nina.

Then again, he'd never really seen her smile, at least not at him. She was always so serious, so intense and the only time her face relaxed and lit up with a smile was when she was engaging with her clients.

This morning she had on a grey pinafore dress with a red jumper beneath, but this was no school uniform! The red stockings and black boots that she wore took care of that. Nina's dark blonde hair was pinned up and her cheeks were red from coming into the warmth of the hospital from a very cold January morning.

'Sorry I'm late,' Nina said, taking a seat at the table opposite him. Just as Jack found himself wondering if the workaholic Nina had actually overslept, she corrected his thought process. 'I got called to go out on an urgent response.'

And, rather inconveniently for Jack, he wondered if there was a Mr Wilson who got annoyed at having Nina peeled from his bed at the crack of dawn by the emergency response team, or even a Ms Wilson, who bemoaned her partner leaving her side. Jack realised then that not once had Nina so much as flirted with him. Not once had she turned those cobalt-blue eyes to his in an attempt to bewitch him, which might sound arrogant, but flirting was par for the course when your name was Jack Carter.

Just never with Nina.

'Right.' Nina glanced around the table. Every person present felt like the enemy in this meeting and so she didn't bother to smile. 'Shall we get started, then?'

Nina really wasn't looking forward to this morning.

Normally she would have spent a lot of the weekend poring over the medical notes and histories, but she had been working at the pro bono centre as well as moving into her new three-bedroomed apartment. She'd hoped to get into work very early this morning and go over the notes again, but instead, at four a.m., just as her alarm clock had gone off, so too had her phone, and now Nina felt less than prepared.

Which was very unlike her.

Certainly, it didn't sit well with her. In a few short weeks her own family would be under the spotlight of a case conference and she wanted her sister and brother's case worker to be as passionate and as informed as she usually was. Still, even if Nina hadn't prepared as meticulously as usual, she was still well informed and, given Sienna was only two weeks old, most of the details of the case were fresh in her mind.

She knew that most of the medical staff were opposed to Sienna being discharged home to the parents. Their concerns had been well voiced and they were repeated again now.

First she heard from Brad Davis, head of the prenatal

unit. Brad had seen Hannah for her very brief prenatal care and had also delivered Sienna, but thankfully he was very matter-of-fact in his summing up.

'Hannah presented to us at thirty-four weeks gestation,' Brad explained. 'She had recently resumed her relationship with Sienna's father, Andy. He was seemingly the one who insisted that Hannah attend Angel's. Andy was concerned about Hannah's drug habit and the effect it would have on their unborn child—Hannah's only concern was feeding her habit.'

'At that time,' Nina responded, and Brad nodded. 'She complied with the methadone programme?' Nina asked, and again Brad nodded, and so on they went.

Nina heard from the midwives and nursing staff and also the addiction counsellors who had been in regular contact with Hannah.

Eleanor Aston, though, was particularly difficult. Always a huge advocate for her patients, Eleanor was perhaps the most insistent that Sienna be removed from her mother's care.

'I looked after her son last year.' Eleanor's voice shook with emotion. 'And I can remember—'

'We're not discussing Sienna's half-brother this morning,' Nina interrupted. She knew that it was terribly difficult to separate the two cases, especially as Eleanor had dealt with Hannah at her very worst and had looked after what had indeed been a very sick little baby boy with a very cold and unfeeling mother, but this was a crucial part of Nina's job and one that made her less than popular at times with the medical staff.

'The difference this time around is that Hannah is

doing her best to get straight and she is also in a very different relationship with this baby's father. As soon as Andy found out that Hannah was pregnant he brought her straight to Angel's and has been rigorously making sure that she keeps up with the programme, and Hannah herself has made a huge effort—'

'When?' They were half an hour into the meeting and it was the first time that Jack had actually spoken. He looked across the table at Nina as he did so. 'When exactly did Hannah make this huge effort that you keep talking about?'

'Since she came to Angel's.' Nina's voice was very calm. She had been expecting Jack to step in at any moment and she hadn't been proved wrong.

'She had nine months to dry out,' Jack said, and then corrected himself. Nina was quite sure Jack's mistake was deliberate. 'Oh, sorry, make that eight months, because it was considered vital that we induce her early due to the baby's failure to thrive in the womb.' Still he stared at Nina, perhaps waiting for her to interrupt, or to speak over him, but she met his cool gaze without words of her own and Jack carried on.

'So, all in all, she actually managed two weeks of antenatal care, mainly because of her boyfriend's efforts, and then two weeks of *huge* effort postnatally, but only with every system and resource available in place.'

'Your point being?' Nina asked, and Jack didn't answer. 'Why wouldn't we offer every resource that we have to this family?' She watched his jaw tighten as she scored a point.

'Hannah has been attending addiction counselling

twice daily. For the first time she actually wants all the help and support that we can provide and there is also an extremely devoted father who, I am quite sure, will put the baby's welfare first. Hannah has broken down with me on two separate occasions and told me that she doesn't want another child taken off her and that she is prepared to do whatever it takes. Now, I know that this is early days—'

'My doctors have been up with that baby night after night,' Jack interrupted. 'I personally have been called in when Sienna has become agitated and distressed.' His eyes held Nina's and she didn't blush or blink but simply met his gaze. 'The baby had severe withdrawal, she was small for her dates due to maternal malnourishment, just like her older brother, and it is my opinion that the last person the baby—'

'Sienna,' Nina interrupted. 'The baby is called Sienna and to date there is nothing that I have seen, from my many observations, to indicate that any of the traits that were a cause for concern with her other children are present now, and the nursing observations verify that....'

Jack drew a long breath as Nina spoke on. Her holistic approach irked him, and he sat, turning his heavy pen over and over as he listened to Nina drone on about how damaging it would be to both Sienna and Hannah if they were separated now, especially as a strong bond had been established. Jack said nothing, though he wanted to point out that a bond surely took longer than a couple of weeks, but he knew he'd be shot down, not just by Nina but by everyone in the room.

Jack really didn't get the maternal bond argument.

His pen turned in his fingers as he thought for a moment of his own mother—she certainly hadn't had one. Instead, Jack had been assigned to two nannies and had only been brought down for dinner and social events.

But instead of dwelling on his own messed-up family, he listened how, from Nina's findings, there was nothing to indicate at this stage that Sienna was at risk and that with full back-up and aftercare, the department had determined that the child should be discharged to the care of the parents.

'So what am I here for, then?' Jack challenged. 'From a medical point of view the baby has put on sufficient weight to be discharged, she is stable, her withdrawal from methadone is manageable now and you've clearly already determined the outcome. You're really not interested in hearing our concerns—'

'Don't!' For the first time this meeting Jack heard the shake of anger in Nina's voice. 'Don't you dare insinuate that I am dismissing the medical staff's concerns.'

Jack rolled his tongue in his cheek. He certainly wasn't about to apologise, but inwardly he conceded that perhaps he had gone a bit too far. At the end of the day the social services department did one hell of a job. They dealt with the most vulnerable children and handled the most difficult cases and had to make decisions that few would relish, so he sat silent as Nina spoke on.

'Every one of your concerns has been listened to and addressed. Every point you have made has been noted.' Nina looked around the table. 'I have to take each case on its own merits and in *this* case I see the mother making a huge effort. She is racked with guilt, witnessing all that Sienna is going through, and—' Nina looked over at Eleanor '—while I accept that she had none of those feelings with the other two children, in this instance it is very different.

'There is a father who is stepping up and a couple who are desperate to keep their child but, yes, there is also a baby who, thanks to her mother's poor choices, has had an appalling start to life. Now, I could arrange temporary placement for Sienna, but I can assure you the foster-care system is not a fairy-tale alternative, especially when we believe that, with support, this family does have a chance.'

'Well,' came Jack's terse response, 'I've voiced my concerns.'

'They've been noted.'

As soon as the meeting concluded Jack stood. 'If you'll excuse me.'

Once outside Eleanor spoke with him briefly. 'Thanks so much for trying, Jack.'

'Nina made several good points.' Jack said to Eleanor, because although he always went in to bat for his staff he could play the devil's advocate better than anyone, but probably, in this instance, he actually agreed with Nina. 'I know that it's hard to step back at times...'

'It doesn't seem that way for you.' Eleanor sighed.

'Yeah, well, you have to be tough to do this job or you'd go crazy,' Jack said. 'Eleanor, sometimes you just have to look at the facts. In this case the mother is doing everything right, albeit too little too late, but, as Nina said, if we take this child from the mother now then realistically they are not going to reunite and though we might think that that might be for the best, who knows where Sienna might end up?'

'She might be placed with the perfect family. She might...' Eleanor started, but her lips tightened and her words halted as Nina came out.

'There's no such thing as the perfect family,' Jack said, and giving Nina a brief nod he stalked off.

'Says the man who comes from one.' Eleanor rolled her eyes as Jack walked off and then stood a little awkwardly when it was clear that Nina was hanging around to speak to her. 'Did you see the Carter family Christmas photo shoot?'

Nina gave a pale smile. Yes, she'd seen it—all the Carters gathered around the hospital Christmas tree, their diamonds gleaming as much as their capped smiles. There had recently been a magazine spread too on Jack's parents, but she didn't want to think about Jack now so Nina got straight to the difficult point. 'I'm sorry that you're upset about the department's decision.'

'Thanks.' Nina watched as Eleanor's eyes filled up behind her glasses as she spoke. 'I've listened to all that you've said and I've just spoken with Jack and he's right—you made some very good points. It's just that I saw what Hannah was like with her son. She was so distant and unfeeling and refused to take any responsibility...'

'Addiction will do that every time,' Nina said.

'I know.' Eleanor nodded.

'And I can assure you that we will be watching Sienna very carefully. The real difference in this case is that there is a loving father on the scene. I really feel that if Hannah goes back to her ways of old and starts using again, then Andy will be the one raising Sienna...'

'Far from perfect.'

'Not so far from perfect.' Nina smiled. 'I think that he'd do a great job.'

As she said goodbye to Eleanor and headed off to find Hannah to let her know about the meeting, she paused for a moment by the water cooler and took a drink, Eleanor's words still replaying in her mind.

Jack Carter thought she had made several good points.

Because she *had* made several good points, Nina told herself, screwing up the small plastic cup and tossing it into the waste bin.

She didn't need his admiration, neither did she need his approval.

The only opinion Nina wanted from Jack was a professional one.

She just had to remember that fact.

CHAPTER TWO

WITH THE MEETING over Jack walked through the maternity unit, restless, angry but not sure why. He was looking forward to getting back to the shield of his office, but his pager stopped him and he halted to use the phone. However, as he waited to be connected by the switchboard he glanced at the handover sheet one of the nurses was working on.

Sienna Andrews. He saw the room she was in and the doctor she was under, that she had been the third pregnancy, and in the comments section was written 'NASS'—which stood for neonatal abstinence scoring system, a method used to gauge a newborn's withdrawal from the drugs they had been subjected to in what should have been the safety of the womb.

Jack concluded his call and walked through the maternity ward, pausing when he came to the room where Sienna was. He looked through the glass to the row of isolettes. Hannah wasn't with her daughter, though a nurse was there, tending to the baby. Jack rarely went into these rooms, only when it was necessary.

Angel's was a free hospital—there was more hope and heartbreak than one building could contain and as

Head of Paediatrics Jack had more than enough to contend with, without getting unnecessarily involved with each and every case.

He had to stay detached, which he did easily.

Jack had learnt the art of detachment long before he had studied medicine—he'd been told by his parents to toughen up at a very young age, and told it over and over again, and so he had, simply refusing to hand over his emotions to anyone.

He had this sudden strange vision of Nina chairing a meeting about his own family and it brought a wry smile to his lips.

There *was* no such thing as a perfect family.

Certainly he never discussed his family life with any of his many lovers—he didn't let anyone close and maintained the Carter image, because the image could be used for good. Jack looked around the unit, saw the cots and the equipment and, ever practical, thought of the cost.

'Do you need anything, Jack?' Cindy, one of the nurses, broke into his thoughts.

'Nope.' Jack shook his head. 'I'm just checking in. How's baby Andrews doing?'

'She's doing really well,' Cindy said, as Jack looked through Sienna's charts. 'She's still a little irritable at times, but seems much more settled now. She'd put on another ounce when we weighed her this morning and mum's given her a bath. How did the case conference go?'

'Same old, same old.' Jack shrugged. 'Home to the parents, follow-up, support systems in place...' He looked at Cindy, who had worked at Angel's for a very long time. They'd slept together once, years ago, but there was no awkwardness between them. Cindy was now happily married and expecting her first baby and Jack valued her opinion a lot. 'What do you think?'

'As I said in my notes, mum's really making an effort...'

'But what do *you* think?'

'That I hope her effort lasts.'

Cindy walked off to check on a baby that was crying and Jack looked down into the cot, stared into the babe's dark blue eyes and wondered, not for the first time lately, if he was in the right job.

Of course the hospital wanted him, he worked sixty-hour weeks as well as juggling a social life that would have most people exhausted. He did an excellent job with the staff, as well as the extracurricular events that ensured the city's goodwill for the hospital continued.

He did a great job.

He just didn't love it.

Didn't know how to fire up, the way Nina had.

He'd heard the tremble in her voice, the passion she had for the family, her willingness to go against the flow and fight for a cause. Sometimes, and this was one of those times, he wished he had even a tenth of her passion.

He looked at Sienna, hoped that for her Angel's had done its best. She'd had the best doctors, nurses, social workers, but would it be enough?

He turned as Nina came into the room.

'How is she?' Nina asked, wondering if he had been called for a problem.

'Fine.'

'Is Hannah around?' Nina asked.

'Nope, I think she's at one of her meetings…'

'That's fine,' Nina said. 'I just wanted to go through the meeting and the conclusions with her.' She walked over to the cot and gave a slightly wary smile to Jack. She wasn't particularly used to seeing him pensive by a cot. 'I was just explaining to Eleanor that we'll be arranging regular—'

'I'll read about it, thanks.'

'Of course you will.'

Nina saw his jaw tighten at her response and she smothered a smile that twitched on her lips as she scored an unfair point. But that was what Jack did—oh, she had no doubt at all that he was a brilliant doctor, he was incredibly respected amongst his peers and she knew that he was considered a brilliant diagnostician.

She'd seen him in action on several occasions, all suited and suave, and then, when he'd delivered his opinion, when the crisis was over, when he'd saved another life, the next time Nina might see him was the way she had this morning in a meeting.

'All the resources that you're putting in place for Sienna and her family…' Jack's voice was steel. 'Where do you think they come from?'

Nina gave a tight shrug. She probably had gone a bit far—she had just wanted to needle him a bit, pay him back for his words in the meeting, and now, clearly, she had.

Jack gave Nina a brief nod and headed off, taking the lift down and walking towards Emergency, where he was meeting with one of hospitals most prominent benefactors.

He was sick of it.

Sick of the smooth talk, sick of the smarming just to get a decent-sized cheque.

Maybe it *was* time for a change.

Thanks to his extremely privileged upbringing and some very astute investments, Jack could easily not work another day in his life.

But then what?

Maybe he should follow in his father's footsteps. Set up his own private Park Avenue practice, screen and choose his patients, patch them up and send them on their way.

A practice where he could fix everything.

Get in at nine.

Do a good job.

Be thanked.

Go home at six.

To what?

'Incoming storm.' As he walked along the corridor Jack was jolted out of his dark thoughts by the sound of a familiar voice.

'Alex!' He shook his colleague's hand. 'It's good to see you—first day?'

'It is.' Alex nodded.

'And?'

'It's going well,' Alex said.

They had trained together at medical school, where

two very ambitious minds had met and had got on well from the start, both admiring the determination in the other—two men who had not settled for a pass mark, two men who had been determined to excel. Jack had chosen the speedier route of paediatrics, while Alex Rodriguez had chosen neurosurgery and had just been appointed head of that department at Angel's.

Jack had used his weight there too in employing his friend—Alex's skills hadn't been the issue, though, more a dark shadow on Alex's past that the board had deliberated over. 'I actually wanted to come and speak to you to say thank you for the recommendation.'

'You didn't need my recommendation,' Jack said. 'You were very impressive at the interviews—Angel's wants you on board.'

'Thanks.' Alex was quiet for a moment. 'And I am grateful to the board for agreeing not to bring up...' His voice trailed off—Alex didn't need to go into detail with Jack, there had been a messy court case in Los Angeles a few years ago that the board had finally agreed to keep confidential. Jack knew it had nearly destroyed Alex, and not just professionally. Still, Jack also knew that there was no one better for the role.

'The past is the past.'

'Yep.' Alex wasn't exactly known for small talk, but just as they were about to head off, Alex spoke on. 'Everything okay with you, Jack?'

'Me?'

'Incoming storm.' Alex's smile was wry. 'I could see it approaching as you walked towards me—it's not the Jack I know.'

'Yeah, well, you've been in Australia for five years. Maybe the Jack you used to know is getting older...' He ran a hand through his hair. 'I've just sat through a case meeting with the most annoying social worker...' Jack rolled his eyes. 'You know the type.'

'Holistic approach?' Alex said, and Jack gave a reluctant smile. 'With the right services in place...' Alex put on his best social worker voice and Jack actually laughed. 'They're the same the world over. Still, can you imagine this job without them?'

'No,' Jack admitted. 'Anyway, right now I've got to go and do some sweet-talking—there's a VIP waiting for a private tour of Emergency.' Jack's words dripped sarcasm. 'I can't wait.'

Maybe it wasn't Social Services that was getting to him, maybe it was this place, or maybe, Jack thought as he saw a pair of red-stockinged, black-booted legs walking very briskly along the corridor, her pager trilling, with Security by her side, it was one social worker in particular.

'Problem?' Jack checked as she dashed past him, but she just gave him a very strange look at his question. Nina didn't generally get fast-paged because things were going well in the world.

And she had *really* hoped for Tommy and his father, Mike, that things were finally starting to go well.

'Just stay back,' Nina said to the security guards as they took the lift to the psychology wing. 'Mike gets very angry at times, but it's all hot air. I'll tell you if I need you to intervene.'

She was met by Linda, one of the most senior child

psychologists. 'I've got another worker in with them at the moment,' Linda said, and then explained what had happened that morning. 'Basically, I noticed Tommy had a nasty cut on his hand. It was covered by a bandage but it came off during play therapy and it looks infected. I think it should have had stitches, but when I suggested we bring Tommy down to Emergency to have it looked at, Mike refused. He got extremely angry and now he's insisting on taking Tommy straight home.'

'How's Tommy?'

'Pale…' Linda said. 'Listless. He's lost weight too. I saw him just last month and everything seemed fine. Things have been going so well between them…'

'I was hoping to close the case this week,' Nina admitted. 'Obviously with ongoing support for Tommy…' She bit back on the expletive that was rising in her throat. She had been sure that things were so much better, had been sure there wasn't a protective issue, and then she heard Mike shouting.

'We're going home.' He had Tommy in his arms and was striding down the corridor. 'Oh, not you!' he shouted when he saw Nina. 'Got your bodyguards with you?'

'Mike.' Nina was calm but firm. 'Tommy needs to have that cut seen. If it's infected, he will need—'

'I'll stop at the drug store on the way home.' Mike didn't let her finish, just marched on towards the lifts.

'Mike…' She walked alongside him, and as he jumped into a lift that was going up, Nina darted in and the doors closed before Security could get in too.

Mike continued his angry rant, not caring that there

was a family with a child in a wheelchair, not noticing Alex Rodriguez, who was in the lift and about to intervene. Nina glanced at his ID and realising he worked at Angel's gave a brief shake of her head. In a confined space it might only make things worse.

'We can talk properly down in Emergency,' Nina said to Mike, because the last thing she wanted was Mike walking off in this mood with his son.

'I'm sick of your talking!' Mike shouted.

'You're scaring Tommy.' She watched as Mike screwed up his face, watched as he tried to contain himself for his son, and thankfully Alex made sure everyone but himself got out at the next floor.

She was grateful to Alex for sticking around while staying back as they walked briskly to Emergency, Security catching up just as they got to the entrance doors.

It was a busy Monday morning in Emergency, Jack noted. He actually wanted to take off his suit jacket and pitch in, but instead he was stuck showing Elspeth Hillier around and telling her what her huge donation, in memory of her late husband, was earmarked for.

'We're hoping to have a supervised play area…' Jack explained. 'It would be used for the siblings of the patient or any child in the care of their guardian. Often the parent or carer arrives with two or three children in tow—naturally they want to be with their child throughout procedures and interviews, instead of having to take care of the other children until help arrives. The patient misses out on the comfort of the carer or, more often than not, the nurses end up babysitting.'

'And it would be called…' Elspeth asked.

'We haven't decided on a name yet,' Jack said. 'But certainly it would be something that honours the Hillier name.'

'Not for me, of course,' Elspeth said. 'I just want Edgar to be remembered.'

'Of course,' Jack duly replied, though he was quite sure it wouldn't be called the Edgar child-care centre or the Edgar Hillier child-care centre… He knew the routine only too well; he'd been raised on it after all.

'So when will building commence?' Elspeth asked, but Jack didn't answer. He was distracted for a moment, not because of a new outbreak of commotion—that was commonplace here—but more at the sight of those red stockings again. Nina was walking through the department alongside a gentleman who was holding a pale-looking child. They were flanked by two security guards and Alex Rodriguez was present too.

Jack tried to answer Elspeth's question but his eyes kept wandering to the group and he watched as a nurse approached to take the child.

'Excuse me for a moment, Elspeth…'

Security were bracing themselves, Alex was hovering, nurses were looking over, and any second now the button would be pressed for the police to be called as the father was becoming more and more agitated. Only Nina stood resolute and calm. He could see her speaking to the gentleman and, as Jack approached, he saw that whatever she had said had worked, for without further demur he handed the child over to a nurse.

Jack was about to head back to Elspeth and even

Alex had turned to go when the explosion hit. 'Who the hell do you think you are, bitch?' The man was right in Nina's face, cursing her and, despite the presence of Security, backing Nina into a cubicle. But even then her voice was, to Jack's ears, annoyingly calm, telling the security officers to step back.

'I can handle this, thank you.'

Er, actually, no, she couldn't, Jack was quite sure. There was well over six feet of angry male yelling at her, telling her that he had trusted her, that she should know him better, that he would never harm his child.

'Take a seat, Mike.' She just stood in the middle of the cubicle as he ranted. 'No one is accusing you of anything, but Tommy looks unwell and needs to be examined. He has a cut that appears infected. No one has said anything about you harming your son.'

'You're nothing but a—'

'Enough.' Jack stepped in between them. 'I'm Jack Carter, Head of Paediatrics. Can I ask what is going on?'

'I've got this, thanks, Jack.' He heard her bristling with anger and held back the slight incredulous shake of his head, because her anger was aimed at him! Still, he happily ignored Nina and looked at the man.

'Sir?' Jack stood patiently, his eyes warning the other man to calm down, and slowly he seemed to a little, but his words were still angry when he answered.

'Tommy had an appointment today with the child psychologist and everything seemed fine but then they decide that the cut on his hand needs to be seen. I just want to take him home, he's tired, and then *she* arrives with security guards in tow and I'm hauled down here just because a four-year-old has a cut hand.'

'It looks infected,' Nina stated. 'It needs to be checked, it's that simple, Mike.'

'How did he get the cut?' Jack asked.

'I don't know.' Mike's temper reared again. 'He's four years old, they fall over all the time.'

'Sure they do.' Jack nodded. 'I'll go and take a look at him myself right now. The thing I want you to do is to calm down before you go in to see him. You've scared your son—he doesn't need to see his father angry and upset.' He gave a brief nod to Nina, who stepped outside with him.

'It's a very complicated history—' she started.

'I'm sure that it is,' Jack interrupted, 'but right now my concern is the child's medical status.'

'The father can be explosive at times, but he's never been that way with his child…'

Jack didn't want to hear her findings at this stage. His only thought was for the safety of the child—well, there was one other thing he would address later. 'I'm going to speak to you afterwards about your own safety. I don't want staff taking risks.'

'I know the family. I knew what I was doing—'

'I'm not arguing about this right now,' Jack broke in. 'I'll speak to you later.'

'If I can just explain about Tommy…'

'Please, don't. Right now I want to go and see that child and find out first hand what we're dealing with.'

So quickly Jack dismissed her.

Other times he blamed her.

But right now she couldn't think about Dr Perfect Never Make A Mistake Carter. Instead she turned to another man, one who had made an awful lot of mistakes that morning, and she watched as Mike sat down, put his head in his hands and started to sob.

'I didn't mean to scare him.' He was beside himself. 'Tommy will be petrified without me…'

'I know that,' Nina said. 'What's going on, Mike?'

'Nothing.'

'When did Tommy get the cut?'

'I don't know, a few days ago… I need to be with him.'

'Not yet. I want you to sit here for a while. Someone will bring you a drink and when things are more settled I'll come and speak to you.'

'I should be with him.'

'You can't be with him because you just lost your temper, Mike!' Despite what Jack might think, Nina was no pushover. 'You can't be with your son because you refused to bring him down for an examination, because you avoided Security and then bullied me into a cubicle. You blew this, Mike, so, no, right now you can't be with him. I'll go in. Tommy knows me, I'll stay with him for now…'

Nina left the cubicle and asked a nurse where Tommy was and was pointed in the direction. She knocked on the examination-room door and was let in.

'Good timing.' She could hear the weary bitterness in his voice. 'I was just about to call you with an urgent referral.' She looked down at Tommy, who was being helped into a gown that was covered with cartoon characters. Nina looked at his pale, bruised body and immediately she could see why she was about to be called. Then she looked over at Jack and she saw it again.

The look he had given her when she had walked into Baby Tanner's cubicle.

The look he would give her if Sienna returned unwell to the department.

It was a look she knew all to well, and one Jack Carter gave her all too often.

I told you so.

CHAPTER THREE

'EXCUSE ME A minute, Tommy.' Jack stepped outside and Nina assumed that she was meant to follow, but of course she had it wrong. Instead, Jack spoke with an elderly, very elegant woman, who looked less than impressed when he headed back towards Tommy's cubicle, offering Nina a brief explanation. 'Lewis is stuck with a multi-trauma, I'm just waiting for the registrar to come and take over. I just want to make sure that there's nothing medically urgent that is wrong.'

'Can I just have a brief word before you go in, Jack?' He gave a slight hiss of frustration as he turned around. 'Tommy is a very guarded child. Initially he had nothing to do with his father and responded only to me, but over the past months…'

She didn't finish; instead she watched as Jack's grey eyes shuttered as they so often did when she spoke. 'You don't want to hear what I have to say?'

'At this stage, no. I want to find out from the child what has happened and given that you have had dealings with the family and that Tommy seems to trust you, I'd like you to assist. Do you think you can?'

'Of course, but—'

'I like facts Nina,' he interrupted. 'I like to explore things for myself and I do not want to walk in there with my thought process crowded by yours.'

'Sure.'

He was arrogant, dismissive, even rude, but there was no mistaking that he was brilliant with Tommy. He didn't rush in, he just chatted to the little boy for a couple of minutes and then asked him something about his parents.

'Tommy's mum is deceased,' Nina said quietly, and had he given her just one moment to speak he might not be feeling such an insensitive bastard right now. At least, Nina hoped that was what he was thinking.

Of course it wasn't.

Jack had been rather hoping Tommy might speak a little for himself, but instead he sat silent and pale, his mop of dark curls unkempt and unwashed. He had dark circles under his eyes and, Jack noted, despite gentle prompting, he remained silent.

'Okay, Tommy,' Jack said, pulling on his gloves, 'we're just going to take a look at that cut of yours.' He looked at Nina and for the first time that day he was smiling in her direction—for the sake of the patient, of course. 'You know Nina, I hear.'

Tommy's eyes darted towards her and she gave him a smile. 'We've met a few times, haven't we, Tommy?' Nina walked over and looked at the cut. It was deep and infected and it was clear that it should have been medically dealt with at the time it had happened. 'That looks sore,' Nina said. 'What happened?' She saw the confusion in Tommy's eyes. 'It's okay,' Nina said. 'We just want to find out what happened so we can make sure it gets better.'

'Where's Dad?' The question was aimed at Nina, and it was the first words Jack had heard Tommy say.

'Dad's just having a seat and a drink in another area.' She made it clear, Jack noted, that his dad was well away and that he could talk freely, and she asked him again about the cut.

'I don't know.'

Gently Jack examined him, probing his little stomach, exploring his rib cage, noting that Tommy winced when he did so. Jack pulled on his stethoscope and listened to Tommy's chest, but looked up as someone stepped into the cubicle.

'Sorry about that.' A woman smiled. 'I'm Lorna Harris, locum registrar.'

'It's fine Lorna, I've got this,' Jack dismissed, but then a nurse popped her head around the door and explained that Elspeth was getting impatient.

Jack closed his eyes in mounting frustration. He opened them to two very dark blue ones and the serious face of Nina, and for the first time that morning he said what was on his mind. 'Do you know what I hate about charity?'

His voice was low and for Nina's ears only, the words not even for her really, they just came from a dark place inside him called frustration, not that she could understand. Jack never expected her to answer. He was already pulling off his gloves, and he certainly never thought that she might get it, but at the sound of her voice he stilled.

'The cost?'

Jack gave a wry smile, noted the small circles of colour rise on her cheeks as still he kept looking. He would have loved to continue this conversation, would have loved to say more, but the world outside waited. He turned and apologised to Tommy, told the little guy that Lorna would take good care of him now.

'Will I see you again later?' Tommy suddenly asked.

Jack had many noncommittal answers that he used to reply to questions such as this one, but apart from Nina he was the only person Tommy had spoken to, and though Jack did his best not to get too pulled in, especially with cases as emotional as this one, for reasons he didn't want to explore, yes, he would be following up on this case.

In detail.

'I'll come and check on you later, but it probably won't be till tonight,' Jack said. 'So you may already be asleep.'

Certainly Tommy was going to be admitted.

He handed over his findings to Lorna and then stepped out. Nina found herself blushing and unsettled by their brief conversation and just the effect of Jack Carter close up. He unsettled her in many areas—filthy rich, filthy morals, combined with a brilliance that somehow, despite his title, was wasted.

She'd always thought him shallow; a spoiled rich boy playing doctor, but she had sensed that he really wanted to be in here with Tommy, not out there talking with a benefactor, and for the first time she wondered if it was always so easy for him. Not that she had long to dwell on it. Despite gentle questioning, Tommy could offer no explanation for the cut and the bruising.

'Yes.' He started to cry when he admitted that his dad had been really cross that morning when he had wet the bed again.

Tommy had stopped wetting the bed three months ago.

Lorna was nice to Tommy, but not as thorough as Nina found Jack to be, and despite Nina telling her the complicated history, it was clear by the time they went into speak with Mike, Lorna had already made her mind up.

'As tragic as their history is,' Lorna said after interviewing Mike, 'we have a child with injuries neither he nor the father can account for, a nasty, infected cut that the father has not sought help for and a father that is hostile and angry towards staff. He already has a history with Child Protection.'

'I've explained why.'

'I know you have, but he's also admitted how frustrated he is that Tommy has started wetting the bed again.' She paused as they were told Tommy's X-rays were in, and as she checked them Nina's heart sank. 'Two fractured ribs.'

They spoke at length and a child abuse screen was ordered—bloods would be taken and a full skeletal survey done, and in the meantime Nina would obtain an order that the father could only visit Tommy while supervised.

It was a long, busy day—the emergency with Tommy was just added to her routine work and by the time Nina had caught up with Sienna the clock was nudging nine p.m., but still there was work to do.

Nina had had a long conversation with Mike, and, despite all evidence pointing to him, something simply didn't sit right with her. Tommy had been desperately upset when his father had left, and Nina had assured Mike that there would be a case worker available first thing in the morning to supervise his access. Then she headed back into the general ward, where Tommy had been admitted, and went over and spoke to him, reassuring him that he was okay and that his father would be back in the morning.

Jack was sitting in the small office, going through Tommy's notes, and he looked up as Nina entered the darkened ward. Her hair, which had been rather more neatly pinned up that morning, had bit by bit worked its way out of the pins and fallen in soft tendrils around her face. She must be exhausted, Jack thought, remembering that she had been called out for an emergency even before that morning's meeting.

He wondered again if there was a Mr Wilson, though, remembering the blush that had spread on her cheeks that moment when their eyes had locked, he was certain that there was no Ms Wilson.

He was so not going there! Jack looked down at the notes he was reading—the last thing he needed was a fling with someone as intense as Nina Wilson.

Don't even think about it. Jack grinned to himself.

Maybe his own lack of sleep was catching up with him.

Still, he did find himself looking at her again, saw

that she was in no rush with Tommy, and wondered how she had the mental energy to be so involved.

And then she looked over towards the office and caught his eye, and Jack, for once, felt a little uncomfortable, as if he'd been caught staring. But he didn't look away, just watched as she made her way over to him.

'Nina.' He gave her a nod and he noted that she closed the door behind her.

'Could I have a word with you?'

'Sure.'

'I'm worried.' She gave him a tight smile. 'Which is nothing new. I always am…but tonight I'm really worried.'

'Go on.'

'I've just spent another couple of hours talking to Mike and I've just been in again to Tommy and I just don't think that Mike's responsible for the bruising.' She looked at him. 'Have you read the notes?'

'I've just started.'

'Have you read my notes?'

'Not yet.' Part of Jack's frustration was that he never actually got a chance to sit down and do that. He was always relying on handovers, catching up. He had read Lorna's findings and wasn't quite happy with the detail of her notes, would have preferred to have thoroughly examined Tommy himself rather than rely on a locum registrar's findings. He looked at Nina, saw the tension in her face and her genuine concern. 'Tell me what you know.'

She actually exhaled in relief before she started talking. 'I've been working with the family for six months, since the mother's death,' Nina explained. 'Prior to Kathy's death, the marriage was in trouble—they had major financial issues and Mike was away all week working, and when he came home at weekends Kathy often went to her mother's, so he hardly saw Tommy. Six months ago, Mike left for a trip after a huge argument with Kathy. He didn't ring her that day, but the next day, when he did, she didn't answer her phone and he figured she still wasn't talking to him.

'When she still didn't pick up the next day, Mike had a neighbour go and check on her. She was dead and Tommy was with her, hungry and dehydrated...'

Jack wasn't shocked, he had heard many stories like this before, but he saw tears well up in her eyes and her involvement in the case unnerved him, challenged him even. 'Given the row and the circumstances, there was suspicion as to Mike's involvement in the death. While Tommy was admitted here, the father was flying back to face police questioning, and Child Protection was naturally called in. That's the reason for my involvement.'

'Okay.' His expression was deadpan, but his mind filtered the information, and, Nina noted, he really was listening.

'Tommy had shut down from the trauma of being with his mother's body, but apart from that there were issues with bonding with his father.'

'Explain.'

She smiled. He didn't waste words, but gave her a chance to speak.

'When I first met Tommy and his father, Tommy

took all his direction from me. He had more connection with me than with his own father. As you know, a child is normally unsure around strangers, but not in this case. Mike had had very few dealings with Tommy and that's what we've been working on, whereas the psychologist has been dealing more with the issues of losing his mother. They've come on in leaps and bounds—despite enormous financial stress, Tommy and Mike are a real unit. He looks to his father now for prompts, he's asking to see him right now...'

'The father clearly has a temper problem. I saw the way he was with you.'

'Yes,' Nina said. 'But never with Tommy.'

'Never?'

'He was cross this morning about the wet bed, but that was out of frustration and fear. He doesn't understand the bruises and the cut. Mike told me that he was terrified that we'd take him away, what we'd think, that's why he didn't bring him in—which, yes, was a terrible call...'

Jack nodded. It had been a terrible call but one he had seen many parents make.

'I remember one child that was referred to us for unexplained bruising had leukaemia...'

'He's had blood work.' Jack shook his head. 'He hasn't got that and leukaemia wouldn't account for two fractured ribs and an infected cut that actually looks as if it's combined with a burn—and that he's resumed bedwetting.'

'Fine,' Nina said, and Jack frowned.

'What does that mean?'

'You've already made up your mind.' She walked out of his office and to the nurses' station and set up her computer to input her notes—God, she was an angry thing, Jack thought. He felt like walking over and tapping her on the shoulder, telling her that, no, he hadn't made up his mind, that he was still trying to catch up on the notes, and that he didn't jump in with assumptions. He looked at all the facts and *then* he made up his mind.

So he started to.

He read the psychologist's notes though they dealt more with the issues surrounding the mother, and then he read Nina's.

They were incredibly detailed and her observations were astute, outlining how Tommy had first responded to her, that he had been precocious almost, sitting on her knee, playing with her lanyard, taking no direction from the father he knew, but in later visits he had turned more and more to his father, so much so that Nina had been about to close the case.

So what had gone wrong these last weeks?

Jack looked up and saw Nina tapping away on her laptop, then she stopped and yawned and gave her head a little shake. He watched as she stood and headed for the water cooler and then came back to the computer, frowning as she read through her notes. Then she must have hit 'send', because an update appeared in the notes Jack was reading.

And he read Nina's account of today.

She was a brilliant report writer. He had expected more passion, a little dig at the medial staff perhaps, but instead she had detailed all that had happened, and her conclusion that, given the injuries and the lack of any explanation, she had obtained an urgent court order that allowed supervised access only for the next seventy-two hours.

And Jack sat and racked his brains.

He shut out all chatter.

He was head of paeds for more reasons than his financial pull.

No one argument swayed him, no tearful plea prompted his signature on anything that he didn't believe in.

Jack walked over to the bedside where Nina now stood stroking Tommy's dark curls as he slept. 'Do you always get this involved?'

'Always.' She didn't look up. 'Right now my department is all this little guy's got.'

'As well as the medical staff.'

'I'm talking about family.' She looked up. 'He wants his father and I've been to court to stop that contact; it's not a decision that can be taken lightly. I have a worker booked for nine a.m. and she will supervise a visit, but really Tommy needs his father tonight.'

'I've been reading through the notes,' Jack said, only he didn't get to finish as he was interrupted by a sudden wail from a sleeping Tommy. Nina looked down, moved to comfort him as his eyes opened and he sat up, clearly terrified.

'It's okay, Tommy,' Nina said, sure the little boy was having a nightmare, but instead Jack told her to step out, already pressing the bell for assistance. He knew long before Nina did what was happening, because Tommy hadn't woken up. He was experiencing an aura, a sudden panic before a seizure, and Tommy nearly bolted from the bed as Jack firmly held him, then laid him back down as his body gave way to spasms…

Nina felt sick. There was no question now that she should go home and she headed to the office, watching as the nurses ran with the trolley, IVs were put up and drugs were given.

Yet nothing seemed to be working.

She heard the call go out for the anaesthetist and then she saw through a chink in the curtains that after only brief respite young Tommy's body was starting to seize again.

A grim-faced Jack came into the office a while later.

'He's anaesthetised and we're taking him down for an urgent head CT,' Jack told her. 'You need to let his father know.'

'What do I tell him?'

'Just tell him to get here,' Jack said. 'I'll be the one to tell him that it's not looking good.'

CHAPTER FOUR

IT WAS A wretched night.

She had to sit with a terrified Mike who arrived after Tommy had gone for his CT scan. Because of the court order, because of the possibility that he had caused the injuries, Mike would only be allowed to see Tommy supervised, and when Lorianna, the duty social worker, appeared in the waiting room to sit with him, although exhausted, the last thing Nina wanted to do was leave.

'Go home.' Lorianna pulled her aside. 'It's after one and you're due back at nine.'

'I want to hear the results.'

'They'll be the same results in the morning.' Lorianna was practical. 'Anything from dad?'

'Nothing.' Nina shook her head. 'I'd just spent the best part of an hour trying to convince Jack that Mike hadn't harmed Tommy and I've just heard a nurse saying that they're flagging brain trauma…' God, she was questioning herself, which Nina did often, but she had been so sure Mike hadn't hurt Tommy. The sight of the little boy seizing had really upset Nina and standing outside the CT area, seeing more and more staff rushing in, in a race to save a little life, had tears stinging her eyes.

'You need to go home.' Lorianna was firm. 'You know that.'

Nina did.

There would be another family or families that needed her tomorrow and it wasn't fair to them if she hadn't at least had some sleep, but it felt so wrong to be leaving, so terrible to just walk away, except Nina knew that she had to.

She said goodbye to Mike, told him she would be back first thing in the morning, and then headed out of the hospital building towards the street, where she would flag a taxi. Really, she should have called Security rather than walk in the hospital grounds this late at night, but right now she just wanted to get home. She questioned her decision, though, as a car slowed down beside her and she walked a little more briskly as the car kept pace with her and the window slid down.

'Can I give you a lift?'

Nina turned at the sound of Jack's voice and saw his luxurious Jag, along with his face. 'No, thanks.'

'I actually want to talk to you—it turns out that you were right.'

'Sorry?'

'Tommy hasn't got a head injury,' Jack explained. 'It's a nasty brain lesion that's been causing the seizures. I expect that's where his bruises and injuries are from. I just called in Alex Rodriguez, he's in there speaking with the father now...' He drove alongside as Nina walked on, her boots making a crunching noise on the icy sidewalk, her breath coming out in short white shallow bursts as she struggled to hold onto both her temper and her tears, but, oblivious, Jack spoke on. 'So there you go—we find out again that things are never as they seem. Nina, let me give you—' He never got to finish.

'"*There you go!*"' She swung around, biting back tired, angry tears. His car halted when she did and Nina said it again. '"*There you go?*" Is that all you have to say?' She should stop speaking now, Nina knew, should just run for the nearest cab, except she didn't. 'Are you telling me that Tommy has a brain tumour?' She was furious and let it show. '"*Oh, hey, Nina, I just thought you might like to know...*"'

'I'm trying to explain—'

'And doing an appalling job at it. Have you even listened to what I've told you? Have you any concept what that family's been through and now Tommy has a brain tumour? Do you expect me to do a little victory dance because I was right that Mike hadn't beaten him? Well, I won't because, unlike you, I don't take cheap shots.'

'Really?' Jack checked, thinking of her little dig about him reading that she had delivered just that morning. 'Or do you not even realise you're doing it?'

'At least I don't gloat over other's mistakes.'

'Now, hold on a minute...' Jack, rather illegally, parked the car in the hospital driveway and as he climbed out she stood there shaking with fury as several weeks of guilt and misery culminated in one very unprofessional row. 'What are you talking about?'

'You know full well what I'm talking about,' Nina shouted. 'Your little *I told you so* look when Baby Tanner was brought back in.'

'Baby Tanner?' She saw his nonplussed face, a frown marring his perfect features as he tried to recall.

'The eight-week-old my department discharged...' Guilt had lived with her since the night he'd been brought back and now, to add to her fury, Nina realised that he couldn't even recall the case. 'You don't even remember, do you?'

'Nina...'

'You really can't remember!' She was disgusted.

'Nina, what you fail to understand is...'

She didn't want to understand him, she didn't want to be inside Jack Carter's mind. She wanted him well away, and so with words she kept him well back. 'You're so bloody distant from your patients,' Nina shouted, 'you're so clinical and detached...' Her temper was nearing boiling point. It was two a.m., she was tired, cold and hungry and, despite herself, she fancied the arrogant man who stood in front of her, could see him so tall and groomed and just so sexy that she was perhaps more angry with herself than with him. 'You know what, Jack?' she hurled at him. 'You're burnt out.'

'Oh, I'm not burnt out, baby—I haven't even fired up...'

Baby! Of all the chauvinistic, unprofessional things to call her—to relegate her... And maybe he realised the inappropriateness of his comment, because he gave a small shake of his head before walking toward her. 'Get in the car.' He was so close she could smell him. 'I'll give you a lift.'

'I don't want a lift.'

'You're upset...'

Nina could hardly breathe she was so angry, so attracted and he was so terribly close. 'I'm more than angry,' Nina said, 'I'm ropeable.'

He had the audacity to smile.

'I'm sure it could be arranged.'

He smiled in the darkness and she could see his white teeth as they both held their breath. For a very long moment she thought he might kiss her, and wouldn't that be typical Jack Carter? Snog his way out of a row, dismiss any criticism with a stroke of his tongue.

She wanted him to, though, and that was what terrified her.

Her feelings for Jack actually terrified her. She simply didn't know how to react around him, didn't know how she felt.

Her eyes were savage now when they met his, as he again told her what she would do.

'I'm going to drive you home and we'll discuss this properly tomorrow.'

'There's nothing to discuss,' Nina said.

'Oh, I beg to differ...' Jack said, 'but not here, not now. Right now you need to calm down.'

He might as well have lit the match. He'd be telling her she was premenstrual next, which, as an aside, Nina realised in that dangerous flickering moment, she was.

But that wasn't the point.

That so wasn't the point.

'Oh, I'll calm down when I'm out of this place and as far away from you as I can get.'

'Nina...' He caught her coat as she turned to go, and swung her around.

'Is this off the record?' Nina checked.

'Of course!' Still, she was sure, there was an edge of a smile on his beautiful mouth.

'Screw you!'

She shook him off, walked noisily on as fast as she could without slipping on ice, which he would just love, Nina thought angrily. Wouldn't he just love watching her bottom up on the sidewalk as he slid past in his silver Jag?

She practically ran out of Angel's, hailed a cab and climbed in, cursing under her breath as he overtook them.

At the same time, a curse come from Jack too.

What the hell was all that about? Jack wondered as he headed for his apartment.

Drama he so did not need.

Yet…

He thought of her angry face, the stamp of her boots, the bundle of passion he'd just witnessed and had actually enjoyed. Jack winced a little as he recalled his own retorts, though, which were so unlike him. He didn't really row with anyone, didn't really discuss, he just told people how it would be.

Still, as he headed for home she soon disappeared from his mind. He was just mildly annoyed that he had dumped Monica that morning, because he could really use a decent unwind…

Detached, clinical, yep, Jack was guilty as charged.

But no.

Nina was wrong.

He was so not burnt out.

* * *

Walking into her apartment, Nina closed the door on the world and let out a very long breath.

She would not think about Jack.

Neither would she think about Tommy.

Quite simply, she *had* to sleep and had learnt long ago that sometimes you simply had to turn off fear and panic and just close your eyes for a little while.

But her hands were shaking as she poured a glass of milk.

Nina wandered through her apartment, hoping it would soothe her.

She had just moved in and it was *everything* to her. She'd fought for eight years to have this, a proper home where finally they could be a family.

She went first to Blake's room, looked at the mountain of boxes that would hopefully soon transform into a bed and bedside table and a chest of drawers, but so far the fairies hadn't been in to build them. She'd hopefully do that tomorrow night, or at the latest by Blake's access visit next weekend.

Then she moved to what would hopefully soon be Janey's bedroom, but instead of feeling soothed her chest tightened in fear when she thought about her sister.

Janey, even before their parents' death, had been a wilful, difficult child, but now at fifteen she was going spectacularly off the rails, and Nina was absolutely petrified for her younger sister.

She wanted Janey close and just hoped and prayed that the case meeting to be held in a few weeks would finally deem *her* a suitable guardian.

Nina had been seventeen when her parents had been killed in a horrific car crash. She had been considered old enough to look after herself, but too young to care for a one- and a seven-year-old and, she now conceded, the department had probably been right.

For two years she had been as difficult and as wild as Janey was now—worse, in fact. Devastated by the loss, not just of her parents but of her brother and sister too, Nina had been unable to keep up with the rent. She had lost her home and had spent a couple of years surfing friends' couches until finally she had found the pro bono centre, which had, quite simply, turned her life around. The people there had counselled her, offered support, both practical and financial, and she had commenced her studies at the age of nineteen and had qualified as a social worker at twenty-three.

But a junior social worker's wage had only allowed for a small one-bedroomed apartment and so she had still been unable to provide a proper home for her brother and sister, having to make do with just access visits and respite care.

Determined that they would be together Nina had scrimped and saved for the past two years, had gone without luxuries and every pay rise had gone towards her savings until finally she had found a three-bedroomed flat she could afford. Now, at the age of twenty-five, she was hoping that, after all these years, the Wilson siblings could be a real family.

But then she'd gone and lost her head with the Head of Paediatrics.

Nina tried to sleep.

Told herself that Jack wasn't going to have her fired—he'd been inappropriate too.

Terribly so.

She lay there in bed and thought of his words, startled that just the repetition of them could have her body aflame.

Nina turned over, screwed her eyes closed and did her best not to think about him. She could not think about Jack like that—except she was.

Her own thoughts startled her. She had never been in a relationship, didn't know how to handle men unless she was dealing with them professionally.

She wasn't thinking professionally about Jack now.

And she hated sex, Nina reminded herself, except she was thinking the sexiest thoughts now, and she moaned out his name. For a breathless moment she lay there, embarrassed and mortified for different reasons now at the thought that tomorrow she might have to face him.

CHAPTER FIVE

IT ACTUALLY WASN'T an issue.

When Nina walked into ICU to check on Tommy, the sight of Mike's grief-stricken face was the only thing that consumed her and she barely noticed Jack speaking with Alex.

But Jack noticed her.

She was wearing a black skirt with a jade top and stockings and flat ankle boots today. She was far paler than yesterday and there were dark rings under her eyes, but even running on fatigue she was a ball of energy.

'How is he?'

Mike shrugged helplessly. 'He's just had some more tests and they're arranging a biopsy. They want to keep him on the ventilator for a few days…' He looked up at Nina. 'I'm so sorry for yesterday.'

'Let's deal with that another time,' Nina said.

'I think I was starting to realise that there was something really wrong with him… I just didn't want to know.'

'Mike, we'll go over all of that later. I've arranged a case meeting for tomorrow morning and we'll look at the supervised access order then, but right now let's just concentrate on Tommy.' Jack noted that she didn't ignore the issue of his outburst, there were just more important things to address right now. 'Have you rung your sister?' Nina asked. 'The one in Texas?'

Mike nodded. 'She's sorting out her children and flying out as soon as she can.'

'That's good.'

Jack had never been a particular fan of the social work department. Oh, he knew that they did a good job, but more often than not he found himself in contention with them. But today he saw that the holistic approach that had irked him so much was vital now.

Mike had no one, had lost his wife, his career and could possibly now lose his son, and he saw just how necessary it was that someone knew that there was a sister in Texas, that there was someone who knew that yesterday had been out of character for him.

He saw how important it was that when Mike was too emotionally distraught to speak that he had a voice, and in this case it came from Nina. He watched as her eyes skimmed past his face and landed on Alex's. 'If I liaise with your secretary, would you be able to attend a case meeting tomorrow?'

'We won't know much more by tomorrow,' Alex said.

'Sure, but I want to sort out the order and bring everyone up to speed,' Nina said.

Alex nodded and got back to the scan he was reviewing, but as Nina walked off Jack halted her.

'I'll catch up with you later, Nina.'

'Sorry?' She turned and frowned. 'You don't need to

be at the case meeting, it was the locum registrar who ordered the child abuse screen.'

'I'm aware of that,' Jack said. 'But I need to be brought up to speed on a few separate issues that arose last night.'

'Sure.'

Damn.

She had wondered how he would handle things—a letter from Admin perhaps, an internal email asking her to attend HR, or, and she'd rather hoped for this one, that her outburst would simply be ignored. Nina really couldn't believe she had spoken to anyone like that, let alone the Head of Paediatrics, Jack Carter himself! She had been completely unprofessional because, Nina knew, her feelings for Jack were completely unprofessional.

Of all the people to have a crush on…

How was it possible to be so attracted to someone that you actually didn't like?

It was a question that she couldn't answer and by three p.m., when her intercom buzzed and she was told Jack Carter was there to see her, Nina was actually relieved that soon things would be sorted out.

She just wanted this over with. 'Send him in.'

Nina took a deep breath, wondering if she should stand to greet him, if she should just apologise outright and explain how tired and emotional she had been yesterday.

She didn't get a chance to do either. The door knocked and as soon as she called for him to come in, he did so.

'You wanted to screw me?'

She had never considered that he might make her laugh, that he might have her smiling with his reference to her parting words last night.

'It's a figure of speech.'

'Oh!' He feigned disappointment. 'I shaved and everything. I even wore my best tie.'

He certainly had shaved, she'd noticed that this morning.

And, Nina reluctantly noted, he smelt fantastic.

He looked fantastic.

Jack would have had as little sleep last night as she'd had, yet there wasn't even a hint of weariness about him. Mind you, from what she had heard about him, Jack Carter was more than used to operating on minimal sleep. As well as his phenomenally busy job, his social life was daunting. If you lived in New York, you knew all about the Carters. They were glamorous, rich and had the social life to prove it. Jack was a regular feature in the social pages, a different woman on his arm each time, and more often than not witty little pieces written about the latest woman he had left in tears.

Nina didn't need to see it in magazines, there were many of his conquests dotted around the hospital, and the last thing she intended to be was another.

'I'd like to apologise for last night.' Nina wasn't as immediate in her apology as she had intended to be, but the fact that he had made her laugh a little made the words more genuine and a little easier to say. 'It came at the end of a very long day.'

'I understand that.' And if she had any hope that

things would be left there, that her apology might suffice, then it was a very fleeting hope, because Jack was pulling up a chair. 'However, it does need to be addressed.'

'Really, it doesn't.'

'Really, it does.' He mimicked her voice and then he was serious. 'I'd like to offer an apology of my own—I shouldn't have told you that Tommy had a brain lesion the way that I did. I thought you would want to know before you went home last night.'

She was somewhat taken aback by his apology. 'How is he doing this afternoon?'

'He's still intubated and his father is with him. Alex is hoping the medication will start to really kick in and that his cerebral irritation will abate over the next forty-eight hours and then he can be extubated. They've taken a biopsy of the lesion.'

'Is it serious?'

'It's too early to say, though I would think that it is. Given the prolonged nature of his seizure, it sounds as if he's been having them for the last couple of weeks—that would explain the bruising and bedwetting. Still, the father has been negligent by not getting the cut and the bruises examined.'

'He was scared.'

'I'm aware of that, but his delay in seeking treatment for his son…' Jack didn't want to argue the point. 'But, yes, I accept that he was scared.'

'Well.' Nina gave him a brief smile. 'Thank you for stopping by and, again, I apologise for last night.' She stood, but Jack didn't.

'I haven't finished yet.'

'I've actually got quite a full workload…' Nina attempted, but could have kicked herself. He was Head of Paediatrics after all, and his diary would be full to bursting.

'Don't we all? But we're going to make some time to sit down and talk about Baby Tanner.'

'I'd rather not.'

'I didn't offer an option,' Jack said. 'And, yes, I'd love a coffee, thank you for offering.'

Reluctantly Nina headed over to her percolator. 'Cream and one sugar,' he called, and when she'd made him his drink and sat down, Jack immediately opened the conversation. 'I've had a look through the notes and it would seem I made a recommendation for Baby Tanner to be placed in foster-care.'

'You did.'

'But the social work department felt that the mother was doing well and with suitable provisions in place…' He gave her a wry smile. 'Does that sound familiar?'

'You don't remember him, do you?'

'A little bit, now that I've looked him up. What I don't understand is why you think that I'm supposed to remember him, why you're so upset.'

'I'm not.'

'I'd suggest you are.' Jack sat back in the chair, took a sip of his coffee as if he had all the time in the world. 'Last night it was clear that you're still furious about it, to the point where you were shouting in the hospital car park at the Head of Paediatrics, "Screw you!"'

'I've apologised for that.'

'And I've accepted your apology. I'm not here to discipline anyone. I'm simply here to find out why you are so upset with me about Baby Tanner.'

'It was what you said when he was readmitted…' Nina shook her head, because that wasn't quite right. 'Or rather it was the look you gave.'

'The look?'

'The *I told you so* look.'

'I don't think so.' Jack shook his head.

'I remember it very well,' Nina said, and took a sip of her own coffee.

'Was it this one?'

She looked over and almost choked on her mouthful of coffee.

Jack Carter was smiling at her and it was a smile she had never seen. He was looking straight into her eyes and his smile was wicked, triumphant. He held that smile till her face was burning, till she had forced herself to swallow the coffee she held in her mouth, till she remembered again to breathe, because for a moment there she had felt as if she were lying under him, felt as she'd just found out what it was like to be made love to by him.

'*That's* my *I told you so* look,' Jack said, and then his face changed. His expression became serious, his jaw tense, his eyes the same they had been the night Baby Tanner had been brought in.

'What you saw was my *I hate this job sometimes, why do people have children if they don't want them, what the hell is wrong with the world that someone can do this to an eight-week-old* look…'

'Oh.'

'They're two very different things and not for a minute was I blaming you for what had happened to Baby Tanner.'

'Okay.'

'And it was the same look I gave you yesterday when you walked in and saw Tommy covered in bruises. Why would you think I blamed you?'

'People often do,' Nina answered tartly.

'Well, I don't,' Jack said. 'And I want to make that clear. There's no simple answer in a lot of these cases…' He would have spoken on but at that moment there was the sound of a commotion outside. The office door opened and Nina heard the receptionist shouting that Nina had someone in with her and that she simply couldn't go in—not that is made the slightest difference.

'Janey!' Nina stood. 'You can't just barge in here…'

'You said I could come by any time.'

Jack looked at the angry teenager who had just burst into the office, heard the challenge in her words, saw the anger in her stance, and decided the social work department really was the hidden front line of Angel's.

'I need some money,' Janey said. 'I haven't got any to ride the subway, and I'm hungry.'

'Wait outside and I will speak with you when I'm finished here.'

'I'm not waiting! Are you going to give me money or not?'

Jack frowned as Nina reached for her bag. 'Hold on a moment.' What on earth was she doing, giving this young woman money?

'Leave it, Jack.'

For a moment he did.

He watched as Nina handed over a few dollars, heard her tell Janey to be careful and that she would ring her later tonight. Then Nina asked her who she was with, where she was going, but all Janey had been interested in had been getting some money and, almost as soon as she had arrived, she left.

'I know I have absolutely no idea about the inner workings of the social work department,' Jack started, 'but I do not like the idea of angry, clearly troubled teenagers feeling they can just storm in here and demand—'

'She isn't a client,' Nina interrupted him. She sat back down at her desk and tried to keep her voice matter-of-fact as she explained to Jack what had just happened. 'Janey is my sister.'

'Your sister? So why is she…?' He never finished the question, realising even as he started to speak that it was none of his business anyway. Though that wasn't the reason that Jack stopped talking. It was because Nina had put her head in her hands and promptly burst into tears.

It wasn't a little weep either.

In that moment everything Nina was struggling with chose to finally catch up with her and she sobbed for more than a minute before attempting to pull herself together. When she did she was mortified that it was Jack who was there to witness her meltdown.

For weeks things had been building up. Janey's behaviour was getting worse and, given her job, Nina knew more than most that Janey was heading rapidly in the wrong direction, yet felt powerless to do anything.

'Please.' There were always tissues on her desk, usually for the clients, but Nina peeled off a generous handful and blew her nose. She couldn't bring herself to look at Jack. 'Can you leave?'

He just sat there.

'I don't want to discuss this.'

'Sorry, but you're going to.' Jack stood. 'But first I suggest—in fact, I insist—that you go home and get some sleep.'

'I can't go home.' Nina shook her head. 'It's impossible, I've got appointments, I need to—'

'You need to go home.'

And she gave in then as she truly was beyond exhausted. She had spent the weekend moving into her apartment, as well as arguing with Janey, as well as working at the pro bono centre in Harlem till late on Sunday, and yesterday had been impossibly long...

'Fine.'

'I'll drive you.'

'I can take the subway.'

'No.'

'I'll take a taxi.'

'I'm not going through this again,' Jack said. 'I'm not on call so I'm giving you a lift and this time you're not going to argue.' He rang down to Switchboard, told them he was out of range for the next forty minutes or so and then walked her out to his parking spot.

She could have taken a taxi, Jack knew that. He really didn't know why he was so insistent on driving her home himself. Rarely did tears move him and exhaustion was frequent in this place.

It was the complexity of her that had him unusually intrigued.

The traffic was busy but Jack negotiated it easily and Nina was actually relieved for the lift, for the silence and warm comfort of his car, and grateful too that he didn't ask any questions.

'Just here,' she told him as they neared her apartment.

'I'll just park.'

'Just drop me here.' Nina was irritated. 'I really don't need to be seen to the door.'

'I'm a gentleman.'

Not from what she'd heard!

A delivery van moved off and Jack dived into the vacant space. Then he walked around the car and as she opened her door he held it for her, before locking the vehicle and walking beside her along the cold pavement.

'You're right,' Nina said as they climbed the stairs. 'I need to be home.'

'Go to bed,' Jack said. 'And I'll pick you up at eight, take you out for dinner.'

'I don't want dinner.'

'You don't eat?'

'I meant—'

'I know what you meant, but I'm not listening. I'm taking you out for dinner.'

'Because?'

'Because by eight o'clock. we'll both be hungry and,'

Jack added, 'we never did get to finish our conversation.'

It was just dinner, Nina told herself as Jack walked off, just dinner between two colleagues who had a few things that needed to be sorted out.

The stupid thing was she almost convinced herself that she meant it.

CHAPTER SIX

A GOOD SLEEP and a lot of talking to herself later, Nina sat opposite him.

He'd chosen the restaurant without consulting her, of course, and it was a really nice one. She knew that even before they were inside because someone opened the car door for her and then took Jack's car to be parked.

It was nothing Nina was used to and nothing she secretly coveted but, despite her values, despite everything she believed in, it was actually incredible to be taken somewhere so nice and, Nina reluctantly conceded as she glanced over at Jack, to be there with him.

He took a sip of the wine he had chosen and ordered after she had asked for a glass of house white and she smarted a bit at that—clearly he thought he knew better. Well, he did know better, Nina conceded as she took a sip too because it was fruity and light and probably fifty times more expensive than the one she would have chosen. But just as she almost started to relax, to believe that they were here to talk about work, Jack asked a very personal question. 'What's going on with your sister?'

'Why would I discuss that with you?'

'Because I happen to know a lot about teenagers.'

'I know quite a bit myself.'

'So you're dealing with this objectively, are you?' Jack checked. 'You're able to treat Janey as if she's a client at work.' He watched her tense swallow and conceded a brief pause. 'Let's order, and if you choose an omelette or a salad I'm going to override you and get the most expensive thing on the menu just to annoy you.'

'Well, can you get the most expensive vegetarian thing on the menu please?' She looked through the menu and... To hell with it, she was out with Jack Carter so she chose what she wanted—a tomato salad for a starter and then mushroom and goat cheese ravioli with saffron cream for the main course.

And, yes, maybe she could use a brain like his if it would help with her sister—she simply couldn't take the emotion out of the equation.

Jack could do it without blinking.

'My sister, Janey, is fifteen and my brother, Blake, is nine. They're both in foster-care—separate foster-homes...'

'So when you say that foster-care is no fairy-tale solution, you're not speaking just professionally?'

'No. Blake has been very lucky for the most part, but in the last year his placement hasn't been going so well. The couple he's with are getting old and their daughter has just returned from overseas with her children and I think they'd rather be spending time with them than Blake. He doesn't say much to me about it, I have him every alternate weekend, but I think he's spending an awful lot of time alone in his room.'

'And Janey?'

'Janey hasn't fared so well in the system. She was moved around a lot, but she's been with a woman, Barbara, for the last four years. In the last few months... I think Barbara's had about enough. Janey's skipping school, arguing, just delinquent behaviour...'

'What happened to your parents?'

'They died when I was seventeen,' Nina explained. 'I tried to get custody but...' She shook her head.

'Too young.'

'Yes,' Nina said, 'but it was a bit more than that. I was very angry at my parents for dying. I was a lot like Janey is now. I lost my temper with the social workers on more than one occasion.' It helped that he smiled a little as she told him, because the guilt of her handling of things back then still ate away at her to this day. 'So I managed to stuff everything up...'

'You were seventeen,' Jack pointed out. 'Do you really think you could have taken care of them?'

'No,' Nina admitted. 'But it just hurt so much that we were separated. My parents weren't well off, there was no insurance, no savings, nothing. I know the department was right to place them, but that was then and this is now. I've just moved into a three-bedroomed apartment and I'm about to go again and try for custody.'

'Without losing your temper this time?'

'Yes,' Nina said.

'Without getting all fired up.'

'Yes.' And this time she smiled.

'You're going to go in there being cool and the amazing professional that you are.'

'Thanks.' She looked over at him. 'It's hard enough

to be dispassionate when you're fighting for a client, but when it's family, well, you can imagine what that's like...'

Actually, Jack couldn't, but he chose not to say anything, just let Nina continue to talk. 'I thought there would be no problem, but Janey ran a way a few weeks ago, and when she turned up on my doorstep I didn't let Barbara or the case worker know where she was. I know I should have rung straight away, I know I was wrong, but I just wanted some time to get to the bottom of what was going on before they took her back. Then the duty social worker turned up at my door and, of course, there she was.'

'Another black mark against Nina.'

'I just want my family together.'

'You'll get them.'

'I'm not sure.' She blew out a breath. 'I work very long hours...'

'Can you reduce them?'

Nina gave a tight shrug. She didn't want to drone on about her finances to someone who simply wouldn't understand. 'I also volunteer at the pro bono centre in Harlem eight hours a week...'

'Well, that can go,' Jack said, and Nina felt her hand tighten around her wine glass. She looked at him, at a man who had had everything handed to him on a plate as he coolly dismissed something that was very important to her.

'I happen to like working there,' Nina said. 'It's extremely important to me. Without them...' She stopped, she just wasn't going to get into this with Jack, but rather than letting her drop it Jack pushed for Nina to go on.

'Without them…?'

'They do amazing work,' Nina said. 'It's run by very passionate, caring people.'

'Unlike me.' Jack grinned. He could hear the barbs behind her words.

'I didn't say that.'

'You think it, though.'

Nina shrugged again.

'I can't afford to get involved, Nina.'

She didn't buy it.

'How can you not?' She blinked at him. 'You're a brilliant doctor. I've actually seen you in action the rare times you're hands on. You and I both know…' She halted. There were some things that should perhaps not be said.

'Go on,' Jack invited.

'I don't think I should.'

'Off the record?' Jack smiled. 'And, no, you can't screw me here.'

He made her blush, he made her smile, he gave her permission to be honest.

'I'm not criticising the other doctor, but I do think that had it been you who examined Tommy…' She took a slug of her wine before continuing. 'Well, things might have been picked up a little sooner.'

Jack would never criticise a colleague and certainly not to a woman he didn't really know—idle gossip was a dangerous thing—but he absolutely agreed with Nina. He'd thought exactly the same thing.

Not only that, he'd had a rather long and difficult conversation with the locum registrar just that morning, not that he could share that with Nina.

'I just think…' She really should say no more, except his silence invited her to go on. Sometimes she was a little too honest and even as the words tumbled out, she wished she could take them back. 'Instead of sucking up to benefactors, you'd be better off with the patients.' She knew she had gone too far, knew from the flicker of darkness across his eyes that she'd overstepped the mark, and she recanted a little. 'Certainly the patients would be better off…'

She was nothing like Jack was used to.

Nothing like anyone he had ever been out with before.

He could not think of one person who had ever spoken to him like this, yet over and over she had.

'Do you ever got involved?' Nina asked a little later, when she was scraping her dessert bowl. 'I mean, do you ever get close?'

'Are we still talking about work?' Jack grinned.

'Of course.' Nina gave a tight smile. She already knew the answer in regard to his personal life. Jack saw the smile, matched it and then upped it, just looked at her and smiled till her face was pink and her toes were curling in her boots.

'No,' he said. 'And no at work as well.' Then he stopped smiling. 'I'm not a machine, Nina. I get a bit upset sometimes, I guess, and some things get to me more than others but, no, I work better by staying back…'

He thought he might get a brief lecture, thought the frown was a precursor to criticism, but then, perhaps properly for the first time that night, her eyes met his. 'You'd be really good at the pro bono centre.'

It was Jack frowning now. 'I already do a lot...'

'No.' She shook her head. 'I'm not asking you to volunteer. I'm just saying that someone like you would be really good.' She gave him a smile when he had expected a rebuff. 'I am sorry for what I said last night— I guess cool heads are needed at times.'

Except his head wasn't so cool now.

And, no, he never got involved on a personal level either. Jack didn't do *dating* and long conversations, and certainly no explorations into someone else's past, except he found himself wanting to know about a younger Nina, found himself asking how she'd fared when her parents had died.

'It was rough for a while, but I got there.'

'How?'

'I had friends.' She gave a tight shrug. 'Couch-surfed for a while...'

'Couch-surfed?'

'Slept on friends' sofas.' He watched her face burn and then blue eyes met his. 'I nearly ended up on the streets.'

Jack could perhaps see why she was so angry at times, why she struggled so much in her efforts to keep families together—given the impact it had had on her life when she'd lost hers. 'So how come—?'

'I'm not going there, Jack,' she interrupted.

'Sure,' Jack said. Usually it was him pulling back,

usually it was him closing off and refusing to discuss things.

And so they chatted about other stuff when he really wanted to know more about Nina. He simply didn't know how to play her, because when he glanced at his phone and saw how late it was, had it been anyone else, they'd have been back at his apartment and safely in bed.

Safely in bed, because that was what Jack knew and did best. He wasn't used to that awkward moment when they climbed into his car, because usually both parties knew exactly where they were headed.

'No, thanks,' she said to his oh-so-casual offer of a nightcap at his place. 'It's already late and I'm the duty worker tomorrow night.'

So not only was Jack not used to going to back to *her place,* neither was he familiar with a smile at the front door and no invitation to come inside.

'Thanks so much for tonight,' Nina said. 'It was nice to clear the air.'

'Oh, we haven't cleared the air yet,' he said, and he gave her the kiss that he should have last night.

Not a gentle kiss, a very thorough kiss, a kiss that meant business.

She should have resisted, Nina thought as she kissed him back. She should have at least made some token protest, but there was something very consuming about being kissed by Jack, something that would make you a liar if you attempted to deny the effect, because like the man himself it was a top-notch kiss, and, like the man himself, very soon it went too far.

His mouth had left hers and had moved to her neck, his hands pulling her hips into him, and he was just as turned on as she was. He made sure Nina could feel it and then his voice was low in her ear. 'Am I going to be asked inside?'

'I don't think so.'

'Can you be persuaded?'

He kissed her again and, no, she couldn't be persuaded, because she trusted her heart to no one and certainly she'd be a fool to trust it to a man like Jack.

She pulled away. 'I'd better go.'

She was playing with fire here, Nina knew it. So she stepped back a little and went into her bag for her key.

'Nina—'

'Thanks so much for dinner.'

And she gave him a smile, stepped into the safety of her flat and closed the door on him. On them.

No matter how she might want to, Nina was so not going there.

These next few weeks were the most important of her life and she was not going into them with a head messed up by Jack Carter. And he would mess it up.

His reputation preceded him.

And she had her family to think of.

CHAPTER SEVEN

OVER THE FOLLOWING days Nina avoided Jack. She didn't return his calls and when he stopped her in the corridor one lunchtime and asked if she wanted to go out that night, she gave a vague reason as to why she couldn't, was polite and smiled and then quickly moved on.

Unused to being rebuffed, Jack didn't like it one bit.

Still, even if he had to face her in a few moments, right now there were more important things on his mind. Jack, Alex and the oncologist Terence were going over the planned course of treatment before speaking with Mike, and on one thing Alex remained resolute.

'I want it made clear to the father that there are no guarantees. I don't want him to be given false hope. Really, we're just trying to buy Tommy some more time here, because even if the chemo does shrink it, I don't know that surgery will be an option. It would be incredibly risky—most surgeons wouldn't touch it.'

'But you take on patients that others wouldn't,' Jack pointed out. 'That's why Angel's needs you.'

They stopped the discussion as there was a knock on the door, but Jack knew full well what was getting to Alex. Still, he wasn't going to discuss it in front of

Terence, and now the oncology nurse had arrived to sit in on the discussion with Mike.

'The father's outside with the case worker,' Gina said.

'Okay.' Jack nodded. 'Tell them to come in.'

Nina didn't blush when she saw him, Jack noted, and, yes, her coolness towards him was grating, her dismissal when he called or spoke to her seriously irked him—perhaps because he wasn't in the least used to it. Still, right now the focus of the meeting was Tommy and his father and preparing them for the difficult months ahead.

'It's basically a marathon that we're asking you to run,' Terence explained. 'It's an aggressive tumour and we're hoping to reduce it, but it's not going to be easy...'

'We're up for it,' Mike insisted.

'We need you fully on board,' Terence reiterated a little while later, because Mike just kept nodding at whatever was said. 'Any bruising or bleeding, a raised temperature, even a cold and Tommy is to be seen urgently.'

'Of course.' Mike sounded annoyed and it was then that Jack cut in.

'You need to listen to this carefully.' Jack was firm. 'Last week you were hiding Tommy's injuries from the hospital.'

'I didn't know what was happening,' Mike admitted. 'I thought you were out to take him away from me.'

'Well, we're not,' Jack said. 'Tommy needs you now more than ever, but we are all going to have to start trusting each other and being honest each with each other, and I'm telling you straight up that I will not accept any outbursts with my staff like the one I witnessed last week, no matter how emotional things get.'

'There won't be any more outbursts,' Mike said, and he looked at Nina. 'I've apologised to Nina, and I apologise again.'

'Mike's going to do the men's anger and emotion course that the pro bono centre runs,' Nina said. 'Aside from what happened in Emergency, I think it will be very helpful for Mike to have that resource in the months ahead.'

And on the meeting went. Terence had to get back to the ward but Mike had more questions.

'But if the chemo works, surgery might get rid of it.'

'It's a possible option,' Alex said carefully, 'but the lesion is in an exceptionally difficult location.'

'Have you done surgery like this before?'

'I've done similar,' Alex said, and Jack stepped in.

'Each case is unique.' He was as calm as always, Nina noted, and, she conceded, sometimes it was a good thing, because the emotion in the room was palpable. 'Each case is continually assessed. We'll know more once we see how Tommy responds to the chemotherapy.'

'But—'

'We're going to do our best for your son,' Jack said, 'but it would be wrong of us to say that this is a straightforward case—it's incredibly complicated. However, you do have the best team and the best resources available to your son. That much I can guarantee you.'

Mike nodded, stood when Alex did and shook his hand.

'Right.' Nina stood too once Alex had left. 'I'll take you up to the oncology ward and show you around.'

'I can do that,' Gina said. 'I'm going there now and I want to go over some of the side effects of the medication with dad.' She smiled at Mike. 'It will be good for Tommy if you're already familiar with the place when we bring him over.'

Which left Nina alone with Jack.

'You've been avoiding me.'

'I haven't,' Nina lied. 'I've just been busy.'

'Well, after work tonight…'

'I'm working at the pro bono centre,' Nina said quickly.

'If you'd let me finish,' Jack said, 'I was going to ask if I could speak with you after work about the pro bono centre—I was hoping to find out some more about it.'

Liar, Nina thought, but she was in no position to refuse him. Someone with Jack's skills would be an amazing coup for the pro bono centre, but she didn't like being manipulated and certainly she wasn't going to go through another dinner with him, or another kiss goodnight, because she knew full well what might happen. So she smiled sweetly back at him, played along with his game, but on her terms.

'Come and watch tonight,' Nina said. 'I'm running a clinic—it might give you a feel for the place.'

'Great!' Jack grinned through gritted teeth, because he'd been hoping to discuss things over a nice bottle of champagne. 'I'll pick you up—'

'I'll meet you there,' Nina broke in. 'My clinic starts at seven.'

'See you there then!' Jack said. 'What time does it finish?'

'About nine, nine-thirty.'

His smile only left his face when she was out of the office. A night at some pro bono centre was something he so did not need, but it would be worth it, Jack decided.

He'd have her in bed by ten.

She hadn't changed, Jack noted, because she had on the same purple stockings and a jumper that she'd been wearing earlier. He stood outside the pro bono centre and as she walked towards him he realised that her entire work wardrobe consisted of a black skirt, a grey skirt, a grey pinafore and then stockings and jumpers of various shades.

He wanted to take her shopping.

He wanted to spoil her, which was a first for Jack.

Oh, he was a generous date and lover. He had both a boutique florist and jeweller on speed dial and had tabs at the smartest bars and restaurant, but somehow with Nina he knew that wouldn't impress her.

And he wanted to.

'You're probably going to be bored,' Nina warned. 'I really deal mainly with paperwork, helping people with social security forms and housing and benefits and things.'

Jack had done a lot of work for charity, but had never actually worked for one. He really had no idea what to expect, a sort of massive soup kitchen perhaps, but he was surprised at the modern offices and the air of organisation.

'There's a doctors' clinic on tonight as well,' Nina explained. 'They're held alternate nights.'

'Well, while I'm here…' Jack said, more than happy to pitch in, but Nina shook her head.

'Sorry. You have to formally apply, your references and registration need to be verified, insurance…' She looked at him. 'It's not a back-street organisation, it's a non-profit organisation with some salaried staff and an awful lot of volunteers.' She gave him a smile. 'You can sit in with me if you like.' She saw his eyebrows arch. 'Though I'll have to ask each client if they mind you being present.'

It was like being a medical student again and Jack felt a surge of irritation. Every minute of his day was accounted for, and now, when he could really help, he was forced to take a back seat instead.

Literally.

He sat in an office as client after client came in.

Nina would explain to each of them that Jack was a senior paediatrician and there to observe, and that he was, hopefully, considering joining the centre. Most smiled and thanked him.

For sitting there.

Some asked that he wait outside.

Nancy gave him a very suspicious look but agreed that he could stay. She was an exhausted-looking lady with a nasty scar over one eye and a nose that had been broken and not reset.

'Where are the little ones?' Nina asked.

'Steven's home and watching them,' Nancy said. 'He's doing good now, much more sensible.'

'How was court?' Nina asked.

'I'm here,' Nancy said. 'No conviction recorded.'

'That's great,' Nina encouraged.

'I'm so grateful. I don't know what I was thinking back then.'

'Four children to feed maybe?' Nina said.

'Nancy left a violent household with her children,' Nina explained. 'They were on the streets for a while and Nancy got arrested for shoplifting. It was then that she was referred to us and we arranged emergency shelter. Nancy has found employment since then, but a conviction would have threatened that. She was represented by one of the centre's lawyers...' And Jack listened and heard how in the year since she'd left home Nancy really had turned her life around. She was out of emergency housing now and in rental accommodation and her eldest son, Steven, was finally attending school and taking it seriously. Nina was going through some welfare forms with her now that her circumstances had changed. 'Things are looking a lot better.'

'They are.' Nancy nodded.

'Now...' As the appointment concluded Nina smiled. 'Do you remember I spoke to you about Dr Cavel?'

'The cosmetic surgeon?'

Jack's ears really did pick up. If they were talking about Louis Cavel, he was renowned, so renowned that he had done some rather impressive work on Jack's own mother.

'We had a meeting a few weeks ago and I mentioned

you to him, as I said I would. He had a look at your photos and he really thinks he can help.' Jack watched as Nancy started to cry and Nina went from her chair and put her arms around the woman. 'He's really looking forward to meeting with you.'

'The truth?' Nancy checked.

'Absolutely,' Nina said.

'I'm so ashamed of my face,' Nancy sobbed. 'I feel people looking at my scars all the time and every time I look in the mirror I remember what he did.'

'Dr Cavel gets that. He wants to help you move on and really put this behind you,' Nina said. 'We're all so proud of the effort you've made this past year.'

'This is the sweet reward.'

'I believe so.' Nina said. 'I've heard that his work is second to none. Now…' Nina stood and went through the file and handed Nancy a business card '…he is holding a clinic here on Thursday. It's strictly by appointment, the wait for him is huge, but he does want to see you, so I've scheduled one. Can you get here on Thursday?'

'Oh, I'll be here.' Despite her tears a huge smile split Nancy's face. 'I wouldn't miss it. I never thought I'd be getting my face fixed.'

'I can't wait to see you when you do.'

As Nancy left, Nina turned at Jack's voice.

'We are talking about *the* Louis Cavel?'

'He donates fifteen hours a month,' Nina said. 'And the difference he makes to lives is amazing. Nancy is already a changed woman, but just wait till she's got rid of those scars, she'll be unstoppable.' She smiled at Jack. 'Louis loves the work he does here—he says it grounds him after dealing with rich socialites who have nothing more to worry about than new crows' feet appearing...'

'He's my mother's cosmetic surgeon.'

Her lack of embarrassment at her faux pas was refreshing, and when she laughed, so did Jack.

'So what will he do for Nancy?'

'A miracle,' Nina said. 'I had a woman last year who had massive, ke-, ke-, I can't remember the name. Really thick scars.'

'Keilod scars,' Jack said.

'That's it, and her nose had been broken numerous times. Louis did the most amazing work, he always does—he gives these women their faces back.'

As the evening progressed Jack was far from bored.

He was, in fact, fascinated.

They didn't finish till after ten, not because of clients but because they actually sat talking and Jack became more and more impressed with what he'd never thought he would be. He started to understand the holistic approach that she favoured so much, and they carried on chatting as Jack drove her home.

'We offer counselling not just to the women and children but also their partners. Some women stay and some men do choose to change.' She saw his disbelieving eye-roll. 'Some do!'

'Perhaps,' Jack said, though he'd have to see it to believe it.

Actually, he wanted to see it to believe it.

'I've got a fundraiser for the burns unit next weekend.' Jack glanced at her. 'Come with me.'

'I don't think so.'

'No, please. You dismiss all the work that I do, just as I dismissed yours, and I would like you to see what I do.'

'Jack…' Her voice was slightly weary. 'I'd stick out like a sore thumb at one of those dos.'

'I can—'

'Please,' Nina broke in. 'Don't offend me by offering to buy me something to wear. If I was a millionaire I still wouldn't drop a thousand dollars on an evening dress and shoes.'

A thousand dollars wouldn't begin to cover it and Jack felt that knot of unease again in his stomach as he thought of the wealth that surrounded him, the money that made money and the games that he played.

'Think about it.'

'Maybe.'

She wouldn't.

'And speaking of men who don't change—' they were nearing the turn-off for her apartment and Jack wanted to drive on '—would you like dinner?'

'I had something to eat at work.'

'A drink perhaps?'

This question Nina did think about, she really did.

She sat with her bottom being warmed on a leather seat and glanced over at him, at his perfect profile. Then, as his hand moved to turn on the music, she saw his manicured nails and the flash of his expensive watch and she remembered that he was everything she abhorred, except still she wanted him.

And Jack was the first man she had ever wanted.

The first.

Avoiding him hadn't cleared her head—her mind was still full of him. The fight to concentrate on anything but him was a permanent one these days and she knew nothing would come of it, knew it would be short-lived, but there were too many less–than-pleasant memories in her head, and Nina wanted a nicer one to replace them.

And so she agreed to a drink.

'Please.'

He had been sure she'd refuse him, and just as he blinked at her acceptance she surprised him again.

'Maybe we could have a drink back at your place.'

It was like a game with two players and they were both assessing the rules.

She walked into his gleaming bachelor pad and Jack Carter was everything she wasn't into.

Not just wealth-wise either.

He undid her coat with this half-smile on his face, made a lot of work of her belt, and that made her tingle in places she shouldn't.

It was a tiny thing, but Nina felt her heart beating in her throat.

'Drink…' Jack said, pouring her one without waiting for her reply.

He watched her at the window, still in her boots and that awful grey pinafore, but, he conceded, he liked the purple.

But it wasn't just her appearance that was different

from that of any woman he usually brought home, it wasn't just that Nina was different.

He actually *felt* different.

Very different.

He just couldn't nail why.

He took off his tie, kicked off his shoes, took a seat on a low lounge and watched as she stood there, looking out at the New York skyline she loved.

'What are you thinking?' Jack asked.

'Nothing. I'm just looking at the view.'

'Come on, Nina, what are you thinking?'

Nina turned. 'Will I be sent to the naughty corner if I don't tell you?'

'Blindfolded.' Jack actually laughed.

'I don't think I like you, Jack.' It was strange she could be so honest, could turn and look him in the eye and say exactly what she thought. 'And I know this isn't going anywhere.'

'Why not?'

'Oh, please,' she scoffed. She didn't need the sweet talk, she really didn't and told him so as she walked over to where he sat. 'I don't know that I'm up for the sexual marathon of the next few days or weeks and then the awkwardness after...'

'I'm never awkward,' Jack said, and watched as she smiled. 'I bet you like really considerate, thoughtful lovers who say, "Is this okay for you, Nina?" as you lie there bored out of your mind.'

'No.'

He frowned.

'So, if you're not sure you like me, why are you here?'

'Maybe for the same reason as you.'

'I'll tell you why I'm here.' And she waited for that beautiful mouth to tell her the reason, for him to say something crude perhaps, yet it was he now who surprised her. 'Unlike you, I happen to know that I like the person I've recently been spending time with. Admittedly, that's taken me by surprise—no offence, but you're not my type.'

'None taken,' Nina said, 'because you are *so* not mine.'

'However…' he was looking at her mouth as he spoke, his hands sliding up between her thighs 'I…think the sex could be amazing, and I actually have no idea where we are going and no idea where this is leading, just that I would like to get to know you some more.'

He was still looking at her mouth.

'I should warn you, though.' He smiled as he did so. 'Those touchy-feely, sensitive new-age lovers you're used to? I'm going to ruin you for ever…'

'Jack, you don't know me at all—there haven't been any sensitive new-age lovers, as you call them. I've never been in a relationship.'

She felt his hand still on her thigh, smiled at the flare of shock and panic in his eyes.

'I'm not a virgin.' Nina couldn't help but laugh at his reaction.

'Thank God for that.' Jack blew out a breath. 'Never?'

'Never,' Nina said. 'I don't really have time.' And she certainly had no intention of telling him about her past or admit to Jack that he was the first man she'd been attracted to in the longest, longest time…ever, really. That the nights spent on friends' sofas had rather too often had a down side in the shape of her friends' brothers or fathers—no, Jack didn't need to know all that.

It was far easier to let him think this was just casual, even if she'd never wanted anything like this in her life before. So that was what she told him, that just for tonight was completely fine. And Jack told himself that he could deal with this. After all, he'd never been in much of a relationship either, but there was a certain disquiet at her honesty that she was only there for sex. Jack noted his own double standards and got over them quickly, his hand resuming its path on her thigh.

If she had thought he would haul her over his shoulder and throw her onto the bed she couldn't have been more wrong. If she had thought he might quickly undress her, she had it wrong there too, because instead he kissed her.

A kiss that was far more tender than expected, a nice kiss that turned into a deeper kiss, but really, though, his kiss was measured and thoughtful and the hand on the back of her head was not bold or forceful, it was the other hand that misbehaved.

It climbed up her stockings, without even pretending to idle, and he stroked her through her pantyhose. He pushed where he could not enter, he fiddled and he probed and he stroked her as, like a gentleman, he kissed her.

And she kissed him back and wriggled on his knee

until she could not stand the tease, couldn't take the frustration any more.

'Tear them...' she breathed into his mouth.

He ignored her.

'Jack...' She pulled her mouth away. 'Tear them.'

'No.' His whole hand cupped her. 'Because I like them and I lied, it will be awkward when I see you in these stocking at work...'

'I've got loads.' But he kept stroking her and kissing her till she wanted to climb off his lap and take the bloody things off herself, except he pulled her down harder to him. She wanted him to undress her, wanted him to take her to bed, wanted to catch her breath, but he did not let her. Jack just kept touching her through her stockings and kissing her, because with his hand working its magic a kiss was all it would take to undo her. And he did not give in even when she tried to move a little to undress him to reciprocate.

'Why are you so stubborn?' Jack said when she held onto her orgasm.

'I'm not.' She could hardly get her breath, yet she refused to just give in to him. She didn't know why she was fighting it, she just didn't want to let go.

She wanted him to let her down, wanted him to be selfish, wanted to fault him in some way so that she could get him out of her mind, but she was failing miserably as she bit her lip, desperately trying not to come. He felt her thighs clamp around his hand, felt her breath rapid in his mouth and he stopped stroking, just enjoyed the small jolts of her body and the triumph of beating her resistance, but more than that, her reluctant pleasure was his.

He angered her.

She didn't know why.

Maybe it was the combination of good looks and wealth and knowing that things came so easily to him.

Even her.

That he simply knew he was that good made her angry and she turned on his lap to face him and refused to simply hand over control, to just lie there when he took her and whimper his name.

So, facing Jack, she kissed him, a different kiss this time. He was detained at her pleasure now, so it was the buttons to his shirt that she opened. He moved her hips up just a little higher so that his erection pressed into her and she kissed down his face to his neck, trying to gauge his collar line, nipping his neck just a little lower and sucking hard. There was a fight for control here and one Jack wasn't used to, but he was up for it, and their mouths found each other as she tackled his belt.

And she didn't just find out what sort of a lover Jack was, Nina found out what sort of a lover she could be.

That she could demand and be met, that she could offer no explanation but be understood. She unbuckled his belt and the top button of his trousers too, freeing him, and he let her feel a lot of him, then his hand moved in and shredded her stockings and her panties too, and she moaned with the pleasure of his fingers inside her and his mouth on her neck, and then somehow Jack made even the search for a condom sexy.

'I've got a little job for you.'

She had to lean over to his discarded jacket, had to find the little silver packet while his other hand stroked her bum, and then she had to rest back on her booted heels with his huge erection between them.

'Here.' She held out the packet.

'I'm busy,' he said, trying to find the zipper to her dress. 'You put it on.'

'You're old enough to dress yourself, Jack.' And she stayed back on her heels and held him, stroked him upwards over and over with both hands, one after the other in an endless tunnel till Jack was the one holding on now, Jack was the one fighting not to come.

'Why are you so stubborn, Jack?' Nina teased.

'Why are you?' Jack said, and lifted her hips enough so that she was over him, till her hands were removed from him and she had to steady herself on his shoulders. Then his hands held her hips and he pulled her down just a little way, just enough to teach her a very hard lesson, and then he lifted her a little and he watched her face as he did it again, and it was then that Nina conceded these were dangerous, reckless games and she never played them, but it was very easy to lose your head around Jack.

He watched as she went to retrieve the packet, but Jack changed his mind.

He didn't want sex on the sofa and neither did he want to be driving her home at two a.m. or calling a taxi, which he was somehow sure that she'd demand, because, unlike others, Nina didn't seem to want an entry pass to his bedroom. Nina wasn't even attempting that futile entry into his heart.

This, it would seem, was all she wanted.

It was Jack, as he kissed her into the bedroom, who wanted more.

He took off her dress in one motion.

And off came the purple jumper too and he looked at the tattiest bra he'd ever seen, and he even made her laugh as he took it off.

'Dressing to impress, Nina?'

'I don't need to.'

She didn't, because never had Jack cared less about the packaging. All Jack wanted was what was inside, but still she resisted.

Not with her body.

Her mouth met his as she undressed him. Nina indulged herself, because he was easily the most beautiful man she had ever seen, or had felt beneath her fingers. He was as luxurious naked as he was dressed. He smelt like Jack but a close-up version that she got to taste, and he acted like Jack, but a more intimate version that she now got to sample.

But, yes, she resisted, because even with Jack inside her, even with her body flaring with heat as he moved deep within her, even while being given the full Jack Carter experience, she held back just one vital piece, and he knew it.

'Nina…' He was chasing something and he didn't know what it was. He could feel her wanton beneath him, every lift of her hips bringing him closer. Her mouth was as probing as his, on his neck on his shoulders, her fingers scratching his back. It was the best sex he could remember, but he wanted something more. She was moaning beneath him and he guided her towards freefall, except he was used to more cheering from the stands, for the chant of his name or shouts of approval, for a giddy declaration as he hit the mark. He didn't need it and never had he actually wanted it, but as she throbbed beneath him, as he gave in to the sheer pleasure, Jack still wanted more.

His tongue was cool when he kissed her afterwards and she lay there, catching her breath for a very suitable while.

So now she knew just how good sex could be and all it did was confuse her, because she just couldn't imagine feeling like this with another man. She looked at Jack and he looked at her and Nina had to be very sure that she held onto her heart, but he had no idea of the gift he'd just given her. Even if soon he'd move on from her.

No idea at all.

'I'm going to get a taxi…'

He almost laughed.

A black laugh perhaps, because how many times had he lain in this very bed, wishing he could hear those words rather than have to do the conversation thing in the morning?

And now he had them from the one woman he didn't want to hear them from.

'You're not getting a taxi, your clothes are all torn…' Jack said. 'I'm not putting you in a taxi with no underwear on.'

'Drive me, then.'

'I will,' Jack said, and pulled her over to him. 'In the morning.'

Most mornings he woke up feeling somewhat stifled, an arm draped around him, or fingers running up his back, or, worse, the smell of breakfast and the sound of talking, except when he woke at six the next morning, Nina was exactly where she'd removed herself about two minutes after he'd pulled her over towards him.

Curled up on the edge of the bed and facing away from him.

CHAPTER EIGHT

IT ACTUALLY WASN'T awkward when Nina saw Jack at work.

She was too busy.

She was allocated several new families and as the days passed her paperwork piled up, but there was always somewhere else she needed to be.

'How are you doing?' She smiled at Tommy, who was looking so much better than he had on admission. The oncology nurse Gina was adding something to his IV and smiled at Nina. The medication had, for now, stopped the seizures and there was some colour in his cheeks, though it wouldn't be for long. Tommy was starting chemotherapy on Monday and from what she had heard it was going to be especially gruelling.

'Good,' Tommy said, and then introduced her to the woman sitting by his bed. 'This is my aunt, she's staying for the weekend.'

'I'm Kelly.' Tommy's aunt smiled. 'I'll be coming back as often as I can. Mike's got a job interview today, but he's coming in this afternoon.'

'That's good.'

It was awful.

Nina couldn't believe how hard it was for this family, couldn't fathom having to look for a job when your child was so sick. She was trying to arrange some accommodation for Mike nearer the hospital for the times Tommy would be here during his treatments, but there was only so much she could do and as she said her goodbyes and walked off, Gina voiced what she was thinking.

'Cruel, isn't it?'

Nina nodded. 'I'm going to look into it all again—see if there is anything more the department can do.'

'The poor man's trying to be in five different places at once, and the only place he wants to be is here with his son.' Gina sighed and when Nina got back to her office she sat with her head in her hands for a moment, because she'd added mandatory counselling to the list of places where Mike needed to be.

And again she questioned herself.

Still, she couldn't dwell on it for too long as she needed to add an urgent addendum to her report for court the next day.

Jack had rung a few times but she'd kept it short, had told him she was snowed under with work, had done everything to not give in to the urge to repeat things with him.

Yes, she had enough to contend with and it wasn't going to get easier any time soon, Nina thought as an angry Janey landed in her office at four p.m., after school, sulking, angry and confused about why Nina now had the three-bedroomed apartment but they still hadn't moved in with her.

'I've applied to be guardian for both you and Blake

and the department has to come and inspect the flat and check everything thoroughly.'

'Yeah, well, I don't believe you,' Janey shouted when Nina told her that she'd put the application in as soon as she'd secured the apartment. 'If you really wanted us, you'd have had us living with you years ago.'

Janey used words like knives and hurled them at Nina regularly, but though Nina had learnt to deflect most of them, these were the ones that hurt the most, because it killed her that she hadn't been able to keep her family together.

'It's not that straightforward, Janey.' Nina did her best to stay calm. 'And it's not fair to Barbara either, for me to just—'

'Barbara's a cow!' Janey huffed.

'I don't like you speaking like that.'

'Well, she is.'

Nina gritted her teeth and not for the first time questioned if she was up to the job of dealing with such an angry teenager. Of course, professionally she was but, as she often said to tearful parents who sat in this office and asked how she handled things so well, she got a break from it, got to go home at the end of each day. If things went well, in a few weeks she could be fully responsible for Janey, and what scared Nina the most was that if she wasn't up to the job, Janey's bad behaviour would escalate.

'Things are moving forward,' Nina said. 'I know it seems to be taking ages but I haven't been in the apartment long. Why don't we go and get something to eat and I'll show the photos I've taken? I've got all the furniture now for your room.'

'I thought you were working.'

'I'm going to be working till late,' Nina said, 'so I can take a break now.'

They took the lift and there were several choices where they could eat—there were a few cafés in the hospital so that parents could come and share a meal with their child if they were able to, or to spend some time away from the bedside with siblings and such. The whole hospital was geared to being not just child friendly but family friendly, but Nina was starting to feel as if her dream of her family being together was fading before it even had a chance to take off. Maybe they'd do better just walking.

'What do you want to eat?'

She was met with Janey's shrug.

They settled for the coffee bar and took a seat at the back where it was a quiet enough to talk. Nina bought Janey her favourite muffin and frappe and herself a regular coffee, deciding she wasn't hungry yet and would get something to eat later.

'Here.'

Should it annoy her that Janey didn't bother to say thank you? Should she let the small things go?

No.

She thought of their parents, how they'd insisted on good manners, but if she said anything, Janey would simply get up and walk out, and not wanting to risk that she let it go.

'I am doing my best.'

'Whatever.'

'I've got Blake this weekend,' Nina said. 'Why don't you come?'

Janey didn't answer. Nina quietly thought that Janey might very well be jealous of the more structured access Nina had with Blake, but that was because of his age and the distance he lived from Nina, which made shorter visits impossible. With Janey it was mainly holidays and the occasional sleepover, especially as Janey's weekends were taken up with sport activities.

'I could take you to netball.'

'I'm not doing netball any more.'

'How come?' Nina asked. 'You loved it, Blake and I were going to come and watch.'

'Yeah, well, don't bother. I got dropped.'

'How come?' Nina pushed. 'You were doing really well.'

'Till I swore at the umpire.' Janey was peeling apart her muffin, not looking at Nina as she spoke. 'And Barbara says that if I'm going to carry on like that then I can spend the weekend sorting out the basement.' She looked up at Nina. 'I guess if you ring her, though, she might let me come…'

'No.' Nina did her best not to be manipulated. Barbara was doing the hard yards, dealing with Janey, and Nina simply refused to interfere in the groundings and early bedtimes Barbara was trying to rein Janey in with. 'Barbara's right not to just let it go. Janey, you loved your netball. What were you doing, swearing at the umpire?'

'She was a stupid cow.'

'Everyone's a cow to you…' Nina tried to hold onto her temper, tried not to upset Janey, but it was impossible. She had no real authority with her sister. Janey pulled all the strings and she started pulling them now.

'Yeah, well, you're the biggest cow.' Janey stood. 'I'm stuck cleaning out a basement all weekend while you're busy spoiling Blake. Thanks a lot, sis…'

And she stormed out of the café and straight past Jack, not that she noticed him.

Jack noticed her, though.

He moved out of the way as a fast-moving, angry teenager stormed past and he looked into the café and saw Nina resting her head on her hands. He wanted to go over to see if she was okay but he'd just been called for a consult in ICU so he'd make time for Nina later.

And he would.

Jack was determined now, because he could not, *could not*, stop thinking about her.

It was an absolute first for him.

Jack's days were too busy to spend time dwelling on one woman, but he woke up thinking of Nina, spent the day with her sort of present in his mind. And the evenings were impossible, because she was *always* busy and sometimes she didn't even return his phone calls.

Another first.

So when he rang at seven that night only to find out that she was working late and didn't have time to stop, like some idiot he found himself walking through a dark social work department to the light from under her office door with a bottle of sparking water and some take-out.

'Jack, I really can't stop.'

'You can't eat?'

He had a good point. That coffee with Janey had been a long time ago, but it wasn't just the timing that was the problem. She was used to Jack looking completely gorgeous and groomed at all times, but she was slightly disarmed at the sight of him in scrubs—he was displaying rather more skin than she could deal with and say no to, so she kept her voice matter-of-fact as she declined him.

'I can eat, but I have to work. I'm due in court in the morning and I have to finish this report...'

'You haven't got five minutes?'

And she remembered her own manners, or she got the delicious waft of food, or it could have been that Jack was someone she found it incredibly hard to say no to, but she gave him a smile and gave in. 'Thank you.'

'How was your day?'

'Busy,' Nina said. 'How was yours?'

'Full on...' He chatted as he served up their meals. 'I've spent most of it up in ICU. There's a little one giving the paed team a headache. Still, we've got her stable now and a plan for tomorrow.'

'Sounds good.' It didn't annoy her any more that he never really used patients' names.

'And there's been progress in other areas,' Jack continued. 'We got the go-ahead on the supervised waiting room.'

'That's going to be so well utilised.' Nina took a forkful of noodles and they were utterly delicious. 'I can't think of the times I've wanted to speak to a parent away from the family, to be able to have the children looked after, even for a little while…'

'It was the one thing the ER nurses really wanted, so it will be good to get it off the ground. So, what have you been up to?'

'Just work,' Nina said.

'How are your brother and sister?'

'Pretty much the same.'

She was nothing like anyone he'd ever dated. Usually it was the woman trying to get Jack to open up or to tease out information from him. He knew full well that Janey had upset her today and yet Nina simply wouldn't share it, and it infuriated him as he swallowed a taste of his own medicine.

They chatted some more about work and Nina finished her food and thanked him for stopping by, but Jack didn't move from the chair he was sitting on.

'Jack, I really need to work.'

'I won't interrupt.'

He sat quietly as she typed and Jack drank sparkling water till his patience waned.

'What's the report about?' Jack asked.

'It's not one of your patients.'

Still he sat there.

Still she worked.

'Tell you what.'

Nina rolled her eyes as Jack interrupted her again.

'Why don't you come back to my place when you're finished?'

'Because I have to go home. I need to wear a suit for court in the morning.'

And he really wanted to see her in a suit! 'Tell you what, give me your keys and I'll go back to your place…'

'Excuse me?' She had no idea the concession he was making, how he never went to a woman's place. Jack liked to be at his own home, never wanted to be too far into anyone's life. 'Like I'm going to give someone I hardly know the keys to my apartment.'

'Hardly know?'

'Jack.' She gave up typing and stood, cleared up the noodle boxes and threw them in the bin. 'I'm going to be here till midnight at least—one a.m. at this rate.' She walked over to him, looked down at him and it was as if he made her feel reckless. She couldn't tell him that she adored the distraction, that right now all she wanted was bed and him, but she could not, must not give her heart over to him.

'I really need to work.'

'And I think you deserve a break.' He pulled her onto his lap and they both knew where that had led last time and again he kissed her.

His kiss remained potent and brought her straight back to the places they'd once been. He was unshaven tonight and she felt the scratch on her face and pulled back just a little. 'I need my face for court…'

'Let me kiss you somewhere else, then.'

He was funny and dark and sexy and she had already proved they could work together, that there would be no awkwardness between them whatever went on in the bedroom, but she was not going to love him—all this her eyes told him as she sat there.

'Nina, I know you don't want to hear this, but I want you in a way I have never wanted anyone else...'

'Have me, then.' She wriggled from his lap and he watched her head lower as she bent and removed her boots and her stockings.

'I meant—' Jack's voice was rising '—I want more of you, I want to go out, to do stuff...'

'Jack.' She stood there, bare-legged, bare-bottomed beneath her dress, but she would not bare her heart to him. 'What is it you want? Do you get a kick out of really making someone fall for you, make sure that they're really head over heels and then the second they're yours you dump them?'

Actually, yes, Jack thought, but decided it was better not to voice it.

Because it *was* different this time.

'This is different.' He settled for that.

'Yes, it is,' Nina said. 'You don't have to pretend this is going somewhere—neither of us do.'

'I didn't just come here for sex!'

'Oh, so you didn't bring condoms...' Nina smirked when he didn't reply. 'Not to worry!' She stood over him and kissed him again and his hands held her hips and then slid down to the hem and up her bare legs.

How could this not be enough? Jack reasoned. She matched him sexually and for the first time there was a woman not asking him to change, or where this was leading.

She dropped to her knees then pulled down his scrubs. Her head moved down with the intention to get him out of her office in the space of two minutes and Jack was actually offended. He had never turned down a blow job, had never thought he would, but as he pulled up her head and kissed her, he was, in fact, thoroughly offended.

This was different, his mouth insisted as he wrestled her to the floor.

This was so different, because his mouth was all over her and she was fighting him again. Not the sex, not the attraction, not the passion—she was trying to pretend it was just sex they were having as he was wrestling for her heart.

And she would not give it.

She kissed him back and when he reached into his scrubs for his wallet, again she smirked.

'Told you!'

'Damn it, Nina.' He was getting cross and with women he never did. He just moved happily on when things got too much.

'Shall I help you?'

He pushed her hand off.

He wasn't just angry, he was jealous, but that didn't quite fit, but her sexuality, her detachment, her *oh, a quick orgasm will do, so let's get it over with* was really starting to get to him.

He prised open her legs with his knees and still she kissed him as he stabbed inside her, and she would not give in to him. It was the strangest of fights and as she lay there beneath him he stopped kissing her and lifted onto his elbows and just watched her face. And she decided that she would just give a little bit…

'You're coming out with me.'

'I don't think so.'

'Yeah,' he said, 'you are. I'm taking you away this weekend…' he was moving inside her '…and we're—'

'We can't.'

'We are.'

'I've got Blake.'

God, at every turn she blocked him.

'Sunday night.' Still he moved deep within her.

'I'm busy.'

'I want more of you, Nina.' He was moving too slowly and she wanted him rapid, wanted him near the end, because any more of this and she'd be crying. Any more of this and she'd be sobbing his name and begging for every piece of him.

So she writhed and moaned and said, 'I'm coming…' And she lay there faking it just to finish him.

'Liar.'

He pushed in slower, harder and watched as the tears sprang in her eyes and the colour mounted on her face, as her hips started to lift. 'Please stop.' They both knew she wasn't talking about the sex.

'I want you, Nina.'

'You've got me.'

'I want more of you,' he insisted, and now he moved faster.

And she gave in to her body then, her legs wrapping around him, her arms pulling him in and her mouth claiming his now because if she didn't kiss him hard then she'd tell him she was crazy for him, that she wanted every second of this man. She captured his mouth so he would silence her and then he just exploded. He moved so fast she couldn't breathe and his moan when he came had her shouting his name when she should not have. It was Jack finishing just as she started and he relished every pulse till she faded.

And afterwards he looked down at her, looked right into her eyes, that smile on his face that said *I told you so* and the crush she'd had on him since first they'd met was at dangerous levels now.

Nina didn't really trust anyone and only a fool would trust Jack Carter with their heart and Nina certainly wasn't a fool—she'd seen and experienced far too much of life.

He was dizzy when he climbed off and lay there for a minute. It was Nina who had a very clear head.

She was not going to let him know how she felt about him; she looked over to where he lay with his eyes closed and decided that she'd save that piece for herself, because he was going to hurt her.

She knew it.

In two days or two weeks he would be out of here, and the only way she could carry on working alongside him was if he didn't know he had her heart. There was a very small part of her that pondered, that allowed herself to think, what if? Except it wasn't just about the two of them—Nina came with rather more baggage than most.

'Thank you for a lovely break.' She smiled at him and kissed him. 'And now I really do have to work…'

She really did.

But Nina stopped for a cry a little bit later, because more than anything in the world she wanted her brother and sister, but she'd have also liked a little time to herself, to have said yes to Jack and be going away for a weekend, to just warm herself in the full spotlight of being Jack Carter's lover.

For however long it might last.

CHAPTER NINE

NINA HATED GOING to court.

No, Nina *hated* going to court.

She dressed in her one court outfit and took more care than usual with her hair. Not that it mattered, because it got flattened by her hat as she battled the freezing rain, and when she arrived there and changed from her boots into her shoes, she was reminded again why she hated it so.

There was a ton of work to do back in her office; there were clients she really needed to see, but instead she spent most of the day hanging around court and drinking way too much coffee. When her computer battery died Nina gave up trying to work and read out-of-date magazines, and joy of joys, there was that Christmas one with the Carters on the cover.

She read the article with new eyes now.

Tried not to compare her life to his.

They were lovely people and so was their home.

Anna Carter was a gracious host, she read, who happily showed the reporter around.

Was she jealous as she glimpsed the sumptuous home Jack had grown up in? Or was she just bitter when she read about this close-knit family? How Jack Senior loved nothing more than a round of golf with his sons and that, yes, Anna couldn't wait until one of her sons gave her grandchildren, which was, she confided, the only thing missing in her very blessed life.

She shouldn't be jealous, Nina reasoned. That wasn't what she was about. She didn't want those sorts of things and, after all, the Carters more than gave back, they were as well known for their charity work as they were for their jet-set lifestyle.

She didn't know how she felt, didn't know why looking at these photos angered her so much. Maybe it was just that she knew she wasn't good enough? Nina had been told that plenty of times in her life, so why would should it be different now?

She felt her phone buzz in her coat, knew it was Jack.

How's court?

Nina didn't answer—after all, she could be in the courtroom now, she reasoned.

How are you?

Nina didn't answer that question either—she simply didn't know.

She'd gone into this thing with him completely aware it was temporary, had shielded herself with that—she just hadn't expected to like him so much. Lust, yes, fancy, yes, but she actually liked him, and maybe she was just fooling herself, maybe it was how Jack played things, but she was actually starting to think that he really liked her, which would be nice and everything, except…

Her phone buzzed again, but it wasn't Jack this time

but Blake, reminding her that she was picking him up at five.

Yes, when she'd far rather be busy, Nina was forced to sit and examine her feelings, because even if Jack might have no intention of ending things any time soon, in just a little while there would be no question of her sleeping over at his place, or long conversations in nice restaurants. There wouldn't even be late nights staying back at the office to catch up on the backlog of work. Instead it would be homework and netball and baby-sitters…

And as much as she wanted her brother and sister, Nina was honest enough to admit that it was going to hurt to give her freedom up, and that was while knowing how much she loved them.

Why on earth would Jack, who didn't?

The fact-finding hearing finally commenced at two p.m. Nina was actually glad at the effort she had put into the addendum and a judge who listened, because a dispositional hearing was scheduled and Nina breathed a sigh of relief as she stepped out and rang the office with the news.

'Are you coming back in?' Lorianna asked.

'I've got Blake this weekend,' Nina said, 'so it will all just have to wait till Monday.'

'I don't think Jack Carter can wait till then…' Nina rolled her eyes as Lorianna teased, 'He's stopped by here twice, looking for you.'

'To discuss Tommy.' Nina was so not going to fan the gossip. 'He starts his chemotherapy next week and

I'm trying to arrange some accommodation nearby for the father.'

She wished Blake's social worker had taken distance into consideration when they had placed Blake. He lived miles from her and, given that she didn't have a car, the trip during peak hour on a Friday night took for ever, as it would when she took him back on Sunday.

She was being ungrateful, Nina thought as she trudged up the Deans' garden path. They were lovely people and had been caring for Blake for the last four years and adored him.

Or had.

When their daughter had emigrated, the Deans had looked into fostering and for three years things had run smoothly. But since their daughter's return from overseas and two new grandchildren to get to know, Blake seemed to be being pushed out more and more. When Nina arrived, Blake was in his room.

'Hi, there, Nina!' Dianne opened the door and invited her in. 'I'll call Blake, he's up in his room.'

Nina stood a little awkwardly in the hallway as Dianne called up to Blake, and though she chatted and was friendly, Nina could hear the laughter and chat coming from the lounge room and knew that Dianne was itching to get back to her family.

'It's my grandson's second birthday.' Dianne smiled. 'We're just having a little party for him.'

'That's lovely.' Nina also smiled.

And it was lovely and completely normal, but she ached for Blake as he came down the stairs. Of course Nina had her doubts at times, of course she questioned taking on so much responsibility, but the second she saw his face any doubts faded.

'Hey, Nina…' He was so pleased to see her and he asked Dianne if he could show Nina a new poster that he had in his room.

'Why don't you show me when I bring you back?' Nina suggested, because she had that uncomfortable feeling that she and Blake were in the way.

She ached for him.

Ached because for the Wilson siblings love never quite made the distance. Instead, they were always having to make do with someone else's crumbs.

Well, not for much longer.

'Are you looking forward to seeing the new apartment?' Nina asked as they trudged through the slush towards their new home. 'I've got to set up your bed and furniture when we get in. Maybe you can help?'

'I want to watch the game…' Blake was ice-hockey mad, and tonight Nina was actually glad of it as she'd get his room set up much more quickly on her own. 'Can we get take-away?' he asked for maybe the tenth time in as many minutes, refusing to let it drop when Nina said no. And as much as she enjoyed her access times, they were incredibly exhausting too. Nina wanted to be firm with him, but she didn't want to spend the weekend arguing either, and of course she wanted to spoil him. It was conflicting and exhausting and she just wanted Blake properly in her life, not these alternate weekend vacations he expected.

She climbed the stairs to her apartment, Blake still moaning about dinner. She was already peeling off her hat and scarf when she saw Jack standing at her door, holding a bottle of wine.

'What are you doing here?'

'I came to talk to you.'

'I told you I had Blake this weekend.' She looked down at her brother, who was grinning up at Jack, and she was not going to discuss things in front of Blake.

'Go inside, Blake.' She turned the key and pushed open the door. 'I'll be inside in a moment.' And then she remembered that Blake hadn't been there before so she could hardly show him his new home by shoving him inside. Suddenly Nina knew how to sort this right here, right now, knew how to get Jack to leave. 'Come in if you want to…'

She was incredibly annoyed that he did.

Blake raced around the apartment as Jack stood a little awkwardly. 'This is your room,' Nina said. 'I'll make up the furniture later. You go and have a wander around and get used to the place.'

She headed back to Jack.

'I'm sorry,' he said when they were alone. 'I shouldn't have just crashed in like that. I honestly thought when you said weekends that you meant Saturday.'

'Nope,' she said. 'I have Blake two nights a fortnight and soon I'm hoping to make it fourteen.'

She was also incredibly annoyed about what his eyes suggested when she took off her coat and she stood in her court outfit, though it was a little less elegant as she'd changed into boots for the journey home.

'How was court?'

'Good,' Nina said. 'Well, there was a lot of hanging around. I read about you in a magazine, actually...'

'Every word must be true, then.'

'This one was devoid of scandal.' She gave him a smile. 'Your mum can't wait to have grandchildren...'

'Well, she can keep right on waiting.'

She heard the dismissal in his voice and again she was reminded about what she was dealing with.

'Are you close to *anyone*?'

He just gave her a smile that spoke of the other night at the office.

'I'm serious, Jack.'

'As I've said before, there's no such thing as a perfect family.'

'What about your brother?' Nina asked, but Jack shrugged.

'There's a six-year age difference.'

'Same as there is with Janey and Blake,' Nina said. 'There's an even bigger one between Janey and I.'

'Which meant we didn't see each other at school.'

'What about at home?'

'We went to boarding school.' Jack knew his words didn't quite wash, given how she fought so hard to unite her family. 'They're difficult people,' Jack said.

'Families are.'

Blake appeared then, asking again if they could get take-away.

'I've already said no.'

'I don't mind going out to get something...' Jack offered, and had no idea why it incensed her so much, had no idea Blake had been begging for it all the way home.

'I'm *making* dinner,' she said.

'Is that an invitation to join you?''

'It's just pasta.'

'Great.'

Nina slammed around her small kitchen as Jack sat on the sofa, chatting to Blake. She could hear them both laughing and it annoyed her further. 'Jack!' she called over her shoulder as she filled a large saucepan with water. 'Can you come here for a moment?'

'Sure.'

He came to the door.

'Go easy on him.'

'Sorry?'

'Blake's really needy...' She was so angry that he'd turned up like this, because two minutes in it was clear Blake was already a huge Jack Carter fan. 'Just don't make any promises you can't keep.'

'Do you think I'm stupid?'

'No,' Nina answered tartly, 'but we're just friends if he asks.'

'Really!' Jack raised his eyebrows. 'I told Blake I worked with you and had a patient that we needed to discuss, but I can upgrade us to friends if you like...'

'Colleagues is fine.'

Trust Jack to have been one step ahead.

Except she didn't trust Jack, because he was terribly easy to like, and from his past reputation terribly quick to leave.

So she made Blake's favourite dinner, herb and breadcrumb pasta.

Quick, tasty, cheap and *nothing* at all like Jack was used to.

She melted the butter in a pan and added a couple of cups of breadcrumbs and then threw in a load of herbs and tried not to listen to the laughter from the lounge as she put the crumbs into the oven and added the pasta to the water.

He walked into the kitchen and searched for a cork-screw then handed her a glass of wine from the bottle he had brought.

She waited for him to kiss her, to be inappropriate, to cross the line, so she could ask him to leave, but he didn't act inappropriately at all.

'Can I help with anything?'

'Hey, Jack…' Blake called out from the lounge room. 'They're live from The Garden…'

'No TV with dinner,' Nina called.

'Spoilsport.'

Yes, she was a spoilsport, she had to be. She drained the pasta and grated the cheese as Blake set up the table, and she added the herbed breadcrumbs and a load of Parmesan and then took the bowl out to the table.

'Jack goes for the Islanders.' Blake was delighted to have a rival right here in the room and Nina was furious with the schedulers too as she sliced garlic bread. Did tonight have to be the night that Blake's team the New York Rangers clashed with the Islanders?

Of course she would have let Blake watch it. They would have been on the sofa, not at the table, if Jack hadn't arrived.

'Please…' Blake begged.

'Fine,' Nina snapped, and on went the television again and off went the dinner from the table, Blake heaping his bowl and Jack too before heading for the sofa. A reluctant Nina joined them.

'Garlic bread…' She put the steaming plate onto the coffee table.

'Not for me.' Jack smiled. 'I don't want garlic breath.'

Very deliberately she took a piece. And another. She wanted her breath to stink for him and he knew it because he held his fingers in a cross and laughed at her efforts.

It was a brilliant game—possibly the best of the year.

It had sold out weeks ago. Nina knew that because she had been hoping to get tickets and take Blake, but not seeing it live was more than made up for that night.

At times Nina struggled with Blake's needy, demanding ways and she wondered how long it would take Jack to tire of the constant questions, but tonight if anyone was noisy and excessive it was Jack, standing and shouting at the television at times, making Blake laugh at others. She stood in the kitchen, the popcorn popping in the microwave, feeling a lot like the chips she was spitting as a roar went up from the lounge.

'Bite your lip!' Jack shouted as a roar went up from the lounge and she heard Jack explaining illegal hits to Blake in a way Nina never had known how to—that if a player made another bleed, then it meant a longer penalty for the opposing team.

Blake was delighted!

In fact, every word Jack said seemed to have Blake fall in love with him just a little bit more.

'I'm going to set up your room,' Nina said, because she could not stand the adoration on Blake's face. She had honestly thought Jack wouldn't come inside, or if he did that he'd clear off pretty quickly. Now, though, he'd won over another Wilson heart.

'I can do that after the game.' Jack stood in the doorway at the mid-game break and watched her angrily setting up the furniture.

'He'll need to go bed when the game's finished,' Nina said.

'It will take me five minutes.'

'You do a lot of DIY, do you?'

'Fine,' Jack said, 'be a martyr.'

'I'm not being a martyr. I'm just trying to set up his room.'

He didn't get her problem. Jack was having a great evening and just didn't know why it angered her so much, but he gave in then. 'Look, sorry I invaded your time with Blake. I honestly had no idea that he'd be here tonight. My mistake. I can go if you want…'

'You're not *invading* my time with Blake, Jack. I don't think you understand how messed up their lives have been, with people tripping in and out, each one promising that this time things will be different. I don't want that for them here. I don't want my personal life invaded.'

'So you're not going to have friends over or date or…?' He shook his head, went to say something, but Blake called out from the lounge that the game was back on. When Jack headed out, Nina sat back on her heels because, no, she didn't want to make up the bed and, no, she didn't want to be a martyr to her brother and sister, but the last thing she wanted was to hurt them, and losing Jack would hurt.

Perhaps he truly didn't see it.

Didn't fully realise the effect he had on her, the effect he was having on Blake—that if he appeared too long in their lives, it would hurt when he left.

But right now the best she could do was enjoy tonight, so she headed out, sat on the couch next to him and tried to simply live in the here and now, which was actually a very nice place to be, because even when Blake's team lost, he told her he'd still had the best night.

'I'd better go,' Jack said, after he'd finished setting up Blake's room.

'No!' said Blake.

Yes, thought Nina as she walked Jack to the door, but of course Blake didn't want him to leave.

'It's time for you to get ready for bed,' Nina called, but unfortunately she was looking at Jack as she said it.

'It's a bit early for me, but if you insist.'

'Ha-ha.' She stood in her hallway. 'Thanks,' she said. 'Blake had a great night.'

'So did I,' Jack said. 'Don't I get a kiss?'

'I smell of garlic.'

She could hear the phone ringing, wondered who it was this late at night, and the panic that was ever present flared just a touch as Jack carried on, oblivious.

'I love garlic,' he said as he moved in for a kiss.

'Nina…' Blake called. 'They want to speak to you.'

She knew in that moment who it was and walked into the lounge with her heart thumping.

'Nina Wilson.' She closed her eyes, because Jack had followed her back into the lounge and now Jack had a ringside seat to her life. 'No, she hasn't been here.' He watched her open her eyes. 'No, I had no idea. Of course I'll ring…' She took a deep breath. 'If Janey calls, I'll let you know.'

And a lovely, albeit reluctantly lovely, Friday night disappeared in a puff. If she had thought her cheap, herby dinner might put him off and had been wrong, then this surely would.

'Janey's run away.'

'Does she run away a lot?'

Nina shook her head. 'She's been skipping school and there's been just that one time I told you about a few weeks ago when she came to my place…' Nina headed to the window, looked out at the freezing night. She could feel panic squeezing her chest at the thought of Janey out there.

'She's probably gone to a friend's,' Jack reasoned. 'Can you think of anywhere that she might go…?' And then his voice trailed off as the door was pushed open and one very angry young lady walked in.

Jack watched as Nina ran over to her, but Janey pushed her off, anger marring her pretty features as she took in the scene—the scent of dinner still in the air, the popcorn on the coffee table, all evidence of all she had missed out on—then she scowled in Jack's direction. 'Sorry to break up your night. Looks like you've been having fun.'

'Janey…' Nina's voice was strained. 'This is Jack, he's a friend from work. We were…' She shouldn't have to explain herself to Janey, so she didn't. 'Where have you been? Barbara's frantic.'

'I'm not going back.'

'What happened?'

'Barbara wanted me in bed at nine. It's Friday night, for God's sake.'

'Why…?' Nina was trying to stay calm, trying to be reasonable. 'Why did she want you to go to bed at nine?'

Janey shrugged and then sighed out her answer. 'I told you, she's annoyed at me for what happened at netball. I've got to clean the basement.'

'That's not all, though,' Nina broke in. 'I've just been told that she grounded you for skipping school today.'

'Yeah, well, I'm not five—I'm not going to bed at nine. I couldn't even watch the game. Vince came in and told me to turn the television off.'

'Because when you're grounded you're not supposed to be lying in bed, eating popcorn and watching ice hockey.' Nina was struggling not to shout. 'Janey, what do you think it's going to be like when you live with me? There have to be rules…'

'Yeah, well, you just carry on enjoying yourselves,' Janey shouted. 'I'm out of here.'

Jack said nothing, just watched, because trouble hadn't just arrived, Janey was in trouble, a whole lot of it, and he'd dealt with enough to know.

'Why don't you ring them?' Janey challenged. 'And tell them I'm here? Then you can get back to your nice night.'

'You know I have to ring them,' Nina said. 'If I don't they'll soon be here to check after last time. Janey, if I am to have any hope—'

'We'll go to my place.' It was the first words he had spoken since Janey had arrived.

'Jack…' Nina was furious. 'You're just making things worse.'

'Come on.' He ignored her. 'Pack some things.'

'Jack, can I have a word please?'

She had more than a word, she had several heated ones, but Jack stood firm.

'Janey needs to talk to you—she needs some time with you.'

'She doesn't want time with me—every time that I speak to her all she does is walk off,' Nina said.

'Because you get too upset.'

'Of course I get upset! Jack, she came to my office today, moaning about Barbara. She was jealous that Blake was coming here tonight. I knew she was planning trouble…' Nina closed her eyes. 'I have to support Barbara in this. If every time she tries to discipline her, Janey comes running to me, things aren't going to get any better. I'll speak with Barbara and suggest that if Janey gets the basement sorted then she can come and spend Sunday night with me.'

'She won't and you know it,' Jack said. 'If you send her back now, or they put her in a temporary placement, she's just going to be a whole lot angrier at you. Now, let's go to my apartment and from there we can sort things, but any minute now you'll have the department knocking, especially if they found her here last time.'

He was right, so Nina grabbed a few things and a few minutes later her little family was sitting in Jack's car, Blake beside himself he was so delighted, Janey angry and silent. Nina just quietly panicked, embarrassed by the chaos of her life and unsure this was the right thing to do.

'We need to ring them.'

'And we will. We're not fugitives.' He turned and smiled at her. 'You've got access to Blake, Janey's nearly sixteen, you're her sister...'

'Could this get you into trouble?'

'No.' He shook his head. 'I'm doing what I think is right and I'll tell that to anyone who asks. I am not having her taken back just to run away again.' He glanced in the rear-view mirror and met the hostile stare of Janey. 'We'll be there soon.'

As expected, she didn't reply.

His apartment was huge, but not designed for children. Blake was at his most annoying, running around, while Janey just sat silently on one of his lovely white sofas. All Nina could think was that they were all so out of place in his perfect life.

Even Jack was wondering what on earth to do with them. Yes, there were spare bedrooms but somehow a luxurious bachelor pad wasn't really conducive to talking, not with a messed-up teenager anyway.

He didn't do the family thing, had never had the family thing himself. The only time he'd done anything remotely family-like had been... And it was then that Jack had an idea and he turned to Janey.

'You're to ring Barbara and tell her that you're safe,

that you're with your sister, and that you're going away for the weekend.'

'Jack!'

He turned to an angry Nina. 'And you're to ring back Janey's worker and tell her the same,' he said to Nina's rigid face. 'She's not in any danger, she's with her sister who has access, so just tell them that you'll bring Janey in on Monday morning to the office.'

'So they can send me back.' Janey looked at him.

'I don't know,' he admitted. 'But running away isn't helping things.'

Janey just turned her head away and carried on staring out of the window and then did the same in the car as they left Manhattan.

Of course he'd have a place in the Hamptons, Nina thought darkly as the car drove through the night.

They stopped for provisions and she was glad that he didn't embarrass her by offering money, just suggested she get a few warm things. She bought some food too as Blake raced around the aisles of the store and Janey just walked silently beside her. As they stepped out into the parking lot she half expected Jack to be gone, but of course he wouldn't do that, Nina knew. He'd probably drop them off at his mansion and then belt it back to Manhattan.

Still, she was grateful to him.

His stern words had helped her handle the department and this small window of time with Janey might mean that hopefully, hopefully she could get to the bottom of things.

'Wow!' Blake was wide awake and admiring the

huge houses they passed. 'Is this yours?' he asked as they slowed down.

'Nope.'

'This one?'

'Nope.'

And then Jack indicated, they turned into a small street and Jack parked.

'We'll have to walk from here.'

It was a tiny house on a large block and they couldn't park in the drive because it was covered in thick snow.

It was actually funny trying to get to the door. Jack put Blake on his back and even Janey laughed as, up to their knees, they waded through snow and he deposited them inside and then went back to the car and got all their bags.

They were all soaked and the house was colder inside than out.

They walked into the lounge and Jack lit a fire that had been prepared and reminded himself to leave a big tip for the cleaning lady who came in and aired the place regularly. They all stood shivering as the fire took. 'There are a couple of heaters I can set up in your rooms…' He looked at Blake and Janey. 'I'll go and check things out. Janey, can you make something to drink?'

Nina followed him, dragging the heaters into the small bedrooms, and she looked around. 'I was expecting a mansion.'

'Disappointed?'

'No, it's lovely, just cold.'

'Yeah, well, not for long. I'm just waiting for planning permission then the bulldozers will be in.'

Once the heaters were on in the kids' rooms he showed her the main bedroom.

'You'll freeze,' Jack said.

'I'll be fine.'

They went back through to the living area and Janey had actually done as she'd been asked and made everyone a drink. By the time they'd finished, it was terribly late and Blake was falling asleep on the sofa. When Nina returned from taking him to his bed, Janey was already heading off to hers.

'Janey, wait,' Nina called, but Janey wasn't hanging around to talk to her.

''Night.'

They sat in the lounge and when finally they were alone, Jack closed the door and spoke to her.

'Are you sure you want to do this?' Jack said, and she sat there silent as he spoke on. 'Are you absolutely sure that you want full custody?'

She looked at Jack and she knew it was their death knell, knew that it would be the end of them, and even though it hurt like hell, yes, she was sure and she nodded.

'Because if I go into bat for you...' Jack looked at her '...you'll get it. I always win.'

'Not always,' she said. 'You didn't win with Sienna.'

'That's because I privately thought you were right,' Jack said. 'If I hadn't there would have been no way Sienna would have gone home to the care of her mother.

I just want to be completely sure that this is what you want.'

'Yes,' Nina said. 'I want my family together.'

'Then we'll sort it out, but right now you need to back off from Janey and stop trying to get her to talk to you.'

'I need to know what's going on.'

'She'll tell you when she's ready. Right…' Jack stood. 'I'm going to drive back.' They headed out to the hall. 'Will you be all right without a car?'

'I don't have a car anyway.' Nina smiled. 'I'm sure I can work out how to call for a taxi.'

'I'm sure you can.' He gave her a kiss, but not a long one as it really was terribly late now. 'I'll pick you up on Sunday afternoon.'

'We're taking up all your weekend,' Nina apologised, her hands loosely together behind his neck.

Jack wasn't quite so tired now. 'You could take up a bit more.'

He watched the smile at the edges of her mouth.

'I don't want you freezing…' Jack moved to her ear.

'It is terribly cold,' Nina admitted.

'Then it's the least I can do.' Jack smiled.

They had never undressed more quickly, though Nina kept her underwear and T-shirt on to take off once they were in bed and they dived under the covers. Jack turned to her.

'You smell of garlic.'

'It was supposed to be a deterrent.'

'Not for me.'

She wriggled away, but he pulled her back. 'We have to keep warm.' He pulled at her T-shirt. 'Skin on skin,'

Jack said, and he peeled off all her clothing. 'That's how you prevent hypothermia. I did mountain rescue once.'

She laughed.

'I didn't really,' he admitted.

But it was exactly how it felt.

As if they were happily trapped on a ledge, waiting, while not wanting the cavalry to arrive, freezing cold and staying warm by the favourite method of all. Afterwards she thanked him for his help with her family and for how he'd handled things tonight.

'I know I try too hard with them,' Nina said. 'You know what it's like with family…' Then she remembered their earlier conversation. 'I thought you all got on?'

'That's what they want people to think,' Jack said. 'We're hardly going to air everything in public but, no, I really couldn't care less about them.'

And he said it so easily, was just so matter-of-fact as he dismissed his entire family, and just a few moments later Nina realised he was asleep. She lay there half the night thinking about the wonderful family he cared so little about and fully realised the impossibility of him ever really caring for hers.

CHAPTER TEN

'DO YOU COME here a lot?' They lay in bed in the morning, before the day had started, and she looked at the man who had brought her family here, who had given them a chance to get away from things properly.

He turned and gave her that devilish smile. 'It depends what this morning brings.' And she simply smiled, except Jack did not. He didn't really want to talk about his time here, but realising all she had trusted him with last night, maybe it was fair to be a bit more open than he would be usually.

'I came on holiday here when I was younger, stayed in a house close to here.' He didn't actually tell her it was the same house.

'Do your family have a property here too, then?'

'They have a property nearby but, no, I came here with a school friend and I stayed with his family.'

'Good?' Nina asked.

'It was great,' Jack said. 'Best summer of my life. We didn't do much really—just the beach most days. I bought this place last year when it came on the market and I thought it was too good to pass up. I'm getting plans drawn up. I want to build up and get the view…'

'And get heating.'

'Oh, yes.' They lay in silence for a moment and then Jack turned and looked at her very serious face, could almost hear her worrying about what to say to Janey, how to approach things with her sister. 'You need to relax.'

'I know.'

'You get too tense.'

'Thanks, Jack,' she snapped, but she knew he was right. 'I don't know what to do today—I mean, she's hardly going to want to build a snowman.'

'There's loads to do here.'

'Like what?'

'Outdoor ice skating,' Jack said, 'and there's a whale tour, it's supposed to be fantastic.'

'How do you know?'

Jack would rather face the freezing morning than deal with that topic. He'd already said far too much, way more than he usually would, and so he pulled back the blankets and climbed out. 'I'm going to get the fire in the lounge going and then sort out breakfast.' He shook his head as she went to climb out. 'Stay there,' he offered. 'I'll bring you in a coffee.'

Jack set to work building the fire and then he headed off to make coffee, and as he returned with two mugs, he nodded to Janey, who was huddled on the couch. 'Still here? I thought you'd be out the window.'

Janey gave a reluctant half-smile. 'Yeah, well, I didn't fancy freezing to death.'

'Did you want a coffee?' Jack asked. 'I just made some.'

Another shrug and then a nod and when she told him she took it the same as Nina he handed her Nina's mug and then went and made a fresh one, then headed back into the bedroom.

'Janey's up, but not Blake.'

'She's up…' Nina went to pull back the blankets, but Jack very deliberately sat down on her side of the bed.

'Leave her.'

'But it might be a good chance to talk to her, before Blake gets up.'

'Which is why she's probably sitting on that couch waiting for the door to open,' Jack said. 'She was waiting for a lecture from me or an, oh, so casual talk from you. Just let her relax…'

'It's so hard, though.'

'Which is why it's good you've got the whole weekend. Look, I'll head back soon and you guys can just have some time—she'll talk when she wants to, Nina.'

'And if she doesn't?'

'Then she was never going to.'

He'd been working with children a long time and was actually very good with adolescents, his slightly aloof, completely unshockable stance giving them confidence. More than most, Jack understood that things weren't always as they seemed—was never blindsided by the persuasive words of the parents.

They drank their coffee and then headed out, only to be met by the delicious smell of breakfast coming from the kitchen. Nina realised that had she got out of bed the minute Jack had told her that Janey was up, had she dashed to the living room for the essential talk, then this might never have happened. Blake and Janey, standing in the kitchen and serving up a delicious breakfast of pancakes and sausages and eggs from the ingedients that Nina had bought from the store last night.

'This looks lovely.'

'I'm starving,' Jack said, and watching Janey serve up he reminded her that Nina was a vegetarian. 'No sausages for your sister.'

'It's…' She felt Jack's hand squeeze hers, realised she must not make too much of a fuss. 'I'll set the table.'

Jack helped, and not just with the cutlery.

'Janey is nearly sixteen,' he pointed out. 'She should be making breakfast, Nina.'

'And she is.'

'And you should be allowed to say you're a vegetarian and that you don't eat sausages.' He looked at her. 'You would have eaten them, wouldn't you?'

'Of course not.'

'Liar.' Jack grinned. 'You'd go against every one of your principles just to please her. You don't have to be her mum.'

'I know that. But she needs more than just a big sister.'

'No,' Jack said. 'She just needs you to be you and she needs to take on some of the responsibility too. What were you doing at that age?'

He left her for a moment to ponder and when he returned with orange juice and glasses she answered his question, because at fifteen years old her part-time job in the hardware store had made a vital contribution to the family.

'Working,' Nina said. 'And going to school. We weren't exactly well off.' And though he appeared unmoved, Jack was far from it, especially when, as they sat eating breakfast, talking and laughing, Janey had mentioned their mum and the Mother's Day breakfast they'd shared just before she'd died.

'Nina did all the cooking then,' Janey said. 'I just got to pour on the maple syrup.' And he felt his stomach tighten as he realised, perhaps properly, all she had been through. That Nina hadn't been much older than Janey was now when she had lost her parents, and the thought of her so young and alone and dealing with such grief brought out a rare surge of compassion in him.

Not that he showed it.

Instead, because they'd cooked, he found out that meant he and Nina were doing the dishes and he grumbled all the way through it. Then Janey grumbled when Nina suggested they go on the whale boat trip.

'You're going,' Jack said in the end to Janey. 'You can miserable with me.'

And though Nina wanted him gone, there was a sigh of relief she held onto because handling the two of them was just so much easier when he was around. Maybe because he was actually old enough to be their parent— the nine years Jack had on her made a big difference.

'Thanks,' Nina said again.

'No need to thank me.'

They were impossible to get out of the house, Jack realised.

Janey took for ever in the bathroom and came out fully made up, while Blake had zero attention span and had to be told five times to wash and get dressed. Nina thought that Jack, with his streamlined life, would get irritated, because it was close to eleven by the time they all headed off, but he didn't seem fazed at all.

Jack talked to Blake in the car about the hockey game the previous night and Janey moaned that the last thing she wanted to see was a group of whales.

'A pod of whales.' Jack turned briefly from the driving seat. 'It's a pod of whales, not a group of whales.'

Nina rolled her eyes, surprised when Janey giggled.

On deck, it was absolutely freezing, but the cabin was warm and there was endless hot chocolate. They took it in turns to go in and out, but it was more than worth it when finally a *pod* of whales was spotted. Far from being bored by them, Janey and Blake stayed on deck for ages—it was Nina and Jack who ducked in for some warmth.

'Thanks for this,' Nina said. 'They've had the best day.'

'What about you?' Jack asked.

'It's been brilliant,' Nina said. 'I really do appreciate it.' She didn't dare ask Jack what sort of day he was having—he'd been so kind to take them on, but surely this wasn't his ideal way to spend a weekend. After all, he had admitted that he rarely used the house and playing carer to two rather troubled foster-children on a rare weekend off no doubt had him wondering why on earth he had got involved with her.

He was very quiet on the drive home.

He told Nina about a couple of local restaurants, but apart from that he didn't say much.

'I'm tired,' Blake said.

'Can we just stay home and eat?' Janey asked.

They'd spent one night there and already Janey had referred to it as home.

It was how he had felt many years ago.

Yes, Jack was quiet.

They arrived back at the house and Jack saw them in.

'Where are you going?' Blake asked when after a quick drink Jack said goodbye.

'Jack's going home.' Nina smiled. 'It's Saturday night!' she said as she followed him out to the hall

'Thanks again.' Nina smiled.

He kissed her more thoroughly than he had the last time they had been in this hall, wondered perhaps if he could be persuaded to stay again.

'Have a great night…' It was Nina who pulled back.

'Sure,' Jack said. 'You too.' He was just a tiny bit rattled and couldn't work out why. 'What do you think you'll do?'

'I'm sure we'll find something, and we might try ice skating tomorrow…' She gave him another kiss. 'See you then.'

'Nina…' He should really just turn and go, really not say what he was about to, but his mouth was moving faster than his brain. 'What was that little snipe for?'

'When?'

'"It's Saturday night!"'

'Well, it *is* Saturday night and I remember you telling me you hadn't had one off in ages that hadn't been taken up by social and networking events,' Nina said. 'It wasn't a snipe.'

'You're sure?' Jack checked.

'Jack…' Nina was not going to get into this. 'I hope you have a good night.'

And he drove off towards the lights of a very busy city. Jack knew how to spend a free Saturday night. And he was free, he told himself when he headed to his favourite bar and met up with a few colleagues. But when he found himself being chatted up by an exceptionally good-looking brunette, whose baggage contained only the lipstick it held, he couldn't seem to concentrate on the conversation. His mind kept drifting back to the house and all that was going on there.

And he was free too to leave the bar alone, even to the pout of the stunning brunette, but Jack was unsettled and even a bit angry.

Nina hadn't even asked him about his plans.

Which was how he wanted things. The last thing he wanted was to get involved in a *relationship* with Nina Wilson, and the irony that he had revised that from *fling* wasn't lost on Jack.

She was carer to two children and he wanted none of that.

He wanted straightforward, uncomplicated, and Nina was none of that either.

'Jack!' As the lift door opened he saw Monica standing there, not in tears this time but wearing a smile.

'What are you doing here?'

'As you said, there doesn't always have to be a reason…'

Jack smiled as she walked over to him, but it sort

of halted on his lips as he said words he'd thought he never would.

'I'm seeing someone.'

He was, and for the first time he said it.

'What?' Monica smiled. 'For all of two weeks? It can't be that serious.' She pressed her lips to him, ran her hands down his chest.

'Yeah, well, it is.' Jack's hands halted hers.

'Doesn't matter...' Monica purred.

But as he kissed her back, Jack knew that it did, that for the first time he was serious about a woman and that he could be about to lose his formidable 'between the sheets' reputation here, because he wasn't even turned on. He stopped kissing her back, because he wasn't enjoying it and because...

'Actually, it does matter.'

He saw Monica to the lift and then let himself in and checked his phone. No, of course Nina hadn't called him.

Neither did he call her, because for the first time he was seeing someone, for the first time things were starting to look serious, for Jack at least.

He had no idea how Nina felt. She seemed delighted to keep things casual, didn't care a bit that he was out tonight.

Jack didn't know what to think.

CHAPTER ELEVEN

'JACK!'

Blake was delighted to see him. 'Janey got hurt.'

'I'm fine,' Janey insisted. 'I fell over, ice skating.' She rolled up her sleeve and showed a rather spectacular bruise, as Nina came through to the lounge and he saw the tension on her face.

'Great, isn't it?' She rolled her eyes. 'I'm sending her back black and blue.'

'It was an accident, ice skating,' Jack calmly pointed out.

'It will be fine, Nina,' Janey said, and he heard the younger sister trying to reassure the older, actually heard the rare tenderness in Janey's voice. And despite appearances, despite the horrible things she said at times, Jack realised Janey really did love Nina.

'So how did you all go?' Jack followed her into the bedroom where Nina was packing.

'Okay, I guess, but Janey took herself off to bed at eight last night and this morning she didn't want to talk. Still, it was fun ice skating till she fell. How was your night?'

'Yeah, okay.' He didn't even have to be evasive, Nina simply didn't want the details.

Everyone was trying to ignore that the small holiday was over, trying to pretend that everything was fine. It was Blake who couldn't hold out.

'I don't want to go back.'

Jack was loading up the car when Blake said it.

'I know,' Nina answered, as she always did, because Blake never wanted to go back, only this time it was different. 'Couldn't we stay another night?' Janey asked.

'We can't,' Nina replied. 'Blake's got school tomorrow and we've got to go and sort things out.'

Nina watched as Jack locked up the house and when he climbed into the car and drove off, he didn't really say much. For once it was Janey who was talking.

'What are we doing tonight?'

'Sleeping,' Nina said. 'And we can set up your bedroom.'

'Jack can do that,' Janey said.

'Uh-oh…' Jack shook his head. 'I've got to head home once I've dropped you guys off.' He glanced in the mirror as he said it and saw Janey's frown, but didn't pay too much attention to it.

'I think I might go back to Barbara's tonight.' Janey's voice from the back seat broke into her thoughts.

'Barbara's?' Nina swung around. 'I thought the whole point of running away was because you didn't want to ever go back there!'

'Yeah, well, I've changed my mind.'

'Janey…' Nina was struggling to keep exasperation out of her voice. 'Let's just leave things as they are. We can have a nice night, just the two of us, and sort things out, talk things out…'

Jack glanced in the mirror again and saw that Janey was back to looking out of the window, realising then that the last thing Janey wanted was another night alone with Nina.

Why?

He said nothing, just kept driving, but his mind was working overtime.

Why wouldn't Janey want a night alone with her big sister? He went through things just as he would with a patient, doing his best to take all the emotion out—except it was impossible to extract emotion from this equation.

Janey was back to scowling and as they approached Manhattan Blake started to cry.

'I'll see you in a couple of weeks.' Nina daren't say it might be sooner, not until she had spoken with his social worker. There was an appointment next week for them to come and see her flat—the wheels tended to move really slowly when a child wasn't in danger. Jack said nothing. He really didn't know how to deal with the situation. He could see Janey's angry expression in the rear-view mirror, could almost feel the daggers she was hurling at him embedding in his back.

'Just here,' Nina said as they approached the house where Blake lived, and Jack wondered how she did this every fortnight. Saying goodbye once was bad enough, but having to do it week in and week out must kill her. He helped her to get Blake's case out of the boot and saw her pale face as she did her best to stay calm for Blake, who was really crying now and clinging to her.

'Of course you can show me your poster.' She glanced up at Jack. 'I might be a while.'

'Take your time.'

'Can Jack come and see it?' Blake asked hopefully, but Jack shook his head.

'I'm going to wait in the car.'

Nina didn't blame him. He wasn't trying to impress Blake, or be his best friend, or proxy father, but she felt the sting of his rejection and it compounded her thoughts that she must end this soon, because after just one weekend Blake already hero-worshipped him. He'd already had enough loss in his life and she didn't want him falling in love with Jack, only to lose him too.

In fact, Jack would've loved to have made this transition easier for Blake, would have happily gone in and looked at his hockey posters, but he had a feeling that there was a rather more difficult conversation to be had and that it was about to take place.

Jack's instincts were rarely wrong.

'Happy now?' Janey demanded as soon as he got into the car. 'You give him the best weekend, driving around in your flash Jag, and then drop him back…' She was going ballistic and Jack just sat there. 'Mr Nice Guy!' Janey sneered, and Jack sat there as she told him how he thought he was better than them, better looking than them and that he was messing around with her sister.

Jack anticipated what would come next, warned Janey that if she spoke like that again, he would get out of the car and go and get Nina, which was when

Janey burst into tears. In the end there was no need for a long talk—all Jack really had to do was listen.

'Can you tell Nina this?' Jack asked.

'No,' Janey sobbed. 'Because she panics about everything, she feels guilty about everything. I know you think she's good at her job, and calm about things, but she loses her temper when it comes to us and she'll go crazy when she finds out…'

And Jack smiled an invisible smile, because Nina would do that. 'I'm scared she'll get into trouble and lose her job or something.'

'Your sister is not going to get into trouble,' Jack assured her, 'and neither are you—you've done nothing wrong.' He was very certain on that. 'Can I speak with Nina about it?' he asked. 'I can come back to the apartment and we can talk about it tonight…'

'No!' Janey begged, her hand moving to open the door.

'Don't run off, Janey.' Jack was stern and she shrank back in the seat. He would have spoken some more but all too soon Nina was coming out of the house, doing her best not to cry, waving to a tearful Blake, and somehow Jack had to sort this, would sort this, but he wondered how best to go about it. Nina was going to freak, he knew that, which meant Janey was likely to run again…

'Please don't say anything,' Janey begged as Nina got into the car, all falsely bright and cheerful.

'Right.' She smiled at Janey. 'Let's get back to the flat.'

Except there was no way Jack was going to drop the two of them off at Nina's flat.

'We could go back to my place,' he suggested.

'No.' Nina was adamant. 'I want to have some time with Janey before we go to the social worker in the morning.'

Jack drove through the wet streets, his mind working overtime, but as they drove past Central Park he knew what to do and Jack indicated and turned into the hospital.

'Do you need to check on someone?' Nina asked as Jack slid into his reserved parking spot.

'No,' Jack said. 'I want to get Janey's elbow examined.'

'It's just a bruise,' Nina said. 'I know I made a fuss, but I was just worried about having to face the social worker tomorrow with Janey covered in bruises. I was being ridiculous. She's fifteen, she fell, ice skating…'

'Still, it's better to get it all documented,' Jack said, getting out of the car and holding the door open for Janey.

Nina frowned, surprised that Jack thought it necessary, but more surprised that Janey so willingly got out of the car.

They walked into Emergency and Jack had a word with one of the nurses to ask which doctors were on.

'She doesn't need to see the Head of Emergency,' Nina said, when she heard Jack asking for Lewis to examine Janey.

'He's a great guy,' Jack said. 'I trust him implicitly.' He gave Janey a thin smile. 'I'll just go and have a word with him. Nina, why don't you get Janey into a gown? He'll need to examine her for range of movement…'

He wanted Lewis to see Janey, and with good reason. Not only was Lewis an excellent doctor and trusted colleague, but he would understand more than most the complexities of dealing with a very troubled young girl.

'I'd rather you hear it from Janey.' Jack spoke briefly with Lewis. 'Assuming, that is, that she talks, but basically we're not here about her elbow.'

'Right.' Lewis nodded.

'And if she doesn't talk to you,' Jack said, 'then maybe she might need a night of observation waiting for the orthos to have a look.'

'Let's just see how it goes,' Lewis suggested. 'She's here with her sister?'

'Nina Wilson, the social worker.' Jack nodded. 'She thinks that I've brought Janey here just to get her arm examined, but whatever happens I'm going to have to step in. I'm just hoping that Janey will talk to you.'

'Sure.' Lewis nodded. 'How about you introduce me?' Lewis called for one of the senior nurses to go in with him and smiled and introduced himself to an anxious-looking Janey.

'Okay,' Jack said. 'Nina and I are going to go and get a coffee. As I said, Lewis is a friend of mine, you're in very good hands.'

It was only then that it dawned on Nina what was happening, or maybe it had started to a couple of moments before. She was about to say no, to insist she was staying with Janey, but she realised then that there was another reason that Jack had brought them here.

She had seen scenarios like this on endless occasions. She was being removed from Janey to give her sister a chance to talk.

'Sure!' Nina choked back the sudden tears that were threatening. 'I could use a coffee.'

Nina waited till they were well away from the cubicle before she spoke. 'Jack, what's going on?'

'Just come in here and have a seat, Nina.'

'You think I did it.'

'Nina.' He shook his head. 'Not for a second did it enter my head that you'd hurt your sister.' Then he was honest. 'I did wonder why she didn't want to spend a night with you, but I think we both know that I don't jump to conclusions.'

He didn't know whether to tell her just yet, but at that moment a nurse popped her head out. 'Jack, Janey wants you to be in there when she speaks to Lewis.'

Nina stood.

'She wants me,' Jack said.

'Why not me?' Nina demanded. 'Why can't she speak to me?'

'Because she's been trying to spare your feelings,' Jack said. 'Because she doesn't love me and she knows I'm not going to get upset or angry or do anything rash, so just have a seat, Nina, and I'll be back to you as soon as I can.'

'Have you any idea how hard this is?' she demanded. 'You gave me no clue. All weekend you never gave a hint you were going to do this.'

'I didn't know then,' Jack said, and he was just so matter-of-fact and calm about everything. 'Nina, she said something in the car that I can't ignore but, please, you just have to trust that I am doing the very best I can for both you and Janey, and right now that means that I've got to go.'

It killed Nina to sit there not knowing what was going on. What on earth had Janey said in the car? Had she threatened to self-harm or was she doing drugs? She'd certainly been withdrawn at times. Or maybe she was pregnant? Nina sat there for what felt like an eternity before Jack finally returned, his face grim. He gave her a thin smile and then took a seat next to her.

'She's fine.'

Nina blew out her breath. 'But?'

Jack looked at her tense face and the bundle of passion that was Nina and didn't blame Janey a bit for not wanting to be the one to tell her.

'Barbara, her foster-mother, has got a new boyfriend, Vince...'

'Oh, God!' Nina stood. She just wanted to dash out there, to be with Janey, but again Jack was stern.

'Sit down, Nina, you need to hear this. First of all, nothing has happened, well, not what you're dreading, at least I don't think so, but you need to listen and then calm down and *then* you can go in and speak to Janey.'

'So he hasn't touched her?'

'He's tried to.'

Jack was very calm and annoyingly matter-of-fact, but sadly he dealt with this type of problem all too often, and though it was upsetting a cool head was needed. Jack was very good at that, except as he went through it with Nina he felt his anger starting to rise, an anger that he had to work hard to keep in check. The detachment that made this job easier for Jack was dissipating by the moment as he told Nina all that had happened.

'When you took Blake inside, she got very angry with me, told me I didn't care, that I'd made things harder for Blake, all that sort of thing.' Nina nodded, because that sounded very like Janey. 'Then she said I was up myself with my flash car and my good looks…' Nina frowned. 'Then she made a couple of suggestions and I told her that if she carried on like that I would get out of the car and go and get you.'

'Suggestions?'

'She was testing me, Nina, being deliberately provocative, and when I was having no part of it she broke down and started to cry. You know teenage girls do that sometimes, and most guys in an authoritative position know how to deal with that.'

Nina started to cry, because of all the things she'd dreaded hearing, this was the one she'd dreaded the most.

'Vince has been coming in to say goodnight to her.' Nina started to retch and he handed her the bin as she struggled to take breaths. She heard stuff like this every day, but it killed her to think it had happened to Janey. 'She didn't like it and she told Barbara, but then she got told off, because Barbara said it was nice that her boyfriend was making an effort. He's been creeping Janey out and she felt that she had to start getting dressed in the bathroom, because he was always finding an excuse to come into her room. Even when she was sent to bed early, or late, or whatever, he'd come in. He's tried a couple of times to kiss her, made a few inappropriate comments, and basically she's been fending him off.'

'I'll kill him.' Nina could hardly breathe. She wanted to go there right now, right this minute, and she told Jack exactly what she'd do when she got there. Jack just sat there as she ranted on for a while till she got back to Janey. 'Why couldn't she tell me?'

'Because she didn't want to watch you retching into a bin, because she knew you'd get upset and feel guilty, that you'd think it was your fault…'

'It is, though,' Nina sobbed. 'It's my job to protect—'

'Nina!' Jack was firm. 'You are not allowed to have your sister as a client for a very good reason. Right now the hospital social worker is coming down to see her, and it will all be dealt with properly. The main thing is, she is not going back there.'

'Can I speak to her?'

'In a moment, when you've calmed down.'

It actually took more than a moment for Nina to calm down. She couldn't stop crying and Lewis came in and had a word with her and confirmed all that Jack had said. 'She's fine, just relieved that she's told someone. In fact, she's more worried about you.'

'I've calmed down now,' Nina said, and she looked at Jack. 'I'm actually glad that she told you. I'd have reacted terribly. It's just impossible to think of it as another job. It's different when it's your family.'

'Of course it is,' Jack said. 'You should go and see her.'

Nina nodded.

She was determined to be calm when she walked in

there, but she burst into tears when she cuddled Janey, and Janey burst into tears too. After a few minutes they calmed down and a while later, Jack popped his head in.

'How are things?'

'Better,' Janey said, and then her eyes filled up with fresh tears. 'I'm sorry for all the things I said.'

'Yeah, well, you had a good reason,' Jack said. 'But what's wrong with my car?'

Janey even managed her first laugh since her arrival at Angel's. 'How was she when you told her?' Janey nodded in the direction of Nina.

'Pretty much as you'd expect!'

'I am here,' Nina said. 'I took it quite well.'

'Oh, God!' Jack impersonated her, and Janey smiled. 'I handed her the bin…'

'I wasn't that bad.'

'You were fine.' Jack smiled.

'Thank you,' Nina said. He really had been marvellous. 'We're going to be here ages, so you might as well go home. Thank you so much for everything.'

'I'll stick around for a while.'

'You really don't have to.'

'It's fine.'

It was a very long night. Things like this were dealt with thoroughly and given that Barbara had two other foster-children, Child Protection went around to speak with the family, but Vince was out and Barbara angrily denied there had been anything inappropriate taking place, Nina was informed by her friend and colleague. 'She's very angry with Janey,' Lorianna told her. 'The usual stuff, but don't worry…'

'I want my sister and my brother in my care.'

'It sounds as if Blake is doing fine.'

'No!' Nina said. 'Blake is not fine, Blake *is* being looked after but he's not being loved. He's clingy and needy and he needs to be with his family.'

Jack listened to her fighting for her brother and sister, saw the determination in Nina's eyes and that she would not back off, would not wait for the department to take its time. This was going to be dealt with, and soon, she told Lorianna.

Jack went and got a drink from the water cooler and just stood and looked around the familiar department, except everything felt unfamiliar. He was glad to be there, glad to have helped, and despite Nina insisting that he go home, Jack actually didn't want to, he really wanted to be here and see things through.

'I thought you were off.' Alex caught up with him at the water cooler. 'How come you're here?'

'Personal stuff,' Jack said, but it was more than personal, it actually felt like family—better than family, in fact.

No one tried to spare anyone's feelings in his family. There were, Jack had long since concluded, no feelings to spare.

Imagine Nina when she met his family—she'd run a mile, Jack knew it. Still, he wasn't going to talk about that with Alex. Instead, he asked about another young patient who, thanks to a certain young woman, had been on his mind of late.

'How's Tommy doing?'

'He's had a good weekend,' Alex said. 'They're starting the treatment tomorrow and hopefully there will be a good response. We should be able to buy him some time.'

'Surgery?'

Alex grimaced. 'I think time is all we can hope for.'

'But do you think it could be an option…' Jack knew he was pushing things, knew what Alex's problem was, but Alex wasn't in the mood to open up either. 'You've done similar surgery before.'

'Thanks for that, Jack,' Alex snapped, but still Jack wouldn't back off.

'If you want to talk…'

'Again—thanks.'

'I mean it, Alex.'

But Alex stalked off. Jack had clearly got to him, but just as he was pondering how better to discuss things, Jack was distracted by an irate man storming through the department. 'Where is she?' Security was pulling him back, keeping him well away from the patients, and Jack walked over to the waiting room where the man was still ranting. Unable to calm him down, Security took him outside.

'She's a lying bitch,' he shouted, and Jack looked at him, felt the anger he'd never felt before slowly building. 'Janey's a liar, I never laid a finger on her…'

And while Jack should have been thinking about his career, the newspapers, the hospital, his role, none of that entered his head. Instead, he just stared at the piece of filth that had tried to touch Nina's little sister and as detached and dispassionate as he could be at times, to-night just wasn't one of those times.

'It was her that came on to me,' Vince shouted, 'flaunting her…' He didn't get to finish.

Jack's fist met his jaw, and two rather startled security guards had to let Vince go. After all, they could hardly hold him as the Head of Paediatrics hit him.

And that was what greeted Nina's eyes when she walked outside.

Vince sprang and lunged at Jack, who met him with his fist again, and Nina stood there just a little bit torn, because she abhorred violence, there really was no place for it in Nina's book, but seeing Jack's fist mid swing and one blackening eye, seeing someone for the first time truly fighting for her family, seeing Jack doing to Vince what she could have so easily done herself, she was hard placed not to stand there cheering.

Still, the fight was broken up quickly and when Vince shouted he that was going to press charges, Nina saw a very different Jack from the one she thought she knew. He was being held back by Security, telling Vince to go ahead, that he was looking forward to seeing him in court where he could explain himself…

Of course there was no chance of keeping things quiet.

Not a hope. It was all around the hospital by the time Jack's closing eye was being treated with an ice pack and even though Nina had tried to keep it from Janey, of course gossip was rife in the corridors and she'd heard people talking.

'Did he hit him?' Janey was sitting on a hospital trolley and was absolutely delighted. 'Did Jack really hit him? That's brilliant!'

'It is so not brilliant,' Nina scolded. 'There's no excuse for violence.'

And there would be ramifications for it too, Nina fretted when she had a word with Lewis a little later. 'Do you think he'll get into trouble?'

'Who, Jack?' Lewis shook his head. 'Not a chance. Really, it's the other guy who needs to be worried. I tell you, I cheered inside. Sometimes in this job you'd love to forget the law...'

'I know,' Nina said. 'Except we don't!' She really couldn't get her head around it, but Lewis was talking about Janey now.

'I've spoken to Social Services and given you already have reprieve access with her, we could send Janey home with you tonight, but I've spoken at length with Lorianna and we both agree that if we do a case meeting in the morning, once they've spoken with Blake's case worker, it might just push things along. It's not the hospital department we're dealing with, but we might stand more of a chance of moving things along than you'll have once Janey is home.'

'I know.'

'So let's keep Janey here and we'll roll the ball a bit harder tomorrow morning.'

He'd been marvellous and again Nina thanked him, before going in to say goodnight to Janey. Jack stood with his keys, trying not to yawn as she said goodbye.

'Jack's going to give me a lift home. We both need to get some rest. It's going to be a busy day tomorrow,' Nina said, and she saw the worry return to Janey's face.

'And I am going to do everything I can to make sure that you and Blake are home with me as soon as possible.'

'Do you think it will happen? Do you think we'll all be together?' Janey asked, and Nina thought for a moment, not as a frantic sister but as the social worker she was. She was their sister who *finally* had a three-bedroomed flat, an older sister who, though it would be incredibly strained financially, actually could support them, there were no protective issues, the children wanted to be there and finally, after all these years, Nina was able to look her sister in the eye and give her real hope.

'I do,' Nina said. 'I actually do.' And she gave Janey a cuddle, knew that nothing was guaranteed, but for the first time Nina allowed herself to get excited. She didn't say it, didn't want to make a promise that she might not get to keep, but she thought it. *Janey, I swear you and Blake are coming home to me.*

Jack was quiet on the drive home and quiet again when she told him he could just drop her off there.

'I want to talk to you, Nina.'

He followed her in.

'Thanks again for tonight—'

'Things will get sorted now,' Jack said. 'I'm sorry Janey had to go through all that...' He saw her struggle to blink back the tears, moved in to hold her, but she shrugged him off.

'I'm really not up for talking, Jack.'

'Fair enough.' His mouth grazed hers, his eyes open and watching hers close, not in bliss but in reluctant acceptance. He felt her tongue in his mouth and her hands move down to his crotch, he heard her fake moan to arouse when she realised that he wasn't hard, and if Jack had been angry before, he was furious now.

'Don't…' She heard the anger in his voice as he removed her hand. 'Don't you ever just go through the motions with me.'

He saw the burn on her cheeks as his fury built inside and he struggled to contain it.

'Did I earn it tonight?' Jack asked, and he struggled not to shout. 'Are you just trying to get it over and done with?'

'Leave if you don't like it.'

And he saw her gutter mouth come out for him, because that was where she'd almost been, saw the scared angry kid she had once been. 'When you say you haven't had a relationship for a long time…' She pushed past him, but he caught her. 'When was the last time you had sex, Nina?'

'Friday night, from memory.' She opened the door. 'Just leave.'

'Before then,' Jack said. 'Before us.'

Nina stood holding the door open, but Jack would not move.

'A while.' Nina shrugged.

'Oh, I think it was a while,' Jack said. 'I'd say about six years. Is that what the pro bono centre did for you? They got you off the streets…'

'I wasn't a hooker, Jack,' she snarled, 'if that's what you're thinking.' He saw all the anger shooting from her eyes and it was merited. 'But there can be a lot of favours to pay for sleeping on a friend's couch…' And then she started to cry.

'And was I the first since that time?' She just stood there.

'What was I supposed to say?' Nina shouted. 'That you're the first person I've even considered fancying, that for two years I've had a thing for you…?' She just looked at him. 'You'd have run a mile.'

Jack didn't know how to deal with this. He just stood there confused, because it *had* been so much more than sex that night.

'Can you please leave?' she said when he walked over to her. 'I mean it,' she said, still holding the door. 'Jack, can you leave?'

And, given what she'd just told him, Jack had no choice but to respect her wishes, no choice really but to do as she asked and leave.

Jack was angry.

More than angry and there wasn't even an actual person he could pin it on. He had been angry enough with what had happened to Janey, but that it had happened to Nina, that there hadn't been an older sister looking out for her, that she had been left to her own devices had Jack's mind working overtime.

There was no one he could speak to about it either.

Jack tried to imagine the reaction of his parents if he tried to talk about what had happened with Nina.

The sneers, the turning up of their noses.

But he knew that the last thing Nina needed was

to see that. He had to deal with this himself, had to work out how best to handle it.

Nina's cheeks fired the next morning when she saw him in the corridor and she just brushed past him. They fired up again a few hours later when her intercom buzzed and Jack was at her door.

And she blushed even more when he sat in the chair where she'd, er, once approached him. And then he did the impossible, just as he had the first time he'd come to her office. Jack made her laugh.

'Is the chair okay or do you want me on the mat again?'

'Very funny, Jack.' She laughed, but she was still cringing about what she had told him last night.

'Nina, don't ignore me in the corridor again. I told you, I don't do awkward,' Jack said, simply addressing the situation between them.

'Thank you.'

And then Jack got to another reason he was there.

'I heard their might be some news.'

There was. The news was still fluttering in her chest, still new and shiny and hard to take in, and she hadn't actually said the words out loud yet.

'I've got custody…' She was shaking just saying it. All those years of study and work and scrimping and saving, just to get to this point, and finally, sooner than expected, she could say it. 'It's temporary custody for now, but they've been to look at the flat, and apparently Blake isn't happy where he is.' She hated so much what they had all been through. 'They're not horrible people or anything, they're just older and can't deal with him...'

'You've got them now.' Jack came and leant on the desk beside her chair. 'They're good kids.'

'They are!' Nina was adamant on that. 'I know Janey can be a handful, but I'm really going to work on her. I'm going to show the department just how much better she is with me.'

And he knew he had to step back here, that it wasn't his place to tell her how to raise them. After all, what would he know? Professionally, yes, he had his opinion, but on family...? He thought of his own family, the complete dysfunction behind the smiling façade, but more than that he needed to do some serious thinking.

Serious thinking.

'Say hi to them for me.' He gave a thin smile. 'Tell them I'll come by and see them some time soon.'

'I think we need some time together...' She saw him frown, saw the slight startlement in his eyes and realised he'd misunderstood what she had said, that he must have thought she was working out a way to schedule some alone time for them, so she made things a little clearer. 'Not us.' God, it hurt to lose him. 'Me and the kids. We need some time to settle in with each other and...' She gave him a smile when she felt like weeping. 'Really, Jack, it might just confuse things if you keep coming round.'

'Yeah, well, I told Blake that I'd get him a Rangers top,' Jack said.

'You can give that to me at work.'

'And I also said to Janey that I'd check in and see

that she was okay, wherever she was…so, tough, I'm coming round.'

He walked back through the hospital and popped into ICU before heading for home, and for Jack things couldn't be more confusing.

He was being dumped and surely he should be sighing with relief, cracking open the champagne and celebrating, because Jack Carter with a twenty-five-year-old, anti-fashion girlfriend, who came with two messed-up kids in tow was so not part of the plan.

And he was still confused when he got home and looked around his tastefully furnished apartment, because all it looked was sterile. He looked into the mirror as he shaved the next morning, saw the fading bruise and decided that if he saw Vince again he'd happily repeat the experience.

He wanted something more from this relationship, wanted something he had never known, and, no, he didn't understand it.

CHAPTER TWELVE

NINA DIDN'T SAY his name. Instead, she pursed her lips when on Friday night Jack came to her door just as she was about to start dinner.

'I rang your office.' Jack smiled. 'They said you left at five.'

'I did.' Nina tried to move out to the hall so that Blake and Janey wouldn't realise that he was there. 'I've got a lot to do, Jack—there's a lot to unpack.' She still hadn't set up the chests of drawers in Janey's room, but she wasn't going to tell him that.

'I thought I might help. Maybe I could go out and get dinner.' He sniffed the air. 'Is that chicken? I thought you didn't eat meat.'

He spoke too loudly so she did move out into the hall as there was no way she wanted Blake to hear him. 'Just because I'm vegetarian it doesn't mean that they have to be.'

'Jack!' Like a Jack-seeking missile, Blake came out to the hall. 'Did you get my top?'

'Blake.' Nina was stern. 'Don't be rude.'

'It's fine,' Jack said. 'No, I haven't got your top yet. I'm working on it.'

He'd probably get one signed by the whole hockey team. Nina could just picture it.

'Are you going to ask me in?' Jack said. 'Or is it chicken for two?'

It was a chicken for three and Nina just had the vegetables. It worried her how much Blake adored him. Janey even asked him for some help with her homework a bit later and Nina heard him ask if she knew what she wanted to do in the future.

'No idea,' Janey admitted. 'Anyway, I think I might have left it too late to get good grades.'

'You're fifteen,' Jack said. 'It's not too late to turn things around. You just need to focus.'

After dinner Nina thanked him for coming over and though she did it nicely it was clear she was asking him to leave.

'I'll be off, then. Oh, and, Nina…' he gave her a smile '…you do remember that you agreed to go to the dinner dance tomorrow for the burns unit…?'

'I didn't agree,' Nina said.

'Well, it's a bit too late to back out now—I've put your name down, bought the tickets…' Annoyingly he smiled. 'It's for a very good cause.'

'I can babysit,' Janey chimed in, before Nina could use that as an excuse, but she shook her head.

'I'm not going out your first Saturday night here and leaving you to babysit.'

'Why not?' Jack asked, and she wished he would just butt out. She could hardly stand here and say that she didn't know if she trusted Janey, but she had no choice but to agree, making it clear that she'd rather he went home now.

'I'll pick you up at seven,' Jack said, and then said goodbye to Blake and Janey.

'You were mean,' Blake said accusingly.

'I wasn't mean,' Nina said, but it was said rather forcibly to override her disquiet, because Jack had seemed to genuinely want to be there and yet again it had been a good evening.

'That's how I used to feel,' Blake said when she went in later to kiss him goodnight.

'When?'

'At Dianne's. I always felt that she just wanted to get back to her family.'

'It's not like that with Jack.' Nina did her best to explain what she didn't herself understand. 'Jack's a very good friend.'

'He's more than your friend.'

'Yes,' Nina said carefully.

'So why were you mean to him?'

'I wasn't mean. The thing is, Jack comes from a very well-to-do family, he's a very...' She stopped because it was impossible to explain.

'You said things like that don't matter.'

'They don't.' Nina blew out a breath. How could she tell Blake that Jack couldn't possibly be ready for this ready-made family? That really, as fun as the time had been that they'd had together, it would be marked in days, weeks at best.

There was not just one but three hearts that could be very easily broken here if she wasn't careful.

'Let's just worry about us for now.' She gave him a kiss goodnight.

'What are you wearing for the dinner?' Janey asked when Nina came out from saying goodnight to Blake.

'I'm not sure yet.'

'Are you going to buy something?'

Nina shook her head. She was already worrying enough about dropping her hours, without buying a new dress, and anyway nothing she could afford could even begin to match the lavish women that would be there.

No, things like that shouldn't matter, but it was going to be an embarrassing way to prove a point.

'There's a nice retro store I know. They have some top-end stuff,' Janey suggested. 'We could go shopping tomorrow.'

And it was the most *normal* suggestion Janey had made, just two sisters going shopping, and of course Blake would come along too but, yes, the thought of having some quality time with Janey and possibly finding a dress that wasn't going to make her stand out like a sore thumb worked on so many levels that less than twelve hours later Nina found herself being bullied to try on dresses that were absolutely not her style.

'It's nice,' Nina said, because it was the best of the bunch, 'but...' She turned around in the mirror and wasn't quite so sure. It was a chocolate-brown dress that looked great from the front but from the back showed rather too much of her spine. She thought of the glossed and buffed women who would be attending, women who would have spent ages in preparation, and suddenly Nina felt more than a little nervous. She had no interest in competing with them, but at the same time she didn't want to embarrass Jack.

'You've got shoes that will go with it,' Janey reminded her. 'And I'm also starving.'

'So am I,' Blake said, thoroughly bored by the whole shopping expedition. 'When can we go home?'

'Okay, okay,' Nina said, but pleased with her purchase she was actually glad Janey had suggested that they come here, and once home and eating lunch she told her so.

'I enjoyed it,' Janey admitted, and then looked at the clock. 'You'd better start getting ready.'

'He's not picking me up till six.' It had been seven p.m. that Jack was to pick her up but he'd texted that morning with a last-minute change of plans. They were going to stop by and have drinks at his parents' house and then go to the dinner from there. The thought of meeting his parents was more daunting than what would follow.

'Which gives you four hours,' Janey pointed out. 'You've no idea, have you?' Janey just stared at her older sister. 'Some of these women will have spent days preparing for this.'

'Okay, okay.'

'And you're going to his posh parents' house—you'll have to look nice for that too.' Janey actually laughed. 'I can't believe he's taking you to meet his family.'

'It's nothing like that.' Oh, she knew better than to read anything into it. The Carters were sociable people and no doubt wanted to briefly meet her before they shared an evening at the same table but, still, it was for that reason that she allowed Janey to paint her finger- and toenails *and* let her do her hair.

'I don't want it straightened,' Nina said as Janey plugged her equipment in.

'I'm not going to straighten it.' Janey rolled her eyes at her very out-of-date older sister. 'I'm going to give you curls.'

Which she did.

Over and over she pulled the straighteners and it was nice to sit in the bedroom as Janey got to work and just chat, to find out that this was the sort of thing Janey liked to get up to with her friends, just spend the evening doing hair and nails and things; that beneath that scowling expression and black eyeliner was actually a very young, very nice young girl. It made her heart thump in her chest to think of what might have happened if Jack hadn't handled things so well.

'You should have a few friends over one night,' Nina suggested as Janey got to work on her make-up.

'So you can interrogate them?'

'No. So you can have some fun with them here.'

'Tonight?'

'No.' Nina knew Janey was teasing, because they'd had some very long conversations. 'Tonight you're in charge of Blake and I'm trusting you to get this right.'

'You mean Jack's trusting me.'

'Okay,' Nina admitted. 'Maybe he did push for it, but I think he's right—you're nearly sixteen you should be able to look after your brother. I'll be home before midnight. Go easy with the make-up,' Nina said, pulling away.

'I have,' Janey said. 'You're done! But you need to see it with your dress and shoes on and everything.'

Nina was somewhat nervous going over to the mirror. While she was all for encouraging Janey, she didn't want to go out tonight looking like a complete clown, but when she stood in the hall and stared into the long mirror she didn't comment for a while.

'You like it, don't you?'

Nina did like it, perhaps because she barely recognised herself.

Her hair, which she usually pinned up loosely or pulled back now fell in loose ringlets and her make-up was amazing. It had felt as if Janey was putting far too much on, but actually it was all very subtle. Her skin looked creamy and her eye shadow was brown, which brought out her deep blue eyes, and her lips were a pinkish neutral. The only place Janey had been heavy with was the eyelashes. From long, fair and invisible, they were now soft and black and really long, and however she looked in the mirror she knew that there was no way she could have put this all together herself.

'You're really good at this.'

'I know.'

'I mean,' Nina said slowly, '*really* good at this.'

'Are you nervous?' Janey asked.

'A bit,' Nina admitted.

'Maybe Jack is,' Janey said, but Nina shook her head.

'These things are no big deal to Jack. He won't be giving it a second thought.'

She could not have been more wrong.

As his driver brought him closer to Nina's, Jack was having serious second thoughts.

He must have been mad to suggest that she come to his parents' for drinks—a table at dinner would have been fine, but to bring her into his home? He'd been thinking of himself, wanting to show Nina first hand what was so hard to explain, except he hadn't properly considered the effect it might have on Nina…until now.

He could just imagine his mother's disapproving eye as she saw Nina in an off-the-peg number. He wouldn't put it past her to even question out loud if her was dress was suitable for tonight.

As the car stopped outside Nina's apartment Jack climbed out and even as he took the lift he wondered if he should suggest they stay at her apartment for a while and just meet his parents at the venue.

'Hey, Jack…' Blake let him in. 'She's been getting ready for ages.'

'You're not supposed to tell me that.' Jack winked. 'Trust me on that one. Here…' He handed him a bag and smiled at Blake's expression and shout of delight as he took out the top. He hadn't had it signed by the entire team but there was Blake's favourite player's signature and a signed photo, and the little guy was so excited he dashed off to show his sisters, leaving Jack standing in the hallway. And after a moment he let himself in.

'I hope you said thank you.'

Jack said nothing. He wasn't trying to get Blake into trouble, but for a moment there he actually forgot he had a voice, because she looked nothing like he could have expected—she looked incredible. Still Nina, still different, but she would turn heads for different reasons tonight.

'You look amazing.'

'Thanks to Janey,' Nina said.

'Thank you, Janey.' Jack smiled.

'So am I going to get paid for being personal shopper, make-up artist and babysitter?' Janey asked as Nina filled her bag.

'No,' Nina said. 'That's what....' She gave in then. Janey had saved her a fortune tonight and in years to come she had her own personal stylist under her roof. What wasn't to love? So she gave her some money and didn't notice that Jack gave her some too, but with a warning that he expected her on her most responsible behaviour tonight.

'I will be,' Janey insisted. 'I want Nina to have a good time.'

So did Jack.

For the hundredth time he wondered what the hell he was doing. He actually felt a bit sick as the car approached his family home, the same nausea he had always felt at the beginning of the school holidays, knowing he would have to spend the summer here, or Christmas...

Jack had far preferred his time at boarding school.

'I'm nervous...' Nina said.

'I know.' Jack helped her out of the car. 'They're pretty daunting.'

It wasn't the answer Nina had been expecting. She'd hoped he'd reassure her that it was no big deal, that he brought friends home all the time, that they'd met so many of his girlfriends that they'd struggle to remember her name for the night, but he said nothing, just took her arm and led her to a front door she'd seen pictured on the covers of lifestyle magazines and Sunday papers and that soon would admit her.

'They're used to this, though.' She was speaking more for her own benefit than his, trying to reassure herself when he didn't. 'You'd have brought a lot of women here.'

'I've never brought anyone back here.' She turned and frowned just as she heard someone approach from the other side of the door. 'I've never brought a friend home, even when I was at school, and certainly I've never brought a date back here.'

'Never?'

'Never,' Jack said. 'And I'm really sorry to put you through this.'

She had no idea what he was talking about.

The door was opened by a servant, who took their coats, and Jack led her through a house that was huge. Then she stepped into the gorgeous lounge that she had seen in the pages of a magazine.

'Jack…' His mother turned as he walked in. She was sipping a glass of champagne and chatting on the phone, but she muted it for a moment and naturally Nina recognised her and gave her a smile.

'Mother, this is Nina Wilson.'

She gave a brief nod in her conversation and it was Jack who introduced her. 'Nina, this is Anna,' he said as she resumed talking on the telephone, bitching about the guests that were going tonight. Nina sat there, cheeks scalding, stunned as everything she thought she knew about the Carters was wiped out of existence.

The father walked in and Jack Carter Senior sort of gave a brief nod in their direction and snapped for a maid to hurry up with his drink.

'What time are we leaving?' were his first words to Jack.

'We're to be there for seven-thirty, so soon,' Jack said, as Nina realised exactly why Jack had been in no hurry to leave her place. They were the coldest, most distant people Nina had ever met. Everything she had read or seen had been an complete act. This was so not the all American family they portrayed.

They were dismissive way past the point of rudeness.

His mother came off the phone but made no attempt to speak with either Jack or Nina, just checked a few details with her husband. They might just as well have not been there, though Jack did make an effort.

He introduced Nina to his father.

Jack Senior just gave a vague nod in her direction.

'Nina does a lot of work at the pro bono centre in Harlem.'

Anna wrinkled up her nose, but Jack pushed on. 'Did you know Louis Cavel donates some time there?'

'I've heard.' Jack Senior nodded. 'I did consider it, of course it would look good, but really...' He shook his head and looked at Nina. 'I suppose you're always looking for donations.'

'We prefer people's time,' Nina responded, but the thought of spending time with this man, knowing it was simply a matter of looking good, and she was more than happy to bend the rules for him. 'Of course donations are always welcome.'

'Louis puts a lot of hours in,' Jack persisted. 'He does scar reductions, resets noses, you really should see the work he does with victims of domestic violence. There's an amazing body of people there...'

'There's a far simpler solution,' Anna said. 'If these women just left their husbands in the first place, they could save us a whole lot of trouble.' Anna laughed at her own joke and her husband laughed too, and Nina realised why Jack had apologised in advance for them— it was truly painful to be there.

The maid came and announced that the car was ready for them and as they stood Anna asked a question. 'What's the dinner in aid of tonight?' she asked.

'The burns unit at Angel's,' Jack said, and his mother gave a little shudder.

'God, I hope they don't do a presentation.'

They were disgusting.

There was no other word for them and Nina was so glad they were travelling in separate cars and had some time alone with Jack before they arrived at the dinner. Nina, who would never usually speak in front of the driver, actually didn't care tonight. He presumably knew the real Carters behind the sparkling façade.

'Are they always like that?'

Jack didn't look at her. He was acutely embarrassed. Nina was the first person he had brought home and his parents had actually been quite civil.

'Believe me, that was nothing.'

'Is that why you don't bring anyone home?' Nina

asked. 'Because you're embarrassed that it might get out…?'

'I couldn't care less,' Jack said. 'There's a strange unspoken rule that what happens at home stays at home but, really, that's not why I've kept people away. I've dated more than a few women who would have happily joined in that conversation.'

'Were they always like that?'

'Always.' Jack nodded. 'Sorry to ruin your night.'

'Thanks a lot.' Nina smiled back.

As they walked into the function she watched his parents turn on the charm and work the room in glittering style, and yet she knew how twenty minutes in their company had made her feel.

Imagine growing up with that?

The place was beautifully decorated, the table gleaming with silverware and gorgeous little chocolate mice, which, Nina found out when she took a bite, were filled with the most amazing mousse. Everything was beautiful or rather, Nina now realised, everything appeared to be.

They sat and ate and chatted and laughed and Nina played her part. They were at a table for twelve and Anna was beguiling them all, and she turned her beams on Nina.

'Stunning dress…'

'Thank you.'

'I can't quite place it.'

'Neither could the sales assistant,' Nina answered. 'The label had been ripped out.' And she made it clear she had bought it at the retro store. Jack watched his mother's face flush beneath her make-up, her eyes shooting angrily to Jack, but he just leant back in his chair, his arm draped loosely over the back of Nina's chair as she carried on with her dinner. 'I offered to get her a dress, but the thing is with Nina, she'd never spend that sort of money on fashion…'

'Very commendable…' Anna gave a vinegar smile.

And while Nina didn't need his mother's approval, his mother felt the need to assure Nina that she'd never have it, or at least to score a few points, because she needled away at Nina when Jack got up to make a speech.

'Yet, for all your altruism, you're happy to sit in your second-hand dress and eat the finest food and drink the best champagne…'

'Very happy to.' Nina met her cool glare. 'It was nice of Jack to invite me and I'm very touched that he did. I work with a lot of families on the burns unit, and this fundraiser will help a lot.'

And she turned from what was unimportant to someone who was, and listened as Jack made his speech. It wasn't a particularly emotional speech. It wasn't designed to pull at the heartstrings but it was to the point and funny at times, and from the reaction of the room just what had been needed to make it a successful evening.

Jack watched the conversation taking place at his table, saw his mother attempting to smile for the room as Nina crushed her with a few words. He had been so right to bring her. Jack knew then that all the doubts of the past few days faded as he had met the one woman who could stand up to his family, because Nina truly did not care what they thought of her. She was the one woman he had met who really was not turned on by money, which meant, Jack realised as they danced a little later, she was turned on only by him.

'Sorry about that,' he said, and she pulled back her face and looked up at him.

'You have *nothing* to apologise for,' she said. 'I might, though. I think I was a bit rude…'

'She has a very thick skin,' Jack assured her. 'Can you do me a favour?'

'Of course.'

'Can you feign a headache?'

'No feigning required.'

They weren't actually leaving that early. People were already starting to drift off. His mother was grimly wringing the last out of the champagne bottle and rather than anger Jack felt an immense sadness as he wished his parents goodnight.

They simply had no idea what was real, and he was only just finding out.

They didn't take a car but walked instead, through the city they both loved but had experienced through very different eyes.

'I'm going to volunteer at the centre,' Jack said. 'Well, I'm going to apply to.'

'Can you afford the time?'

'Not at the moment,' he admitted, 'but I can cut back on some other things.' They sat in Central Park and looked at the couples going past on the last of the night carriage rides and then up to Angel's and all that was going on unseen behind the windows. 'I don't think I'm right as Head of Paeds,' Jack admitted. 'The board is happy because I'm bringing in a lot of funds but, really, my role should be more hands on…'

'You can make it that way.'

'I'm going to,' Jack said. 'I'm going to pull back on the fundraising stuff and put in some hours at the pro bono centre, but I don't think I'm practising medicine the way I want to. I know I'm good at what I do, but…' he let out a breath '…I want to do more.'

'You will, then,' Nina said. She had, for so long, thought him cold and arrogant and, yes, in recent times she had seen a different side to him, but tonight she really was starting to understand why Jack was the way he was. 'What was it like, growing up with them?'

'Messed up,' Jack said. 'But at the time you think it's normal. I was told off for crying, for any display of emotion really. I think I finally worked out how far from normal it was when I was eight and stayed with that family for a week. I saw how different things should be.'

'Yet you didn't go and stay with them at Christmas?'

'Because it's easier not to know how bad things really are sometimes,' Jack explained. 'I understand how angry Janey was last week—how an amazing weekend away just made it harder to go back—that was how I felt after my holiday.'

'So much for the perfect family,' Nina said. 'Maybe there is no such thing.'

They hailed a cab and as they approached her apartment Jack just sat there as Nina went to climb out.

'Aren't you coming in?'

'Am I invited?' Jack asked, and Nina took a breath.

'For coffee.'

'Then yes.'

Blake was asleep and Janey was watching a movie, but after a brief chat she went off yawning to bed.

'Here.' Nina handed him his coffee and she felt incredibly awkward, embarrassed to be alone with him, with the man who knew so much about her past.

But was somehow still there.

Jack looked around the shabby apartment that had been so fought for and cherished by three people, and he knew why—it was home.

'Thanks for these past couple of weeks, Jack.' Nina made herself say it. 'I really do mean that.'

'You're welcome,' Jack said, and took a mouthful of coffee before speaking. 'Thank you too.'

'For what?' Nina grinned.

'Oh, a few things spring to mind—changing my career path for one.'

'Sorry about that.'

He drained his coffee. 'I'm going to go.'

He really ought to do exactly that, the sensible part of him knew that as he stood, or rather the sensible part of the Jack he had been a couple of weeks ago, who had looked out at the ward and chastised himself for even considering a fling with Nina Wilson, knew that he should just get out now. Except he'd done more thinking these past weeks than he had in a long time, and more thinking that he'd ever thought he would about a woman in the days since she'd asked him to leave.

''Night, Nina.'

He moved in to give her a kiss, just a friendly kiss that started on her cheek and then moved to her mouth, and she felt the graze of his lips, felt her own tremble to his mouth, but then he removed it.

''Night.' He smiled and his arms let her go.

Except she wanted some more of his mouth.

'Jack…' she called as he headed to the door. 'You said things would never be awkward between us.'

'They won't be,' he assured her.

'You don't have to go,' Nina said. 'I mean, if you want…'

'Tell me what you want, Nina.'

Her cheeks burnt as she said it, as she told him exactly what she would like to happen. 'I'd like you to stay.'

'Or we could just have a kiss and see where that leads?'

And her cheeks burnt some more. She felt the wrap of his arms around her and then his lovely mouth and she kissed him in a way she never had. His tongue slid around hers and his mouth tasted divine, so she kept right on kissing until it wasn't enough, till she wanted him to kiss her harder, but still he just kissed her slowly and when her hands left his hair and tried to work down his body, Jack halted them, held them down by her sides and just kept kissing her till she though she might die from the pleasure. She gave in then, till the pleasure was too much and not enough at the same time, and Nina pressed her body into him, except Jack pushed her hips back and then stopped.

'What do you want, Nina?'

'I want you to stay.'

'In that case,' Jack said, 'I'd love to.'

And he entered the hallowed turf of her bedroom and kissed her again, just as blissfully as he had out in the hall, except she wanted more.

'Jack...' His hands were back holding hers down. 'Please.'

'What do you want, Nina?'

'For you to undress me.'

'I'd love to.'

And he was way too slow, just so painfully slow because she wanted to be on the bed with him, but instead he was slowly unzipping her dress and then taking off her underwear, very, very slowly, with no kisses in between. His touch was tender, just not enough, and when he knelt down and carefully took off her shoes, she could have wept at the slight graze of his hair on her thighs when she wanted his mouth.

'Please, Jack...' She went to the buttons of his shirt, but his hands stopped her. 'Please.'

So he undressed himself while still kissing her and frantically she helped him, closing her eyes to the bliss of their naked skin pressed together and she simply could not stay standing and she knew what he was doing and just gave in to it now.

'I want you to take me to bed.'

'I'd love to.'

And Jack was old enough to dress himself, and she watched and held onto his shoulders as he protected them then kissed her, moving her onto the bed. She wanted to hold him, to touch him, yet still he restrained her. Then he began to move his hands over her body, until she was crying and dizzy, and then his hands were still and hers led him to where she wanted them to be, because tonight it was all about her.

'What do you want, Nina?'

'You to…' His hand went over her mouth and he spoke into her ear and reminded her she was a lady. He felt her mouth stretch on his palm into a smile and then he felt the heat of her skin as it flared into a dark blush.

'What do you want?' he checked.

'For you to make love to me.'

And so he did, and Nina didn't care about tomorrow as he moved inside her, as he took her completely, because whatever happened from this point he had given her tonight—a night when she didn't hold back, when she moaned and writhed beneath him. And Jack didn't hold back either. Maybe it would be awkward at work in the future because, when they came, he was telling her he loved her and she was telling him the same. Afterwards they lay there, Nina burning from the pleasure and just a bit embarrassed because, yes, she loved him, she just hadn't really wanted him to know how much.

'What do you want, Nina?'

She frowned and turned her head to him, had thought that delicious game was over.

'Tell me,' he insisted.

She looked at the playboy on her pillow and would love him for ever, but she knew there were limits, knew that the truth couldn't fully come out here. 'What I can't have.'

'How do you know that?'

'I know that.' She smiled, and watched as he turned onto his elbow and then gave her a little telling-off.

'You need to start saying what you want,' Jack said. 'You need to be able to say what you want.'

'I know that.'

'So say it.'

'I'd like to see more of you.'

'How much more?'

'I don't know.'

'I think you do.'

'And I think it's impossible...' She forced another smile. 'I've effectively got two kids...'

'Forget them.'

'I can't,' Nina sobbed, because she couldn't and never would, even if it meant that she and Jack couldn't have a future together.

'Forget about your brother and sister and my reaction, and just tell me what it is that you want.' Jack was insistent.

And at the risk of him running from the bed and grabbing his suit, at the absolute risk of him running off and life being terribly awkward in the morning, she told him.

'I want you to be a part of my family.' She said it and Jack listened and he didn't run. He'd done that in the past few days when he had carefully thought about all he might be about to take on, and as he looked down Jack knew he had come to the right decision and her honesty only proved it now.

'I'd love to be.'

'Don't say that…' She didn't want a heat of-the-moment thing, she told him.

'It isn't,' Jack assured her. 'I've thought about it, I've done nothing but think about it, and, yes, it's a bit overwhelming, but…' He had never been so honest either. He told her about Monica the other night, how empty he had felt, how empty he had been till she'd come into his life.

'Your mother's going to hate me!' Nina grinned, starting to believe this might be true.

'I know.' Jack grinned. 'I just can't wait to tell her!'

And then he told her that he was going to go and buy a ring, but figured she'd want to choose… 'I can't really win,' Jack moaned. 'If I spend too much you'll get upset, but I'm not donating for trees somewhere or buying goats instead, like I know you'll suggest. I want to take you out and spoil you.'

'How can I say no to that?'

'You can't.'

She couldn't.

So, instead, Nina said yes.

EPILOGUE

JACK LOVED FRIDAYS.

He always had and he always would, but he was especially looking forward to this one.

Blake and Janey were off at summer camp and tonight he and Nina were flying to Hawaii for a delayed honeymoon. He walked up the garden path of their large Brooklyn home after a very full week working at the pro bono centre.

Nina had been right.

His rather more analytical mind had been exactly what the centre had needed and Jack was part of the team that allocated funds as well as running two night clinics a week, and he loved it.

Jack didn't miss Angel's. He was often there, consulting on a patient he'd had admitted or stopping by to take Nina for lunch.

'How was work?' Jack asked as Nina woke up from a doze, stretched on the sofa and yawned.

'Exhausting,' she admitted. 'I think I got everything done before we go away, but the trouble with working part time is that you end up doing a full week's work in half the time. Though it was a good day. I saw Tommy and Mike…'

'And?'

'Tommy's finished his chemotherapy and the doctors are really pleased with the results.'

'Is he having surgery?'

'I'm not sure,' Nina said. 'I think there's a big case meeting next week, but for now, at least, things are going better than expected.'

Everything was going better than expected.

Nina had been a Carter for a few months now, but as of this week so too were Janey and Blake. A few days after they'd announced they were getting married, Janey had flared up at something, and shouted that Jack had no say, that he was only her sister's boyfriend, or her brother-in-law.

'We'll see about that!' Jack had snapped back, and so earlier in the week they'd all stood in front of a judge who had smiled as broadly as all of them for the photo to capture the moment Jack officially became a father.

And now Nina had to somehow tell him that he was about to become a father again.

She didn't know how she felt about it, had wanted to wait a while, but that option was closed to them now.

'So,' Jack said, 'are we packed?'

'I am.' Nina smiled.

She followed him into their bedroom and he laughed when he opened the case because it contained two bikinis, a sarong and not much else. Jack threw in a couple of things too.

They would have their own very private pool and had no intention to leave its side.

'It's going to be nice to have some time on our own,' Nina said, but Jack didn't really comment. He loved the busy household they had made, loved doing sport with Blake and just having a childhood thirty years late. He knew she was fishing, knew Nina was waiting for him to admit it was too much at times.

He never did.

Still, there were some advantages to having the house to themselves, because he had her try on her new bikini and then had the pleasure of taking it off, and all without having to think and close the door, and afterwards, as his hands traced her body, he noticed the tiny changes, the slight fullness to her breasts, and he wondered when she was going to tell him.

'We'd better get ready.' He caught her as she went to get off the bed, and pulled her back to him.

'When are you going to tell me?'

He watched the colour spread first on her cheeks and then down to her chest, watched her rapid, confused blink. 'What?'

'That I'm going to be a father of three?' Jack smiled. 'How long have you been holding out on me?'

'Jack!' she wailed in frustration. This wasn't how it was supposed to be. 'I was going to tell you on holiday…' She shook her head in exasperation. 'I only found out this afternoon.'

'I've known for a week.' Jack grinned. 'I thought you just weren't telling me. I knew at the courtroom….'

'How?'

'I can't tell you.'

'You can.'

'I really can't.' Jack grinned. 'Because you'll accuse me of being a chauvinist.'

'You are a chauvinist!' Nina reminded him. 'But I'm working on it.' She didn't understand. 'How did you know before I did?'

'You forget sometimes that you're married to a brilliant diagnostician,' Jack said. 'Okay, I'll tell you. Remember our case was pushed back, remember how that woman in the coffee shop pushed in line…?'

'Yes.' She was sulking before he said it.

'And it was a tense day and I knew that your period was due, but you were lovely…'

'Don't!' Nina dug him the ribs with her elbows. 'Don't you dare…'

'I'm not,' Jack said. 'I'm just saying…'

And he was arrogant and rude and chauvinistic at times, but he was also the best thing to have happened in her life and she wouldn't change a single piece of him.

'Are you okay with it?'

'Delighted,' Jack said. 'Who'd have thought that night when we rowed that in a few months I'd be married, a father of two, with one on the way, and we haven't even been on our honeymoon yet?'

'Me,' Nina broke in, and for the first time she told him the truth, a truth she'd kept hidden from herself.

That it hadn't been just a crush that she'd had, and she hadn't just fancied him either, that the whole problem she'd had was…

'I loved you from the start.'

* * * * *

NYC ANGELS:
HEIRESS'S
BABY SCANDAL

BY
JANICE LYNN

To my editor, Lucy Gilmour. Thanks for all you do!

First published in Great Britain 2013
by Mills & Boon, an imprint of Harlequin (UK) Limited.
Harlequin (UK) Limited, Eton House, 18-24 Paradise Road,
Richmond, Surrey TW9 1SR

© Harlequin Books S.A. 2013

Special thanks and acknowledgement are given to Janice Lynn
for her contribution to the *NYC Angels* series

ISBN: 978 0 263 89881 1

Harlequin (UK) policy is to use papers that are natural, renewable
and recyclable products and made from wood grown in sustainable
forests. The logging and manufacturing process conform to the
legal environmental regulations of the country of origin.

Printed and bound in Spain
by Blackprint CPI, Barcelona

Dear Reader

Okay, I'll admit it. I'm a sucker for a cowboy. I mean, really, there's just something about a gorgeous man in a cowboy hat that makes my heart go thump-thump-thumpity-thump. Make that man gorgeous, good-hearted and the owner of a sexy Texan drawl and I might just have to turn up the AC. Tyler Donaldson is just such a man. Ty was my first cowboy hero, but I seriously doubt he'll be my last. I had a lot of fun researching his character. Really, I did. Have I mentioned how much I love my job?

Ty and Ellie's story also presented me with another new experience as this was my first continuity series. Working closer with my fellow Medical Romance™ authors was great, and I loved watching as each of our stories developed. What an amazingly talented group!

I hope you enjoy Ty and Ellie's story as much as I enjoyed researching (grin!) and writing their story. Drop me an e-mail at Janice@janicelynn.net to share your thoughts about their romance, cowboys, or just to say hello.

Happy reading!

Janice

NYC Angels
Children's doctors who work hard and love even harder…
in the city that never sleeps!
For the next four months, step into the world of NYC Angels

In March New York's most notoriously sinful bachelor Jack Carter
finds a woman he wants to spend more than just one night with in:
NYC ANGELS: REDEEMING THE PLAYBOY
by Carol Marinelli

And reluctant socialite Eleanor Aston makes the gossip headlines
when the paparazzi discover her baby bombshell:
NYC ANGELS: HEIRESS'S BABY SCANDAL by Janice Lynn

In April cheery physiotherapist Molly Shriver melts the icy barricades
around hotshot surgeon Dan Morris's damaged heart in:
NYC ANGELS: UNMASKING DR SERIOUS
by Laura Iding

And Lucy Edwards is finally tempted to let neurosurgeon
Ryan O'Doherty in. But their fragile relationship will need
to survive her most difficult revelation yet…
NYC ANGELS: THE WALLFLOWER'S SECRET
by Susan Carlisle

Then, in May, newly single (and strictly off-limits!)
Chloe Jenkins makes it very difficult for drop-dead-gorgeous
Brad Davis to resist temptation…!
NYC ANGELS: FLIRTING WITH DANGER by Tina Beckett

And after meeting single dad Lewis Jackson, tough-cookie Head Nurse
Scarlet Miller wonders if she's finally met her match…
NYC ANGELS: TEMPTING NURSE SCARLET by Wendy S. Marcus

Finally join us in June, when bubbly new nurse Polly Seymour
is the ray of sunshine brooding doc Johnny Griffin's needs in:
NYC ANGELS: MAKING THE SURGEON SMILE
by Lynne Marshall

And Alex Rodriguez and Layla Woods come back into each other's
orbit, trying to fool the buzzing hospital grapevine that the spark
between them has died. But can they convince each other?
NYC ANGELS: AN EXPLOSIVE REUNION by Alison Roberts

**Be captivated by NYC Angels in this new eight-book continuity
from Mills & Boon® Medical Romance™.**

**These books are also available in eBook format
from www.millsandboon.co.uk**

CHAPTER ONE

Uh-uh. There was absolutely no way Dr. Eleanor Aston was wearing that itsy-bitsy, teeny-tiny scrap of sparkly spandex her sister had sent for her to wear tonight!

"Take it back," she ordered Norma, the darling, elderly woman who'd headed up the Aston household for over twenty years and a woman who was more like family than—well, than Eleanor's biological family.

Looking out of place and uncomfortable in the hospital doctors' lounge where Eleanor had pulled her to talk in private, Norma shook her head. "Sorry, but I can't do that. Brooke gave me specific instructions. You are to wear that dress and those shoes to the ribbon-cutting ceremony."

Right, because she could squeeze her more than generous curves into the dress. Eleanor shuddered just at the mental image.

"I'm giving you specific instructions, too. Take it back, because even if I could squeeze into that..." She eyed the glitzy red dress and matching stilettos her sister had picked out. "Well, it's not exactly my style, is it?"

Staring at Eleanor with her almost-black eyes, Norma

shrugged her coat-clad shoulders. "Perhaps your sister thinks your style needs an update."

Norma's tone implied that Brooke wasn't the only one who thought that.

Ha. No doubt about it. Media darling Brooke Aston definitely thought her sister's style as ugly duckling in the midst of a family of swans should change. Mostly because Brooke thought Eleanor's usual wardrobe of hospital scrubs to be the bottom of fashion's totem pole.

Eleanor loved her hospital scrubs.

For so many reasons. Never had she felt more proud than when she'd donned a pair after she'd completed her training as a pediatrician specializing in neonatology. Plus, shapeless hospital scrubs hid a lot of body flaws.

"A lot" being the key words. She'd never be a size two like Brooke and she'd quit beating herself up over that years ago.

She eyed the scrap of fancy material again, crinkled her nose and shook her head. "I'm sorry my sister wasted your time, but you can keep the dress because I'm not going to wear it, or those torture devices my sister calls shoes." She glanced at her watch. "Sorry to run, but I've got to get back to the NICU. My patients need me."

Norma winced, but didn't look surprised by Eleanor's answer. "Brooke won't be happy."

Was her baby sister ever happy with anything that didn't involve all the attention being on her? Too bad she'd had an allergic reaction to some new beauty cream that had left her unable to bask in the limelight of Senator Cole Aston's latest publicity project.

At least this time Eleanor agreed with how her father was spending his money. Actually, she was quite pleased, which was the only reason she'd agreed to take Brooke's place at the ribbon-cutting ceremony this evening. He'd donated an exorbitant amount to build a new neonatal wing for premature babies at the Angel Mendez Children's Hospital where she worked.

She loved being a part of something as wonderful as Angel's, New York's first and finest free children's hospital. Working with her preemies left her with a feeling inside that no other aspect of her life had ever achieved. She felt needed, whole, as if she made a difference. In her patients' families' eyes, she did matter, was the most important person in their tiny baby's world.

Her patients didn't care that she wasn't glamorous or wearing the latest Paris styles. They didn't care if her hair was plain black and always clipped tightly to her scalp in a bun. They didn't care that she never bothered with makeup or taking time to put in her contact lenses so her thick-framed glasses didn't hide her dark brown eyes.

Neither did they care that she'd never be beautiful and svelte like her petite sister, not with her bone structure and too-generous curves that no amount of starving herself seemed to cure. So she just maintained a healthy diet and lifestyle and ignored that the media liked to point out the differences between her and her Hollywood-thin, perfectly coiffed sister.

Pain knotted Eleanor's gut at the recall of some of the comments that the gossip rags had made about those differences over the years.

Her sister might love the limelight, but Eleanor detested it, did everything she could to avoid putting herself in the media's glare. Yet tonight she would be representing her family at a very important event for Angel's. The press would be there in droves.

What had she been thinking?

The sheer impact of what she'd agreed to do hit her, made her hand shake, reminded her that she was being forced to attend a social event. Still, think of all the families the new wing would benefit.

She took a deep breath, praying a full-blown panic attack didn't hit. "Brooke isn't going to be happy anyway, Norma. She's not the one cutting the ribbon this evening."

Having been a constant fixture in their lives and knowing them as well as their own mother did, probably better, a semblance of a smile played on Norma's twitching lips at Eleanor's accurate assessment of her sister.

"Agreed, but you're going to have to return that dress yourself." At Eleanor's frown, she continued, "If I'm going to have one or the other of you upset with me, it's going to be you over your drama-queen sister."

Eleanor took another deep breath and exhaled slowly. Hadn't it been that way her whole life? Brooke always managed to get her way one way or another, whether it was with their parents, the hired help, the media, or the many enamored people who flocked to be close to such "perfection" as the lovely and superfun Brooke Aston.

Eleanor had spent a great portion of her life in the shadows. Fortunately, she liked it there.

She glanced at her watch again. She'd been away from the neonatal unit too long already. "Fine. I'll deal with this later."

* * *

Eleanor's heart squeezed as Rochelle Blackwood's tiny fingers wrapped around her pinky finger. So precious.

Even with the tubes and wires attached to the twenty-six-weeks-gestation little girl, nothing was more beautiful or precious to Eleanor than new life.

Not so many years ago, Rochelle wouldn't have had any chance of surviving outside her mother's womb short of a miracle. Thanks to advances in modern medicine, the little girl's odds had greatly increased, although certainly she was high risk. Still, each day she survived raised those odds.

Eleanor intended to give her tiny patient everything in her favor that she could.

"What do you think, Eleanor?" Scarlet Miller, the head neonatal unit nurse, asked from beside the tiny heated incubator. "Is she going to pull through?"

Rochelle had been born with part of her intestines outside her abdomen, with underdeveloped lungs and eyelids that were paper-thin and not yet open. She couldn't eat or breathe on her own. But the little girl had a strong will to live. Eleanor felt the strength of her spirit every time she was near the baby.

"I hope so. She's a fighter, that's for sure."

Rochelle's mother had been sideswiped by a drunk driver and had suffered multiple crush injuries. Rochelle had been in trouble and the decision had been made to deliver by emergency cesarean section. Sadly, her mother hadn't survived the night.

Eleanor felt a special bond with the baby, perhaps because the five-day-old baby's father was grieving the loss of his wife and had yet to visit the little girl who'd already undergone multiple surgeries and treatments during her short life. The medical staff of the NICU was the only human contact the baby had.

"Agreed," a strong masculine Texan voice drawled from behind her. "I hope you don't mind, but I've been keeping tabs on this little darlin'."

As it always did when Dr. Tyler Donaldson was around, Eleanor's face caught fire. Not literally, of course, but it may as well have for how hot her skin burned anytime the man was near.

Just as it also always did, her tongue refused to do anything other than stick to the roof of her mouth, leaving her unable to answer him and feeling like an awkward teenager with a first crush.

Urgh. How could one sister be such a consummate flirt and known for the many hunks wrapped around her manicured finger and the other sister be a shy, inept mute just because a good-looking man spoke to her? Not even spoke to her about anything personal but about a patient. Yes, she really was pathetic.

Probably taking her silence as disapproval—or who knew what he thought of her since he usually ignored her—Tyler stepped closer to the incubator. "I was on duty the night she made her entrance into the world. She's such a sweet little darlin', ain't she?"

His Southern accent got to her, just as it did most of Angel's female staff. In a big way. His voice was so inviting, like a fire on a cold winter's night. She just wanted to bask in the warmth of everything about the man. Which was crazy. He was a total player who charmed women right out of their pants. Yet all his exes still adored him. Go figure.

She risked a look at him and immediately wished she hadn't. Just as if she really did stand next to a fire, her face burst into a new wave of flames. If there was a pill to cure blushing she'd be first in line at the pharmacy, because she hated the nervous reaction almost as much as she hated her panic attacks.

"You met her father?" Tyler asked, his warm brown gaze focused on the baby.

Still unable to prise her tongue off the roof of her mouth, Eleanor shook her head.

"Guess he still ain't been by." Tyler sighed, making the sound long and as drawn out as his speech, as if every sound that came from his mouth had to stretch the span of his home state of Texas. "Can't help but feel bad for the guy. Losing his wife that way and afraid that he'll lose this li'l sweetheart, too."

Her tongue still not cooperating, Eleanor nodded.

"I'm glad she got assigned to you, Eleanor. She got lucky and got the best." Without looking up, he brushed his finger gently across where the baby still clung to Eleanor's finger.

Sparks shot up her arm and her breath caught in her throat.

She'd been so engrossed in the man beside her, in his unexpected compliment, she'd completely forgotten she was still touching the baby until his skin made contact with hers.

Wow.

Just wow.

Thinking she had finally prised her tongue loose, she turned to try to say something witty, but just as she opened her mouth, he flashed that half-crooked grin of his. At someone walking up beside them.

Someone else female.

Because he was Dr. Tyler Donaldson and that's what he did best.

With every single female in the NICU except for dumpy, boring, *mute,* too-curvy Eleanor Aston.

Where was the black dress she'd brought with her that morning?

Panic raced through Eleanor as she stared at the contents of her staff locker.

It had been ransacked.

In the place of her gym bag, the black dress that she'd neatly hung that morning and the pair of black flats she'd planned to quickly change into was a note in familiar handwriting.

A note that made smoke billow from her ears.

You're gonna look so hot, sis. You can thank me later. B.

Thank her? Ha. She was going to strangle her sister. How had Brooke gotten into the doctors' lounge? Gotten into her locked locker? Not that her sister had been there herself. No way would Brooke risk being seen or photographed with her face red, swollen and peeling.

Yet her sister had wiped her out.

Even her purse was gone.

There were three items in the locker other than the note. The red dress and stilettos that her sister had so thoughtfully sent over and a square white box that covered almost the entire bottom of the locker.

Dare she even open the lid to see what lay inside?

She glanced at her watch, knew she was running out of time and snatched the lid off to stare at the items inside.

Underwear. Eleanor wrinkled her nose. Leave it to her sister to know that if you were going to wear an itty-bitty dress you had to have itty-bitty underwear to go with it.

Plus, a red clutch purse that matched her dress and shoes and a too-big, too-flamboyant hair clip meant more for adornment than to actually be useful.

And makeup. Lots of makeup.

Acid gurgling in her stomach, Eleanor shook her head. This was her place of employment, the hospital where she worked.

Okay, she'd jump in the shower and pray that when she was clean, her belongings would be back.

They weren't.

"What's wrong?" Scarlet asked, doing a mad make-over dash of her own to get changed for the ribbon-cutting.

"My sister has gone too far this time." Eleanor tightened the towel she had wrapped around her body. "How am I ever going to be taken seriously again if I wear that?"

Scarlet's gaze ran over the dress then over Eleanor from head to toe. "I'm pretty sure if you wear that there's going to be a lot of people taking you seriously. Maybe one person in particular."

Eleanor's chest tightened. "What do you mean?"

"Don't give me that. I've seen how you look at him."

"Who?" Had her voice just squeaked?

Scarlet laughed. "Dr. Donaldson."

"He barely knows I exist."

Scarlet motioned to the dress. "You wear that and there's not going to be a man alive who isn't aware you exist."

Eleanor crinkled her nose. Brooke she could see putting her into a dress she shouldn't be in, but she trusted Scarlet. "You really think so?"

Scarlet gave her a *duh* look. "Hurry up and get changed and I'll help you do your makeup and hair. You have great eyes and hair. We'll play them up to draw attention to them."

Great eyes and hair? Right. Had Brooke bribed her friend to say that? Next thing she would be telling her she had a great body.

"Of course, with a chest like yours it's going to be difficult to keep attention anywhere but on your cleavage."

That she knew. Which was why she never wore anything revealing or clingy. Her breasts were too big, but they matched her curvy hips and thighs.

But Scarlet was right. She was running out of time and it wasn't as if she had anything else to wear. Plus, she felt ridiculous talking while wearing only a towel.

She let her gaze go back to the items in her locker. If she was going to look a fool, she might as well go for broke. "Why not?" She smiled at her friend. "We'd better hurry. Thanks to my father for being out of town and Brooke not being able to make it, yours truly is sort of the guest of honor."

"You're going to totally knock the socks off Dr.

Donaldson," Scarlet mused as Eleanor stepped into the dress. "It's a perfect fit."

Eleanor blinked, then put her glasses on and stared at herself in the mirror. "Yeah, but where's the rest of the dress?"

She tugged on the material, trying to cover some of her cleavage, but only managed to hike the skirt higher up her thighs.

Dear Lord, if she bent over someone might get a glimpse of those tiny scraps of underwear Brooke had left her no choice but to wear or go commando.

Mortification set in. "I can't go out in public like this."

Scarlet inspected her then nodded. "You're right. Hand 'em over."

"Huh?"

"Your glasses. Give them to me."

One hand protectively holding on to her frames, Eleanor shook her head. "I can't see without them."

Scarlet tsked. "You should get contact lenses. You have gorgeous eyes."

"I have contacts." She wore them for sports and exercise, but rarely when she was at the hospital as she was more comfortable behind the shield of her glasses. "But since my sister took my purse, I couldn't put them in if I wanted to."

"Not a problem." Before Eleanor could stop her, Scarlet had plucked her glasses off her face and refused to give them back. "Now, let's get you to the ribbon-cutting because you're already five minutes late."

Eleanor glanced at her arm, realized she wasn't wearing her watch and frowned. Late? The senator was not going to be happy with his elder daughter.

During the whole walk to the new wing, Eleanor told herself that all the stares she was getting was because she was wearing a fancy red dress in a children's hospital.

She knew better.

Thank goodness she'd decided to carry her heels because if she'd had to walk in those things over to the new wing, she'd have fallen flat on her face and probably split the seams of her dress in the process.

"Quit fidgeting," Scarlet ordered from beside her. "You look great."

She looked a fool—not that she could see how foolish she looked, not without her glasses.

Only this time was much worse than past embarrassments because she was at the hospital where she worked, surrounded by the people she worked with, people who, until today, had respected her as Dr. Eleanor Aston.

Dr. Tyler Donaldson grinned at the cute little nurse who worked in the obstetrics department and considered the possibilities.

Just as he knew she was sizing him up.

No doubt she'd heard about his reputation.

Everyone at the hospital knew he was a love-'em-and-leave-'em kind of man.

He liked it that way. Truthfully, he was pretty sure most of the women liked it that way, too, although they'd never admit it.

He was a good time waiting to happen, but not a keeper.

However, the blonde was looking at him as if she wouldn't mind keeping him occupied for the night.

"I can't believe Dr. Aston isn't here yet," she chattered, although Ty was more interested in what her eyes were saying. Those eyes were saying *you and me, bub, hot and sweaty between the sheets.*

Although he hated admitting it, lately he'd been getting bored with women.

"I never would have thought she'd be late."

Dr. Aston? No, he wouldn't have pictured her the type to be late either. She seemed much too uptight to be anything other than punctual. Unless something had come up with one of her tiny patients and then Ty could see the dedicated pediatrician blowing this celebration altogether. He'd be hard-pressed to name a more dedicated doctor.

"It's so difficult to believe she and Brooke Aston are really sisters."

He'd have to live in another country not to know who Brooke Aston was. The media loved her. The image of a blonde bombshell came to mind. Yeah, accepting that the two women came from the same DNA pool was difficult to believe.

"Brooke was supposed to have been here to cut the ribbon, but she caught a virus or something while volunteering at some charity event for sick children," the blonde prattled on. "I hope it's nothing serious."

From the things Ty had seen about the infamous senator's daughter, he had a hard time envisioning her getting close enough to sick kids to have actually caught something from them.

"Maybe one of them was adopted," he suggested to make polite conversation. With the publicity for the new wing, he'd heard about the family connection prior to this evening. As Eleanor didn't make a bleep on his possibility radar, he hadn't paid much attention to the hospital gossip.

But something about her irked him. He couldn't quite put his finger on what it was about her, just that he'd decided to steer clear.

"Oh, my word!"

At her gasp, Ty's attention jerked back from thoughts of a woman who crept into his mind more often than a woman who didn't make a bleep on his radar should to the OB nurse. Her gaze was fixed beyond him to the hallway leading into the new wing. He turned to see what she was looking at and found his own breath catching in his throat.

It took him only a moment to realize who he was looking at. Even then he had to do a double take before he could convince himself that he wasn't wrong. But once he realized that it was really *her,* his chest tightened, making him gulp for much-needed oxygen.

"I don't believe it," the nurse next to him muttered. Neither did Ty.

He didn't believe he'd totally missed that Dr. Eleanor Aston had been hiding a killer curvy body beneath those baggy scrubs she wore. Wow.

Bleep. Bleep. Bleep.

Hell, what was his possibility radar doing? He was not interested in Eleanor. Not in baggy scrubs or in a body-hugging red dress that ought to be labeled lethal. Not with her gorgeous brown eyes wide and uncertain rather than hidden behind her glasses as she faced the crowd. Not with her glossy black hair flowing loosely down her back rather than tightly pinned to her scalp.

Only he was and maybe he had been all along.

Bleep.

CHAPTER TWO

"I'm sorry I'm late," Eleanor apologized to the hospital CEO, to the hospital medical director, to the NICU director and several other hospital bigwigs whose titles she couldn't quite recall. "I—I worked, and then I had to shower and change." She glanced down at her barely there dress and way-too-exposed body as if that explained everything. "And then my sister had…"

She stopped, realizing she was rambling, realizing that they all stared at her as if she'd grown a second head and spoke in foreign tongue. Or maybe they were all staring at her too-ample bosom overflowing out of Brooke's idea of a sick joke.

Eleanor couldn't be sure because she couldn't see any of their faces clearly. Which was probably a good thing because she was pretty sure disapproval marred their expressions. They'd never take her or her suggestions for the hospital seriously again.

"Dr. Aston, how do you feel about your father donating the money for the new wing?" A man poked a microphone in her face.

Bile pooled in her stomach. The press. She'd known she'd have to deal with them, both at the ribbon-cutting and at the reception afterward. She wanted to shrivel up and become invisible in the hope they'd go away and not notice her.

Fat chance of that when she was essentially the guest of honor.

Not her, really. Just Senator Cole Aston's daughter.

Which technically she was, but if someone had told her she'd been accidentally swapped at birth, she'd have no trouble believing them as she was so different from her socialite mother, power-hungry father and media-darling sister.

She much preferred being Dr. Eleanor Aston, who was someone she was proud to be most of the time.

She didn't feel proud at the moment.

She felt awkward and uncomfortable and like she might throw up.

She looked at the reporter, wanted to be like Brooke and deliver a smooth, witty line about how proud she was of her father for making such a wonderful contribution to the hospital and community.

But she wasn't Brooke and under the best of circumstances she wasn't witty.

Half-naked and surrounded by people who'd once dubbed her "Jelly Ellie" didn't come close to being the best of circumstances.

Why had the bane of her childhood reared its ugly head now? For years she'd kept that much-used media label out of her head. She wouldn't let it back in, wouldn't let the slurs back into her mind, wouldn't let them degrade the woman she'd become. So she wasn't a skinny Minny and never would be. She was average, of healthy weight and her curves were fairly toned thanks to the hours she spent in the gym each week. The press could get over their craze for too thin.

Thankfully, the hospital CEO grabbed her by her elbow and whisked her toward the ribbon that partitioned the new wing from the rest of the hospital. A big bright red ribbon that perfectly matched her dress. Had Brooke planned that? Probably. Her sister had an eye for detail.

"We're already a little behind schedule." The CEO didn't actually say that it was her fault but she felt the weight of his implication all the same. He was getting his slam in on Dr. Eleanor Aston being late, but wasn't going to say anything specific to Eleanor Aston, daughter of Senator Cole Aston. "So we'll get the show on the road."

Fine. The sooner they got this started, the sooner they'd finish, the sooner she could go home and try to figure out how she was ever going to face her co-workers again.

Wondering if everyone could see how her legs were shaking, Eleanor stood next to the CEO while he droned on and on about the hospital and what a blessing it was in the community.

Then he did something horrible. He turned to Eleanor to give a welcome-and-thank-you speech.

Immediately, the full-blown panic attack she'd been fighting most of the day took over. Her heart picked up pace, doubling in tempo. A hot sweat broke out on her skin, making her palms immediately feel sticky wet. Her tongue attached itself to the roof of her mouth and refused to budge.

She took a deep breath, reminded herself that the

rapid pounding of her heart was just anxiety and not that her heart was really going to explode from fear of being in the spotlight.

Although the blonde at his side felt it necessary to continue to chat softly to him, Ty's attention was focused solely on the woman standing next to her bosses. His bosses.

In direct opposition to the low-cut-cleavage and long-leg-revealing dress, her ethereal face looked fragile, pale, out of place.

Ty didn't have to see the pulse jumping at the base of her throat or the tremor of her knees to know she was nervous.

Nervous? More like petrified.

She appeared as delicate as a butterfly's wing and just as beautiful with those big brown eyes of hers and that full mouth.

A mouth made for kissing.

She'd always kept to herself so much that he'd taken it as a sign that she wasn't interested.

Was it possible he'd mistaken shyness for disinterest?

She stirred something within him, but he'd just labeled it as curiosity, considering she was the only female he knew who didn't fall into flirt mode whenever he was near.

He was definitely curious. Beyond curious.

More like intrigued by the plethora of contradictions that defined his colleague.

The CEO waited for Eleanor to speak.

The rest of the crowd waited for her to give her speech.

A too-long pause settled over the crowd.

"H-hello. It—it is…" A few stuttered words began escaping her quivering lips. "An honor…an honor to be here. Today. This evening, I mean."

"She sure isn't her sister," a man next to Ty with a camera in his hands grumbled under his breath.

Surprisingly, Ty's fingers curled, the man's comment rubbing him up the wrong way. Why he felt so protective of a woman he wasn't certain he even liked, he had no clue. But he found himself wanting to speak up, to defend her. How could you defend someone you didn't really know?

Still, he shot the man a silencing look. "Not everyone is a polished speaker, but Eleanor is a fantastic doctor and woman."

The man's bushy brows drew together then he shrugged. "Whatever, pal." Then he went back to snapping photos.

Not looking anyone in particular in the eye, Eleanor began speaking again, and Ty found himself letting out a breath he hadn't realized he'd been holding.

"Th-thanks to everyone for coming to this wonderful occasion where we're celebrating the opening of a new neonatal wing at the Angel Mendez Children's Hospital." She paused, swallowed hard, then smiled what he knew was a forced smile before she continued. "M-many of you know pediatrician Federico Mendez started this hospital during the depression after the death of his much-loved son, Angel, who suffered from polio. My father, Senator Cole Aston, wishes to continue the tradition started by Federico Mendez."

Her expression tightened and she cleared her throat, pausing too long yet again.

Come on, Eleanor, he mentally willed her on. *Just thank everyone for coming again and be done.*

"It is with that same generous and caring spirit that my father donated the funds for this new neonatal wing in the hope that—that..." Between stutters, she thanked everyone for coming to the ribbon-cutting. Then, not seeming to know what else to say, she turned imploring eyes on the CEO.

Imploring eyes because she was begging to be rescued.

How was it possible that a woman who'd had to grow up in the public eye could be so socially backward? Surely Cole Aston would have enrolled her in some prep courses to prepare her for public speaking?

And the stuttering? Was that lifelong or something she just did when she was nervous?

Tyler wished he knew. Wished he knew lots of things about the enigma showcased in a flashy red dress.

Rather than rescuing her, the CEO looked as if he had no clue at how on edge she was. Instead, he made another big hoo-ha, then handed Eleanor a large pair of showy scissors.

Immediately, she almost dropped them but managed to recover in the nick of time. One of the men beside her rolled his eyes. Ty saw red and not just the red of Eleanor's hot dress and cheeks.

His gaze shot back to hers, saw the fear, saw the shaking of her hands, the sheen of perspiration that glistened on her skin. Something moved inside him.

Literally, something in his chest shifted.

Dear heavens, she was going to pass out.

Ty might be known as a womanizing son of a gun, but he was a chivalrous son of a gun. His momma, God bless her big Southern heart, would have beaten his hind end otherwise, and rightly so.

He might have left his horse in Texas but, hell, no one else was stepping in to save the good doctor.

Despite the fact that he was feeling a little off-kilter himself at just what a knockout body she'd been hiding under her scrubs, at whatever that odd sensation in his chest had been when he'd looked at her just a moment ago, at admitting to himself that he'd been interested in her all along, playing the role of white knight to Eleanor's damsel in distress came as natural as counting one, two, three.

Eleanor couldn't breathe.

Couldn't move.

Wasn't even sure how she was hanging on to the scissors that she'd somehow managed to position over the ribbon.

All she had to do was close her hands and the ribbon would slice.

So why weren't her fingers cooperating? Why weren't they closing around the handle?

She needed cooperation, needed to get out of there before she toppled over on her face or sagged to a humiliating puddle at the feet of her bosses. Not to mention that her dress would burst wide open if she made any sudden movements. Wouldn't the press have a field day with that?

Jelly Ellie's belly exposed yet again.

She winced, fought back the horrible thought of the photo of her happy, pudgy, eight-year-old self hanging out of her bathing suit while hugging her cute and cuddly little sister forever captured by the paparazzi. She reminded herself she wasn't that little girl anymore who'd been crushed by their cruel jokes and taglines that she carried too much weight. She was an accomplished woman, a doctor. She could do this.

Make the cut. Just squeeze your fingers together and cut the ribbon.

Nothing happened. Except that her palms grew more and more clammy. Any second the scissors were going to slip out of her sweaty hands and fall to the floor.

Headlines around the city would read *Senator Cole Aston's daughter doesn't make the cut*. Folks would nod their heads in agreement, make comments that they'd known she wasn't good enough to get the job done, that had the lovely Brooke Aston been there all would have been well.

"Dr. Aston?" the CEO prompted from beside her, his low tone warning for her to get on with the program.

She wanted to. Really, she did. But panic had seized her and, except for the trembling within her, she stood frozen in place.

The room began to spin, to darken. She was going down. She'd be mortified. Her father would blame her. Brooke would blame her. The hospital would blame her.

She prayed that when she went down she would bump her head and lose her memory, that she'd lose all recall of the day's events. Amnesia would be a blessing.

But rather than fall to the floor, a strong pair of hands closed over hers, applying pressure and closing her fingers over the scissors handles. The ribbon split in two and each end drifted toward the floor in a dainty float that Eleanor watched as if in a surreal dream.

The sound of the applause and cheers—and was that a sigh of relief?—came from some faraway surreal place, too.

When she turned her head and looked up into the twinkling brown eyes of her savior, she was definitely somewhere other than reality.

Because Tyler Donaldson winked at her and drawled a breathy, "Hi, there, darlin'."

As if it was the most natural thing in the world for his hands to be over hers, he motioned his head slightly toward the crowd. "Better paste a smile on that pretty face of yours 'cause there are a lot of folks capturing the moment for posterity."

Who was this man and what had he done with the real Dr. Donaldson, who never spoke except in regard to patients?

She gawked at him a second longer, then turned and forced a smile to her face the same way she'd done a hundred times before. She thought of happy times. Thought of medical school and how hard she'd worked, at how proud she'd been to accomplish something her daddy's money and power couldn't buy, something she'd had to do on her own. Something that didn't require glamour, glitz or a hot little body.

Although her smile stayed on her face, her mind didn't go to her happy place. Oh, no. Her happy place was all tangled up in Tyler's hand still covering hers, holding hers, of the electricity and warmth burning into her at his touch.

He gave a squeeze as if he wanted to reassure her that she was going to be okay, that he was there and wouldn't let her fall on her face.

Oddly enough, she believed he wouldn't.

Which was crazy. He flustered her, barely knew she existed, so how could he possibly be rescuing her from total mortification?

Her knees weakened, and she swayed.

Tyler's hand immediately went to her waist, steadying her, resting low on her back. "Just smile, babe. You're doing just fine. It's almost over."

Easy for him to say. She had to face the reception afterward, mingle with the bigwigs while representing her father, her family.

But Tyler didn't leave her side.

He stayed and smiled right there with her. He kept his hand at her back and his strength gave her the fortitude to keep her smile in place even though she really just wanted to curl up into a ball and cry.

When the photographers finally had their shots and moved on to their next victim, Eleanor let out a long breath and looked at her rescuer.

"Th-thank you."

One side of his mouth lifted crookedly in a half grin. "No problem, sugar. You looked like you needed a helping hand."

Speaking of hand, his still rested against the curve of her back, burning through the thin red material and branding her skin.

"I don't like crowds." Were those the first words she'd ever actually formed around him without stuttering, grunting or mumbling? Finally, coherency.

"I noticed."

She smiled despite the nervousness still chipping away at her resolve. "Now, if only this party were over."

"Over?" He glanced around at the smiling, laughing people and shook his head. "Why would we want the party over when the night is so young?"

"I don't like crowds, remember?" She crinkled her nose and frowned up at him. Goodness, the man was tall. Probably about six-four. Maybe everything that came from Texas was big.

He grinned down at her, then tweaked her nose with the tip of his finger. "I tell ya what, darlin', you just relax. Have some fun. I'll handle the crowd."

She glanced around at the people making their way into the room that had been decked out for the celebration. "But surely you have someone with you? You always have someone with you."

"You're right. I do." He winked then leaned close to her ear. "Tonight that someone is you, Eleanor. My friends call me Ty, by the way, and you and I are definitely going to be friendly."

CHAPTER THREE

ELEANOR LAUGHED OUT LOUD for what seemed like the hundredth time that evening. Honestly, she couldn't recall the last time she'd laughed so much.

Had she ever?

"You are very pretty when you laugh, Eleanor."

Now, there was a comment worth laughing at.

"Because you keep saying funny things," she told Tyler, not quite meeting his eyes. He'd complimented her repeatedly during the evening. Good thing she knew his reputation, that he was an incurable flirt.

With a grin that was way too intoxicating, he touched her face. "I want you to laugh at what I say, but only when I'm saying something worth laughing at. I was serious. You are a very beautiful woman, Eleanor."

Despite the fact that she was sure he didn't mean her to laugh, she couldn't suppress the nervous little giggle that spilled from her lips. "Yeah, well, th-thank you."

Because, really, what else could she say?

"Tell me about that," he urged in a slow drawl.

She bit her lower lip, hoping he wasn't asking what she thought he was asking.

"Your stutter."

Face flaming, she shook her head. "Nothing funny about my stuttering so let's not talk about it."

"Have you always stuttered?" he asked, as if she hadn't just spoken.

"Perhaps you didn't hear what I just said. I don't want to talk about me."

"But I do. You fascinate me."

Had he been drinking? The hospital wasn't serving anything alcoholic, but perhaps someone had spiked the punch.

"When I was younger, I—I stuttered all the time. These days it usually only h-happens when I'm in a stressful sit-situation."

He studied her a moment. "Am I a stressful situation?"

"Men are always stressful," she answered flippantly, because she didn't want to label anything at all about the way Tyler made her feel. Not the way he'd made her feel before tonight and especially not the way he was making her feel at that very moment.

He leaned his long frame against the hospital wall they stood near, crossed his arms and regarded her. "Ya know, I just realized that during the entire time I've been at Angel's I've never heard a thing about you and a man, Eleanor. Is there someone special in your life?"

Had the room suddenly grown hot? Her skin had certainly grown clammy.

"Not at the moment."

"Lucky me."

Not sure what to say, Eleanor glanced around the lobby that had been converted into a reception area for tonight's gathering. The crowd had started to thin and most of the press had left.

"I should probably quit monopolizing your company," she said, realizing that he hadn't left her side the entire evening.

"Please don't, darlin'."

She glanced up at him.

"I want you monopolizing my…company."

Her breath caught. He was flirting with her. Really flirting. If she'd had any doubts earlier, now she didn't.

The only problem was that Tyler Donaldson flirting with her was way out of her league. As in she wouldn't know how to flirt back if her life depended on it.

So she just smiled and took a sip of her punch.

He had the audacity to laugh, causing her gaze to return to him. When their eyes met, she found herself laughing back.

She wasn't sure exactly what they were laughing at, but a giddy happiness flowed through her, along with a shared connection with Dr. Tyler Donaldson that was both unexpected, a bit magical and so exciting she could barely breathe.

"Who's the hunk?"

Totally lost as to what Brooke meant, Eleanor glared at her sister across the Aston penthouse's breakfast table. Brooke's face was masked by a thick layer of medicated cream.

Eleanor had gotten up that morning determined to accomplish one thing. To kill her sister.

Not literally.

Maybe.

But seriously, Brooke had gone too far this time. Even though the night had turned out nothing short of wonderful thanks to Ty, that didn't mean Brooke wasn't going to get an earful.

"Don't try changing the subject," she warned, tapping her finger against the glass tabletop covering the rich mahogany. "You broke into a hospital doctors' lounge and stole my clothes."

"I," her sister put great emphasis on the pronoun, "didn't do anything. And don't change the subject." Brooke's head bobbed with attitude, which should have come across as ridiculous, with her platinum hair tied up and flying every which way, thick white cream covering her still-swollen face and her body wrapped in a fuzzy pink terry-cloth robe, but which somehow didn't look ridiculous at all.

Even while suffering from an allergic reaction, her sister managed to pull off cool.

Brooke slid that morning's paper across the breakfast table. "Who is he and where can I get one? He's yummy. Introduce me."

"What are you talking about?" But even as Eleanor finished asking she saw exactly what her sister referred to.

More like who her sister referred to.

Oh, no.

Oh, yes.

A photo of Eleanor and Ty was splashed across the top of the society section of one of New York's top newspapers.

Not just any photo but one that appeared to have

been edited because she knew they hadn't really been looking at each other in that manner.

Okay, so she might have been looking at Ty that way because, let's face it, he was hot and *friendly*.

"Although," Brooke mused, frowning, "he's looking at you as if he's about to sweep you off your feet and find the closest place to get you alone. Who is he?"

In the picture, he was looking at her as if he thought her the sweetest thing since chocolate syrup and he'd like to cover her in that syrup and lick her clean.

Wow. No wonder Brooke wanted to know who he was. But, no, her sister couldn't have him. Not Ty. Which was a crazy thought because if her sister wanted Ty, she'd have him. Brooke always got what she wanted. Especially when it came to men.

"It's a trick of the camera." Perhaps it really was. Although, recalling how wonderful Ty had made her feel, perhaps it wasn't. The man knew how to make a woman feel as if she were the only woman in the world. No wonder all the female staff at Angel's adored him.

"Huh?" Brooke's collagen-enhanced lips pouted. "He isn't really that scrumptious?"

"He is, but…" She trailed off, her stomach sinking. She'd meant that he hadn't really been looking at her as if he found her irresistible. Maybe he really wasn't, but he had helped her get through what had started as a horrible evening but, because of him, had ended almost feeling enchanted.

She glanced at the photo again. She was looking into Ty's face as if she found him enchanting. Although you couldn't see his hand, she knew that his palm had rested low on her back, that his thumb had traced lazy patterns over the smooth material of the red dress. That his hand had been somewhere on her body at most points during the evening. Her lower back, her arm, her hand, her face. He'd touched her almost incessantly.

Almost possessively.

He'd felt sorry for her and his Southern good manners had demanded he rescue her. That had to be it, right?

"I couldn't be more pleased."

Both girls spun as their father entered the room.

Entered? Ha. More like invaded the room. Because when Senator Cole Aston entered a room even imaginary dust took cover. A trail of servants followed, all scurrying to serve the great man his breakfast and to meet any need he might have before he could even voice his desire.

"Morning, Daddy," Brooke cooed, blowing an air kiss in his direction as she popped a bite of melon into her mouth.

Glamour girl Brooke had always been their father's favorite. Eleanor couldn't blame him. Although the "it" party girl, Brooke never went so far as to cause their father to do more than shake his head with an indulgent smile. Her, on the other hand, he just didn't understand. Why would she want to work so hard getting her medical degree when her financial security wasn't an issue? Why work such long hours at a free hospital that she collapsed exhausted into sleep night after night when she could live a life of leisure, travel at whim as her mother and sister did?

She knew she was a disappointment and had been for most of her life. She'd been the pudgy, geeky, plain-

Jane misfit who'd had to stand next to her handsome, intimidating father, her elegant, classically beautiful mother and her glamorous, much-loved and ever-popular, beauty-queen sister.

Yeah, she was pretty sure she'd been swapped at birth.

There was some dull, plain, geeky family out there scratching their heads at how they'd ended up with a beauty-queen daughter who thrived on the limelight.

"I didn't realize you were back," Eleanor ventured. He'd been in Washington, D.C., in meetings all week, which was why he hadn't been able to attend the ribbon-cutting himself.

"Daddy, aren't you going to say good morning?" Brooke pouted, tucking her leg beneath her in her chair and turning more fully toward him.

For once, the senator ignored Brooke and smiled— or as close as he got when a camera wasn't present—at Eleanor. "I flew in late last night. You'll bring him to my campaign fund-raiser next week, of course."

Him? Then she noticed what he carried. A copy of the same newspaper Brooke had shoved at her. The one with the picture of her and Ty. Her father was happy about that? Really? Then again, he was probably just amazed that some man had paid attention to his elder daughter.

"He's just a friend. Not even that, really. More of an acquaintance." At the arch of his salt-and-pepper brow, Eleanor rushed on. "We work together at the hospital. He's nobody, really."

"He's somebody all right, and I want him with you at the fund-raiser."

Eleanor's gaze met her sister's. A still-pouting Brooke shrugged, obviously not having a clue what their father was talking about either.

"His family owns about half the state of Texas. If I ever throw my hat in to run for president, he'll be our ace in the hole."

She didn't know which shocked her more. That her father already had her paired off with Ty, that Ty was wealthy or that her father thought he might someday run for president.

That he'd plan her life choices around what best garnered votes didn't shock her in the slightest. She'd dealt with that her entire life.

"How do you know anything about Dr. Donaldson?" she asked slowly, knowing she wasn't going to like his answer.

Her father's gaze narrowed slightly at her calling Ty by his proper name. "I figured the son of a gun was just after your inheritance so I called my attorney first thing this morning and had a background check run."

Because her father hadn't believed any man would want her for herself, only for her cut of the Aston fortune. Great. Had he ever had any of Brooke's many beaus checked out?

Probably not, since her sister never seemed interested in the same man for more than a week or two. Then again, perhaps the senator did have each one thoroughly investigated and perhaps that's why none of them lasted more than a week—because they weren't worthy of his precious baby girl.

"He checked out," her father announced, sounding somewhere between smug and surprised.

"You've already gotten a report on his whole life history? Wow. That was fast work." Head spinning, she took a deep breath. "Well, you wasted your time and money, because Dr. Donaldson is a colleague from work." Sure, they'd had a great time the night before, but it wasn't as if she expected him to actually call and ask her out. They were friends. Sort of. "Nothing more."

Not liking being ignored, Brooke tapped the newspaper picture again. "This doesn't look like just work."

Her father smiled in that way that didn't convey happiness, just arrogance that he was right and that he would get his way because he was Senator Cole Aston. "I should have known you'd be contrary."

Shocked at his comment, Eleanor stared at her father. Because she was known for her contrariness? Hardly, unless he counted her going to university, getting a medical degree and actually working for a living. If he counted that then, yes, she was quite the contrary child.

"No matter." He waved his hand dismissively then took a sip of his black coffee. "I've already taken matters into my own hands."

That didn't surprise her in the slightest. However, the implications of his comment terrified her.

"What do you mean, you've taken matters into your own hands?"

"I sent the car for Dr. Donaldson. He should be arriving…" he glanced at the slim gold watch on his wrist "…any moment."

Brooke squealed, her eyes widening. She jumped to her feet. "Daddy! You can't invite people here when my face is all messed up."

The senator ignored his younger daughter, his gaze

instead boring into Eleanor. "Perhaps you'd like to go freshen up before he arrives?"

Heat rose to the tips of Eleanor's ears. Her father had sent the car for Ty? How had her father even known she'd be here? Had he cared? If her father said that he would be arriving any moment, that meant Ty had gone along with her father's request. Then again, Cole might not have requested anything. He'd probably demanded that Ty come.

Great.

She'd thought she was going to die of total mortification last night, but perhaps that honor had been saved for this morning.

Ty had ridden in a limo a few times during his life, but none of the luxurious caliber of Senator Cole Aston's. Although he definitely preferred Ole Bess, his affectionate nickname for the Ford pickup he'd driven since first getting his license, he couldn't deny that he'd been impressed.

But, then, he was pretty sure that had been Senator Aston's intention.

That and to perhaps intimidate him.

Not that Ty was easily intimidated. Only his own father seemed capable of achieving that.

Obviously, Eleanor's old man had seen the picture of his daughter with him and wanted to know his intentions.

He had no intentions.

Not toward Eleanor. Not really.

Yeah, she'd piqued his interest last night and once she'd gotten over her shyness she'd been funny and intelligent. He'd enjoyed the evening more than he would have believed possible.

He'd found her incredibly intriguing and, yes, he'd admit it, he found her sexy as hell.

But that didn't mean he had any intention of seeing Eleanor outside the hospital. Something told him she wouldn't be a love-'em-and-leave-'em-smiling kind of experience.

He didn't do any other. Which meant he should stay away from the good doctor. Which was why he hadn't made any move on her at the end of the evening, despite the fact that he'd wanted to kiss her repeatedly. Hell, he'd wanted to do a lot more than kiss her.

But he'd settled for a goodbye hug and he'd gone home alone.

The senator had nothing to worry about.

The elevator ride to the penthouse of one of Manhattan's most prestigious apartment complexes overlooking Central Park was an experience in and of itself. Ty had to smile at the seat along one wall and wondered if he was wicked for thinking of all the fun ways that seat could be used by him and...

He stopped, realizing that rather than some random hot babe popping into his head, the woman making use of that seat with him was Eleanor.

Which shocked him. Hadn't he just reminded himself that she wasn't his type?

Senator Cole Aston's daughter.

How had Eleanor ended up shy, sweet, compassionate and hardworking when she'd grown up in the lap of such luxury?

Then again, thinking about what he knew of Cole

Aston, perhaps Eleanor's childhood had been more hellish than his own.

Which wasn't exactly fair, because his childhood hadn't been bad. Not really. It hadn't been until he'd gotten older, known his life was going in a different direction than his family envisioned that the problems had started with his father. The rest of his family was… things he wasn't going to think about. Not right now when he was about to get his butt chewed for latching on to Eleanor the night before.

The Aston penthouse suite was something straight out of a magazine on luxury living. The fancy living quarters probably had been featured in a magazine. Several of them. Ty almost felt as if he should take his shoes off before stepping onto the shiny hardwood floors.

Following a well-dressed woman who'd introduced herself as the head housekeeper, he entered a large room containing a long mahogany table, with Senator Aston sitting at the head and Eleanor to his right. Fresh flowers adorned the elaborately set table.

The bright red splash of color that infused Eleanor's cheeks and the quick way she averted her gaze told him she hadn't been behind his summons.

Perhaps she didn't even want him here.

Was that disappointment shooting through him?

No way. He hadn't really thought Eleanor had sent for him. He hadn't even expected her to be here as she'd told him the night before that she lived in an apartment of her own. Ty had known it was her father planning to whip out the shotgun and tell him to keep his good-ole-boy hands off his precious daughter.

No worries. He'd already decided to do that.

"Glad you could make it, Dr. Donaldson." The senator stuck out his hand and Ty shook it firmly. "Have a seat. Next to Eleanor, of course."

Senator Aston had a future in acting should he ever opt out of politics because no way was that welcoming tone real. Had he really just invited Ty to sit next to Eleanor?

Wondering what he'd gotten himself into, he sat.

"Can we get you some breakfast, son?"

Son? What the…?

"No, thank you, sir. I've already eaten."

"Coffee, tea, juice?"

What was with the host with the most?

Eleanor was now shooting daggers at her father.

"No, thanks." He searched her face, but she wouldn't even look his way. When she finally stopped glaring at her father, she just stared at her breakfast, which it didn't look like she'd much more than touched. So he met Senator Aston's eyes and decided to cut to the chase. "You asked to see me?"

The man smiled and a shiver ran up Ty's back.

"I wanted to meet the man who spent the night with my daughter."

Ty didn't wince or glance away from the man's penetrating gaze. He wouldn't show weakness around this man who was obviously used to everyone bowing to his command. "Eleanor is a grown woman and surely makes her own choices as to who she spends her time with."

Which wasn't what he should have said. He should have pointed out that they hadn't spent the night together. Only a very public evening. Something about the man got Ty's hackles up.

"Until I saw this morning's paper I hadn't realized she was spending time with anyone," the senator countered smoothly, taking a sip from his coffee cup. "She tells me you work together."

Her shoulders having dropped at her father's words, Eleanor's face now glowed rosier than any bloom in the flower arrangement. Once again, Ty found himself feeling protective.

"Yes, she's a brilliant pediatrician. One of the best Angel's has."

Senator Aston waved off Eleanor's accomplishments and focused on the real reason he'd summoned Ty. "What are your intentions regarding my daughter?"

That's more like what he'd come expecting to hear.

"Daddy! Please." Eleanor scooted her plate back, stared at her father. "I told you that Ty and I are only work colleagues."

Ouch. Why did Eleanor's words sting?

"Ty?" Her father's brow arched, then his dark gaze settled directly on Ty in question.

Here was his opportunity to set the record straight and get the hell out of Dodge.

"It's too early to say what my intentions are regarding your daughter." Which wasn't what he'd meant to say, but those words had somehow come out anyway.

"What?" This had come from a very shocked, very red-faced Eleanor. "But you…you didn't…" Her voice trailed off, not verbalizing that Ty hadn't kissed her when they'd said goodbye.

Ty's gaze remained locked with her father's.

"I'm very protective of my daughters."

Ty bit back a grin. "I imagine so."

Eleanor's father leaned back in his chair, eyeing Ty as if he were sizing up an opponent. He took a sip of his coffee and calmly announced, "I want you to accompany Eleanor to my fund-raiser ball next week."

That surprised him, but Ty only shrugged. He wouldn't be bullied by this man. "I'm busy."

"Get unbusy," the senator ordered, as if whatever Ty's plans were they couldn't possibly be more important than his.

"Eleanor may have other plans."

"She doesn't." Had there been humor in the man's tone? "This is important to my career and the perfect opportunity for me to get to know what type of man my daughter is spending her time with."

Ty wasn't sure how he felt about going to the fund-raiser. He liked Eleanor, but hadn't he already decided that he needed to stay away from her? That she would expect more from him than he'd ever give? But there was something about the way her father was discussing her as if she weren't in the room that got Ty's hackles up, made him want to puff out his chest and stand in challenge.

What was it about the woman that gave him all these protective, testosterone-filled urges?

"I prefer to arrange my own dates."

The senator sat his coffee cup down on the table and eyed Ty intently. "Fine. Arrange one. Now is as good a time as any. I'm sure Eleanor is available the night of my fund-raiser."

"Daddy." Eleanor's voice sounded so humiliated Ty

wanted to whisk her out of the room. Hell, he knew exactly how she felt. Hadn't his own father loved to put him in his place every opportunity he got?

His father. His family. Which only served to remind him of his own family issues and the fact that his mother wasn't letting up on him coming home to attend Swallow Creek's annual rodeo, which his father was hosting. Just the thought of going home, seeing the shame in his father's eyes as he expounded on what a disappointment Ty had turned out to be, turned his stomach. It would be the first time he'd be face-to-face with dear ole Dad since their big row about Ty moving to New York.

He'd be damned if he was going to face it solo when presented with such a golden opportunity.

"Fine," he agreed to the senator's suggestion, liking the idea that had struck him. "I'll go to the fund-raiser." Just as the pompous man started to smile, Ty added, "On one condition. I want Eleanor to go to Texas with me six weeks from now to attend a rodeo my family is hosting."

With her by his side, his family would be on their best behavior, would be distracted by him bringing a woman with him, and maybe, just maybe, his father wouldn't launch into how he'd screwed up his whole life and let the entire family down by following his own dreams rather than to follow in his father's footsteps.

"Done." Smiling again, the senator stuck his hand out for Ty to shake.

"What?" Eleanor's chair flew back from the table, almost toppling she stood so quickly. "Th-this is crazy. You're talking like I'm not even here." She glanced back and forth between them. "You're both crazy. I'm not going to Texas."

Wondering what the hell he was doing, Ty shook Eleanor's father's hand before any of them could come to their senses.

CHAPTER FOUR

ELEANOR AUSCULTATED ROCHELLE'S tiny chest, distinguishing each sound and praying the baby's lungs remained clear of fluid or pneumonia despite her many risk factors.

"Hey, you."

Eleanor jumped, startling the baby. Talking softly to Rochelle and stroking her finger over the baby's tiny hand, she mentally gathered her wits. What she needed was someone to talk softly to her and calm her nerves before she acknowledged who'd surprised her.

"Don't do that," she ordered, spinning to face the man she wasn't quite sure what to think of. Not that she hadn't thought of him. She'd thought of little else since yesterday morning when she hadn't been able to take any more of her father bargaining a date for her.

That she understood.

What she couldn't understand was why Ty had agreed, why he'd even suggested her going to Texas with him.

That made absolutely no sense at all to her. No matter how many times she'd tried to work out his reasons, she kept coming up blank.

Looking as gorgeous as ever, Ty grinned that sexy Southern grin that, along with his Texan drawl, had all the NICU nurses swooning over him. Eleanor's body did a little swooning of its own, too.

"Sorry, darlin'." His eyes twinkled. "Didn't mean to startle you or the babe. How's our girl doing?"

At his "our girl" Eleanor's throat clogged shut. Why, she didn't know because it was the silliest of phrases and she knew he meant their patient and… Oh, what was she prattling on in her mind for? Just answer the man and be done with it.

"She's holding her own." A complete sentence and no stutter—yeah! If nothing else, spending time with him at the ribbon-cutting and reception seemed to have cured her of that habit around him.

He nodded his understanding. "A babe's fighting spirit makes all the difference."

"Speaking of fighting spirit, why did you agree to my father's crazy suggestion that you go to his fund-raiser ball?" She tried to keep her voice light, as if his answer was no big deal. "They aren't that much fun."

He shrugged. "Maybe good ole country boy me just wanted to see what it's like to hang with the big city-slicker politicians."

Eleanor rolled her eyes. "You can cut the good-ole-country-boy act. The big city-slicker politician ran a background check and obviously liked what he found. He could probably tell me what type of baby formula you were raised on."

"I wasn't."

She stared at him in confusion. "You weren't what?"

"Raised on formula." He puffed his chest out. "My momma breast-fed me and my brother."

"I didn't need to know that." Actually, she had a hard time envisioning Ty as a baby, as anything other than the gorgeous man he was.

"Sure you do," he countered. "Can't have you showing up in Texas as my date and not knowing a thing about me."

As his date?

"That's another thing." Her brows pulled tightly together. "Why on earth would you want me to go to Texas with you?"

He didn't seem concerned, just pulled his stethoscope out of his scrub pocket then met her gaze. "Why not? We had a nice time together at the ribbon-cutting reception and you'd be doing me a favor."

"Just as you're doing me a favor by going to my father's campaign ball?"

Ty's gaze cut to hers. "He really wasn't going to take no for an answer. I just worked a Texas travel buddy into the bargain."

"A travel buddy? If you think I'm going to—"

He held up his hand. "Stop right there. I'm not thinking any such thing, but am quite shocked at how quickly your mind went to the gutter, Eleanor." He tsked, his eyes full of naughtiness.

As much as she wanted to, she couldn't hold back her smile. "Try selling your innocence to one of your many fan clubs, Dr. Donaldson. I'm sure they'd be impressed."

His brow arched. "Not much impresses you?"

Tired of fidgeting nervously with her stethoscope, she put the tubing around her neck and shoved her hands into her lab-coat pockets. "Lots of things impress me, but not your innocence. I've seen snakes with more saintly backgrounds."

"As in the background check your father did? He couldn't have turned up anything too bad or he wouldn't have been rolling out the red carpet." His grin took on a mischievous little-boy gleam. "Sure, I tipped a few cows in my younger days, but—"

"Tipped a few cows?" She hadn't read her father's report. He'd offered, but she'd refused on principle. Perhaps she shouldn't have been so haughty.

"You should see what we did to the sheep." Ty's brows waggled.

His outlandish comment had Eleanor smothering a laugh and a few of the nurses looking their way.

"Quit distracting me from the real issue," she warned. "Why do you want me to go with you to Texas?"

This time he was the one fidgeting with his stethoscope. "I like you."

Her cheeks grew hotter than asphalt on a midsummer day. "You like me? What's that supposed to mean?"

He liked her? Not meeting Eleanor's eyes, Ty stalled by checking out Rochelle, listening to her tiny heart, lungs and surgically repaired belly, which still had various tubes and drains in place.

Very unlike him to hesitate to give an answer.

Usually he was smooth with the lines with the ladies. Usually.

Maybe it was because he wasn't exactly sure what he wanted with Eleanor that he was thrown.

That was exactly what was throwing him.

He'd decided not to pursue a relationship with her but had ended up with a date to her father's campaign ball and with her going home for the weekend with him. Not exactly consistent with staying away from her and avoiding the attraction he felt toward her.

He glanced up, studied her slightly flustered expression, uptight hairstyle, thick-framed glasses and tried to go back to seeing her as just Dr. Aston and not the intriguing woman he'd spent an evening with.

But he couldn't.

He couldn't look at her and not see beneath the surface to the woman she hid below. Couldn't not want to peel away the layers to let that woman out, to free her, and to sit back and watch the explosion.

More than watch, he wanted to experience that explosion in every shape, form and fashion.

"What are you thinking?" She licked her lips nervously.

That he wanted to lick those soft pink lips, to taste her mouth, to take his time and kiss her all night long.

He cleared his throat. "That our girl is going to make it."

After frowning at him a moment, Eleanor took his bait and cut her gaze to the baby. "I hope so. She's such a sweetheart."

"They all are."

Surprise flickered in her gaze. "You really like babies, don't you?"

The question seemed a no-brainer to him, but he understood what she meant. A big macho Texan like him choosing to take care of babies. Could a man choose a more emasculating profession? Not according to his father. In Harold Donaldson's eyes a man might as well chop off his big boys as to "play with babies all day."

Ty didn't quite see things the way his dad did and hadn't from the point he'd realized he wanted to be a doctor. During his early academic career he'd discovered he specifically wanted to be a neonatologist. Despite his father's hee-hawing and ho-humming about the "shame of having a son who played with babies," not once had Ty felt less of a man because of his profession.

He liked what he did at Angel's, liked making a difference in his tiny patients' lives and their families' lives. He'd been blessed with a God-given talent and he was where he was supposed to be in life.

Only he had no choice but to go home for the rodeo. His mother had threatened to have the entire crew converge on him in New York if he didn't. Of course, seeing his father in downtown Manhattan might be worth it.

Then again, those skyscrapers might bow in the presence of his giant of a father.

"Ty?"

He blinked, realizing he'd totally blanked out on Eleanor. "Sorry. I got lost in my thoughts."

"I noticed." She smiled tentatively and the gesture tugged at something in his chest.

She was pretty. Why had it taken him seeing her all decked out for him to notice those eyes, that generous mouth, that porcelain skin? That phenomenal body?

"Would it help to talk about it?" she gently offered.

"Hell, no." His mother had talked about the problems between him and his father till Ty was blue in the face. Nothing was going to make his family understand his need to be a doctor.

He sure didn't want to talk about his reaction to her since the ribbon-cutting. How could he explain to her what he didn't understand himself?

"I didn't mean to pry." Obviously embarrassed, Eleanor's eyes dropped. Her chest rose and fell with a deep breath.

Ty knew his gaze shouldn't drop to watch the shifting of the material across her body, but it did. A crying shame when a grown man was jealous of a cotton scrub top, but he was.

Guilt hit him on several counts.

"Offering to listen isn't prying," he countered, smiling at her and hoping she took his peace offering. "Besides, if you're the little darlin' doing the listening, I'd be happy to give talking a whirl."

Her gaze lifted and she stared at him in confusion. A slow smile curved her lips. "You would?"

"Oh, yeah." Which surprised him, but for some reason he enjoyed talking to Eleanor, enjoyed seeing the uninhibited emotions play across her lovely face. "Go to dinner with me tonight?"

Hands digging deeper into her pockets, she eyed him suspiciously. "Is my father paying you to be nice to me? To take me out?"

Ty laughed, put his hand on her lower back and led her away from Rochelle's incubator. "Is that how your sister has a new beau every week?"

Eleanor's face lost some of its sparkle. "If you have to ask that, you obviously left my father's place without having met my sister."

Brooke hadn't made an appearance during the few minutes Ty had remained after Eleanor had disappeared.

"If she's anything like you, she's a knockout."

Eleanor's eyes rolled behind her thick-framed glasses. "Right."

"Definitely."

When had they fallen into step together? Where were they even headed? To the new wing, he realized. More and more of the neonatal unit was being transferred to the area.

"Seriously, if it means going to dinner with you, I'd spill my guts on all the reasons why I want you to come to Texas with me."

She considered him a moment, then nodded. "Okay, Ty, you have a deal. You get to feed me and I get to listen."

"I get the better end of that deal."

Her brow lifted and she grinned with an almost flirty gleam in her dark eyes. "You haven't seen me eat."

Watching Eleanor eat should be X-rated.

Ty was positive he'd never seen a woman take so much delight in food. Most of the women he knew barely picked at the few scraps of lettuce put on their plate, much less actually enjoyed each bite with such unabashed pleasure.

He was also positive that he'd never been turned on at watching a woman eat, but he was turned on.

Majorly turned on.

Each and every time Eleanor's mouth closed around her fork, her eyes closed and joy lit up her face. Had she moaned with her delight in the food he wouldn't have been surprised.

She opened her eyes, caught him watching and pink splashed her cheeks. "Sorry."

"For?"

"Making a glutton of myself. I like to eat. I did warn you."

"Enjoying your dinner isn't making a glutton of yourself."

She pushed her plate back, eyeing the remaining food with regret. "Yeah, but if I want to fit into my dress for my dad's campaign fund-raiser, I'd best stop."

Immediately his mind was brought back to the tight red dress that had wrapped around her body so delectably at the ribbon-cutting.

"You fill a dress out just fine."

"Yeah, that's the problem." She sighed a bit self-derisively. "I fill it out."

"Why is that a problem? Admittedly, I've only seen you in one dress, but you looked great." More than great. She'd been hot. "Ever since then I've been considering requesting a change to hospital policy just so I can see you in a dress on a regular basis."

Snorting softly, she toyed with the napkin in her lap. "You can't help yourself, can you?"

"Hmm?" he asked innocently, knowing he hadn't been innocent since his sixteenth birthday when he and seventeen-year-old cheerleader Casey Thompson had made out after a football game.

She folded the napkin and placed it neatly in her lap. "Whenever there's a woman around you just have to spew out compliments."

"Is it wrong to tell a woman she looks beautiful with her glasses off so that I can see those amazing eyes?"

Those amazing eyes lowered. "I wear my contacts for sports. I just didn't change back to my glasses afterward, that's all. Thank you for the compliment, but you don't have to say things like that. I don't expect you to."

Ty considered all she'd said, trying to decide which subject he wanted to tackle. The fact that she wasn't used to compliments was the one that bugged him most, but for now he opted to go with one that would hopefully have her relaxing again. He wanted her relaxed, wanted her to enjoy their dinner as much as he was.

"What sport do you play?"

Her relief was palpable and he was glad he'd not pushed. He'd liked the easy camaraderie between them, the easy flow of conversation as they discussed everything from the new hospital wing to the New York Knicks, who, to his surprise, Eleanor loved.

"Tennis and racquetball mostly. I was on the swim team and ran track during my high-school years. I still do both, but only for the exercise."

He picked up her fork, loaded it with food and held it out to her. "Then I'd say you're allowed to finish your dinner."

Eyeing the fork of North Atlantic salmon with longing, she shook her head. "I can't."

"You can," he said temptingly, moving the fork toward her mouth.

"Really, I shouldn't." But her eyes said she wanted to.

"You should, darlin'." He brought the food to her lips and they parted. He barely bit back his groan when her eyes closed and she savored the melt-in-the-mouth entrée.

He convinced her to have dessert under the pretense

of them sharing it. He enjoyed immensely having the excuse to feed her bite after bite, watching her reaction as the cheesecake hit her tongue.

Watching Eleanor Aston eat could quickly become an obsession.

"You promised me an explanation about why you wanted me to come to Texas with you," she reminded him, dabbing her mouth with her napkin.

"That I did." Somehow in the course of their dinner and the enjoyable company he'd forgotten all about the trip to Texas. That alone was testament to how wrapped up in watching Eleanor, in talking with her, he'd been. "My family is hosting the local rodeo this year. I need a date."

Her gaze narrowed suspiciously. "You're never short on dates, Ty. Why would you choose me?"

"Why wouldn't I?"

"Because we're not dating."

"One could argue that technically we're on a date at this very moment."

She seemed to consider that a moment, then met his gaze again. "I'm not your usual fare."

"Exactly."

She frowned. "What's that supposed to mean?"

He laughed at her expression, quite enjoying how her every thought was broadcast so plainly in her eyes. "Quit looking so perturbed, Ellie. I meant it as a compliment."

If anything, her frown deepened. "Don't call me that."

"What? Ellie? It fits." He spooned another bite of the

cheesecake, but she wouldn't even look at it, just shook her head, practically wincing.

"I don't want any more and, no, that name doesn't fit."

He started to tempt her, knew he could, but realized there was more going on than she was telling him, something profound.

"I'll make a deal with you," he offered, watching every emotion flicker across her lovely face.

"What's that?"

Had her voice broken? Her eyes were sparkling and not from looking at him but as if she was fighting back tears.

Ty reached across the table, took her hand in his and laced their fingers. "I'll only call you Ellie when you steal my breath with your beauty."

Not looking at him, she snorted. "That's a deal I'll gladly make, because I don't want to be called that." She took a deep breath, pulled her hand free of his and slipped on what he supposed was her game face. "Now, tell me more about this trip to Texas."

Ty wanted to dig, wanted to know what made Eleanor tick, to know what had upset her, but now wasn't the time for digging for details. At least, not into Eleanor's life. His was another story altogether as he'd promised her the goods.

Eyeing Eleanor's quiet expression, he couldn't resist saying, "For the record, I wouldn't count on not hearing me call you Ellie again. You're a very beautiful woman. On the inside and the outside."

She ignored his implication and his compliment. "So the trip's for an entire weekend?"

"We'll fly up on Thursday morning and can safely sneak out on Sunday afternoon under the need to get back to our patients. Should be a breeze, right?"

Four days with Ty Donaldson. Could she survive it? Because the man was a natural-born charmer and she really wasn't equipped to deal with the likes of him. It would be so easy to believe in his quick lines.

To believe in the way he looked at her.

Because he looked at her as if he found her attractive. If she'd thought she'd imagined it the night of the ribbon-cutting, she'd been wrong. He was looking at her the same way right this minute. As if he found her interesting, desirable, beautiful—inside and out.

When he'd fed her, she'd almost died. No man had ever fed her, ever taken pleasure in doing such a simple act, but Ty had. When she'd opened her eyes after that first bite, she'd seen the pleasure in his eyes. He'd enjoyed feeding her every bit as much as she'd enjoyed him doing so.

Don't read anything into it. You've seen how he's gone through women at the hospital. You're just this week's flavor.

"Where I come from," Ty continued, "the local rodeo is a very big deal. My brother and I grew up wanting to be rodeo stars, but we're too tall."

"Is that like one of those carnival rides where you have to be this tall to ride, only in reverse?" she teased, trying to picture Ty as a young boy.

He grinned. "You're funny. Actually, most cowboys on the rodeo circuit are under five and a half feet tall."

Her eyes widened. "That's pretty short for a man."

"But just right if you're going to ride a bronco."

If he said so. In her mind, she preferred thinking of cowboys as tall, dark, ruggedly handsome. Like Ty, actually. Which set off a whole slew of cowboy fantasies. Not good.

She could see Ty in worn jeans that fit just so, in a Stetson that sat upon his head just so, with no shirt on, of course, because in her mind he was all six-pack-and-muscle bound. And feeding her some light and flaky calorie-free delicacy that only paled in comparison to him.

She picked up her napkin, started to fan her face with it, realized what she was doing and dropped the cloth back into her lap.

"My father said you grew up on a ranch so I imagine you do ride, even if you are too tall to be a rodeo star," she said, taking a sip of her water in the hope of moistening her dry mouth and cooling her libido, which was in overdrive.

"I was riding a horse before I could walk." His grin widened, making her wonder if he could somehow read her thoughts and knew exactly the effect he was having on her body.

"Well," he continued, his eyes twinkling, "not alone, but I've seen the pictures of me sitting on a horse in one person or another's lap. Donaldsons pretty much go from birth to horse."

"What about cows?"

"Nah, we don't ride cows until we hit at least elementary-school age." His lips twisted with amusement. "My nephew's competing in the sheep-riding competition."

"Sheep-riding? How old is he?" For the life of her, Eleanor couldn't picture a wild bucking sheep trying to throw someone off its back. But what did she know about ranch life or rodeos?

"Don't look so horrified. William is four. Feel sorry for the sheep. That kid is hell on wheels."

The love in Ty's words was strong, making Eleanor wonder yet again why he'd stayed away from Texas so long. "Takes after his uncle Ty?"

"Nah, that would make him the black sheep of the family."

His answer startled Eleanor.

"I can't imagine any family not being proud of your accomplishments." Then again, didn't her own parents look at her as if she was demented for working for a living?

"I should prepare you. My father and I had a disagreement, shall we say, about my career choice and where I chose to work."

"Because he wanted you to practice in Texas?"

Ty's face lost its playful edge. "Something like that. Quite frankly, darlin', the man scares the daylight out of me."

He said it jokingly, but there was no humor in his voice.

"Because you're easily scared?" Her fingers toyed with the napkin in her lap, twisting one end back and forth.

"There's a reason I work with babies." Although his tone was teasing, something told her there was more to what Ty said than his actual words.

"I'm glad you work with babies, Ty. You're an excellent doctor and your patients are very blessed to have you overseeing their first few months in this world."

His smile was genuine and her compliment softened his eyes. "Ditto, Ellie."

She frowned at his use of the nickname, but his grin held and he shrugged as if to say he couldn't help himself.

"A deal's a deal," he reminded her.

Right. Because he'd looked across the table at her and she'd stolen his breath by her beauty and had felt the need to let her know.

"Tell me about your brother," she rushed forward, not wanting to let her mind go down the "Ellie" path. They'd been there once too often that evening already.

"Harry is great. The spitting image of my father and the golden boy of Swallow Creek. All his life, he's excelled at everything he's done, especially bowing to my father's whims. On paper, he runs the ranch, but I've no doubt my father still pulls the strings."

His words held no sarcasm, no malice. She could tell that he genuinely loved his brother, yet so easily his words could be taken as sibling rivalry. Or worse.

"He's older?"

Ty nodded. "By three years."

She considered her next words carefully. "Must've been tough growing up in the shadow of such a successful sibling."

Ty shrugged. "I never was much for standing in the shadows."

At the thought of a younger Ty daring twice as much to keep up with his gifted older brother, Eleanor smiled. "I thought that about you."

The corner of Ty's mouth lifted. "What about you? Must never have been boring growing up with Senator Cole Aston as a father."

"No, I can't say I was ever bored." Just never quite part of the family. "He is constantly into something."

"Like donating the money to open the new hospital wing?"

"That's one of the few things he's done that makes me very proud to be an Aston."

"The few?"

She shrugged. "He's a politician. He does what he needs to do to get votes. My whole life was planned around what would help Daddy most in the polls."

Ty regarded her for long enough that Eleanor wanted to squirm, but didn't.

He leaned back in his chair, eyed her curiously with a glimmer of bedevilment dancing in his eyes. "Tell me, Eleanor. Come election day, do you vote for dear old dad?"

Her jaw dropped. Never had anyone asked her that. They just assumed...

"I'd answer that," she began, keeping her tone even, "but then I'd have to kill you. So I'm just going to plead the Fifth."

Ty burst out laughing. "Like I said, you're funny. I like you, Ellie."

Yeah, she liked him, too.

Except for the nickname, which she could do without, although there was something about the way it rolled off his tongue that was starting to get to her.

She only hoped that later down the road liking Ty didn't come back to haunt her.

CHAPTER FIVE

ELEANOR HAD SEEN Ty several times around the hospital, had even grabbed a few quick cups of coffee with him in the cafeteria and twice they'd shared lunch.

She'd heard the rumors that were flying around, had fiercely denied them, but everyone knew Ty's reputation.

"Just be careful, Eleanor," Linda Busby, a registered nurse in her early sixties who worked in the NICU, warned. "Dr. Donaldson is wonderful. I swear every woman he's gone out with still sings his praises, so I know he's a great guy. However, you don't play the dating games most men and women do, and I don't want to see you get hurt."

"We're just friends." They were. Not once had Ty attempted to kiss her or hold her hand other than the brief moment at the restaurant. Actually, on the night of the ribbon-cutting he'd touched her more than he had all the other times they'd seen each other since then combined.

"Watch him," Linda warned, her hands on her hips. "He isn't known for being just friends with pretty young girls."

Seeing Ty behind the nurse and knowing her friend

was unaware of their eavesdropper, who was nodding his head in agreement with everything Linda said, Eleanor bit back a smile.

"Then you might want to watch out for him, too. I hear he's into the whole cougar thing."

Linda spun at Ty's teasing comment, her face turning beet-red. She playfully smacked his arm. "You, young man, are bad."

His grin killed any argument anyone tried to make to the contrary. "Wanna be bad with me, darlin'?"

Linda shook her head, turned to Eleanor. "Like I said, watch this one. He uses that good-ole-boy Southern charm to boil our Northern-girl blood. You'd be wise to steer clear."

"You know you love me," Ty teased her.

Linda and Eleanor both rolled their eyes, making Ty laugh out loud.

"I've got work to do." She gave Ty a well-meaning glare and pointed her finger at him. "You behave."

"Yes, ma'am." He gave her his lopsided grin.

Linda walked away smiling, shaking her head and mumbling something about God having blessed Texas.

"You here to check on the new twenty-four-week preemie?" Eleanor asked him, wondering why her heart was beating so fast in her chest just from Ty being near.

His expression sobered. "I am. The family given him a name yet?"

She'd taken a peek at the newborn herself just a few minutes prior to Linda giving her advice about spending so much time with Ty.

"No." Eleanor shook her head, walking with him to the little boy's incubator. "He's just Male Griffin at the moment. Linda told me they say they aren't going to. They think that will only make them get more attached."

Glancing toward her, Ty winced. "They've not been to see him?"

"The father has, but he refuses to let his wife come. Her nurse says she asks continually but that she won't go against her husband's wishes."

His eyes assessing the tiny baby he'd watched be born and had immediately taken charge of, Ty sighed. "He's trying to protect her, but how is she not supposed to already be attached to a baby she carried inside her body for twenty-four weeks and built a lifetime of dreams around?"

"He knows her better than we do, but if she wants to see her baby, he shouldn't keep her from doing so. If he dies and she hasn't seen him even though she really wanted to, she may never forgive herself."

"Exactly my thoughts," Ty agreed.

Eleanor couldn't imagine the fear the baby's parents must be going through, the worries, the doubts. Her heart went out both to the parents and to the little boy who very well might not live.

Ty examined the baby, discussed his immediate care with Eleanor, asking her opinion on a few points and then they stood next to the incubator, watching the baby struggle for each second of life, alive only by the technology that kept him that way.

Even though she dealt with similar cases routinely, just looking at the tiny baby was enough to make Eleanor's heart clench.

As if maybe he'd had a few heart clenches of his own,

Ty inhaled sharply, then turned toward her. "Pick you up at six for the fund-raiser tonight, right?"

Her pulse jumping for no good reason at all except for the way his gaze held hers, Eleanor shook her head. "My father insists on sending his limo for you."

Ty's dark brows drew together. "Will you already be in that limo?"

Eleanor shrugged. "I have no idea what order my father has planned. I thought perhaps you two had discussed the arrangements." She'd barely spoken to her father since the morning he'd summoned Ty to the Aston penthouse. "I just know that when he called me this morning he insisted on providing our transportation. For us both to be ready so we wouldn't be late arrivals. He wants us to make a big media splash."

Apparently her father planned to milk her having a date for all it was worth. Just the thought of being in the crowded ballroom, of all the backslapping and paparazzi that would be there was enough to make her heart do that funny little flipping sensation that always preceded a full-blown panic attack. She hated crowds, hated that as the senator's daughter she'd be photographed. At least tonight she'd have Ty at her side. Perhaps for that she should thank her father because she couldn't have made it through the ribbon-cutting without him.

Ty's lips twisted with displeasure. "For future reference, I need to let your father know that I prefer to pick up my own dates."

Future dates? As in dates her father arranged between them? Or real dates? As in dates that he asked her to go on with him because he wanted to be with her?

Better yet, why did she desperately wish tonight was a real date?

Ty supposed there were advantages to arriving to pick Eleanor up from her apartment in the Aston limo. For instance, he didn't have to find parking while he ran inside to collect her.

Although a nice apartment complex, Eleanor didn't live in the grandiose style of the Aston penthouse. Not that he actually saw the inside of her apartment. The doorman buzzed her and she insisted on meeting him in the lobby. Fine, nothing was going according to how he'd pictured it in his mind.

He'd look a dork for bringing flowers and handing them to her in the lobby, but so be it because he'd wanted to do this right. Whatever right was.

The moment his gaze landed on her stepping out of the elevator he felt like a country hick come to the big city and about to meet a glamorous star.

"Hello, Ellie," he greeted her in a worshipful whisper.

Her forehead creased. "I told you not to call me that."

"And I agreed to only do so when you stole my breath, darlin'."

She reached out, placed her palm near his nostrils. "Still breathing, so don't let it happen again."

But her demand was tempered by the way her eyes had lit up when he'd reminded her of their deal.

"You are beautiful, by the way," he added, thinking truer words had never been spoken. She'd clipped her hair up, but much looser than she wore for work. Although her dress was much more demure than the red number she'd worn for the ribbon-cutting, she still looked supersexy in the silky black number clinging to her body.

"So are you."

At her response, Ty glanced down at his tuxedo. A black-and-white penguin suit when he was more comfortable in scrubs or a pair of well-worn jeans. Nothing beautiful about him. But Eleanor was truly gorgeous. She looked as if she should be gracing an ad for a classic movie much as Audrey Hepburn would have or Grace Kelly. Eleanor shamed them both.

"Nice flowers." She smiled softly at him when he just stood staring at her.

Wondering at how his chest tightened at her shy smile, Ty grinned back. "Yeah, darlin', I think your doorman has a thing for me. He insisted I take these…" he held up the bouquet "…although I'm pretty sure he stole them out of one of the floral arrangements in here." He held them out toward her. "You better stash them in your apartment to save me from getting in trouble, just in case."

She took the flowers, closed her eyes and breathed in their fragrance, then smiled in a way that really put his chest into lockdown. "Thank you, Ty, but you didn't have to bring me flowers. It's not as if this is a real date."

Not a real date? Hadn't they already been through this the night they'd gone to dinner?

"What is it, then?"

Cheeks pink, her gaze averted. "A deal you and my father arranged."

Was that how she saw tonight? As something he and her father had arranged? Did she not want to be with him? He'd thought… Never mind what he'd thought.

"I still think you should have just asked one of your women to go with you to Texas. You'd have saved yourself a lot of trouble." She walked over to the front desk, gave the flowers to the smiling older man there, leaned over and kissed his cheek.

When she returned to where he stood watching, Ty scratched his head. "My women?"

"One of the women you've taken out for real."

Enough was enough. "This is real."

Not responding, she just smiled as if she was humoring him. She probably was.

"Come on, darlin'," he said, not liking the frustration moving through him. He took her hand. "Let's go get the party started. For real."

Eleanor laughed at Ty's latest corny joke. He'd been telling her silly little jokes all night. If she found herself feeling panicky or uptight, he'd lean over and whisper something totally outlandish in her ear just for her to hear.

"You're beautiful.

"You're one sexy woman, darlin'.

"I'm the luckiest man at the fund-raiser because I'm with you.

"Just in case there's any doubt, let me remind you. This is a real date."

Champagne had been flowing freely at her father's

announcement that he planned to run for another senate term. As if anyone had thought otherwise. Eleanor needed to have stopped drinking prior to her last glass of bubbly because her insides felt a little too warm and cozy. Because Ty's whispered words were starting to get to her, were starting to make her want to do some whispering back into his ear.

Things like, "You're gorgeous, Ty," and "You're one sexy man, darling," and "I'm the luckiest woman at the fund-raiser because I'm with you." And "I'm so glad this is a real date, because I'd really like you to kiss me before the night is over."

"Wow!" he exclaimed, drawing her attention away from her daydreaming. "That's your sister? The papers don't do her justice."

Ty's words pulled Eleanor right out of her dreamy euphoria. Here they went. How many times throughout her life had she been interested in someone only to have them meet Brooke and forget she even existed? How many times had she been used as a means to get an introduction to glorious, glamorous Brooke?

"You want me to introduce you?"

Her words must have tipped him off, because he shifted, dragged his eyes away from Brooke and looked fully at Eleanor, searching her eyes.

She didn't look away, didn't back down.

For once she wasn't going to be all nice about a man who was with her but wanted Brooke instead.

"Only if you want to, Ellie. Only if you want to."

She gritted her teeth. The nickname only served to remind her of the contrast between her and her sister.

Forever she'd be Jelly Ellie when put next to beauty-queen Brooke.

"Oh, yes, I want to. Let's go." Might as well get it over with. Probably, if the truth be told, an introduction to Brooke had been on his agenda all along. Didn't he realize all he'd have had to do was mention to the senator that he preferred slender blondes and Cole would have had him taking Brooke to Texas instead?

Brooke held court in the midst of about twenty people, mostly besotted men. She barely paid any heed to Eleanor joining her. Until her gaze landed on Ty.

"You brought Dr. Yummy to meet me." Brooke's gaze ran suggestively over Ty. "Goody."

Goody, indeed. Eleanor wanted to gag. Why was she doing this? She liked Ty. Really liked him. Why was she serving him on a silver platter to her silly, immature sister?

Better to get it over with now than to get her emotions more entangled and then discover she had just been a means to get to her sister.

She already knew how that felt.

"Actually, it's Dr. Donaldson," Ty smoothly corrected with an easy smile. He slid his arm around Eleanor's waist, his hand resting possessively at her lower back. "But as I'm your sister's date for the evening, you can call me Ty."

"As in tie me up and tie me down?" Brooke flirted, still eyeing Ty and making no pretense that she was interested.

Gag. Gag. Gag. Did men really find that attractive?

Looking at her sister in her figure-hugging blue dress and flawless appearance, Eleanor decided that if you looked like Brooke men would overlook almost every-thing. And did.

But rather than respond to Brooke's obvious inter-est, Ty lifted Eleanor's hand to his lips, pressed a kiss to her fingertips and winked at her. "Only if Ellie is the one doing the tying."

It was a toss-up as to which sister's jaw hit the floor first.

"Pardon?" Brooke blinked, sure she'd misunder-stood, glancing back and forth between him and El-eanor.

Eleanor couldn't speak. Had Ty really just dissed her sister in favor of *her?* In public? Had he gone mad?

"Sure thing." Ty smoothly misunderstood Brooke's comment, whether feigned or real Eleanor wasn't sure. "We were headed to the dance floor anyway. Nice to meet any family member of Ellie's."

His hand stayed low on Eleanor's back, guiding her toward the dance floor. She was too blown away to put up any kind of argument, instead instinctively wrap-ping her arms around his neck.

Ty's arms settled around her and they swayed in time to the music. "She always like that?"

Wondering at how their bodies had so naturally fallen into rhythm together, at how he had just done something no man ever had—chosen to spend time with her rather than Brooke—Eleanor shook her head.

Maybe she really had drunk more champagne than she'd realized. Maybe she was so drunk that she'd imag-ined everything that had just happened. Maybe she was really passed out on the ladies' room floor.

"No?"

Automatically, she opened her mouth to defend her sister. It was what she'd done her whole life. But when her gaze met Ty's she found the truth spilling from her mouth. "Usually she's worse." Oh, yeah, she'd drunk one glass of champagne too many. "Although really it's not her fault." Old habits died hard. "Everyone spoils her so it's only natural that she expects everyone to bow at her feet." Eleanor shrugged. "They usually do."

Holding her close, Ty shuddered. "Tell me you took after your mother."

All too aware of the strong arms around her, of the muscular body against hers, of the wonderfully male scent filling her nostrils, Eleanor laughed. "Because my mother is the only immediate family member you've not met and maybe there's hope yet?"

His husky laugh warmed her insides. "Always knew you were one sharp cookie, Ellie."

"I wouldn't hold my breath if I were you because she's here and no doubt you'll meet her before the night is through. I saw the senator and her looking our way earlier. And do not call me that name."

"Don't glare at me, *Ellie*." His lips twitched. "I'm just keeping to our deal."

"You've called me Ellie four times in the past five minutes," she pointed out, frustrated at his insistence on the name. Sure, the way it rolled off his tongue always made her breath catch, but she didn't like the name.

"Exactly."

His one word sliced right through the past. She couldn't look away from the sincerity in his eyes. Ty found her attractive, had chosen her over Brooke—

something that she'd never dreamed would happen—and he was holding her close to his body.

His wonderful, warm, hard, fantastic-smelling body that was obviously affected by holding her close.

"You are a very beautiful woman, Ellie Aston, and you have taken my breath away from the moment I arrived to pick you up this evening."

Eleanor's insides melted to ooey-gooey feminine happiness and for once she didn't even glare at him for using the nickname she despised.

After all, a deal was a deal.

"When you look at me like that you make me feel beautiful," she admitted, wondering if she was a fool for revealing so much, wondering if perhaps she should have cut off the champagne long ago because he couldn't really be looking at her that way. Could he?

His fingers lifted her chin. He studied her face, her eyes, until she wanted to squirm away. He leaned forward and pressed the gentlest of kisses to her forehead. So soft she could almost think he was hesitant, but he wasn't. He was strong and confident. His kiss had revered her as if she were something fragile, precious.

How would it feel to kiss Ty for real? On the mouth? To have him enthralled in passion, touching her, kissing her as if he craved her lips more than the air he breathed?

His hand pressed against her back, holding her close to him. Her cheek rested against his chest. She breathed in his musky fragrance, the smell of him intoxicating her much more than any alcohol she'd consumed.

He bent, spoke close to her ear. "I want to kiss you, Ellie, but not here. Not with all the photographers. I want our first kiss to be just between us, not fodder for some gossip page."

She wanted to be kissed. Desperately. By Ty. She wanted that first kiss. Thousands more.

"We can leave anytime," she offered.

He leaned back enough to look her in the eyes, as if trying to decide exactly what she was saying.

"Now," she clarified. "Let's leave now."

"Oh, yeah."

Hand in hand, they headed out of the ballroom, through the glitzy foyer, got their coats. Ty helped her into hers then they walked out onto the sidewalk.

As soon as Eleanor finished asking the attendant to call for the limo, Ty lifted her hand to his lips.

"Thank you for tonight, darlin'."

The brisk night air grasped at her and she shivered. Reality began to set in, to wash away the effects of the alcohol haze that had enveloped her. Self-doubt set in.

"You don't have to do that, you know," she told him. "You've more than done your duty."

His eyes darkened. "Done my duty?"

"As my escort for the evening. You were wonderful."

"If I hadn't wanted to come with you tonight, darlin', I wouldn't have." His eyes glittered. "I'm here because I want to be. Because this was a date. A real date."

Had he drunk so much that he'd fallen into the same fantasy as she had?

"My father is a very persuasive man. Maybe you just think you want to be here."

"What? He used some kind of super-politician force to trick me into thinking I wanted to spend my evening with his lovely daughter?" Ty shook his head, blew a puff of cold breath into his hands, then smiled wickedly at her. "I don't think so. We Texans are made of stronger stuff. I'm here because I want to be with you. No other reason."

Eleanor blushed. "Thank you."

"No. Thank you, Ellie." Then he surprised her by pulling her to him. He kissed her fully on the mouth despite the fact they stood on the street and Lord only knew who might see them.

She didn't care. Later she might, but at the moment all that mattered was that he was kissing her. Finally.

His lips were firm, confident, sure in their movements over hers. He tasted of heaven. He tasted of fire.

She wanted more. Much more.

Her fingers wove into the hair at his nape. Soft strands with just a touch of curl. She'd done so throughout the evening while dancing, but now she latched on, clasping the locks tightly within her grasp, needing him closer and closer still.

Vaguely she was aware of the limousine pulling up to the curb, of her and Ty separating long enough for him to generously tip the attendant and to help her into the back of the car.

Then he joined her and she was back where she wanted to be.

In Ty Donaldson's arms.

Ty moved in a blur. A desire-driven blur.

One spurred on by a woman he foolishly hadn't realized capable of such passion.

Ellie had passion.

He pressed his lips to her throat just so, and she

moaned, spurring him on. He traced his hands down her body, touching places he'd carefully avoided while holding her on the dance floor.

"You are so hot," he breathed against her throat, caressing his way to the sweet indention at her clavicle.

"Because you're touching me," she answered in a husky tone, her fingers threading through his hair, holding him to her. "That makes me feel hot."

Somehow they made it into his apartment still dressed.

Once he closed the door and secured the lock, he made haste with her dress, letting it drop somewhere on the way to his bedroom.

He pushed her back onto his bed, loving how she looked lying there, watching him as he stripped off his clothes in record time.

"Wow," she breathed, reaching her hand up to run over his abs. "You're perfect, Ty."

"You're what's perfect," he corrected, joining her on the bed and pressing his body against hers. "So very perfect. See how you fit against me? Perfect."

Her mouth and hands were all over him, leaving trails of goose bumps, making waves through his nervous system, rewriting his definition of pleasure.

Pushing her bra aside, he closed his lips around one pert nipple, then the other, taking turns laving her until she arched off the bed.

"Ty." Her fingers cradled his head. He suckled harder, taking great pleasure in her breasts, in her passionate responses to his every touch.

"Tell me what you want, Ellie," he encouraged, wanting to give her every pleasure, wanting to give her everything within his power to give. "Tell me where to touch you, how you want to be touched."

For the briefest moment she stiffened in his embrace, her eyes searching his, then she relaxed and guided his mouth to hers.

She kissed him long, hard, deep, leaving him breathless.

"I. Want. You."

He wanted her, too. He was pretty sure he told her somewhere during the time he stripped off her panties and then his boxers.

The way Eleanor's eyes ate up his bare flesh set him afire, made him ache for her touch, for her body.

She looked at him as if she couldn't wait another moment to feel him against her. To feel him inside her.

Maybe she couldn't because she tugged on his shoulders, pulling him to her and wrapping her delectable legs around his.

Hands were everywhere.

Mouths were everywhere.

They touched desperately.

They touched with need, committing each other's bodies to memory, learning every nuance, lighting fires that burned wickedly hot.

When Ty couldn't stand another moment, he thrust deep between her welcoming thighs, plunging into almost blinding pleasure, knowing she'd rewritten much more than his definition of pleasure.

Ellie's cry of satisfaction was everything.

CHAPTER SIX

WHAT HAD SHE DONE?

Not that Eleanor didn't know.

She'd spent the night in Ty Donaldson's bed. Now she knew exactly why all his exes smiled and thought he was the most awesome thing ever.

He was.

Wow.

She rolled over and looked at his sleeping form lit by the streaks of early-morning light. He was beautiful. Truly deep-down beautiful. One of God's loveliest creations.

She wanted to reach out and touch him, to stroke her finger over the strong planes of his cheek, to feel the soft wisps of his hair, to feel the full softness of his lips. But she kept her hands to herself.

She wouldn't risk waking him. No way did she want to see the disappointment that would dawn in his eyes when he realized what they'd done, who he'd spent his night with.

Then again, spending the night with a woman was no big deal for Ty. Just because it was something she never did, it didn't make their night out of the ordinary for him.

To Ty, she was just another of a long string of women he'd made love to.

Had sex with.

Sure, with the way his hands and mouth had worshipped her body, she'd felt like she'd been made love to. But she wasn't so naive as to not realize the truth.

Somehow she managed to get out of the bed without waking him. Desperate for a fast escape, she snatched a pair of way-too-big drawstring running shorts and a T-shirt from the floor, gathered her gown and clothing.

Her heart pounded faster, harder. So loud she couldn't believe Ty didn't wake. Maybe he only faked sleep because he didn't want to face her any more than she wanted to face him. Maybe he wished she'd hurry and get out of his apartment.

The muscles in her chest tightened, squeezing her rib cage almost painfully. Her hands sweated so badly that she almost dropped her clothes.

She sucked in one last breath, storing the vision of the sheet draped low on his waist to memory, knowing that seeing him like this, his beautiful body relaxed and completely loved by her, would never happen again.

Buzz. Buzz. Buzz.

Oh, hell! Her heart pounding, Eleanor desperately dug in her purse for her cell phone, which was obviously still on vibration only. In the silence of the room the buzz sounded as if it should register on the Richter scale. She almost clicked the phone silent, then realized that the only calls she ever got in the early-morning hours were emergency calls. Her heart pounded all the harder.

"No need to leave the room," a sleepy-sounding Ty

drawled from behind her, causing her to freeze halfway to the door. "I'm awake."

Eleanor's pulse thrummed in her ears as she answered and listened to the caller. "I'll be right there."

She clicked her cell phone off. Taking a deep breath, she slowly turned to face him, dreading whatever she might see on his face in the early-morning light.

"Mornin', darlin'," he surprised her by drawling, his gaze taking her in as he scooted up in the bed. The bedsheet rode even lower on his hips, barely covering his impressive bottom half. His very impressive upper half shamed the six-pack fantasy she'd had of him. He patted the bed, motioning for her to climb in next to him. "From your end of the conversation, I figure that was the hospital. Before you go, give me a proper good-morning kiss."

A proper good-morning kiss? As if she even knew what that was.

In her mind, she tossed everything she held on the floor and dived back into bed with him, smashed her lips to his, rubbed her body all over his until he gave her a proper good-morning everything.

But, um, she couldn't do that.

So she cleared her throat and wished like crazy that she'd not lingered quite so long taking in how beautiful he was. Whereas he was gorgeous in the early-morning light, she imagined her hair was wild, her eyes puffy from lack of sleep, makeup smudged from not having been removed, and how sexy could she possibly be standing there in his too-big clothes?

She was just plain, ordinary Eleanor Aston, nothing

like the glamorous women he was used to who probably gave him glorious mornings-after.

Breathing got more and more difficult. Her palms
grew more and more clammy.

Oh, yeah, she really just wanted to click her heels
together and be far, far away from Ty Donaldson and
all memories of the night they'd shared.

Ty stretched his arms over his head, enjoying the light
ache in his muscles from the night's activities.

The night's very enjoyable, rather vigorous activities
with the siren standing in his bedroom.

Wearing his gym shorts and T-shirt.

Holding her dress, shoes, purse and phone.

Looking like a deer caught in headlights.

The happiness within him dwindled.

"You were leaving, weren't you?"

Her wide eyes and guilty face answered before her
stuttering lips did. "I—I need to go to the hospital."

He shook his head, anger replacing every good feeling he'd awakened with. "Really? You were just going
to sneak out without so much as 'Thank you, Ty'?"

"I…" She glanced down, took a deep breath. "Thank
you, Ty."

His jaw clenched. "For?"

She shrugged. "What is it you want me to say?"

That she'd enjoyed last night as much as he had. That
she hadn't been going to creep out of his apartment
without waking him. That what she'd really like was a
repetition of how they'd spent the night, that she'd felt
all the things he had.

Because even as angry as he was, just looking at her,

at seeing how his T-shirt stretched over those amazing breasts of hers, at seeing the long span of her legs beneath his running shorts, he wanted her. Wanted to pull her back into the bed beside him and kiss her until she was breathless, make love to her until she cried out his name and begged him for more.

Until sneaking out of his house while he slept off the effects of their night together would be the last thing she'd ever consider doing.

He ran his hands through his hair, took a deep breath. "Ellie."

Her weight shifted, drawing his attention to her bare feet. He'd kissed those feet, massaged them and worked his way up her calves and…

"Look, Ty," she began, wincing when his gaze lifted to hers. "I—I have to get to the hospital. One of my patients coded and they couldn't revive her. The family wasn't there, but they've been called and asked to come to the hospital. I need to be the one to tell them."

Ty nodded. As frustrating as he found her leaving without them talking, he understood. He'd feel the same.

As if his thought conjured a call of his own, Ty's phone rang. The hospital. If not for the seriousness that would have prompted the call, he'd have laughed.

He took the call then clicked off his phone.

"There's been a multicar wreck in one of the tunnels. Multiple injuries, at least two of which are infants and another's a pregnant woman. Looks as if you aren't the only one who has to head to the hospital. Let me grab some scrubs for both of us and we'll share a cab."

* * *

Eleanor stepped to the curb as the taxi Ty had hailed came to a screeching halt.

He opened the cab door and waited for her to step in. He'd barely said two words to her since he'd gotten out of bed and grabbed clothes for them both. He was upset that she'd been going to leave without waking him. What had he expected? That she'd snuggle up next to him as if they were longtime lovers? Or that she'd awaken him with kisses and promises of an early-morning repeat?

Was that what he was used to?

"Where to?" the driver asked, eyeing the heels and gown Eleanor carried then letting his midnight gaze travel over the baggy scrubs she wore. With the drawstring waist they weren't too bad and she'd rolled up their long legs to make them work.

Without meeting the driver's gaze, because Lord knew he had to know how she'd spent her night, she spat out the hospital's address.

Ty slid into the backseat next to her.

The cab smelled of years of use badly disguised with an air freshener hanging from the rearview mirror.

So how in the world was it that the one scent that stood out in her mind was that of the man next to her? A scent that filled her mind with memories of the night before.

"You okay, darlin'?"

"Fine," she answered, without glancing toward him. Really, what was she supposed to say? That this was awkward and that, yes, she'd kissed him all over the night before but now she didn't know what to say to him and would like to crawl under the seat?

At least she hadn't stuttered.

Eleanor couldn't keep her eyes from watering as she sat across from the young couple on the sofa. The young couple to whom she'd just delivered devastating news.

"Did she…?" The young woman's head bowed, then her tear-filled eyes lifted to Eleanor. "Did she suffer?"

Shaking her head, Eleanor reached over and took the woman's hand. "No. She died in her sleep."

The baby's body just hadn't been strong enough to maintain life outside her mother's body. She'd lived a week, but only with the aid of the respirator and numerous other machines performing the bodily functions her tiny underdeveloped body hadn't been able to.

"I should have been here," the woman said between tears. "I shouldn't have left the hospital."

"Your family wasn't wrong to want you to go home to get a good night's sleep. Your body is recovering and needs rest," Eleanor assured her, squeezing the woman's hand. Her poor husband had his arm around her but looked as if he was about to burst into tears himself at any moment.

Eleanor spent a few more minutes with the couple then left the room to give them a few minutes of privacy. And to collect her own emotions.

Because she was a mess.

Losing one of her patients always tore her heart to bits, but her heart had already been in tatters before she'd even gotten to the hospital.

"There you are," Ty said from right behind her.

She faced him, couldn't help but immediately be struck with the memories of what they'd done only hours before.

"You okay, darlin'?" he asked, looking and sounding the same as he always did. Like handsome, charming Dr. Tyler Donaldson. Because for Ty last night hadn't been anything out of the ordinary. But he'd probably rightly assumed that for her last night had been extraordinary.

Which was why she had to save face, to pretend she hadn't seen stars when he'd made her orgasm, to pretend that last night hadn't been the best time of her life.

Ha. As if she had that many comparisons. A quickie during her freshman year at college with a short-term boyfriend. Short-term meaning he'd dumped her immediately after their one and only time together.

No way was she letting Ty Donaldson do the same. Not when she had to work with him. Already she'd had to field questions from Scarlet and several other co-workers who'd seen photographs of her and Ty in the society pages. The last thing she wanted was her friends and colleagues to feel sorry for her.

"Of course I'm okay." Which sounded great, but she couldn't bring herself to look into those gorgeous eyes, neither could she prevent the heat burning her face. "Why wouldn't I be?"

His expression tightened. "You just left the family, right? The family of your morning code?"

Eleanor fought putting her hands over her face in shame. He'd been talking about work and she'd been... "Yes. You're right. I—I…"

Oh, please, don't let the stuttering start. He'd know how nervous she was.

He raked his fingers through his hair, glanced around the unit, then for once seemed at a loss. When his gaze met hers, the fatigue she hadn't seen earlier was etched on his handsome face. "I have an emergency C-section that came in this morning. Twins. The pediatrician for the second baby's team isn't here yet. Go in with me in case there are complications?"

Despite the fact that being anywhere near him was the last thing she wanted, she couldn't refuse. Not when a baby's life might be on the line. "Sure."

In silence they scrubbed and went into the obstetrics surgery room specially designated for preemies. Every second that ticked by, Eleanor felt more and more awkward, more and more as if the nurses must be able to look at her and Ty and know what they'd done.

The first baby was delivered without any major birthing complications, but his Apgar score was only a seven. Ty assessed the baby, cleared his throat and examined him all in a matter of seconds.

Watching him work, Eleanor couldn't help but admire his skill, his finesse, the way his big hands were so gentle as they handled the baby. Just as they'd been so gentle when they'd touched her.

He was a gentle man and she hadn't been anything special, just the result of too much champagne and the next notch on his belt. Nothing more.

She closed her eyes, forcing her thoughts from her mind. When she opened them, her gaze immediately collided with Ty's. He stared at her for a brief moment as if trying to read her thoughts, then that sexy crooked grin of his slid into place as a peace offering of sorts.

But Eleanor couldn't smile back.

She just couldn't. Sure, the sight of his generous mouth curved upward made her want to smile back. Instead, she hardened her resolve. He might be used to women thinking he was amazing after a night of his loving, but she needed distance to survive emotionally.

Ty's smile waned. A nurse spoke to him, pulling his attention away from where he still looked at Eleanor as if he wanted to probe inside her head.

The second baby, another boy, made his entrance into the world. Eleanor focused her attention on the newborn, giving him a thorough once-over and realizing his lungs weren't as developed as his brother's.

Telling the nurse her intentions, she gave the baby a few breaths with a manual respirator, hoping to stimulate his lungs, but was unsuccessful in her efforts.

"You want me to intubate him?" Ty asked from beside her. He was so close she could feel his body heat. If she leaned just a little she'd brush against his arm.

"I can do it," she assured him, having done it many times previously and wondering why he'd offered, wondering why she so desperately wanted to lean into him.

"I'm sure you can. Just wanted to help you."

"This is my job," she reminded him. "I'm good at what I do, Dr. Donaldson, but thanks for the offer."

The nurse assisting Eleanor glanced back and forth between them and Eleanor fought against blushing.

She threaded the tiny tube through the baby's nostril, checked placement, then secured the line. She turned to where Ty stood, but he was no longer there. She supposed he'd gone with his team to the NICU, but surprisingly she'd not been aware when he'd walked away.

Good, the less aware she was of the man, the better.

"I know you've had a crazy morning with the code, then talking with the family, then working the trauma delivery with Dr. Donaldson, but you are extraordinarily quiet this morning." Linda stepped up beside Eleanor while she examined a thirty-two-week preemie who was now a month old and would be going home within a week if all continued to progress well. "The fundraiser for your dad run late last evening?"

Frustrated at the recurrent reminders of the night before, Eleanor thought she might scream. She straightened from examining the baby. "How is it that everyone knows where I spent my evening?"

Lord, she hoped they didn't know where she'd spent her night.

Staring at her a little too closely, Linda's brow arched high. "Should I assume that you didn't attend your father's fund-raiser ball, then?"

Sighing with frustration and remorse that she'd snapped at her coworker, Eleanor stroked her fingertip over the tiny baby's precious cheek, loving how his reflexes kicked in and he turned in the direction she'd touched. Developing reflexes was a sign of progress, of increased survival chances.

"No, sorry, you're right," she relented, knowing that she was being overly sensitive, that she just wanted this crazy day to end, and it wasn't even noon yet. "I was there."

"It's not like you to be cranky." Linda's eyes were way too astute. "Things didn't go well?"

"Things went just fine." Hoping she would take the hint, Eleanor made a fuss of continuing to check the little boy, talking to him softly as she did so.

"Dr. Donaldson came, too?"

Oh, he came all right.

Eleanor winced at her crude thought. Her very inappropriate thought. She knew she shouldn't have reacted, that Linda was too keen to have missed the telltale expression.

"Let's not talk about him, okay?" she settled with saying. "I want to know about Rochelle. How is she?"

"She's holding her own." Linda paused for effect, then continued, "You should probably know that he was looking for you after he finished up with the twin."

Eleanor fought to keep from sucking in air. "Maybe he wanted an update on the other twin or something."

"Or something," Linda mumbled as she walked away from the incubator, shaking her head as she went.

Turning back to assess the baby, Eleanor bit her lower lip. What was Ty thinking? Was he relieved that what he probably considered the worst mistake of his life wasn't making a fuss?

She finished examining the baby, entered her notes into the computer, thoroughly cleansed her hands, then moved on to her next little patient.

But before she started, she spotted Ty entering the unit. Her breath caught. The man was way too beautiful. Tall, dark, handsome, fantastic in bed.

A flashback of her naked body tangled with his

flashed through her head. Images of their bodies molded together, gyrating, thrusting, exploding. How was she ever going to look at Ty without remembering? Without thinking of all the marvelous ways he'd touched her body?

He headed straight for her and although she might have tried had she thought she'd be successful, there was no place for her to hide.

"We need to talk about what happened last night."

Hoping no one was close enough to overhear their conversation, she glanced around the nursery. No one seemed to be paying them the slightest attention, but looks could be deceiving.

"Can't we talk about this later?" She really didn't want to talk about it at all. She just wanted to forget.

"Tonight?"

She shook her head. "I'm busy."

Ty's face clouded. "All night? Or you just don't want to spend the evening with me?"

"I have plans." Did reading the latest medical journal and going to the gym count?

His lips pursed. "Cancel them. We need to discuss what happened last night."

Knowing they had to be attracting attention, even if only Linda's, she glanced around the room again. "No, we don't, and especially not here."

Seeming to recall where they were, he glanced around, sighed. "Fine, then go out with me tonight so we can talk somewhere that's not here."

"No." She couldn't risk going out with him again. She wasn't that strong, might end up begging him to kiss her, touch her, take her to heights previously unknown. "But if you insist on having this conversation right now, let's at least go somewhere private."

"You have time for a coffee?"

If it got them away from the prying eyes and ears of their coworkers then she'd make time.

"If we make it quick." She glanced at her watch as if she was doing him a favor by agreeing. At least, she hoped that's how it came across. Every instinct within her told her to not let Ty know how he'd blown her away the night before, to protect herself. "Let me finish my assessment and I'll be right with you."

Hands shaking, heart thumping, blood raging through her vessels, she examined the baby, entered in her notes and new orders, then headed out of the NICU. For coffee.

With the man she'd touched all over with her mouth.

With the man who'd touched her all over with his mouth.

Best she forget. He probably wanted to take her out so he could make sure she knew last night meant nothing.

"Or something," Linda reminded her of her earlier comment with a grin when Eleanor walked by the smug nurse.

Eleanor's face flamed, but she kept walking, not meeting her coworker's eyes.

Yeah, the sooner she got the coffee break over with the sooner she could forget the previous night had happened.

At least, she hoped she could forget.

Ty ordered two coffees, grabbed a couple of sweetener packets and cream and sat down at a table.

"Hey, Dr. Donaldson," a cute little brunette from the surgical floor greeted him, stopping at his table and smiling prettily at him. "You want some company?"

Automatically he grinned at the woman, but he shook his head. He gestured to the second cup of coffee. "I'm meeting Dr. Aston."

Looking disappointed, the woman nodded as if she understood. "Maybe next time."

Although usually he would have flirted back with her as naturally as taking his next breath, Ty didn't say anything, just stirred sugar into his steaming cup of coffee. He hadn't even called her darlin'. What was up with that?

"We can do this later if need be."

He glanced up and knew exactly what was up. Ellie and the night they'd spent together. The amazing, out-of-this-world night they'd spent together.

Her face was red, her gaze wouldn't meet his and she sounded agitated. A new wave of frustration hit him.

"Why would we need to do that?" He took a deep breath, reminded himself that patience was a virtue even if his had felt in short supply from the moment he'd awakened and realized she was skipping out on him.

She gestured in the direction of the departing woman.

He pulled out the chair next to his. "Have a seat."

She sat. Not in the chair next to his but in the one directly opposite. He almost laughed at her bullhead-edness. Any moment he expected her to cross her arms and glare at him in her stereotypical fashion.

If he knew what the hell he'd done to deserve her antagonism, it would be one thing, but as best he could recall, the night had been amazing all the way around.

With care, he slid the cup of coffee across to her along with two packets of sweetener and one cream.

Surprise flickered across her face. "You know how I take my coffee?"

His lips twitched. "We've had coffee together several times over the past week. I pay attention to details."

She tore the packets of sweetener open and poured the contents into her cup. "You'll get no argument from me on that one."

"Meaning?"

She popped the top of the creamer, her face blazing red. "I'd think it obvious. You knew how I take my coffee so you must pay attention to details."

She made a production of stirring, then taking a sip. Ty had to force his gaze away from her mouth to keep from staring, to keep from remembering where that mouth had been during the night.

Why had she been leaving that morning without waking him? Why was she acting as if she was angry with him? Had she not felt the same things he had?

"About last night," he began, but she held up her hand.

"Don't worry about it." She took a slow sip of her coffee as if to stress her next point. "Last night was no big deal."

Ouch. He studied her pale face, trying to read her thoughts, but, as she had for most of the morning, she held her emotions in check. Her face was a blank slate.

"You're sure?" He wasn't. Every aspect of the night had felt like a very big deal. Like something new and wonderful.

"Positive." She set her coffee cup on the table, looked

into his eyes, but quickly glanced away, toying with the empty sweetener packet papers. "We drank too much champagne and got caught up in the celebration."

Sounded feasible to him, except that nothing similar had ever happened before and he hadn't had that much champagne.

As he searched Eleanor's eyes, her claim didn't feel right. Just as the blank expression on her face didn't feel right. Not after having seen her so alive just a few hours before. He wanted a glimpse of her smile, just to see if he'd imagined how his pulse reacted. He wanted to touch her to see if he'd imagined how his body responded to her skin against his.

"Okay, so we drank too much and got caught up in the moment." He didn't buy it, but he'd go with the flow for now. "You were leaving without waking me. Why?"

What was wrong with him? Mornings-after were no big deal. At least, they never had been before.

"If we hadn't gotten called in to the hospital, I would have made you breakfast," he added with a grin, but the gesture didn't feel natural.

Just as she hadn't in the delivery room, Eleanor didn't respond to his grin other than to get pink splotches on her otherwise pale face. "Is that what you usually do? Cook breakfast for your…guests?"

He had cooked breakfast for women before. Several times. But never at his place. He didn't have women at his apartment. Going to their place kept things simpler. Easier to walk away when it wasn't your place you were leaving. He had brought Eleanor to his apartment, made love to her in his bed and she'd been the one who'd been going to walk away. He hadn't liked that one bit.

Ty sighed. He'd had a great time the night before. Not just the sex, but the entire evening. Truthfully, he wouldn't mind a repeat—several repeats. Obviously, she wasn't of the same mind. She'd seemed to enjoy herself well enough, but maybe the champagne really had been why she'd relaxed and smiled so freely at him.

It seemed she wasn't overjoyed that she'd spent the night with him. Actually, she was acting as if he'd been one big disappointment all the way around.

That was a feeling he was all too familiar with.

Well, hell.

"Breakfast?" Ty downed the rest of his coffee in one gulp, not caring that the hot liquid scorched his throat, then stood and answered her question. "Not always, but at least you got a cup of coffee out of the deal."

CHAPTER SEVEN

LEANING BACK IN her chair and staring at the computer screen, Eleanor brushed a loose hair away from her face. Her entire body ached with fatigue and she'd been fighting nausea all morning.

She'd been at the hospital since about 4:00 a.m. Not that she'd been sleeping much since the night she'd spent with Ty. Sleep evaded her and when she did finally drift into sleep, memories haunted her dreams.

She rubbed tight muscles in her neck and left shoulder, forcing herself to quit thinking about Ty yet again. She'd survived five weeks without him and she'd survive the rest of her life, too. She just needed to focus on one day at a time, focus on work.

Rochelle wasn't doing well. The tiny little girl had taken a turn for the worse and nothing Eleanor did seemed to be making a difference.

She studied the baby's chart, looking for anything she might have missed, anything she could try that she hadn't tried already.

There wasn't a logical reason why Rochelle had taken a turn for the worse. The baby had been getting a little stronger each day and then she'd just stopped.

The baby's father hadn't been to see his tiny daughter, was still grieving the loss of his wife and couldn't bear becoming attached to a baby he felt certain wasn't going to live. Eleanor had called him, told him that she was concerned about Rochelle's sudden failure to thrive and that she wasn't sure if they were going to be able to turn the baby's prognosis around. She'd asked him to come to the hospital, but he hadn't made any false promises.

"I heard you were still here."

Eleanor's heart jerked, slamming hard against her rib cage. She hadn't heard Ty walk up to where she worked in the small, private dictation room.

"You not talking to me?"

Taking a deep breath, she glanced up from the computer screen she'd pretended to study to keep from looking at him. She wanted to look so badly it scared her. She wanted to throw herself into his arms. Perhaps never having been the center of all that sexy Texan charm would have been better.

"Sorry," she said slowly, thinking about each syllable in the hope of preventing a stutter. "Just thinking."

"About Rochelle?"

About anything and everything to keep from thinking about him. But she wasn't about to admit how much she'd missed him when he'd obviously not missed her, had obviously moved on with his life, with her not having made a speed bump's worth of difference.

So she told him about the tiny baby girl who she feared had taken a turn for the worse she wouldn't pull back from. "She's dropped weight over the past week."

Ty sank down in the chair next to hers, stretched out

his long legs. "I thought she'd pull through. That she was going to be a success story."

He was so close. Close enough she could smell the spicy clean scent of him. Close enough that his body heat radiated toward her. Close enough that all she had to do was reach out to touch him, to feel his skin beneath her fingertips.

She swallowed. Hard. "Me, too."

In silence, he studied the baby's record. "You've done everything possible."

She knew that the very nature of what they did meant they wouldn't always be successful. "I just keep thinking I've missed something, but I can't figure out what."

"Maybe it's more who you've missed rather than what."

Her breath catching in her throat, her gaze jerked toward him. "I haven't missed you."

Much.

She'd missed him like crazy.

She'd relived every touch shared between Ty and herself, and had cried more tears than she cared to recall.

"Darlin', for the record, I was referring to Rochelle's father." The corner of Ty's mouth twitched, but she wasn't sure if it was with annoyance or an almost smile.

She felt his gaze on her, but she refused to meet his eyes. She just couldn't. "Oh."

"But since you've brought up the subject of missing me—"

"Perhaps you misunderstood," she interrupted, feeling sweat pop out on the back of her neck. "I said I hadn't missed you."

"Perhaps we should discuss just how much you haven't missed me."

"What?" She squinted at him from behind her glasses. "That makes no sense."

"About as much sense as you avoiding me the past few weeks."

Maybe she should take pity on him. After all, he had attempted to talk to her a few times in the NICU when their paths had crossed, but his expression had seemed so forced, his conversation so stilted and underlying with anger that she'd wanted cry. So she'd held fast, avoided him, refusing to become just another woman Ty loved and left by beating him to the punch and keeping distance between them.

"I didn't see you seeking out my company," she pointed out, knowing she probably sounded accusatory.

"Did you want me to seek out your company?"

Had she?

"No."

"Would you have granted me your company if I'd sought you out? Because I got the distinct impression that you wouldn't." He sighed, took her hand in his and studied their locked fingers. "I'm here to find out if you're still going to Texas with me next week."

She'd wondered if he'd want her to, but then had written off the possibility as crazy. Of course he wouldn't want her there. Not after what they'd done. Not after five weeks of awkwardness between them. When she couldn't do more than stutter and blush around him.

"I could see why you might want to reconsider our agreement, but I did keep my end of the deal, which means you owe me."

He really expected her to go with him? Why did that secretly thrill her as much as it scared her? Because she'd missed him and felt desperate for his attention? Lord, she hoped that wasn't it, but feared it just might be.

"Well," she began, glancing toward the computer screen and focusing on a random word, "technically, it was a deal between you and my father, but a deal is a deal, so I really have no choice."

"There's always a choice. If you don't want to go with me, I won't hold you to it."

That got her attention. "Is that your way of telling me you don't really want me to go?"

His expression darkening, he shook his head. "If I didn't want you to go, would I be here talking to you? I want you to go."

What was one weekend with Ty in the grand scheme of life? She could do this. She'd prove to herself and to him that she could do this and then they'd go back to being just colleagues. Plus, maybe the awkwardness would disappear. "I'll go."

"Hey, Dr. Aston?" With a quick rap on the open door Linda poked her head into the dictation room. "I think you'll want to see this." Noticing Ty sitting next to Eleanor, she added, "That you will both want to see."

Silently, they followed the nurse, pausing just outside the nursery.

"Look who stopped by for a visit," Linda whispered excitedly. "Apparently whatever you said to him when you called made all the difference."

Eleanor's heart quickened at the site of Rochelle's

father standing next to his tiny daughter's incubator. It was the first time he'd seen her.

Ty grinned. "I always did think you were one smart woman, Ellie."

Her breath caught at the use of the nickname and she found herself wishing she really did take his breath away each and every time he called her that name. Ellie. How crazy that rather than flinching at the nickname, she wanted to grab the moment and hold it close to her heart?

She cleared her throat. "Babies are smarter than we give them credit for. Rochelle needs her father."

They watched as he gowned, gloved, masked and eyed his baby girl in the incubator. He spoke in a low voice to the little girl. The glistening emotion in his eyes told Eleanor everything he was saying without her being able to hear his actual words.

This was what Rochelle needed. What no tube or medicine or surgical correction could give. She needed her father, the interaction between parent and child.

As if sensing that he was being watched, the man turned, his gaze meeting Eleanor's. "Can I hold her?"

Yes! was all Eleanor could think. Oh, yes! Rochelle needed her father to bond with her, to hold and love her.

Eleanor joined him at the incubator, aware that Ty stayed just a couple of feet back. She gently went over the proper way for Rochelle's father to hold her, then she prepared the baby to be removed from the isolette.

"If you want to sit in one of the rocking chairs, I'll bring her to you."

Looking uncertain, the man nodded, then did as she'd asked.

"Oh, Rochelle, honey," she told the sweet baby girl. "Today is the day you've been waiting for since you were born. Today you met your daddy and now he's going to hold you and fall hopelessly in love with you."

"You want me to get a bottle to let him try to feed her?" Ty asked from beside her, helping to straighten a wire as Eleanor repositioned the baby.

She glanced at him, smiled. "That would be perfect. She's not been taking much by mouth for the past few days, only by her feeding tube, but maybe, just maybe, today is a day for miracles."

She unhooked what could be unhooked, bundled the babe up and with Ty's assistance they brought the baby to the waiting father.

"You won't go far, will you?" he asked, his eyes full of fear when Eleanor lowered the baby into his arms.

"No, Dr. Donaldson and I will be close. No worries," she assured him, understanding his anxiety as many parents of preemies experienced those same fears. Rochelle's dad probably more so than most as he'd waited weeks to see his daughter. No doubt the man was terrified that his coming here might somehow jinx his baby girl's chances. "If anything changes, we will be right here."

Ty watched the pleased smile spread across Eleanor's face and wondered at the pleasure spreading through him. Of course he was happy that Rochelle's father had finally come to visit his baby girl. But the wonder spreading through him had more to do with the woman he watched.

"Look," Ellie whispered, grabbing his shoulder, her voice breaking with emotion.

Ty's attention returned to Rochelle and her father. The man held the little girl awkwardly, but his eyes were filled with awe, with love.

With unshed tears.

"He's talking to her. I wish I could hear what he's saying," Ellie continued, her voice low, full of just as much emotion as Rochelle's father's.

Ty could almost feel the excitement bubbling through her.

"They're bonding."

Ellie glanced at him, smiled beatifically. "Isn't it wonderful?"

Her smile was wonderful.

Her touch on his shoulder.

The light in her eyes.

He'd missed her.

Something in Ty's chest shifted, blossomed, and he realized that if she'd said no to going to Texas, he'd have talked her into it.

He wanted her with him, wanted to show her his family home, introduce her to his family and, more than anything, he wanted her at his side during the weekend. He'd have begged her to go if that was what it would have taken.

That thought worried him almost as much as the thought of seeing his father again did.

On a plane.

With Tyler Donaldson.

On the way to his family's ranch in Swallow Creek, Texas.

Not feeling a hundred percent as she was fighting a nervous stomach.

How were they going to get through the next few days?

Those were the thoughts running through Eleanor's mind while she pretended to be asleep in the first-class airline seat next to Tyler's.

Pretending to be asleep was easier than trying to make polite conversation as they'd done when their paths had crossed since the day Rochelle's father had come to the NICU. They'd shared a moment of truce when Rochelle's father had been present, but otherwise the awkwardness lingered and made her stomach churn even now.

Then again, everything seemed to make her feel nauseated these days. As a child she'd often had stomach issues when she'd got really nervous or upset, but she'd thought she'd outgrown that during her late teens. Recently, that old habit had returned. As if having to deal with her memories wasn't enough torture.

She snuck a quick peek at the man she couldn't keep from her mind.

And caught him staring at her.

"Good nap?"

"Um, yes. Thanks for asking." Heat infused her face at the way he watched her. As if he knew exactly what she'd been doing.

He couldn't possibly know she'd been faking sleep, could he?

Probably. Somehow Ty seemed to know everything.

The plane hit a bit of turbulence and her stomach lurched. Her face must have paled, because Ty's expression instantly grew concerned. His hand covered hers where she clutched at the armrest.

"You okay?"

For answer, she unbuckled her seat restraint and hurried to the lavatory, grateful that no one was there or she'd have had to make do with the little bag provided on the back of the seat in front of hers.

Once inside the small lavatory, she prayed the other passengers couldn't hear her spilling the meager breakfast she'd forced down.

She prayed Ty couldn't hear.

She delayed in the restroom as long as she dared occupy the only lavatory in first class, but the empathetic gazes that met hers when she left the sanctity of the private space told her everyone had heard.

That Ty had heard.

Great.

Without looking directly at him, she sank into her seat, closed her eyes and said a little prayer that her nerves calmed down. Spending the weekend with Ty was stressful enough. Spending the weekend with him with an upset stomach just went off the charts of bad luck.

"I thought it was me," he mused, "but now I'm wondering if perhaps you just don't enjoy flying."

Her gaze shot toward his. "I'm fine."

"Yes, ma'am," he agreed, his eyes studying her. "I can see that by the ashen color of your skin and the way you're holding your stomach."

Why couldn't she be suave and sophisticated around this man? Why did she continually embarrass herself?

She dug through her purse, searching for a breath mint and popping one into her mouth prior to answering him.

"My stomach acts up sometimes when I get nervous."

"You don't like flying?"

"Th-that's not it."

He considered her answer, then asked, "You're nervous about this weekend? Isn't that my job? You never have to see these folks again. They're my family. I'm stuck with them."

That got her attention, made her stomach lurch. For Ty their relationship was truly temporary. When they returned from Texas, whatever this was between them would well and truly be done. They'd deal with each other at the hospital and nothing more. Which should be just fine by her since she hadn't really expected more of the weekend than fulfilling her end of a deal, had she? She hadn't fantasized that Ty was going to take her into his big Texan arms and tell her he'd missed her as much as she had missed him and that they'd go back to New York as a couple. Nope, no way had she been that gullible and naive.

Willing her stomach to settle because, really, there couldn't be anything left in there, she watched him. "I know you said you and your dad had an argument, but surely you're excited to see your family?"

He didn't look sure.

"How long has it been since you've been home, Ty?" Her question was soft, but had the impact of someone shaking the plane.

"Years." Had Ty made a run for the lavatory and retched, Eleanor wouldn't have been surprised.

She placed her hand over his, meaning to comfort him but only managing to send her pulse into orbit at the flesh-to-flesh contact. Would touching him always affect her so? Always pull her back to memories best forgotten?

They both stared at where her hand covered his, at how her thumb had begun to trace a pattern over his. No, she definitely hadn't had any false hopes where the weekend was concerned.

"You've told me a little about your family, but I'd like to know more before we arrive."

He didn't speak at first and she thought he was going to ignore her or tell her to mind her own business, but finally that sexy Texan drawl of his began to tell her about his life.

"My mother is the greatest woman. Kind, loving, strong. There's nothing the woman can't do. Growing up, I was just as likely to see her out breaking a horse with my father as I was to see her inside, canning vegetables. She wins the bread-baking contest at the county fair every year and has for as long as I can recall. She worked from dawn to late into the night every day, but always found time for my brother and I." He smiled as if a good memory was playing through his mind. "Rarely was there a night that went by that we weren't read a bible story, made to say our prayers, tucked in and kissed good-night by her."

Eleanor smiled at his idealistic-sounding childhood. How wonderful it must have been to grow up in such a loving family environment. "You said your brother is three years older than you? He's your only sibling?"

He nodded. "Mom wanted more, but there was just us two boys. Probably just as well as we kept her running."

"She sounds wonderful."

"She is." Which meant his mother wasn't anything to do with why he dreaded going home. Then again, he'd already said who it was he didn't get along with.

"Tell me about this father who scares you."

Leaning his head back against the plush first-class seat, Ty snorted. "I was kidding when I said that."

She couldn't imagine him afraid of anything, but there was definitely something off in his relationship with his father.

"Your tone changes when you speak of him," she pointed out in what she hoped was a gentle voice. The skin tightened on his face, too, but she didn't point that out.

He sighed, shifted his hand to where their fingers laced. "I don't talk about my father usually. Life is better that way. Actually, you're the only person I've talked to about him other than my mother and brother."

Why did his admission make her feel as if she was different from the other women he'd been with? That maybe she hadn't imagined just how special their night had been?

"But," he said with another sigh, "since I'm dragging you into the middle of my life, I should prepare you. Can't have you walking in unawares and being blindsided."

"Being blindsided?"

"I told you that the last time I was home my father

and I had a disagreement." His lips twisted and a flicker of hurt flashed in his eyes. "I left swearing I'd never set foot in Swallow Creek again."

He still looked at her, but Eleanor wasn't so sure Ty saw her. He looked lost in the past, a dark, unpleasant place that held a tight grip on his present.

She lifted a shoulder. "That's a silly thing to swear about a place where the people you love live."

He blinked, clearing whatever had momentarily come over him. He laughed at her comment, but the sound didn't come out as natural. "You're right, and here I am headed back, ready to eat my words."

Still fighting nausea, she let his admission soak in, trying to understand the man sitting next to her, holding her hand as if she were his lifeline rather than the other way around, as it had been earlier. "Why now? Why go back after all this time? Because of the rodeo?"

He took a deep breath. "My mom's been on me from the moment I left to come back, but she understands my love of medicine." He smiled, thoughts of his mother obviously easing some of his tension. "But lately she's been pushing more and more. With Dad hosting the rodeo this year, she wouldn't let up until I promised I'd be there."

His poor mother must have missed him like crazy and been frantic to repair the rift within her family. But at no point had Ty sounded as if he wanted this trip home.

"Why did you agree if you don't really want to do this?"

He glanced at her, seeming surprised that she'd

pushed further. She knew there was more than he was telling her.

"Lots of reasons. I do miss my family." He frowned, then added, "Mostly. Plus, if I don't come home, she and my whole family are going to come to New York for an extended visit."

"Would that be so bad?"

That lopsided grin lifted one side of his handsome face. "Ask me that again after you've met my family."

She smiled, glad to see his usual smile back in place and hating it that something he'd said nagged at her brain. Hated it because she suspected when she asked him about it his smile was going to slip, but she wanted to understand this man beside her. Which was crazy. After this weekend, they'd probably go back to barely talking to each other.

"You said your mother understood your love of medicine."

There went the smile.

"Does that mean your father doesn't?" she pushed, wondering if her suspicions were correct.

"Let's just say I'm not the son who makes him proud." His jaw working, Ty gave a nonchalant shrug, as if her question was of little consequence, as if his answer was of little consequence. But she saw the clench of his jaw, the quickening pulse at his throat, felt the slight unsteadiness in his hand. His answer revealed a vulnerability in him that made her feel protective, as if she wanted to shield him from anyone who dared to treat him with less than the utmost love and respect.

Which really was crazy.

Ty was a six-foot-four Texan hunk. Not some wall-flower who needed her to run interference.

Despite him rescuing her at the ribbon-cutting, the time they'd spent together at the hospital, the fund-raiser and afterward, well, really, they barely knew each other.

Yet she did feel as if she knew him. That he knew her. Really deep down knew each other.

Which was even crazier.

She fought leaning over and taking him into her arms. It was what she wanted to do. She doubted he'd welcome her sympathy, her comfort.

She settled with giving his hand a gentle squeeze and saying quietly, "Then your brother must be an ex-ceptionally amazing man."

CHAPTER EIGHT

THANK GOD HE'D brought Ellie with him, Ty thought for the hundredth time since they'd arrived in Texas. Everyone was so busy falling over themselves to meet the woman he'd brought that no one had mentioned the last time he'd been home.

His mother's welcoming arms squeezed him tightly.

"I'm so glad you're home, son." Her voice broke just a smidge, causing his chest to constrict more than a little. Then she pecked his cheek and turned to the quiet, elegant woman standing at his side. "Eleanor, that's the prettiest skirt I think I've ever laid eyes on. Wherever did you find it?"

First looking at him as if to gauge how he'd responded to his mother's hug and to make sure he was okay, Eleanor turned to his mother and smiled.

"There's this fantastic shop just a couple of blocks from the hospital. It's owned by a family I met when their son was born a couple of weeks early. We've stayed in touch." Her face became animated as she launched into a tale of some of the other bargains she'd found there.

Ty couldn't help but think how pretty she looked. Beautiful, actually. Ellie was beautiful.

He was so glad she was at his side.

From the moment they'd arrived at the airport and been greeted by Harry, Eleanor had been truly wonderful. Despite her bout of travel sickness on the plane, she smiled at all the right times. She asked questions at all the right times. Surprisingly, his shy, quiet Eleanor had even kept up the conversation during the few short, awkward moments that had passed between him and his brother when their father had come up in the conversation.

By the time his brother had helped load their luggage onto the small private twin-engined plane in which Harry would fly them to the ranch, they'd been conversing like, well, like long-lost brothers.

"I'll have to fly up to the city for a shopping trip with you," his mother suggested, still going on about Eleanor's skirt.

Harry and Ty both laughed. Their mother shopping in New York City? She was the most no-nonsense woman they knew, rarely even made it into Houston to shop, and that was only a couple hours' drive away. She rewarded them with a motherly frown.

Ellie glanced back and forth between them, obviously confused by their laughter. She smiled politely at his mother. "That would be nice, but if you do, I'll introduce you to my sister. She's the expert shopper."

Based on the dress she had told him that Brooke had arranged for the ribbon-cutting ceremony, Ty couldn't argue. That dress had accented Eleanor's curves superbly, but the truth was it didn't matter what she wore.

Over the past six weeks, seeing her at the hospital in her shapeless scrubs hadn't helped one bit. He knew what she hid beneath and just the memory of her curvy body had his hands itching to touch, had him wanting to beg her to reconsider.

Ty's mother hustled them toward the large eat-in kitchen. When Ty stepped into the room, he breathed in the smell of being home. The room held a lot of memories. Good memories of sitting in here with Harry and his mother while she cooked their breakfast on school mornings. Not-so-good memories of the last row between him and his father, which had also taken place in the room.

Odd, but most of the major conversations of his life had taken place in the Donaldson kitchen.

As if his mother knew exactly what he was thinking about or, more aptly, who, she patted his shoulder. "Your father hated not being able to be here to welcome you home, son, but he had to go to the rodeo to make sure things are coming along on schedule. He's swamped with last-minute details." Her eyes didn't quite meet his, but she pasted another bright smile on her face and hugged him yet again. "Now, let's get the two of you fed. I've left lunch out because I know you must be starved."

Ty's gaze went from his mother to Eleanor. Her thick lashes swept her cheeks. She probably was starved after her bout of travel sickness on the plane. She'd disappeared into the ladies' room at the airport long enough to freshen up and to put her contact lenses in. That had surprised him, but he'd been grateful because nothing blocked his view of her face.

Plus, seeing her without her glasses reminded him of the night of her father's fund-raiser. Which was really a reminder of what had happened after the fund-raiser.

Which made Ty realize he was starved.

But not for food.

Ellie was all he hungered for.

Despite the awkwardness between them since the night they'd spent together, he hadn't stopped wanting her. He missed her and wanted her in his life. And not just at the hospital. Seeing her face light up with a smile did odd things to his insides and he wasn't in denial now.

He wanted her, was going to thoroughly enjoy the next few days of her company, and use the time to convince her they'd shared something special.

"Come along, Ellie. Let's see what my mother has rustled up for us." Ty took her hand in his and grinned at her surprised, pink-cheeked expression at his use of her nickname. Along with the entourage of family who tagged along behind them, he led her to the long solid oak table that matched the cabinets and woodwork.

Harry's son, William, had taken an instant fascination with Eleanor and climbed into the chair opposite hers, staring at her as if she were some big-city goddess. The four-year-old had almost doubled in size since the last time Ty had seen him.

Nita, Harry's wife, chatted a mile a minute about the one time she'd visited New York and how she'd like to come along for his mother's suggested shopping trip, too. His mother busied herself with hostess duties. His brother had kicked back and was watching all the commotion with a lazy grin on his face. Their eyes met and they shared a grin.

Ty's heart squeezed. This was his family. He'd missed them a whole lot more than he'd acknowledged. He should have come home a long time ago, been here for the holidays, been here where William wouldn't have had to rely on the multitude of family photos all over the house to remember who his long-lost uncle Ty was.

But he knew the moment his father got home he'd recall all the reasons he'd left, that within seconds he'd most likely be ready to hop on the first plane back to New York.

"Ellie." His mother used the name she'd heard Ty call her by, concern in her voice. "Is your food not to your liking, dear? I'd be happy to cook something else for you if there's something you'd prefer."

Ty's mind jerked to the present, stunned to realize that he'd demolished every scrap of his mother's delicious home cooking but Eleanor had barely touched her food.

Looking a little pale, she shook her head. "Everything is delicious. I just wasn't that hungry. I'm sorry."

"Don't be sorry, child." His mother's eyes softened as they regarded Eleanor. "If you're not hungry then you're not hungry."

William nudged his mother's arm. "See, Momma, I shouldn't have to clean my plate when I'm not hungry. Grammy says so."

Leaning forward, Harry winked at his son. "You're a growing boy and need your meat and potatoes to make you grow up strong like your old man."

"What he means is like your uncle Ty," Ty corrected,

but his eyes never left Eleanor. Her skin had grown pasty, almost a pale gray. "You okay, darlin'? Is your stomach acting up again?"

Bright red color splotched her cheeks as she lifted pleading eyes to him. Eyes that begged to get her somewhere private pronto. Purplish smudges darkened beneath them, almost as if her skin was bruised, and guilt hit him. He'd been so self-absorbed that he'd totally missed that she still wasn't feeling up to par.

"A little," she admitted. "I've never traveled well. Sorry."

His mother must have read her look accurately, too, because before Ty could do more than reach for her hand, she jumped in. "Ty, take this poor girl to your room and let her rest for a bit. She looks exhausted."

His and Ellie's gazes met as realization dawned. He hadn't really thought about where his brother had put her bags. Not in one of the guest rooms as there would be more family coming in for the rodeo and the house would be at full capacity, as would the guesthouse and the bunkhouse. Harry had put her belongings in Ty's room.

Because everyone had assumed she was his girlfriend and that that was where he'd want her sleeping.

That was where he wanted her sleeping. With him.

Of course, if Ellie was in his bed, neither of them would be doing much sleeping.

Then again, with how frail she looked at the moment, he should keep his hands to himself. And other wayward body parts that had a predilection for her.

As much as he wanted her, at the moment he just wanted to take care of her.

"Come on," he said, standing from the table and taking her hand. "Let's get you upstairs for a nap. It's been a long day already since we left LaGuardia this morning."

"I…" she started to argue. He knew that was what she was about to do because her phenomenal etiquette would think it rude to disappear so quickly. But she stopped, which told him just how poorly she felt. Another wave of guilt hit him. How could he have been so lost in his own homecoming misery that he'd been oblivious to her exhaustion and just how much effort she was making to hide how ill she really felt? He felt a grade-A jerk.

He *was* a grade-A jerk.

Because when he'd not been lost in the past, he'd been thinking about the night they'd shared and how he'd been wanting a repetition ever since.

"After our trip this morning, resting for a short while would be heavenly. Thank you." Still, she turned to his mother. "Can I help you clear the dishes before I go?"

His mother beamed at her perfect manners, shot Ty a thumbs-up, I-like-this-girl look. "No, Carmelita has already taken care of everything else so there's only these. She and I will get everything cleaned up in a jiffy. Nita will help."

Watching the conversation curiously, Ty's sister-in-law nodded her agreement.

"You go and rest so you will be refreshed for the rodeo this weekend and meeting the rest of the family. They're all looking forward to meeting the first woman Ty's ever brought home to meet us." As if she couldn't stop herself, his mother pulled her into her arms for a big hug. "We are so glad to meet you, Ellie, and to welcome you to our house and family. This is just wonderful."

Eleanor bit back both her wince at Ty's mother's use of "Ellie" and the nausea she'd been fighting from the moment she'd smelled food. What was wrong with her? Usually her bouts of nervous stomach didn't last so long.

Then again, usually her bouts of nerves weren't triggered by a trip to Texas with a gorgeous hunk she'd spent a night naked with several weeks ago.

Ha, it had never been triggered by that until Ty and this trip. She'd truly believed he'd have invited someone else or have gone alone.

Not that he'd been linked to anyone since her.

Or if he had, she hadn't gotten the gossip memo.

Since Ty seemed to be Linda's favorite topic of conversation these days, Eleanor was positive she would have heard if Ty had so much as looked in another woman's direction. He hadn't.

Why hadn't he?

He led her up a majestic curved gleaming oak staircase to the second story of the sprawling Texan mansion that spoke of wealth, functionality and family.

Because unlike the magazine picture-perfectness of her parents' various homes, the Donaldson mansion was filled with love, with family photos and knickknacks that, without asking, Eleanor knew had special meaning. The house was lived in and full of love.

"I like your family," she said when they were almost to the top of the stairs.

Holding her hand tightly in his, Ty snorted. "You

may want to withhold judgment until you meet my father. He's the scary one, remember?"

Eleanor's heart squeezed at the pain she heard in his voice. All her life she'd lived knowing that she didn't quite fit in with her family, but never had she doubted that they loved her in their own way. Even Brooke had her loving-family moments such as when she'd insisted upon helping Eleanor pack yesterday and had given Eleanor a pair of bright red designer boots for her trip to Texas. Ty's voice didn't convey that same knowledge of love. Not where his father was concerned.

"You want to talk about it?"

He shook his head. "No, I just want to get you into bed." He waggled his brows and grinned. "For once not so I can take your clothes off you. Seriously, Ellie, you should have told me you still weren't feeling well. We didn't have to do the whole family thing right then. They can be a bit overwhelming. You could have rested first."

Although she knew he was purposely distracting her from the conversation he didn't want to have, she let him. If he didn't want to tell her about his relationship with his father, what right did she have to pry? After all, she was only the date he had bartered with her father for.

Plus, she really did feel exhausted and so nauseated that she really might throw up again. She hoped not. How embarrassing would that be?

"Honestly, I felt better until we walked into the kitchen. When I smelled the food I just…" She paused, realizing what she'd said and feeling horrible. "I didn't mean that there was anything wrong with your mother's cooking, just that—"

He grinned. "Relax, Ellie. I know what you meant and it's okay." He winked, then opened a door and stepped back for her to enter first.

Immediately on stepping into the room, she was overwhelmed with Ty. With his past and his present. There were all sorts of paraphernalia from his life scattered throughout the darkly masculine room. Obviously at some point his mother had thought the room needed updating to her grown son's tastes, but she hadn't been willing to let go of her little boy either.

"You used to compete in the rodeo?" she asked, walking up to a shelf that was filled with various trophies, plaques and photos of Ty on horses, of Ty roping a calf, of a teenage Ty sliding onto the back of a monstrous-looking cow. "I thought you said you were too tall."

Although he'd paused on stepping into the room, his room, which he hadn't been in for years, that crooked grin of his slid into place. "I'm a true, full-blooded Texan, darlin'. Of course I competed in the rodeo. Besides, I wasn't always this tall."

She gestured to the vast display of awards. "Looks like you were pretty good."

His grin widened and mischief twinkled in his eyes. "Was there ever any doubt?"

She gave him a small smile. "Never. I bet you always won the cow-riding events."

He burst out laughing, slid his hand around her waist and turned her toward the bed. "It's bull riding, darlin'," he corrected her. "Come on. You can check out all this stuff Mom keeps out later. Right now, I want you resting."

He led her to the king-size bed that suddenly domi-
nated the room. They both stopped, stood staring at it.

"You grew up sleeping in this giant bed?" Had her
voice just broken?

He shook his head. "Early on Harry and I shared
bunk beds. Later, when we went into rooms of our own,
I got this furniture. Guess Mom expected us to keep
growing."

"She's tiny, so your dad must be a giant of a man."

"He is."

Ty's soft words twisted her heart, made her want to
wrap her arms around him and hold him tightly to her.

"You look exhausted, Ellie."

She did feel worn out, which was unlike her. It was
probably that she hadn't slept well due to nerves the
night before and the travel sickness on the plane had
also taken its toll. Yet she couldn't bring herself to climb
into Ty's bed so she stood, staring at the big bed.

"Here, let me." He yanked the deep brown comforter
back, then gently pushed her down onto the bed in a
sitting position.

What he did next surprised her. More like stunned
her.

He dropped to his knees, slipped her shoes off her
feet and set them aside. His hands slid up her calves,
massaged along the way, paused at her knees, leaning
forward and kissing each one, then, over her skirt, up
her thighs, her hips, to her waist.

He placed his palms against her upper arms and
gently guided her backward. "Lie back, Ellie, and take
a load off."

She did, letting him pull the covers around her and

tuck her in as if she were a small child, then he straightened, stood staring at her with an odd look in his eyes.

Suddenly she felt terribly alone in the big bed.

"Ty, hold me."

His brows went together in a surprised V, but he kicked off his shoes and slid into the bed next to her.

He wrapped his arms around her, held her close to him in spoon fashion and dropped a kiss on her hair. "Now, close your eyes and be very still, Ellie, or else we're going to have a problem."

It only took her a second to realize what he meant. Giddiness bubbled up inside her. She twisted around to face him, stared into his beautiful eyes and couldn't keep from smiling.

"You really find me attractive, don't you?"

He gave her a quizzical look. "Why wouldn't I find you attractive? You are a beautiful, amazing, sexy woman, Ellie. Any man would have to be blind not to find you attractive." He slid his palm over the curve of her hip. "Of course a blind man would have to feel his way. Then he'd know how hot you were firsthand, too."

Eleanor's insides melted. Unable to stop herself, she stretched forward and closed the distance between their lips. Just a soft brushing of her lips against his. It was the first time they'd kissed since the night of the fundraiser. Instantly, longing shot through her. Longing for the way she'd felt that night. Longing for the way she felt at this very moment, touching him.

"Now you're just tempting fate," he warned in a low voice. "You're supposed to be resting."

She blinked at him, not so innocently. "What if I don't feel so very tired anymore?"

Amazingly, she didn't. That was crazy, as moments before just holding her head up had almost required too much effort, but lying in Ty's arms, kissing him, energized her, cured her finicky stomach.

His brow arched, a boyish grin on his face, his eyes twinkling with delight. "Darlin', were you playing possum to get me into bed and take advantage of me?"

Her gaze not wavering from his, she shook her head and with great clarity knew exactly what she wanted. "No, but kiss me, Ty. Kiss me as if you mean it."

His expression growing serious, his eyes darkened. "I do mean it, Ellie. When I kiss you, I mean every touch."

She wasn't sure what he meant by his words or even what she'd meant by her request. Not until his lips touched hers.

Then she knew.

He kissed her softly and slowly, yet with an undercurrent of urgency that let her know he wanted more, that he struggled to keep from deepening the kiss. His hands ran over her body just as softly and slowly, as if she were a prize to be treasured.

That was how he made her feel, how he'd made her feel that night. Like she was the most important woman in the whole world to him. Like she was the only woman.

For now that was enough.

That was everything.

CHAPTER NINE

ELEANOR'S NOSE WRINKLED even before they stepped inside the long sheet-metal building they were headed toward, which Ty called the main barn. There was a definite outdoorsy smell to the cold, crisp February Texas air. Fortunately, her nausea had completely passed.

As had her fatigue.

Amazing what phenomenal sex did for a person.

And the sex *had* been phenomenal. Part of her had wondered if her recall of how fantastic Ty was had been due to too many glasses of the champagne she'd consumed.

Definitely not.

They'd napped for an hour or so afterward. Now she just felt great.

She snuggled more fully into the thick coat Ty's mother had insisted she wear when they'd headed out the door and she'd only had her overcoat. His mother had also found her a pair of boots to put on so she didn't have to worry about soiling her shoes.

"I like your family, Ty." Not that she'd met his father yet. The great man had yet to return from the arena where the rodeo was being held. Her breath made a puff of smoke in the crisp air.

"Good." He clasped her gloved hand. "They like you, too."

Her gaze cut toward him as they continued their trek toward the barn. "Am I really the first girl you've brought home?"

Staring at her from beneath the cowboy hat he'd donned before they'd left his bedroom, he feigned a sigh. "Caught that, did you?"

"What can I say?" She smiled, despite the frigid air stinging her face. "Smart chick, remember?"

He turned to look at her, his eyes like molten chocolate. "I remember everything about you, Ellie."

At the warmth in his voice, her insides lit.

"But to answer your question, there were a few local girls during high school who came to the ranch. But during college and afterward…" he shrugged beneath the heavy work coat he'd donned "…I just didn't meet anyone I wanted to bring to Swallow Creek."

"You brought me." Her heart slammed against her rib cage. She knew it didn't mean anything, that she'd only been a convenient, uncomplicated buffer between his family and the circumstances under which he'd left Swallow Creek.

Only more and more her relationship with Ty wasn't feeling convenient or uncomplicated.

Sex complicated everything.

"A wise decision on my part."

Uncertainty hit her. "Because of what happened in your room?"

He pushed an aluminum door open, pulled her inside

the building. Warmth swamped her as she stepped onto the concrete floor. Her idea of a "barn" was nothing like the extensive heated metal building in which they stood. This was more like a minibusiness complex. She supposed it was. At the far end she could see areas that appeared to be stables, but at this end there were office spaces and everything was quite meticulous.

Ty shed his gloves, unzipped his jacket and pulled it off. "What just happened was fantastic, but that wasn't what I meant. I meant because I enjoy being with you— your company, your smile, just holding your hand."

"Oh."

Grinning, he rubbed his finger across her cold nose. "Yeah…oh."

After taking her coat, gloves and scarf and hanging them, along with his, in one of the small offices, he took her hand and showed her around the main barn, one of several barns on the Triple D, apparently. He introduced her to some of the hands, let her feed an apple to a mare, then proudly showed her his stallion, Black Magic.

"Why have a horse when you've not been home for years, Ty?"

He stared at the horse, his expression contemplative. "He's a Thoroughbred and a champion, so he brings a high stud fee." He'd shown her a room earlier where those stud fee samples were kept frozen. "That more than pays for his upkeep, but maybe you're right. Maybe I should sell him as I'm not around."

Eleanor glanced back at the magnificent animal that snorted and grunted as if giving his own feedback to his long-gone owner. Something in Ty's tone said he didn't want to let the horse go, that really he was ready to heal past wounds, but perhaps Ty himself wasn't even aware of what she heard.

"Or maybe," she suggested softly, hoping she wasn't overstepping the boundaries of their tentative, confusing relationship, "you should come home and ride him more often."

Ty held Ellie's hand tightly in his as they walked into the Swallow Creek Arena where the rodeo was being held. Tonight's agenda was more about family fun and kicking off the rodeo than actual competitions. There were kids' events, exhibits, a barbecue cook-off and a barn dance.

From the time they made their entrance, familiar faces greeted Ty, introduced themselves to Eleanor and told him how good it was to see him.

No one mentioned his father.

But no doubt about it, he'd be seeing his father soon.

Acid gurgled in his stomach.

He glanced at Ellie in her jeans and Western-style snap-up that his sister-in-law had insisted she wear. It seemed his whole family was planning to dress her before the weekend ended, but Ellie took it all in her stride, smiling and going along with their wardrobe suggestions.

The jeans were a little snug and looked good clinging to her body. The shirt did nothing to hide her generous curves and looked even better. Ty's mouth watered just recalling what those curves felt like in his hands, his mouth, pressed to his body.

And the boots. There wasn't a single practical thing about Ellie's red boots but hell if they weren't his favorite part about her outfit. Somehow the bright boots suited her, the real her, the passionate woman beneath the surface.

"You okay?" she asked, her big eyes looking up at him.

"Fine," he answered, squeezing her hand gently. "I'm fine, darlin'. Just so long as I have you at my side."

Which crazily enough was true. Having her next to him both excited and calmed him.

"Just thinkin' how much I liked your boots." He grinned, liking how her gaze dropped to her boots and a blush that almost matched their bright color spread across her cheeks. "And what's in 'em," he added, just to watch the color in her cheeks deepen.

"Ty Donaldson?" a familiar feminine voice called out from behind them with a distinctive Southern drawl. "Is that really you?"

"Layla?" Ty spun, surprise filling him at the sight of the pretty little blonde barreling toward him. He held his arms out and she stepped into them. "Layla! What are you doing here? Last I heard you were practicing in Florida."

She hugged him then smiled up at him as if he was a sight for sore eyes. "I'm still in Miami. How about you? You still a big-city doc up North?"

"Absolutely. Angel's is where I was meant to be. There's no place in the world I'd rather practice than at that hospital."

Ellie shifted at his side and he put his arm at her waist, proudly pulling her close to him. "Excuse my been-away-from-the-South-too-long rudeness, Layla.

This is Dr. Eleanor Aston. She's a pediatrician at Angel's. One of the best. Y'all have a lot in common."

Eleanor told herself that it didn't mean a thing that Ty introduced her as a coworker and not as his weekend date. Or that he'd introduced her as "Eleanor" rather than the "Ellie" he'd taken to calling her by. Or that when he'd said they had a lot in common she'd instantly wondered if he meant they'd both slept with him.

She was just being overly sensitive when there was no reason. But when the petite woman had launched herself into Ty's arms, Eleanor had felt overly sensitive, gawky and jealous.

Jealous. Her. She really wasn't the jealous type.

She winced. She had no claims to Ty. None whatsoever. Yet…

She was jealous of the slender young woman Ty grinned at as if she were his long-lost best friend.

"Layla is the daughter of Swallow Creek's longtime mayor, Rick Woods. She was one of my closest friends from school."

Okay, so maybe she was his long-lost best friend. Or did he mean closest as in former girlfriend? Hating the way she was reacting, Eleanor pulled in her little green monster and accepted the smiling woman's outstretched hand.

"I have Ty to thank for encouraging me to go into medicine," Layla said, shaking Eleanor's hand with enthusiasm. "I owe him big-time."

"Hmm." Ty scratched his chin. "Then maybe you should consider moving up North so you can pay your debt."

Eleanor's gaze jerked to him, but she couldn't read anything beyond the friendly grin on his relaxed face. Was he flirting with the woman? What was she thinking? Of course Ty was flirting. It was what he did with every woman.

Layla gave him a confused look. "What would I do up North?"

"More good than you'd believe possible. You should come and work at Angel's."

Layla gave him a thoughtful look. "Why do you say that?"

"Although nothing's official, the current head of Pediatrics is going to make a career change. Soon. You'd be the perfect person to take his place."

Interest flickered on the blonde's face, but she still looked hesitant.

"You'd like working at Angel's, Layla. Those kids reach in, grab your heart and don't let go. The entire hospital is about serving others, giving to those in need. If ever I question my life choices, all I have to do is step into that hospital to know I'm exactly where I'm meant to be, helping those who can't help themselves."

Eleanor bit her lower lip. Ty was right, of course. There was no place like Angel's. While she stood, feeling more and more out of place, they chatted about Angel's awhile longer, about Ty's family, about a couple of mutual friends.

"Have you seen Luke since you've been home?"

Her smile fading and her expression growing guarded at Ty's question, Layla shook her head. "I'm just here for a few days to visit with Mom and Dad."

"That going okay?"

A smile that Eleanor could only describe as sad slid onto the woman's face. "Probably about as well as your visit. How's your father?"

"Right." Ty laughed, put his arm around Eleanor's waist, instantly making her feel a little better. What was wrong with her? She shouldn't be jealous of his easy camaraderie with the woman. It wasn't as if she hadn't seen him talk to hundreds of women at Angel's. Then again, perhaps she'd never really liked that either.

His thumb rubbing across the indent at Eleanor's lower back, toying with the waistband of her jeans, Ty's gaze remained on Layla. "Why don't you come grab a seat with Ellie and me? We'll tell you more about the Angel Mendez Children's Hospital and why you should think about joining our team."

Ellie. He'd called her Ellie. Instantly, the tension that had been gripping her shoulders eased and she let out the breath she hadn't even realized she'd been holding. Who would have ever thought that the nickname would make her feel better instead of worse?

"You're sure I wouldn't be intruding?" Layla looked back and forth between Ty and Eleanor.

Reining in the remainder of her green monster, Eleanor shook her head. "No, please do. I want to hear all about Ty's youth. Maybe you could tell me some good stories for me to tease him about."

Layla smiled back, hooked her arm through Eleanor's and began to do just that.

Later, Eleanor admitted that she liked the beautiful young doctor from Ty's past. It hadn't hurt that he'd kept Eleanor close, holding her hand while they talked, asking for her input regarding Angel's. That Layla had been sweet, friendly and not once had she looked at Ty in any way that made Eleanor feel uncomfortable. Once she'd gotten over her initial jealousy, she'd realized that nothing more than friendship had ever existed between the two.

The three of them had eaten barbecue and laughed at some of the children's antics during the kids' events. They'd laughed at some of the animals' antics, too.

With a heartfelt sigh Layla excused herself when her mother motioned to her. Eleanor and Ty continued to check out exhibits, talk to his old friends and generally enjoy the chaos that was apparently the rodeo. They remained all smiles until a giant of a man stepped up beside them and slapped Ty on the back

Without really looking at the man's features, Eleanor knew who he was.

Ty's body language did a one-eighty from relaxed and happy to tight and agitated. All without the man saying a single word.

Just a touch and his father sent him into an obvious tailspin.

"You ready to pack up and come home from that big city to be a real man?"

Had his father's first words to Ty in years really been those? Next to her, Ty's spine straightened and she felt the tension bristling within him.

She wasn't exactly sure what she should do, but she knew she needed to do something to defuse the situation before sparks flew. She stuck out her hand and politely introduced herself. "Hi, I'm Eleanor Aston. You must be Ty's father."

The older man turned astute golden-brown eyes

toward her. Definitely, she'd have recognized him as Harry and Ty's father. The likeness was strong with the man's handsome but more weathered face and tall-body build. But that was where the similarities ended because, whereas Ty was always smiling and oozing charm, this man's face bore a scowl that appeared permanently etched into his features.

"You are?" he asked.

Ty's jaw clenched and she could feel him counting forward, backward, asking for patience to keep from reacting to his father.

"Ty's big-city guest from New York. Born and raised and absolutely love it there." Had that confident, almost sassy reply really been her? Without a single stutter? Wow. Generally, she was all about keeping the peace but this man obviously had no real appreciation for the wonderful son he had. Any man who was too blind to see Ty for his true self didn't register too highly in her opinion.

His father's expression remained unreadable, but before he could respond Ty spoke. "Great to see you, too, Dad. Layla's home for the rodeo, too."

Ignoring the first part of Ty's comment, his father shook his head as if in disgust. "A shame that you two were raised right and both took off for parts unknown to take care of babies. Her I can understand. She's a woman." His expression slipped into one of true confusion. "But you? My son? Babies?"

Apparently Ty's dad lived in another century. Eleanor slipped her hand into Ty's and gave it a reassuring squeeze. "That's what neonatologists do. There's no nobler profession than to save lives and who better to save than precious newborn babies?"

"Ellie—" Ty began, but didn't finish as they were interrupted.

"There you two are!" His mother stepped up, all smiles, but her gaze went back and forth anxiously between Ty and his father. "Harold, Harry was looking for you. William is up in a few. He thought you might have a few words of advice prior to his turn. You're so good at that kind of thing."

The giant of a man Ty called his father looked at his wife as if he knew exactly what she was doing, but he just nodded. "Fine, I'll go talk to the boy." His gaze went back to Ty, dropped to where his and Eleanor's hands were clasped, then he shook his head. "Ain't like there's a lot to riding a sheep, though, and he didn't need my input when he won the calf-roping competition. That boy may only be four, but he has been taught right."

His father mumbled a few more things that Eleanor didn't quite catch before he disappeared through the crowd to go and encourage his grandson. At least, she hoped he was going to encourage his grandson. After how he'd interacted with Ty she had to wonder if the man knew how.

His mother gave them an apologetic look, then took off after her husband, no doubt to grill him about what he'd been saying to Ty. Good. Eleanor hoped she gave him an earful.

"Wow," she breathed, glancing up at Ty. "You weren't kidding when you said he didn't approve of your medical career."

"Nope."

Ty's expression remained tight, withdrawn. She didn't like it, wanted back the closeness they'd shared all evening, all day really. But she didn't know what to say because she didn't understand Ty's father's reaction to his son. How could any man not be proud of a son like Ty, who dedicated his life to helping those in need?

Since words failed her, she lifted his hand to her lips and pressed a soft kiss there. "You are a wonderful doctor, Tyler Donaldson. Your patients and their families think you are wonderful. You have a special gift and everyone at Angel's benefits from you being there. Me included." She paused, took a deep breath. "Actually, me especially."

His gaze met hers, darkened. "Thank you, Ellie. I needed that." His hand slipped around her waist, pulling her in for a hug. He bent, whispered in her ear, "I needed you."

Ty held Ellie tightly in his arms, his face close to her hair, breathing in her lightly seductive scent while they danced on the crowded dance floor.

All evening he'd found himself touching her. Her hand. Her face. Her arms. Her back. Anywhere just to reassure himself that she was really there, that she was real.

All evening he'd found his gaze meeting hers, knowing what she was thinking, sharing secret smiles, laughing at her comments over some of the events, proud to show her off to his childhood friends and family, anxious to get her home so he could peel off her jeans and have her and those red boots all to himself.

"I know I'm not the best at Texas two-stepping." Her

startled voice broke into his thoughts. "But did you just growl at me?"

Ty grinned at the woman in his arms. Tonight could have been horrible, a blast from the past, but, thanks to her, it hadn't. With the exception of when he'd come face-to-face with his father, he'd actually had a great time. "Maybe. Did I?"

"I believe you did."

"I guess you bring out the growl in me."

Her arms around his neck, her face bright with happiness, she laughed. "Thank you, Ty."

He couldn't help but want to lock the magical sound away inside him to pull out on some rainy day. Ellie's laughter could chase away clouds, could chase away Texas tornadoes.

"I've had fun tonight," she continued, missing a step and landing on his toes. "Oops!" She gave him a little apologetic look, then smiled and added, "More fun than I can remember having in a long time."

"Me, too, Ellie." He slid his fingers beneath her chin, lifted her face, stared into her lovely brown eyes. "But for the record the night isn't over and what comes later is a lot more fun."

Her gaze locked with his, she nodded her understanding, smiled. "Promises, promises."

"No worries, darlin'." He dropped a kiss on the tip of her nose. "I'm a man of my word."

"You really were good at riding, weren't you?" Eleanor asked later that night while lying in the crook of Ty's arms in his big king-size bed.

His bare chest rumbling with amusement, he tickled her side. "You should already know the answer to that firsthand."

Feeling almost decadent, she giggled and squirmed against him. "I am not a horse or a cow, Tyler Donaldson."

Within seconds he had her pinned beneath him and grinned. "No, but you ride like a—"

Laughing, her mouth dropped open and she feigned looking aghast, and his head lowered, brushed a kiss across her parted lips.

He waggled his brows. "Sorry, couldn't resist."

"Try harder next time."

"I'll give you hard." Proof of his claim pressed against her hip.

"Ty!"

"Now, say it again," he teased, his eyes telling her exactly what he meant, what he intended. "This time with more feeling."

He kissed her. Over and over.

When his name next left her lips he didn't have to ask for more feeling, for more of anything.

She gave him everything she had within her to give.

CHAPTER TEN

THE NEXT MORNING Ty woke with a jerk as Ellie shot out of bed and rushed to the bathroom. Startled out of a deep peaceful sleep, his bare feet had barely hit the cold hardwood floor when the sound of her retching met his ears.

Was she okay? Too much barbecue and sex the night before? Or had her travel sickness not ever completely cleared?

Without a word he entered the bathroom, got a cold, wet washcloth and placed it to her clammy forehead.

Looking miserable, she knelt next to the toilet, her shoulders slumped, her body quivering, her eyes closed.

"I'd ask if you're okay, but obviously you're not." He hated the thought of her not feeling well. He was a doctor, should be able to do something to ease her symptoms. "You want a drink of water?"

She nodded ever so slightly as if she was afraid that any movement might trigger another round of losing any remaining contents of her stomach.

He took a disposable paper cup from a dispenser on the sink and filled it with cool water. She took the cup, swished the water around her mouth and spat in the toilet several times.

"I'm so embarrassed," she said in a weak voice, her eyes squeezed tightly shut. "I hate that you saw me like this."

"Now I know why you don't stick around for mornings-after," he teased in reference to the morning she'd tried to leave before he'd awakened.

To the morning several weeks ago.

The morning after… Oh, hell.

The floor shifted beneath Ty's feet and his toes gripped the cold tile in the hope of maintaining his balance.

"That's not why I was leaving that morning," Ellie moaned, sounding miserable, oblivious to the crazy thoughts rushing through his head. "I just didn't know what we'd say to each other or how you'd feel. Or—"

"Ellie," he interrupted, his hand against the wall to balance himself. Sweat popped up on his brow, on the back of his neck. "Are you sure you just have a nervous stomach?"

Please say yes.

Misery on her pale face, she shrugged. "I've had a nervous stomach on and off most of my life. It just hadn't bothered me in years until…"

His heart slammed against his rib cage in thunderous bursts. His mind raced ahead, drawing what he hoped were inaccurate conclusions. "Not until the past couple of weeks?"

Face pink, she nodded again. "Yes. I was anxious about coming here with you, Ty. I'm really sorry I woke you up to this. I kept lying there thinking my nausea would pass, but it just kept getting worse. I couldn't hold it back any longer."

His heart beating faster and faster, his insides shaking, his knees threatening to buckle, he sank down to the floor next to her, placed his hand on her thigh. "Ellie, have you had a menstrual cycle since the night we first made love?"

Her lips didn't move, but they didn't have to. The widening of her eyes and blanching of her skin answered for her.

She hadn't.

Dear Lord, Ellie might be pregnant with his baby.

Eleanor shook. Her entire body *shook*.

Pregnant.

Was that even a possibility?

Well, of course it was a possibility. She and Ty had had sex. About a month ago.

She had missed her menstrual cycle.

She'd been so lost in thoughts about the night she'd spent with Ty, about this upcoming trip, that she'd never even noticed that she'd skipped a period. Could she be any more naive?

"I'm probably only late due to stress." Surely that was the only reason she hadn't gotten her period.

"Are you usually regular?" He sounded so calm, so logical. If not for the tremble of his hand where he touched her thigh, she might think him completely unaffected.

She closed her eyes and nodded. "Yes. Usually I'm like clockwork."

"Have your breasts been more sensitive?"

She so did not want to be having this conversation.

Not while crouched on the bathroom floor. Naked. With Ty. Naked. With her having just thrown up.

Under the best of circumstances she didn't want to be having this conversation, but definitely she didn't under the current ones.

A new wave of mortification hit her and she wrapped her arms around her body, trying to cover herself, wishing she could just crawl back into the fantastic dream she'd been having prior to waking and making her mad dash to the bathroom.

"Ellie," Ty whispered, wrapping his arms fully around her and holding her tightly to him. "Oh, Ellie, you're pregnant, aren't you?"

"I…I don't know. It—it never occurred to me that I might be." She kept her eyes tightly squeezed shut, hating that hot tears stung her eyelids, hating that she'd stuttered. "It's possible." She sucked in a breath, praying she didn't hiccup or sob. "I'm sorry, Ty."

She felt his fingers clasp her chin, felt him lifting her face, but she didn't open her eyes, couldn't bear to see what was in his eyes.

"Look at me."

She prised her eyelids apart, not surprised that the moment she did so the waterworks started down her cheeks.

"Don't cry, darlin'." He wiped at her tears. His hands were soft, gentle, attempting to comfort, but just the thought of what might be had her insides crumbling.

"If you are pregnant, you didn't get that way alone," he continued. "I'm as much to blame as anyone. More so."

To blame. Because this wasn't something good. Wasn't something planned for. She might be having a baby and rather than it being a joyous discovery, she sat naked on a bathroom floor, being coddled by a man who couldn't possibly want to be here but was. He was being sweet and wonderful rather than angry.

Which made her feel all the more guilty that she hadn't been suave and sophisticated like the women he was used to, like no doubt her own sister was.

"We weren't exactly thinking straight that night," she whispered, offering him an out.

"All I was thinking that night was that I wanted you, Ellie, but that doesn't excuse me making love to you without a condom. All I can say is that I've never done that before. I've never wanted someone so much that I lost control that way."

She bet he didn't want her now. Not after seeing her like this. She probably repulsed him.

But rather than pull away, he just held her to him for long moments, kissing the top of her head and gently rocking her in his arms while she cried.

Which probably only added to how bad she looked.

When he stood, he got another damp washcloth, knelt and gently cleaned away her tears. "You feel like standing up?"

She took a deep breath and nodded, although really she wasn't sure of anything. Her legs felt weak and her head spun, but they couldn't stay like this forever.

He took her hand and helped her to her feet. "Let's get a shower, get dressed, then we'll go into town and buy a pregnancy test. No use worrying about this until we know exactly what we're worrying about. Maybe it really is just your nerves."

He didn't sound hopeful, but perhaps…

Really, if it was just her nerves, that would be best

all the way around. Yet the idea that Ty's baby might be growing inside her... She placed her hand on her belly. Was there a baby there? Her and Ty's baby?

Why did she hope not?

But, even more confusing, why did the thought not seem so horrible either?

When he'd suggested taking a shower, she'd thought he'd meant alone. Honestly, she wanted to be alone, to have a few minutes to herself to think, digest the morning's events. But he must have been afraid to leave her, because he turned the walk-in shower on, tested the temperature then pulled her in with him.

He didn't say a word, just washed her hair, her body, rinsed her clean, then did the same for himself while she watched.

When he was done, he wrapped her in a large bath sheet and they silently dressed.

She wished she knew what he was thinking. Considering what might be happening inside her body, he'd been wonderful, sweet, very understanding.

But he couldn't be happy about the possibility of her being pregnant with his child. Of all the women he'd ever been with, he'd surely have chosen someone different to have conceived his child.

What about her? How did she feel about all the things bouncing around in her head?

What if before the end of the year she was going to give birth to Ty Donaldson's baby?

"You've barely said two words since we left the house," Ty pointed out as he maneuvered Ole Bess into downtown Swallow Creek.

Ellie sat with her hands folded in her lap, staring out the passenger window at the various businesses they drove past. "At this point, I'm not sure what to say."

She'd been quiet all morning. Somehow she'd made it through breakfast with his family, although she'd barely eaten a thing until his mother had yet again offered to have something different prepared. Red-faced, Ellie had forced down some eggs and a biscuit, but he'd seen the effort she'd put into doing so, had held her hair away from her face as she'd paid for those efforts in the lavatory not twenty minutes later.

Had he done that to her?

"If you are pregnant, we'll figure something out, Ellie." Guilt rode him hard. "You have to know I won't leave you to deal with this on your own."

"I won't have an abortion." For the first time that day her voice had strength and she met him square in the eyes. "I won't do that."

"I wouldn't ask you to." Ty winced. Had she thought he would when they worked day and night to save babies?

"I'm sorry." She turned away from him, stared out the window, her hands clenching and unclenching in her lap. "I didn't mean to imply that you would. I was just stating a fact."

"I understand."

He did. If she was pregnant, her entire life would change. His, too, but Ellie's in a more immediate way as her body grew with their baby.

Their baby. In his mind, she was already pregnant.

Ellie was pregnant.

In his heart, he knew she was. He'd been around

animals his entire life, had dealt with nature on the ranch. He should have recognized the possibility of her being pregnant when they'd been on the plane and she'd been sick.

Then again, she'd written off her illness as a nervous stomach so perhaps he could be forgiven.

"Do you even want kids, Ty?"

Her voice was tiny, vulnerable, so full of need that he pulled into the parking lot of a general mart and killed the truck engine, rather than driving to the other side of town to the chain pharmacy where they might have a little anonymity. They probably wouldn't have, but it had been a thought.

He undid his seat belt and turned to her. "I can't say that I've given much thought to the idea of having kids, Ellie. Maybe I thought I would someday, but up to this point in my life, taking care of the babies at Angel's has been enough."

She nodded as if she understood. Perhaps she did. Perhaps she felt the same.

"But if you are pregnant with my child, I will want our baby and I will do right by you and our child. Don't doubt that."

"With your…" Her startled gaze met his, wide-eyed and full of shock. "There's no possibility of my being pregnant by anyone other than you."

"Not what I meant." He raked his fingers through his hair, wondering if he was destined to repeatedly say the wrong thing today. "Let's go buy the test. See if there's a reason for us to discuss this further and we'll go from there, okay?"

Her cheeks pink, she nodded.

Of all the stores in Swallow Creek, he would have to choose the one where Nita just happened to be.

"Ty? Ellie?" she exclaimed when she spotted them in the checkout line. "I didn't know y'all were headed to town."

Ty considered putting the box behind his back, but figured that would only draw Nita's attention to what he held. Not that he needed to worry. She noticed anyway.

Her eyes growing huge, Nita's jaw dropped, her hands clasped together.

"Are you pregnant?" she gasped, much louder than Ty would have liked. Surely everyone in the general mart was now staring, waiting for Ellie to answer.

Ellie's cheeks glowed a bright pink and she didn't seem capable of answering. Perhaps she wasn't.

"Mind your own business, Nita. Besides, if we knew the answer to that question, we wouldn't have need for this, now, would we?" He motioned to the rectangular box he held.

Looking way too excited, Nita said, "Your mother said Ellie was pregnant, but I didn't—"

"Mom said what?" he gasped. If Ellie was pregnant, they needed time to digest the news, time to figure out what they wanted, time without his family butting in. His mother knew?

A sinking feeling gripped his gut. If his mother knew, his father would soon know.

Nita smiled, knowing she'd snagged his attention. "Yesterday, after the two of you went upstairs after lunch, she said that Ellie was pregnant, but the rest of us thought she was just doing some wishful thinking out loud."

His entire family had been debating the possibility of Ellie being pregnant before either of them had suspected a thing?

"Wishful thinking?" he muttered, still trying to wrap his mind around how his mother was so observant she'd figured out quickly what he'd missed. He was a doctor. Then again, she'd lived on a farm or ranch her entire life and was on a first-name basis with Mother Nature. He was pretty sure they sat down for tea on a regular basis.

"You know how she wants more grandkids to spoil rotten," Nita reminded him, beaming at Ellie.

"So you and Harry give her a few more."

"Ty?" Ellie's voice sounded panicky. She reached out, clutched his upper arm as if for support.

His gaze immediately went to her pale face.

"I think I'm going to pass out."

Then she did.

He caught her just before she hit the floor.

Two blue lines. Pregnant.

Eleanor was grateful she was sitting on the shiny oak floor of Ty's bathroom, that she was leaning up against the wall, that Ty sat beside her, holding the test so they could look at the results together.

His hand shook as he held it out for them both to read.

She closed her eyes, took a deep breath and looked at the results again.

There were still two blue lines.

Positive.

Eleanor Aston, the other Aston daughter, the quiet, shy Aston, pregnant out of wedlock.

The media would have a field day.

Her father would have a fit.

Recalling how he'd arranged her date with Ty, perhaps he wouldn't have a fit. Perhaps he'd find an angle, hand out cigars and ask for votes in his upcoming election. Or he'd take out his proverbial shotgun and demand Ty make an honest woman of her, probably just so he could marry her off to a well-to-do Texan while he had an excuse to push the issue.

Her mother would be mortified and remind her not to eat too much because losing baby fat wasn't going to be an easy feat.

Brooke would… What would her sister say? Probably high-five her on getting "knocked up by such a scrumptious man." But that was Brooke. Always thinking in the short term, never the long term.

Then again, maybe she was more like her sister than she'd thought. Because she certainly hadn't been thinking the long term on the night she'd gone to Ty's apartment.

Everything had been about short-term pleasure.

Now there were long-term consequences.

She was having his baby.

"I'm sorry," she whispered, for lack of knowing what else to say as she stared at the test he held in trembling fingers.

"Quit saying that you're sorry, Ellie." He almost sounded angry that she'd done so again. "I don't want you to be sorry."

She winced. Poor Ty. She'd gone out like a light in the general mart and he'd carried her back to the truck while Nita had paid for the pregnancy test. How many times had she apologized for that one? At least a few dozen on the ride back to the ranch. No doubt his entire family knew what had happened by now. Probably the entire town knew. Ty's hometown, and she'd embarrassed him. She was pregnant with his baby. Her face flamed.

"But it's true." She wished she could convey to him how humiliated she felt that she'd passed out, how sorry she was that she wasn't sophisticated enough to have prevented pregnancy. After all, she knew better, but on the night they'd made love she just hadn't been thinking. She'd like to blame the champagne, but she wasn't sure how much had been alcohol and how much had been pure Ty. "I didn't mean to get pregnant."

He set the test down on the floor beside him. "I know that, but we're talking about a human life that we've created." His expression gentled. "Don't be sorry for a new life. Don't ever be sorry for that."

"But it wasn't intentional." She needed to be sure he understood that.

"Most babies aren't intentionally created. You know that. That doesn't make those babies any less special, any less lovable. We made a baby, Ellie. A new life isn't a bad thing."

She stared at him, wondering if she was dreaming. If, when she'd passed out, she'd hit her head and was now living in some fantasy world. "You're taking this too well."

He leaned his head back against his bathroom wall, took a deep breath and gave a slight shrug. "Honestly, I'm not sure how I'm taking anything, Ellie. I'm blown away."

That she understood.

"We're having a baby."

Not that she was having a baby, but "we're." He'd said "we're."

She closed her eyes. "What are you going to tell your family?"

Head down, he snorted. "Nita will already have told Harry and my mother that she saw us at the store. Plus, my mother already knew. Hell, you heard Nita. The entire family was debating if you were or not."

She dropped her head forward, resting her forehead against her knees.

"I didn't know." How could she have been so oblivious? Then again, why should she have suspected? Pregnancy wasn't something she'd given any thought to. "I honestly hadn't considered the possibility of being pregnant until you asked about my cycle. I feel stupid that I hadn't, but I just never…well, you know."

He laced his fingers with hers, held her hand tightly within his, rubbing his thumb gently over her skin. "I know. Shock was written all over your face."

"Better you were looking at my face than the rest of me this morning," she mumbled, recalling how horrid she must have looked on the bathroom floor.

Odd that they were back there now. At least now they were fully dressed and she hadn't just thrown up the contents of her stomach.

Although certainly the news that she was pregnant was enough to have her stomach pitching and rolling.

Ty squeezed her hand. "I happen to like looking at the rest of you, darlin'. I like it a lot. Perhaps you noticed. I did a lot of looking yesterday afternoon and during the night."

He sounded so sure, so sincere, yet he couldn't be, could he? Yet he had acted as if he enjoyed her body. Maybe he was just one of those men who loved women, period, and it didn't matter how curvy they were.

"I'm going to gain a lot of weight." Just the mental image of what she'd look like in a few months made her want to cringe. "I won't be one of those cute pregnant women who maintain their body with a basketball for a belly. I'll just look like the basketball. A big, giant basketball."

His gaze narrowed and he forced her to look at him. "Your body is going to change into the body of a pregnant woman who is carrying my child. Mine. There's nothing more beautiful, Ellie."

Her insides quivered, and she found herself wanting to lean on him, put her head on his shoulder and put her trust in him. "I want to believe you, but..."

"But?"

"I know I'm not exactly the stuff of legends right now. How are you going to want me when I'm larger?" The tears had started flowing. Lots and lots of tears. Must be another side effect of pregnancy because she rarely cried, yet couldn't seem to stop today.

"Of course," she blabbered on. "That's making wild assumptions, isn't it? You might not even want me anymore now. I mean, after seeing me this morning and now." She hiccuped, wiped at her eyes with her free hand, thinking she probably looked pathetic with her red, wet eyes and runny nose from crying. "I really should just shut up, shouldn't I?"

Ty stared at her, shaking his head as he pulled her onto his lap and wrapped his arms around her. "Ellie, and I do mean Ellie because you do steal my breath, there is no one I want more than you. Haven't you figured that out yet?"

She sniffed. "Why would you want me, Ty?"

"Are you kidding me? Why wouldn't I?"

Should she write him a thesis? Or perhaps just send him the abbreviated version?

"You are a beautiful, intelligent, sexy, fun, wonderful, caring woman, and I know it, so you should, too."

Yep, she was dreaming, so she might as well enjoy her dream. She buried her face in his chest and let him hold her, let him soothe the part of her that had never quite felt good enough for her family.

In Ty's arms, she felt good enough.

She felt perfect.

She didn't know how the future would play out. For the moment the future didn't matter. All that mattered was that Ty made her feel complete, as if she belonged. He made her believe in herself, made her stronger than she'd thought she was.

CHAPTER ELEVEN

TY DREADED GOING downstairs, but knew eventually he would have to face his family. Part of him was surprised he and Ellie hadn't been interrupted by the whole Donaldson clan. Each of them would have something to say to him, no doubt.

Things he'd really rather Ellie not hear.

He'd convinced her to lie down. He'd lain down with her, held her sleeping body spooned up against him for almost an hour before he'd slipped out of the bed. He liked how her body fit against his, how holding her in his arms felt so right.

His brain had been racing from the moment he'd realized she might be pregnant. There were so many things to consider that he didn't want to rush what he said to her, didn't want to possibly say the wrong thing and inadvertently create problems.

A baby.

He'd dedicated his life to caring for babies, for nurturing and providing care for innocent new lives. Now he was going to be responsible for a new life.

A baby.

His and Ellie's baby.

Really, before he faced his family's various reactions, he'd like a little time to figure out his own emotions and to clear his head. Black Magic called to him. Big-time.

Somehow he made it out of the house without bumping into anyone, but the moment he stepped into the barn, his brother slapped him on the shoulder.

"Wanna go for a ride?" Harry asked, probably knowing that was exactly where Ty was headed.

"Absolutely." He went into a tack room, grabbed his saddle. When he'd gotten his gear, he wasn't surprised to see his brother had already mounted his stallion. Black Magic waited impatiently.

He spent a great deal of time getting the horse ready for the ride, taking time to talk gently to the stallion, to allow him to bond again with his too-long-gone master.

When he sat on the horse, old memories and emotions hit him. He'd loved this horse, but first medical school then moving to New York had kept him away.

But really what had kept him away had been much more than physical location and distance.

His father's disapproval had been what had driven him away.

In silence, he and his brother rode out across the fields, riding toward nowhere in particular, yet neither was surprised when they stopped at a pond where they'd often ridden out to, fished and played at as kids.

Although the air was brisk, the sun was shining and light glimmered across the water's surface.

"You wanna talk about it?" Harry asked when they'd both dismounted and stood next to the pond just as they'd done hundreds of times in the past. They'd swum in this pond, played in this pond, camped at this pond.

Removing his gloves, Ty picked up a rock, skipped it over the water. One. Two. Three. Sink. He found another flat stone, tossed it toward the water. "Ellie's pregnant."

"Yeah, I heard." Harry bent and studied the ground until he found a rock that suited him. "My wife isn't known for her discretion, God love her."

Ty shrugged. "Mom already knew."

"Mom has this way of already knowing everything." Harry gave his stone a fling and it skipped farther out than Ty's had gone. "So, what are you going to do? You going to marry her?"

"I'm not sure." He wasn't even sure that if he wanted to get married whether Ellie would marry him. She didn't need some man complicating her life. Not that he hadn't already complicated her life enough by getting her pregnant. "Her father will likely get out his shotgun when he finds out."

"His proverbial one, maybe," Harry agreed. "I may not know Senator Aston, but I do know of him. Shooting you would cost him too many votes, so I think you're safe."

Despite his brother's teasing tone, Ty didn't smile. "She deserves better than me. A lot better."

Harry stopped in midsearch for another stone, looked up at him and frowned. "Because she's an Aston?"

"Because she's Ellie." Which summed up everything. He couldn't care less that she was an Aston. What he cared about was the woman herself. He cared about Ellie.

Straightening, Harry seemed to consider his answer. "She could do worse."

"Yeah." Ty gave the stone he'd been holding a hard fling. "She could have ended up with you."

Harry grinned. "Nah, Nita wouldn't have been happy 'bout that. I'm a taken man." His brother hit his shoulder. "It's not so bad, you know. Having a kid, being married. You might like it."

"This coming from the man who still lives with his parents." Ty could have bitten his tongue off the moment the words had left his mouth.

Harry's face paled, then his cheeks splotched red, and not from the cold.

"I didn't mean that the way it sounded."

"Sure you did," his brother countered, cramming his hands into his jacket pockets. "In some ways, you're right. I do live in that big house with Mom and Dad, because you know what? I love it there. I love having my wife and child grow up on this ranch, because I love it here. I love Swallow Creek, the Triple D, and there's no place on earth I'd rather be than right here with my family."

Ty didn't say anything. He figured he'd already said too much.

"But that life isn't for you," his brother surprised him by saying. "The ranch has never been in your blood the way it has in Dad's and mine. William's, too, actually. But living on this ranch isn't what I was referring to. I was talking about having a family, a place where you belong."

That Ty understood. "I belong at the Angel Mendez Children's Hospital."

"Really?" Harry's brows formed a V and he sank down on a fallen log, picked at a piece of loose moss before glancing up and meeting Ty's gaze. "That's enough? Your career?"

"It always has been."

"Before Ellie."

Before Ellie. The words seemed to echo across the plains, strumming louder and louder in Ty's head.

"She's a part of Angel's," he said slowly, wondering why the words wouldn't quit sounding through his mind. *Before Ellie.*

"Ellie is your family, Ty. She's carrying your baby."

Ty sank onto the log next to his brother. "Tell me about it."

"So, I ask you again," Harry said with that calm big-brother voice of reason of his. "What are you going to do? You need a game plan, bro. Because we both know that when Dad finds out you've gotten a Northern girl pregnant out of wedlock, he's going to hit the roof."

"Of all the stupid, irresponsible stunts that boy has pulled, this one tops them all!"

Ty winced. Yep, Harry had been right. His father was hitting the roof. Ty had barely stepped back into the house from his ride with his brother and didn't really have his game plan formed. He'd wanted to talk to Ellie prior to doing that. To tell her his thoughts and how he felt about her, to ask what her thoughts were, what she was feeling.

Unfortunately, he doubted he was going to get the opportunity. At least, not before a confrontation with his father.

His mother replied in her usual steady voice, encouraging her husband to calm down, that having another grandchild was a good thing.

Good ole mom, always coming to his defense.

"The boy is living in New York City. What kind of place is that to even consider raising a family? Too many people, too much pollution, no grass to grow beneath one's feet."

Ty felt his father's shudder as much as he heard it.

"And rather than have a real man's job, he takes care of babies for a living." Another shudder, this one much more pronounced. "What kind of example is that going to be for my grandchild?"

A new jab poked into an old wound. Hadn't this been exactly the argument that had led him into leaving Swallow Creek? Into swearing he wouldn't return? He didn't have to be a rancher to be a real man.

Except in his father's eyes, that was.

Ty took a deep breath and prepared to go into the kitchen where his parents were talking. Might as well get this over with rather than leave his mother to take all the flak.

No doubt she'd taken enough of that over the years since he had moved away.

"A good one."

Pausing in midstep on his way into the room, Ty's ears perked up at the steady voice that responded to his father's question.

Not his mother's voice, as he'd expected, but Ellie's.

"What did you say?" His father's voice boomed, obviously shocked and awed that someone dared speak up.

Ellie's voice didn't waver, neither did it stutter. God

bless her. "I said Ty would be a good example for our child."

His father harrumphed. "A good example would be for that boy to get his act together and get his butt home so he can help take care of family responsibilities."

Without so much as a pause, he heard Ellie's sweet voice continue to defend him.

"He has new family responsibilities now. To me and our baby."

"To you? Hell, woman, he's not even got a ring on your finger and you're knocked up. I don't think he can be accused of facing his family responsibilities or doing right by you."

Ty cringed, wondered why he was still standing just outside the room, yet he wanted to hear what Ellie would say. He needed to hear what she would say.

"Ty is a man of honor."

His heart swelled at her confident words. God, he would do his best to do right by her. Somehow. Some way. He would do right by Ellie and their baby.

"A man of honor doesn't abandon his family to move out of state to take care of babies."

"A man I admire and respect," she continued as if his father hadn't spoken. "A man who works hard and gives all he has to help those around him, a man who will be a good father and not judge our child based upon outdated, chauvinistic ideas that a man has to live off the land to be a real man."

Pride surged at Ellie's staunch defense. Knowing how her anxiety tended to flare, he was again amazed that not once had she stuttered. Hell, he'd seen his father make grown men stutter and quake in their boots. Yet Ellie was standing her ground, defending *him*.

Ty closed his eyes, picturing her in his mind, her smile, her eyes, the way she looked at him when he kissed her.

The way he knew he looked at her. As if she meant the world to him.

Because she did.

"You've known him, what, a few months? Don't pretend you know my son better than I do."

"Harold, don't do this," Ty's mother begged, speaking up for the first time since Ellie had come into the conversation. "Don't say such things."

"You know I'm right. That foolhardy boy always had his nose in a book when he should have been doing other things."

"Other things such as being like you, Dad?" Ty hadn't consciously decided to step out of the shadows, but he couldn't risk his father launching into Ellie. He wouldn't risk it. She was too fragile.

Too precious.

As timid as she'd always been around the hospital, recalling how panicked she'd been at the ribbon-cutting ceremony, he was amazed at how she'd defended him, at how her shoulders were high and her gaze bright, confident. Had she been wearing a long red cape and the wind blowing in her hair, he wouldn't have been surprised. Ellie was his heroine.

His father's lips pursed and his gaze narrowed as it settled on Ty. "A boy could do worse than to grow up to be like his old man."

True. His father was a hardworking man who had

always provided for his family, had always given as much as he demanded of others. But that didn't mean Ty had to follow in his footsteps.

"I'm not like you, Dad."

"Ty," his mother began, her nervous gaze going back and forth between her husband and her younger son, "perhaps we should have this conversation later."

"Why, so that we can sugarcoat the fact that my own father is disappointed in me?" Had he ever said those words out loud before? He didn't think so. Maybe he'd never even mentally acknowledged them, but something about Ellie's defense of him made him acknowledge a lot of things.

"No, thanks. We've been doing that for years and it's not helped one bit. And if it's for Ellie's benefit, don't bother. She's already seen how he feels about me. Hearing the words only confirms what she has already figured out."

"Don't you be rude to your mother, boy."

"I'm not a boy," he countered, not really thinking he'd been rude to his mother and certainly not intending to have disrespected her in any way. But his father's chest puffed up and his gaze narrowed.

Out of years of deferring to the man he'd been taught his whole life to respect, Ty automatically zipped his lips.

Ellie, on the other hand, did not.

"He's right," she said with that easy confidence again that surprised him. "Ty is a man. A very good man who is going to be a father. A very good father to our baby, who can grow up and do anything he or she likes in life, whether that be a baby doctor or a rancher or a garbage collector. What's important is that our child grow up healthy and happy and knowing that he or she can do or accomplish anything and that self-worth does not come from how others see you but how one sees oneself."

Ty bit back a smile at the shocked look crossing his father's face and took a step forward in Ellie's direction. Hell, he wanted to wrap his arms around her and spin her around for the staunch way she defended him.

But she was oblivious to him and focused solely on his father. Her shoulders lifted, her eyes burned with dark intensity and she met his father's gaze squarely.

"If you want anything to do with our baby, you will learn to appreciate the wonderful man you have for a son because he is a brilliant doctor and an honorable man," she warned, her hands on her hips and her expression serious. "I will not have my child around someone who obviously has so little appreciation for a man who does so much good for so many."

Blood pounding in her ears, Eleanor wondered if Ty was going to read her the riot act for daring to be so outspoken to his father, but she didn't care at the moment. Anger burned too hotly in her veins for her to hold her tongue. Really, how could any man be so obtuse?

No wonder Ty had moved so far away.

She'd awakened, realized Ty was gone, and that he must have been for some time because the bed barely held an imprint of him having been there. She'd gone downstairs to find him.

And stumbled on Ty's parents, discussing him.

Discussing being the mildest of ways she knew how to put what Ty's father had been doing.

Degrading his son.

Tearing him down.

She hadn't been able to stand it.

How dared he say such things about the most wonderful man she had ever known? About the man who made her view life differently?

If the blustery old man thought he was going to have anything to do with her baby when he treated his son so callously, he was wrong.

Because she might have only known she was pregnant for a few hours, but she loved this baby and would protect him or her with her life. No way would she let some overbearing, pompous man berate her child.

Or her child's father.

"Ellie, dear, perhaps you and I should go to the den and let the men have this discussion?" Ty's mother suggested gently, her worried gaze going back and forth between her son and her husband. She moved toward Ellie, put her arm gently on her shoulder.

Eleanor risked a look at Ty. His face was dark, cloudy, upset.

Coldness doused the flame that burned within her.

She had overstepped her boundaries.

Hadn't she known she had?

She might be pregnant with Ty's baby, but she'd been talking to his father. Blood was thicker than water. Didn't that always hold true?

Still, she wasn't going to apologize. Not when she so strongly disagreed with how Ty's father treated him.

"Actually, I need to do some things upstairs," she ventured, not wanting to go with Ty's mother so that she could be scolded for overstepping her place. Plus, tears burned at her eyes and she wanted to get away, far away, before they fell. No way did she want to show weakness in front of this family. If for no other reason, she didn't want them to think they could browbeat her in regard to her baby. They couldn't. She held her head high. "If you'll excuse me…"

Without pausing, she headed back toward the stairs she'd descended only minutes before.

She hadn't mentally made any decisions, but when she got back to Ty's room, saw all the things from his childhood and past, she was struck with homesickness.

Immense and utter homesickness.

Perhaps her family was odd. Perhaps they each had their own quirks and faults. But they were her family.

She wanted them.

Before she even consciously thought about what she was doing, she had her suitcase out of Ty's closet and had begun methodically packing her things back into the case.

"What are you doing?"

She spun at the sound of Ty's voice. "Going home."

Filling the entire doorway with his tall frame and broad shoulders, he didn't look happy. His gaze narrowing, he stepped into the room, closed his bedroom door behind him.

"Why?" he asked, turning the lock.

She almost winced at the sound of the lock clicking into place. Why? Ha, did he really have to ask why she'd want to leave?

"Because I don't want to be here any longer." Truer words had never been spoken. She wanted to be far away from the Triple D ranch and Texas.

His hands on his hips, Ty stood just inside the door, staring at her with an expression she couldn't quite read. "Because of what just happened downstairs?"

"Because I want to go home, Ty. I want to be back in the city, back at Angel's." Back where she belonged. "I don't like it here."

"This is my home."

"Yes, and hasn't it been a lovely homecoming for you?" She hadn't meant to be sarcastic or to say anything derogatory. Lord knew, he got enough of that from his father. But the words had slipped out before she could stop them.

His lips tightened. "With the exception of my father, yes, it has been."

Exactly. The rest of his family had been quite lovely. She shouldn't have said what she had. Shame filled her. Shame and frustration and the overwhelming need to be in her own environment, to have time to process all the things that had happened over the past few days, over the past few weeks since Ty had rescued her at the ribbon-cutting.

Her entire life had turned topsy-turvy.

Her life would never be the same again.

She was going to be a mother, to have Ty's baby.

"Well, good for you." She forced a tight smile to her lips, pretended she wasn't falling apart on the inside, because really she wanted to be strong. "I'm glad that you have had a good visit, but I want to go home."

He stared at her as if he was looking at a stranger. "We're not supposed to leave for another two days, Ellie."

"Don't call me that!"

The name did her in. Emotions were battling within her and hearing him call her that when the single word could bring her so far down or so high up thanks to him was just too much.

"But—"

"No buts, I've asked and asked you not to call me that, but you're just like your father. You think you know what's best for other people so you do what you want anyway. Even when that person has asked you repeatedly not to call her that." Over twenty years' worth of frustrations and hurt spewed forth all at once. "Well, guess what? I don't like it, so don't!"

"What's wrong with you, Eleanor?"

The way he enunciated her name grated on her nerves like fingernails on a chalkboard. "Nothing."

"Is this about the pregnancy? It's normal for you to feel emotional."

Emotional? Yes, she felt emotional. Overflowing with emotions. All of which centered around the man staring at her as if he wasn't quite sure what to think.

"Sure, I'm probably just hormonal." She actually felt hormonal. She felt overwhelmed. Sad. As if every nerve ending in her body was in motion.

He raked his fingers through his hair, leaving dark tufts in disarray. "I don't understand what's going on, why you're doing this."

She glanced at the open suitcase on the bed. "I'm packing my bags so I can go home. I don't want to be here. I don't want to be with you. I just want to go home. Now."

He flinched almost as if she'd struck him. His lips tightened to a thin line. He sighed, seemed to come to some decision. "Fine, I'll have Harry fly you to the airport. If he can't because of the rodeo, I'll fly us there." At her look of alarm, he added, "It's been a while, but I have my pilot's license. Harry and I took lessons at the same time during our teens and have flown since." He paused, stared straight into her eyes. "You're sure this is what you want?"

At the moment, leaving was the only thing she was sure of. She needed to be moving, to be taking action, to soothe the anxiety rising within her that was threatening to go into a full-blown panic attack, to get home to where she could dissect the emotions rushing through her.

"Get me home, Ty." She wanted to be as far away from Texas as she could possibly get. New York sounded just about perfect.

She watched walls slide into place as he shielded his emotions behind an expression she'd never seen on his face before. One almost of indifference.

"Fine." He sounded as if he couldn't care less, that what she did didn't matter to him and he'd just as soon she leave as stay. "You want to go home. I'll get you home."

CHAPTER TWELVE

ELEANOR SAT ON Ty's bed, uncertain about what she needed to do. He'd disappeared more than thirty minutes ago, saying he'd be back for her when the plane was ready. She'd finished packing and had been sitting on the bed ever since.

A light knock sounded on Ty's door. Much lighter than Ty would have done. Not that he'd have knocked to enter his own bedroom anyway.

Although she didn't want to face anyone, she refused to show any remorse over her confrontation with Ty's father. She'd meant every word.

"Ellie," Ty's mother called through the door. "May I please come in? Please."

Taking a deep breath, Eleanor crossed the room, opened the door and moved aside for the woman to enter.

When inside the room she looked as uncomfortable as Eleanor felt.

"I suppose you think my husband is terrible."

Eleanor didn't speak. Really, what could she say?

"He isn't. He was just raised a certain way and sees the world in black-and-white with no shades of gray."

"Ty being a doctor isn't a shade of gray."

His mother smiled, surprising Eleanor. "I heard the two of you argue. I wasn't intentionally eavesdropping. I came to find you, to tell you how happy I am Ty has a strong woman like you."

Eleanor wanted to laugh. Her, strong? Ha. Ty's mother had her confused with someone else.

"So the fact that even now you defend him, well, it makes this mother's heart sing with joy." Then she surprised Eleanor even further by wrapping her arms around her. "Please reconsider leaving. My son loves you. Stay and talk this out with him."

Eleanor reeled at the woman's words. "Ty doesn't love me."

She supposed the woman might think that as he'd brought her here when he'd never brought a woman home. Then there was the whole thing of being pregnant with his baby.

"Has he not told you?" Then his mother frowned. "Have you told him how you feel? That you're in love with him?"

"I don't love Ty," she denied, but even as she said the words, she realized that she did.

That perhaps on the night he'd rescued her at the ribbon-cutting she'd fallen hopelessly in love with Ty Donaldson.

Standing just inside the open door of his bedroom, Ty recalled exactly why he'd been taught not to eavesdrop.

He flinched at the words that stopped him cold.

Hearing Ellie say she didn't love him cut straight through his chest, right to the soft center of his heart.

Hell, he was making a habit of eavesdropping today and nothing good had come out of it yet.

Squaring his shoulders, he cleared his throat.

Both women spun toward him.

"Ty!" Ellie gasped, her face flushing, her eyes bright, guilty. Guilty because she didn't love him and he'd heard her say so.

Thank God he hadn't poured his sappy heart out to her earlier.

"The plane is fueled up and Harry is going to fly you to Houston. I've booked you a seat on the first available flight back to New York."

Her gaze dropped, then she nodded. "Thank you."

"Ty," his mother said, stepping toward him, "I was just trying to convince Ellie to stay. Don't you think that's a good idea?"

"Her name is Eleanor and, no, I don't think her staying is a good idea at all." Never would he be accused of forcing a woman to be with him when she'd so plainly said she didn't want to be.

His mother let out a loud sigh. "You're as stubborn as your father." With a shake of her head she hugged Ellie. "For whatever it's worth, I hope you change your mind and decide to stay. This family needs to heal and you started that process today. Please don't leave without seeing it through."

Heal? His mother thought what had happened between him and his father had been healing? Wrong. The confrontation had been like ripping the scab off a deep wound. Nothing more.

Looking torn, Eleanor hugged his mother back. "Thank you for welcoming me into your home." She hesitated. "With the baby, I'm sure our paths will cross in the future. Please take care." Then she turned to Ty. "I'm ready to go."

She reached for her suitcase, but Ty beat her to it.

"No way am I letting you carry that."

"I'm pregnant, not an invalid."

He shrugged. "Makes no difference. You're not carrying it."

When they reached the bottom of the stairs, Ty's mother stopped them.

"You can't leave without saying goodbye to William. He'd be heartbroken."

Yeah, well, his nephew wasn't the only one who was going to be heartbroken when Ellie left.

"He's in the pool. I'll go get him if you'll wait?"

Eleanor nodded.

She and Ty stood in silence, then she sighed.

"We should have just walked out to the pool instead of her having to drag William inside."

She nodded, sure he was right.

"Ty!" His mother's scream echoed through the house.

Both Ty and Eleanor took off toward the door that led out to the pool.

What met their gazes made Eleanor's stomach tighten into a nervous ball.

Ty's father was in the pool, holding a lifeless little body to his chest but apparently frozen with fear and unable to move further.

Ty immediately jumped to action, crossing the distance and jumping into the pool.

"Give him to me," he demanded of his father.

His pain-filled eyes dropping to the lax body of his grandson, he did so.

Ty took William, prayed he wasn't too late, assessed him while carrying him from the pool.

As best as he could tell, there wasn't any trauma or neck injuries. God, he hoped William hadn't dived into the pool, injured his neck, been paralyzed and drowned.

But his nephew had drowned.

No heartbeat. No respirations.

A pain unlike any Ty had ever experienced slashed across his chest, but he drew on years of experience with dealing with medical emergencies to move automatically.

"Oh, Ty," Ellie cried, as he laid William's tiny body on the concrete and began performing cardiopulmonary resuscitation.

Ellie pulled her cell phone from her purse, dialed 911 and realized she had no idea what Ty's address was.

"The Triple D Ranch," she told the emergency worker. "We're at the Triple D Ranch."

Behind her, Ty's mother gave the address and Ellie carefully repeated it to the voice on the other end of the phone line.

She handed the phone to Ty's mother and bent beside him, meaning to help him with the CPR, but her gaze caught on Ty's father.

The man still stood in the pool. She didn't think he'd budged since he'd handed William over to Ty.

Worried that more might be going on than just shock, she called out his name, but he didn't even look her way.

Kicking off her shoes, Ellie went into the pool to Harold Donaldson.

"Mr. Donaldson?" She touched his arm.

He jumped, seeming to come out of the trance he'd been in. He glanced around, his eyes landing on where Ty was working on William.

"I didn't know what to do," he began, his voice trembling.

Despite her differences with the man, her heart squeezed with compassion. She put her arm around him. "Come on. Let's get you out of the pool."

Ty counted compressions in his head, gave a breath at the appropriate times and prayed. In his mind, he prayed and prayed and prayed.

But nothing happened.

No lub-dub of William's heart.

No gasp of breath or sputtering or cough.

Nothing.

He couldn't let this happen. Couldn't not revive William.

Couldn't ever forget the pallid color on his father's face, the pain in his father's eyes as he'd taken William out of his shaking arms.

Never had Ty seen a weak link in his father's armor. Never had he seen the man not know exactly what to do.

His father was a man of action, a decisive man who never questioned, just did.

Ty gave another breath.

Nothing.

The longer he couldn't revive William the less likely he was to be able to.

How long had the boy been in the pool? How long had his father just been holding his lifeless body?

From the corner of his eye he saw his mother go to his father, wrap her arms around him and start talking to him. He saw Ellie reassure herself that nothing more was wrong with his father than fear, then she moved to him, knelt next to where he desperately tried to save William.

"Let me help." She didn't wait for him to answer, just bent and gave William a breath, counted his compressions out loud and repeated the breath.

And a miracle happened.

Nothing could convince Ty that anything short of a miracle had happened.

Because William coughed.

Weakly at first, then stronger as his lungs cleared the water.

"Oh, Ty, he's alive."

At Ellie's exclamation, Ty's mother cried out and his father sank to his knees.

"Harold!" His wife sank down next to him.

"Check him," he ordered Ellie, not willing to leave William's side but afraid the stress of what had happened might be affecting his father's heart.

William's eyes opened, he coughed more. Deep, rattling coughs that shook his tiny frame.

Ty turned him, beat on his back, trying to assist in clearing the fluid.

"Uncle Ty?"

Ty let out the breath he hadn't realized he'd been holding.

Stepping out of the house, Harry and Nita took in the scene before them.

"What the hell is going on here?"

Eleanor could recall very few times of sitting in a hospital waiting area. At least, from her current point of view as an anxious family member waiting to hear news.

Family member.

She wasn't really family.

But the baby inside her was William's cousin, was a part of this family.

She glanced at Ty. He sat slumped over, eyes closed. He'd barely said a word to her since they'd followed the ambulance to the hospital. His mother had sat in the front seat next to him and she and Nita had shared the backseat of the king cab Triple D pickup. Harry had ridden in the ambulance with his son and father.

When they'd arrived, Ty's mother had been allowed to stay with her husband while he was checked over just to make sure his reaction had only been one of stress. Harry and Nita were both with William. Which left Eleanor and Ty alone in the emergency room waiting area.

Ty opened his eyes, caught her watching him. His expression tightened. "I'm sorry you missed your flight."

"Really? You think I'm worried about my flight?"

"I thought you were all set to get out of Texas as quickly as possible."

Eleanor's eyes closed and she prayed for strength to see her through the rest of this stressful day. "I thought you were upset with me and I panicked."

"Why the hell would I have been upset with you?"

"Because of what I said to your father."

"When you defended me? Hell, darlin', I thought you were great. Brilliant. I didn't want you to leave."

"You weren't upset?"

"At you? Never," he answered without hesitation. "My father is a different story altogether. Hell, we'll both just leave. I'll go back to New York with you."

"But the rodeo—"

"The rodeo was just an excuse to get me home," he interrupted, sitting up in his seat. "My mother hoped my father and I would work things out, but that's never going to happen. We're too different. He is never going to understand me and I quit trying to make him understand years ago."

He stood, moved next to where she sat.

"Thank you for trying, though, Ellie."

Ellie. He'd called her Ellie.

That's all it took for the dam of emotions to break loose within Eleanor. She'd been holding them at bay so staunchly, trying to be strong during all the afternoon's drama, but hearing the nickname destroyed all her resolve.

Because when Ty had called her Eleanor earlier, she'd hurt. Deep down hurt.

Because she wasn't Eleanor.

Not with Ty.

She was Ellie.

Not Jelly Ellie, but Ellie, the woman who stole Ty Donaldson's breath.

Because when he looked at her, said her name, that's exactly how he made her feel. As if she really did steal his breath.

Just as he was looking at her right this moment.

"I didn't mean to make you cry." He touched her face, brushed away tears that she hadn't realized had fallen. "I'm sorry, Ellie. Sorry you had to deal with my father. Sorry you want to leave. Sorry you don't love me."

The last one had her looking up at him. "Why would that matter?"

He gave a soft laugh. "What my mother said earlier was right."

He knew she loved him? "But how?"

He brushed his thumb across her cheek. "How could I not?"

She supposed he saw the truth in her eyes every time she looked at him, every time she'd kissed him, touched him.

Because she did love him. Even now the way she felt about him was probably shining in her eyes.

"I'm sorry, Ty. I didn't mean it to happen."

"It's not your fault."

Perhaps not, but she didn't want him feeling sorry for her. Which apparently was what was happening. He'd overheard what his mother had said and was taking pity on her just as he'd done at the ribbon-cutting.

Or maybe he was just being nice because of the baby.

Either way, she didn't want his pity. She wanted his heart.

"I know you didn't intend me to fall in love with you. I just did."

As Ty's words registered, the room spun around Ellie and she worried for a brief moment that she might pass out again. "You fell in love with me?"

He gave an ironic laugh. "As I said, how could I not? You're wonderful, Ellie."

"But I thought…" Her voice trailed off, a thousand thoughts hitting her at once. That Ty loved her was the foremost one. Ty was in love with her. "You really love me?"

"It's okay, Ellie." He shrugged off her question. "I heard what you told my mother. It's not a big deal."

He started to turn away but she grabbed his arm. "Ty Donaldson, it's a very big deal. If you love me, it's the biggest deal of my entire life."

Facing her, he searched her eyes, his soft and vulnerable as understanding dawned. A lopsided grin lifted one corner of his mouth. "Oh, really? The biggest deal, eh?"

"Really," she said, hope building higher and higher within her at how he was looking at her, at what she saw shining brightly in his eyes.

He stood, pulled her to her feet. "I love you, Eleanor Aston."

Her heart burst with joy at his words, but she shook her head. "Not acceptable."

His smile fell.

"Tell me again," she demanded, staring up at him. "Only this time get it right."

It only took Ty a second to realize exactly what she meant. Taking her hands in his, he stared straight into her eyes, straight into her heart. "I love you, Ellie Aston."

She smiled. "Much better."

"Agreed." He grinned, pulling her into his arms. "I've never understood why you protested so much anyway. Ellie fits you."

Knowing the past no longer mattered, she told him

about "Jelly Ellie," watching as anger darkened his expression.

"Whoever called you that has a lot to answer for and had better hope like hell they never have the misfortune of crossing my path."

She smiled. "The name doesn't bother me anymore, Ty. When you called me Eleanor earlier, it…" Her voice broke and she shrugged helplessly. "It tore me to bits because I'm not Eleanor anymore. I'm Ellie and I like who that woman is because she's your woman."

"Always, Ellie. You're always going to be mine." With those words, he kissed her. The sweetest, most possessive kiss Eleanor had ever had the pleasure of experiencing.

"Tell me," he breathed against her lips. "Say the words to me."

Placing her palms on each side of his face and staring directly into his beautiful eyes, she smiled. "I love you, Ty Donaldson. Always and forever."

"I like the sound of that."

"Ahem."

Both Ty and Ellie spun at the sound of his father clearing his throat.

"Dad."

Ellie didn't have to be a rocket scientist to hear the relief in Ty's voice.

No wonder. His father's normal robust color was back and he looked fit enough to take on the world. Thank God.

"They tell me they are going to keep William overnight for observation but that he's going to be just fine."

Ty nodded. That's what Harry had told them earlier, too.

An awkward silence filled the lobby as the three of them stood there, no one saying anything.

"Perhaps I should step out. Get a cup of coffee." Remembering her pregnancy, she changed it to, "A glass of juice or something."

As she went to step past Ty's father, he grabbed her arm. "No, young lady, you need to hear this. Have a seat."

Young lady? Ellie winced. Was Ty's father really going to start in while they were in the emergency room waiting area?

Ty glared at his father's hands on Ellie's arm. He wasn't one bit surprised when she failed to sit, though. Ellie was developing quite a backbone.

But she didn't need it.

Because if his father thought for one minute that Ty was going to let him say one negative thing to Ellie, one negative thing to him, he was wrong.

Not today. Not ever again.

"Calm down, son," Harold ordered, apparently reading Ty's expression correctly. "And have a seat because I have something I need to say and you need to hear this. Both of you need to hear it."

A war waged within Ty, but he sat, taking Ellie's hand as she sat in the seat next to him. He couldn't say he liked his father towering over them, but he'd had a long day so Ty would give him that advantage.

"I know we've had our differences."

To put it mildly.

"But what you did today…" His father paused, looked every one of his years as he met Ty's gaze. "Son, I was wrong."

Ty's breath caught. Ellie's hand squeezed his. Was his father saying what he thought he was?

"My whole life I've thought I knew what was best for you boys, what was right, but today you proved to me what a fool I've been."

"I just did my job."

"Exactly. A job that I've never given you any credit for. Just as I never told you I was proud of how well you did with your studies and medical school."

From the corner of his eye he saw Ellie dab at her eyes. Ty clenched his teeth, determined he would not let his father's words get to him.

"But I was always proud of you, Ty. Proud that no matter what anyone said you went after your dreams and the rest of the world could take it or leave it. I was proud that you were your own man with your own mind and that you aced everything you did."

Ty wanted to hit the side of his head to clear his ears, because he was certain he hadn't heard correctly.

"Today, what you did, Ty, son, I can't begin to tell you how in awe I am of what you do, of how proud I am of the fine doctor you are."

A tiny sob escaped Ellie. Her fingers dug into his.

"I…" He glanced around the empty lobby. "Well, that's all I came to say. That I am proud of you and I'm sorry for not telling you sooner."

He turned to leave the lobby but Ty stopped him, wrapping his arms around his father's stiff body.

But after just a second Harold took over the hug in

true Harold Donaldson fashion and hugged Ty so tightly that he could barely breathe.

When his father had left the lobby, Ty turned Ellie and pulled her to him.

"Did you say something about being mine for always and forever, darlin'?" he asked, holding her close to him.

"Seems like I recall saying something along those lines." Ellie smiled, knowing that always and forever with Ty sounded about as close to heaven on earth as one could get.

EPILOGUE

"YOU READY for this?"

Checking to make sure his tuxedo was straight, Ty grinned at his brother. "I've been ready for this for months."

"Yeah, a shame it took you that long to convince the bride to make an honest man of you."

It had taken him way too long to convince Ellie to marry him. "Stubborn woman wouldn't agree until after Levi was born."

"Yes, because every woman wants to be pregnant in her wedding photos."

Ty could have pointed out that he'd have marched Ellie down the aisle on the day he'd first told her he loved her, on the day that she'd first told him she loved him.

He'd known he wanted to spend the rest of his life with her. In the months that passed, he'd not changed his mind or his heart. The way he felt about Ellie just kept growing, getting stronger with each day that passed.

Ty and Harry joined the rest of the wedding party on the lawn of the Triple D. Row after row of white chairs were filled with Texans in their best Sunday duds and New Yorkers in the latest European fashions.

His father held Levi in the front row. Ty grinned at the tiny white Stetson that his dad had insisted the six-month-old wear. William fidgeted next to Harry, toying with the ring pillow he held.

The live band began to play the wedding march and all eyes, especially Ty's, went to where Ellie rode up in a white carriage with crushed red velvet seats. Her beaming newly reelected to the Senate father stepped up to the carriage and assisted his lovely daughter down.

Ty's breath caught at the beautiful woman who would officially become his during this ceremony. In reality, she'd been his from the moment they declared their love and he'd been hers.

He took in her long dark hair in a mass of curls about her neck and cascading down her back. Her gown was strapless and accented her beautiful curves and nipped-in waist. Never had a bride been more beautiful.

Never had a woman been more loved.

Her gaze met Ty's and she smiled.

A smile that told him everything words never could convey.

A smile that told of a love that would last always and forever.

* * * * *

A sneaky peek at next month...

Medical Romance

CAPTIVATING MEDICAL DRAMA—WITH HEART

My wish list for next month's titles...

In stores from 5th April 2013:

☐ NYC Angels: Unmasking Dr. Serious — Laura Iding

& NYC Angels: The Wallflower's Secret — Susan Carlisle

☐ Cinderella of Harley Street — Anne Fraser

& You, Me and a Family — Sue MacKay

☐ Their Most Forbidden Fling — Melanie Milburne

& The Last Doctor She Should Ever Date

— Louisa George

Available at WHSmith, Tesco, Asda, Eason, Amazon and Apple

Just can't wait?

Visit us Online

You can buy our books online a month before they hit the shops! **www.millsandboon.co.uk**

0313/03

Welcome to the world of the NYC Angels

*Doctors, romance, passion, drama—
in the city that never sleeps!*

Redeeming The Playboy
by Carol Marinelli
Heiress's Baby Scandal
by Janice Lynn
On sale 1st March

Unmasking Dr. Serious
by Laura Iding
The Wallflower's Secret
by Susan Carlisle
On sale 5th April

Flirting with Danger
by Tina Beckett
Tempting Nurse Scarlet
by Wendy S. Marcus
On sale 3rd May

Making the Surgeon Smile
by Lynne Marshall
An Explosive Reunion
by Alison Roberts
On sale 7th June

Collect all four books in this brand-new Medical 2-in-1 continuity

Find out more at **www.millsandboon.co.uk/medical**

Special Offers

Every month we put together collections and longer reads written by your favourite authors.

Here are some of next month's highlights— and don't miss our fabulous discount online!

On sale 5th April

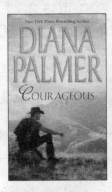

On sale 15th March

On sale 5th April

Save 20% on all Special Releases

Find out more at
www.millsandboon.co.uk/specialreleases

Visit us Online

0413/ST/MB410